FOREVER DAMNED

BY

ERIN K. PUGH

To Donna,

Warm Regards,

Erin K. Pugh

MARTELL PUBLISHING, INC.
SAN DIEGO, CA

Forever Damned

Copyright © 2007 by Erin K. Pugh
All Rights Reserved

No part of this book may be reproduced in any form or by any means without permission in writing from the publisher, except in the case of brief quotations embodied in critical articles for reviews. For information contact:

Martell Publishing, Inc.
3333 Midway Drive
Dept. 104
San Diego, CA 92110

Manufactured in the United States of America

ISBN: 1-893181-71-5

DEDICATION:

*For my brother, Ricky –
so missed in my life, so loved in my heart*

ACKNOWLEDGEMENTS

There is not space enough available for me to properly thank or show my love and appreciation to all who have played a part in supporting and encouraging my writing. But I would like to mention those who have gone above and beyond and made the road to publication a more easily traveled one for me.

Firstly, my family has been there from the beginning. Both my brother and sister have read my novels and offered their advice and an honest view of the writing. Any my nieces have always been ready with their opinions and advice when I'm figuring out plots. My mother's done her share with help on editing and helping to organize my files of chapters into a more workable format – she was more help than she knows. My family shares a great love for reading and I consider them well-informed as to what makes a good read, and I count on their love and support.

To Kristal and Shannon, my lifelong best friends, my family -- precious few know me better; thanks for your never-ending support, love, and good humor. From our childhood to this day, our bond has sustained me. I treasure it and both of you. And to your husbands, Dann and Wade, you guys make me both laugh and wonder, but most importantly, you make these great women happy. For this, you'll always have my affection and appreciation. And to your mom, thanks for the use of your computer throughout countless weekends in the very early days of more than a decade ago during the writing of this, my first book.

To Frank, Nick, and Lance, brothers in my heart, you guys and your wives have always been there for me. What you all mean to me, and your place in my life, can't be overstated. We're family, if not by blood, then certainly by bond. To Mila and Shirley, the only two people who have read this book in its unedited, as I wrote it, chapter by chapter, entirety. Thanks for your invaluable feedback; now everyone can read the story we fell in love with so long ago.

To Dr. Steven Gelfand and his tireless staff -- you have treated me well as both a patient and friend. Without your excellent medical care, the simple act of typing would be impossible and too painful to contemplate. Just saying thank you seems inadequate, so I will state a simple fact – were it not for you, Dr. G, I would not be physically able to do what it is that I love. To Dr. Lake -- you've helped me tackle many difficult tasks, not the least of which is tempering my impatience. A valuable asset to be sure, and difficult to attain, and you know why. I'm on an easier path now, and walking it with a new perspective. And that is in large part thanks to you. And I would be remiss if I did not mention the out-patient physical therapy staff at Indiana Regional Medical Center. I received top-notch care which makes my life much easier – my appreciation and thanks to all.

A special thanks to David, my studious and capable hands-on man in California. You, my friend, are a lifesaver. Lastly, but by no means least, thank you Ed Johnson. Your guidance on the road to publication is most appreciated. I have learned much from your wisdom and experience. Thanks for your faith in my work and the chance to share my work with the world.

Warm regards, and affection to all,

Erin

FOREVER DAMNED

Erin K. Pugh

The wind was blowing furiously outside the tinted window of the Rolls Royce and Andrew Carter frowned in disgust as he slumped in the back seat of the large car. It was a disappointment to still be fighting the cold weather in late April.

He wasn't always able to get out of the mansion. He just hated for this weather to spoil it for him. The view outside was reminding him too much of his old home in England, a place he sorely missed but to which he could never return. It was a punishment worse than death and a punishment he had richly earned.

When he left Cambridge so many, many years ago the townspeople were glad to see him go. The red carpet reserved for his great grandfather eighty years before was absent, forcing him to leave by the family's private jet in the dead of night. His father had promised him that it would only be for a short while, but as the door to the jet closed behind him, he knew that he would never be able to return home again. Those were the memories that brought the taste of bitterness to Andrew's mouth as his car made its way through the streets of New York. Would he ever be able to forgive and forget? The people of his homeland blamed him for things that were beyond his control. They would never understand. He would never understand.

The sudden whine of the brakes snapped him back into reality. "Thomas....Thomas what in bloody hell is going on out there?" he demanded. "Are you trying to get us killed?" Maybe it was time for him to interview for another driver. Thomas would do well for the mansion, but maybe he was no longer capable behind the wheel, he thought.

The graying man behind the wheel glanced nervously into the rearview mirror. "I'm sorry, there seems to be some trouble up ahead," he said desperately. There was no escaping one of his master's moods. When he was upset it was best to just ride it out. "We'll soon be safely at home, don't worry." Thomas Leavy had been with Andrew since the day he was born and had chosen to go with him when he was kicked out of Cambridge. And despite some rather foul moods, Master Andrew was really quite good to him and he would never leave him, thought Thomas.

Andrew was feeling guilty about having snapped at poor Thomas. The poor soul was sixty two years old and he had always been very loyal and warm. He was the father he missed and could only hope to have. Without Thomas he'd be lost. "Sorry old chap. I'm just a bit tense, forgive me." He smiled warmly when he met Thomas' eyes in the mirror. He looked at his watch. Ten more minutes and I'll be home, he thought.

Leaning back against the seat he released a deep breath and tried to relax. He pulled his wallet from the breast pocket of his one thousand dollar suit and removed his driver's license. He read it over and smiled. It was all true enough, he supposed. He was six foot one, his hair was black and his eyes were green, born 9/30/60. He shoved it back into his wallet when he felt the car come to a stop.

It seemed like forever before Thomas came around to open his door for him. It wasn't that Andrew was lazy or spoiled and he didn't want to open his door for himself. It was simply that the back doors had no inside handles. As his father once told him, 'people who can afford to own and ride in a car such as this could bloody well afford to have someone open the door for them'. He pulled his coat tightly around himself to ward off the bite in the air, and stepped from the car into a long canvassed archway that lead directly to the main door of the mansion. He walked quickly beside Thomas. He wanted classical music and a chilled glass of wine.

The Carter mansion was beautiful, elegant and quite large. It contained six stories with sixty rooms. Three of those floors were his company offices. Andrew had everything he would ever need or want in this fortress he called a home. If it weren't for his own peace of mind he would never have to leave the protection of its walls. He purchased it for a tidy sum of five million dollars. Another three million to redecorate both the business and personal levels of the building but it had been a good investment.

He made back the money he spent in one short year. He was obscenely wealthy so money and its value meant little to him. Over the years it had become just another curse for him, one that brought him much shame. He could never accept that he had earned it when he only had to look around the streets to see people more deserving than himself. So he gave very hefty checks to various charities every year to ease his troubled conscience. One thing he could not fight was the fact that his life style demanded his billion dollar bank account. And as he made himself comfortable in his large living room he was resigned that it would be a long life without much real happiness.

Andrew finished his first glass of wine, poured a second. And turning up the volume on Chopin, he prayed for night to come.

*

What a day, Monica Banebridge thought, stepping out from behind her desk and scanning the printout from the news room. She had waited two years for her own office and still was awestruck at the size of her spacious surroundings nearly two months after her move. Finally the general manager of WNYC had given her the chance she'd been waiting for since the moment she walked into the station. Monica knew she had a lot to prove and she could do it, she thought as she drummed her fingers on the edge of the desk restlessly.

The desk meant everything to her. It was her father's old desk and had been well used by him during the thirty-five years he spent in various news rooms during his journalistic career. He had it shipped to her from Ireland the year after his retirement. At thirty she was the youngest on air reporter at the station, and on this family desk is where she would someday write the story that would bring her respect and make her a household name.

Distracted by bittersweet memories of her father, she hadn't heard the receptionist calling her on the intercom. Snapping back, Monica quickly pressed her finger down on the button, "Yes, Sue?"

"Ms. Banebridge, Mr. Philips would like to see you in his office at three."

She lifted a brow, curious. "Fine, tell him I'll see him then. Sue, do you have any idea what it's about?"

"Nope, he just asked me to give you the message. Maybe it's a promotion," Sue laughed. That was the running joke between her and Monica.

"Very funny," Monica slipped her finger off the intercom button and collapsed into her chair. She suddenly had a headache, the same headache that always took root when unplanned meetings with her boss came up.

What could this be about she wondered as she made her way through the halls shortly before three o'clock later that day. As far as she knew her work had been excellent, but she always felt as if Mr. Philips was just waiting for a legitimate excuse to fire her. Well, it doesn't matter what he has up his sleeve, she decided walking into the small waiting area outside his office. She would let her work speak for her.

"Hello, Monica. He'll be ready for you in a moment," the cheery person behind the receptionist desk beamed. "Just have a seat."

Monica smiled in reply and took the seat offered to her. The cheery woman's name was Denise. She had been Mr. Philips secretary for the past eleven years and his mistress for the past eight. Everybody knew it. They often made no secret of it. It was the station's private little dirty joke. She was a sweet person who deserved more from a relationship than Mr. Philips could ever give her. But she seemed very happy with the arrangement, so why rock the boat, thought Monica.

Mr. Philips finally called her into his office ten minutes after she'd arrived. He waited until she took a seat then he offered her a cup of coffee. She accepted and once he set a cup down in front of her he came to the reason why he called her there. "Monica, you've been with us for two years now, right?"

"Two years one month and ten days," she corrected.

"Right," he smiled at her like he would a child. "Well, I've got an assignment in front of me that no one wants. They all think it will be too tough to handle. And you've always been my one reporter with a lot of spunk, so I thought you might be interested in the story. Would you like to know more about it?"

Monica wasn't sure what she was getting herself into, but what the hell, she thought. "Sure."

"I'm sure you've heard of Andrew Carter, the billion dollar business tycoon?" Mr. Philips asked with a grin.

Monica straightened her skirt and took a drink of her luke warm coffee. Hadn't the man ever heard of a hot plate? "Who hasn't heard of him," she replied.

He handed her an envelope, "I want you to do an interview with him; an extensive interview, for an in-depth story to hit the air in three months." His smile was wide but he could see her wheels already turning.

Monica couldn't believe what she was hearing. It was no wonder nobody wanted it. It was an impossible story. "Andrew Carter doesn't give interviews."

He shrugged, "Apparently he does now. One of his people called one of our people and set it up."

"Andrew Carter wants to give us an interview?"

"Yep."

"And you want *me* to do it?"

"Yep."

This wasn't going to be an easy assignment but it could be the one to launch her career. Andrew Carter was a business legend. She knew very little about him beyond the surface. He was tall, dark and handsome and extremely intelligent and business savvy. She couldn't pass this up. "When do I get started?"

"Fantastic, I'll set the ball in motion and let you know." He clasped her hand between his and grinned, "This is going to be great kid, wait and see." Mr. Philips led her out of the office. "Research'll dig up everything we've got on him so you can get prepped."

*

Andrew was pacing in his robe, his hands shoved deep into the pockets, his brow knit with worry. He was nervous and upset and second guessing his decision to do the interview. Thomas just sat on the couch and watched helplessly. Just another one of his master's foul moods. Back and forth he would go past the fireplace. "Whose idea was this anyway?" he muttered.

Thomas got up, crossed the room, and poured a glass of wine to ease his master's nerves. Stepping in front of Andrew he handed it to him, "It was yours Master Andrew. It's what you wanted, remember?"

"Yes, damnit, I bloody well remember. Thomas, how could you let me make such a damn fool mistake?"

"Oh, just me being silly again," he smiled at Andrew and soon they were both laughing, "Really, it won't be that bad."

He took a drink and with his smile quickly fading he said, "I hope not." So many things could go wrong. He could say too much or have to give explanations that he didn't have to give. Much of his life he had been trying to forget and for very good reason. His story was not a simple one to tell or even believe, so he would have to be very careful with this reporter. Pure and simple disaster could await him. Andrew had been to the abyss before. He could not go back.

*

Mr. Philips startled Monica when she looked up and found him in her doorway, "Good morning. I thought I was the only one who came in this early. I guess I'm just a little anxious about this afternoon." Terrified was a better description.

"What do you have to be nervous about? You should be able to do this interview with your eyes closed," replied Mr. Philips.

"I just might do that," laughed Monica.

"Don't worry. Is there anything I can do for you? Are you ready?"

"I'm as ready as I'll ever be."

"You'll be great. I'm sure you'll make quite an impression on Mr. Carter."

"Just pray it's a good one."

Soon she was alone in her office again and that gave her more time to worry about the questions she was going to ask. Were they going to keep him interested or would he become bored and lose interest? Monica looked at the clock. In five hours she would have her answers.

*

Thomas had chosen some rather casual clothes for Andrew to wear. Andrew was glad, the last thing he wanted to do was intimidate the reporter and get off on the wrong foot. He decided to wear the brighter shirt now and change into the darker, more relaxed shirt and cardigan for the interview. He dressed, took a deep breath and rolled his shoulders to get comfortable.

He would make an appearance at the office and check into a few of his overseas dealings. It would do him good to keep himself distracted. He couldn't stay at home for the day and twiddle his thumbs. Thomas would make sure the home was presentable to company, as it always was because Andrew Carter always wanted perfection.

Yes, business would be the best thing for him right now, he thought. It would relax him to get elbow deep in the daily running of his company. His employees would be expecting to see him, and he wouldn't disappoint them. For them it was just another ordinary day. For him there might never be another one as important as this.

The buzz of Carter enterprises greeted Andrew like a warm hug from a mother to a child. He smiled and instantly the urgency humming around the halls relaxed him. This truly was what he was on this earth to do; his calling. The pleasant exchange of smiles between himself and his employees was a morning ritual. Sarah, his right arm at the office, had a steaming cup of coffee waiting for him on his desk when he arrived.

He settled himself in his chair and buzzed for Sarah to join him in his office with her steno pad and pen. It was time to get to work. There were several letters he wanted in the mail by the end of business today. The calendar on the corner of his desk reminded him that an annual charity dinner that he and Thomas attended every year was the following evening. Sarah came smiling through the door and took her usual seat across from Andrew's desk and they began the day's dictation.

*

Andrew read the cryptic e-mail with stunned disbelief. He read it through three more times and cursed under his breath. Anger bubbled up in him unlike any he had ever felt before. Just like the sonofabitch, he thought bitterly, and he'd be damned if he let him get away with it. Damned if he let him play his games.

He wasn't a scared little boy anymore. He would deal with him as he should have long ago, with a heavy, and if necessary, lethal hand. Father or not, he could be eliminated.

*

Monica stared in amazement as an elderly, but strong looking man led her through what appeared to be a dimly lit hallway. He asked her to watch her step when they stopped in front of two large colonial looking doors. She couldn't believe this place. Once they were inside she checked her watch, 1:15. Their meeting was running a few minutes behind schedule but she didn't care. This place was amazing. If Andrew was anything like his home she couldn't wait to meet him.

In another part of the mansion Andrew Carter waited, trying to settle his nerves and will his tense muscles to relax. He wanted wine, much more wine. He spun around on his heels at a sound behind him to find Thomas entering the room with a beautiful woman on his arm. This was not what he had been expecting. The expression on Thomas's face showed that it hadn't been what he was expecting either.

She was gloriously beautiful, blond hair that seemed to fall in waves to her shoulders, green eyes that even at a distance he could see held a depth to get lost in, milky skin and a perfect mouth. His breath backed up in his lungs when she crossed the room and offered her hand. Her smile could light up the room, he thought, taking her hand in his. He knew it the moment he saw it on her face.

She shook it firmly. "I'm Monica Banebridge of WNYC channel 12 news."

He knew his mouth was hanging open. He knew he was staring holes through her, "Andrew Carter, it's a pleasure to meet you. Forgive me if I'm staring, to be honest you're not what I was expecting." He offered her a seat on the sofa behind her.

"Don't worry, I'm never what people are expecting," she smiled at him and that seemed to break the ice. She made herself comfortable on the sofa and prepared the recorder she took from her bag. "You have a lovely home, Mr. Carter. I'm sure you take great pride in its beauty," Monica said.

Andrew smiled as his gaze swept the room. "Yes, I suppose I do. And please no more Mr. Carter. My friends and beautiful women can call me Drew."

Surprised, Monica said, "Well, since we've just met I thank you for the compliment, Drew." He wasn't what she had been expecting either, much less reserved and much more approachable than his reputation would have the public believe. Monica knew he was handsome, but the pictures she had seen in the paper, didn't do him justice. "Shall we begin?"

He crossed his legs and took a deep breath. "I'm ready when you are, Ms. Banebridge."

She motioned for the cameraman to get ready. "It's Monica." She gave him a broad smile. "And you can relax, I don't bite."

He laughed. "Okay, Monica."

*

"Hello, New York. I'm Monica Banebridge and I'm here today in the estate of Andrew Carter, prominent businessman and chairman of some of our city's most promising renewal projects." The camera angle widened to include Andrew with a backdrop of his fireplace. "This is the first you've agreed to do an interview, so we here at WNYC feel very honored. Thank you for having us Mr. Carter," she said, sliding smoothly into her professional voice and with a confidence that was second nature, looking into the camera.

"It's my pleasure, Monica. I've come to realize over the past few years that many people of New York don't really know much about me, and to my dismay that's lead to some very interesting rumors. All of which are untrue I can assure you."

"What rumors are you referring to?"

"I'm sure you've heard them," he laughed, finally relaxing in her company and letting his natural charm come through.

"Some of them, yes," she replied with a chuckle. "So you're not terribly afraid of people or germs from the outside world?"

Andrew grinned and for the first time acknowledged the camera, "Oh heavens, certainly not. But it would definitely make life much livelier wouldn't it?"

"Yes, I guess it would. Why don't you tell us something about yourself?"

"Well, let's see, I was born and raised in England where I remained until I came to America to seek wealth and respect."

"Tell us about your family, do you have siblings? What're your parents like? Tell us about them."

Thomas was watching from the doorway as Andrew's expression changed suddenly. What he feared most was about to happen. "Please Master Andrew stay calm," he said softly under his breath.

She saw the change in his eyes. "Are you all right Mr. Carter?" Monica asked becoming concerned.

It took him a few moments but he snapped from the trance like state he was in and was grateful when the cameraman shut off the camera. "Ah, yes…I'm fine. I'm an only child. My mother and father were killed in an airplane crash, years ago. I've never spoken of them since that time."

He seemed so upset she wondered if she should continue. "I'm very sorry. Should we stop for today?" she asked softly, feeling bad for the abrupt shift in his mood she'd caused. How could research overlook information that was so important?

"No. Let's continue, but I would like to take a break, if you don't mind?"

Andrew fought the lump in his throat with a cough and very nearly leapt from his chair. "Thomas!" he bellowed. The gentle man appeared in the doorway. "Bring me some wine. Would you care for something, Monica?"

She was staring at him, intrigued. "Ah...some wine would be

nice. Thank you."

"Bring her something from the '87 stock, I'll take my usual." Once Thomas disappeared from view Andrew smiled softly at Monica. "I'm sorry for my behavior, forgive me. It's just that I speak so little of my parents and the last place I want to discuss them would be on television with all of New York."

"I understand, Drew," Monica replied. He didn't seem like a business legend now. He seemed like a man who was used to hiding his pain. Losing his parents clearly devastated him. She could see that. "I'm sorry for your loss."

"It was a long time ago," Andrew said walking over to the fireplace. "I'm not usually so affected by it."

Thomas soon returned with two glasses of wine on a silver tray. One was white and the other was red. He set them down on the coffee table and quickly left the room.

"He didn't have to open up two bottles of wine, red wine would have been fine with me," she said taking a sip from her glass.

Andrew picked up his glass, took a long sip and licked his lips. "This wine is quite bitter. It's an acquired taste. It took me years to get used to it." He drained his glass and set it on the mantle.

After they finished their drinks Andrew took Monica on a tour of his home. She seemed in awe of its vastness. She was full of dozens of questions. She was asking them so fast that he didn't get a chance to answer them. He marveled at her curiosity. His home was something he saw every day. Something that he was unimpressed with, Monica on the other hand had never been around such an abundant lifestyle. It was as if she was in a fairy-tale and this was an enchanted castle.

She noticed that the decor matched the man who had chosen it. The colors were deep and the furniture spoke of his English background. And even for its immense size it offered warmth she hadn't been expecting.

When they returned to the living room, Thomas had the crumpets he had baked earlier that morning displayed on the serving tray. They looked as if they were something to admire and not eat. Tea replaced the wine they had shared. Monica was again surprised by the swiftness with which Thomas could move and make every gesture seem so effortless. She sat across from Andrew at the table Thomas had moved into the room while they went on their tour.

"You seemed so surprised by all of this, Monica. Someone so beautiful should be exposed to this type of thing all the time," he said, dropping a sugar cube in his tea.

She smiled at him, "Thank you, but I'm afraid I'm more of a 'reheat last night's dinner in the microwave' kind of a girl."

"That doesn't sound very healthy."

"It's not."

"Good health is essential to beauty."

"I'll remember that."

"Good." He felt better, like he had his legs under him, his tricky emotions under control. He had an idea and went with it. "I was wondering if you had plans tomorrow evening. There is an annual charity dinner which Thomas and I attend every year, and I thought you might like to accompany me? It will give you a chance to see me in a different environment; you'll get a better feel for me that way. Please come with me, I'm sure you'll enjoy it."

"I really shouldn't impose. I mean it wouldn't be right."

"It's not an imposition when you're invited. And we'll call it a business dinner if that would make you feel any better."

"I guess that would be fine, if you're sure Thomas wouldn't mind," Monica said as she ripped another piece from the crumpet on her plate.

"Thomas will be thrilled for the company. We attend so many functions together he would be happy to walk in the door with a lovelier face than mine," Andrew quipped. He leaned back in his chair and looked at Monica Banebridge. She was lovely. There was no question about it. And when the thought entered his mind another burst through and destroyed the pleasant feeling. He couldn't do anything about his feelings. He could never love a woman. Not as long as he lived. There would be too much danger for her, and ultimately him.

"You seem a million miles away right now."

"Not a million, just a few thousand," he replied with a smirk.

"Thinking about your parents?" she asked.

"No, but I was thinking about how much I missed England," Andrew said getting up from the table.

Monica set her cup of tea down and looked at Andrew. "So why don't you go back for a visit?"

Andrew turned around and faced his lovely visitor. "When I

left England so long ago, well, I guess I knew then that I would never return," he replied softly.

"Why?" Monica listened intensely as she began taking mental notes of the conversation.

"There's nothing there for me anymore, I'm afraid it's very hard to explain. I'm not sure I can understand it." He saw the intensity on her face. "Taking mental notes?" he asked.

A blush rose to color her cheeks. "How'd you know?"

"I've been around long enough to recognize the look Monica." Andrew knew she felt uncomfortable. He put his hands in his pockets and walked to the table. "Don't feel bad, you're better at it then most. Why do you think I stopped giving interviews?" he asked.

"Well, I'd hate for you to think I'm only in this conversation for a story," Monica said in her own defense.

"That's what reporters are supposed to do, right?"

She smiled, "I do have some more questions for you though; mind?"

"Ask away."

"Why live in the same building where you work everyday?" her voice began to take on that reporter tone she'd become known for.

"Practicality for one; and why travel unnecessarily if I don't have too, particularly if I tout environmental concerns at every opportunity? I simply practice what I preach, Monica," he said in a fatherly tone.

Monica laughed, "In my own defense, I usually take the subway. Around town you're referred to as the billionaire hermit. The talk of the town is that you rarely leave your estate during the day. Why?"

"Everything I need is here. And I value my privacy. If I'm to leave just to satisfy the wagging tongues about town then I'll have to pass." These answers were good. He was just grabbing them out of thin air. Telling her the truth would only land him on the 'Hard Copy Exclusive' list.

"Fair enough," she had to raise an eyebrow. He wasn't telling her something; "The canvassed hallway?"

Andrew knew that Monica would ask these questions, because if he were the reporter he would ask the same ones. He paused, took a drink of his English tea. "I got tired of all the bloody photographers snapping my picture every hour of the day and night. The hallway allows me the privilege of a leisurely walk from my car to my door. And I can be sure my picture won't end up in Star magazine."

They talked for another hour, bouncing from one subject to another. When her cameraman cleared his throat and pointed to his watch she knew time had gotten away from her. "I think I better get back to the station, Drew. What time shall I meet you at the dinner tomorrow night?"

Andrew stood and walked her to the door. "A gentleman always picks a lady up at her home." He helped her on with her jacket. "My car will be at your home at 7:30 sharp. Just leave your address with Thomas."

Monica buttoned her jacket. "See you at 7:30 then." She heard the sound of a phone ringing in the distance, breaking the lock on their eyes. "Walk me to my car?" she asked.

"I would love too, however, the ringing we just heard is the conference call I've been waiting for and Italy hates to be kept waiting. Please forgive my rudeness." He walked quickly to his study once his guest had left. What a day, he thought.

*

Thomas served dinner later than usual because his master was still anxious from his visit with the reporter. If he didn't know better, Thomas would have sworn that his Master Andrew was smitten with Ms. Banebridge. He did know better. The poor lad could never act on his feelings even if he wanted too. The results of such a thing could be disastrous for everyone involved. It was such a cruel fact of life for him. When would the madness end?

Andrew had been climbing the walls since she left. Why? Why had he done such a stupid, stupid thing? What was he thinking? There was no way out of it for him. He watched Thomas set up his plate and silverware. "You shouldn't have bothered old chap. I'm not hungry."

Thomas spoke with authority, "You must eat."

Andrew slumped into his chair, "I'm afraid I've done something dreadfully stupid."

Thomas put his lamb chop in front of him, "Really?"

"I've invited Ms. Banebridge to accompany us to the charity dinner tomorrow evening. She's accepted." Andrew closed his eyes waiting for the roar to erupt from Thomas.

Thomas filled Andrew's wine glass and cleared his throat. "I see. What makes you think that's so terrible? I can think of worse things than her coming to a stuffy dinner with us. But it must end there Master Andrew. You know as well as I that it must go no further. The temptation would be too great for you; we cannot allow what happened in Cambridge to happen here too." After he finished his speech he took his seat across the table from his master.

"I know Thomas." He took a bite of his lamb chop. "Don't worry."

*

The apartment that Monica loved so much the day before, now suddenly felt dirty and cramped. It didn't compare to where she had spent the afternoon. Now as she lay in her bed, she couldn't get Andrew Carter out of her mind. What was it about him? His charm was very appealing and his accent was like music to her ears. There was something mysterious about him. Only she couldn't put her finger on what it was exactly.

She had to figure out what she was going to wear to the charity dinner the next evening. She wasn't in the poor house, but she didn't have a closet full of Armani's best either. She could only imagine what the women at the dinner would be wearing, probably dresses that cost more than she makes in a year. I had to open my big mouth, she thought.

*

The fresh air from his bedroom window hit Andrew in the face and he gladly inhaled deeply. It felt wonderful, he looked up at the moon and it danced with his eyes. The moon and he were friends now, but back in England so many years ago they were enemies. For when the moon would rise in the sky, his nightmares would begin. His madness, that wasn't his at all. It was all because of his father and his dirty little secret.

He turned away from the window in disgust. "He made me what I am," he said softly. Thoughts of his father always unsettled him, and he received proof this afternoon that he was determined to make his presence known, whether Andrew liked it or not. And he didn't like it, not one bit. He pressed the intercom button that would connect him with Thomas's room. It was a few moments before he heard any response.

"Thomas, I have a job for you. I want my father, bring him to me. I don't care what you have to do or who you have to buy, find him!!"

"Master Andrew, it's after midnight," Thomas pointed out.

"First thing in the morning then."

"Are you sure this is what you want?"

"Quite sure, Thomas. Quite."

"Very well then."

Chapter 2

Andrew was up early. This was one day he wouldn't need Thomas to wake him. He didn't sleep all night, not that he had really tried. He felt distracted. He was looking for anything to do to keep his mind off of the decision he'd made the night before.

Thomas was surprised to see his master come through the kitchen door. He wasn't sure what had happened to change his master's mind concerning his father, but it must have been something important. The first pot of coffee hadn't finished brewing yet and the two of them were avoiding speaking to each other because they weren't sure what they could say. Andrew was going through the cabinets as if he knew exactly where to find things.

The coffee finished brewing so Thomas poured his master a cup of black coffee and handed it to him. He was on his hands and knees looking through one of the cabinets for a mixing bowl, when he heard the question he'd been waiting for.

Andrew asked the question matter-of-factly. "Did you make the call?"

"Three hours ago. We should hear something soon," he replied, getting to his feet.

"Don't look at me like that," Andrew complained, sniffing his coffee. "I know what I'm doing." He'd seen that look on Thomas' face many times over the years. It was the distinct look of disapproval.

"You realize that once that phone rings, there's no going back?" Thomas said over his shoulder. He broke some eggs and began whipping them for French toast. "You can still change your mind."

"I won't change my mind, and you cannot change it for me. It's time for me to deal with this head on, old boy."

"You could be opening yourself up for all kinds of pain."

Andrew laughed. "Thomas what do you call what I've already been going through in the last twenty years? He took my life and twisted it into something that he thought it should be and he's still trying to. Thanks to my father this life I'm living isn't a life at all. It's a bloody living hell!!!" He hadn't meant to get so upset. The rage he felt towards his father after all these years finally came spilling to the surface.

"I understand how you feel, Andrew. I begged your father to let you live in peace. He wouldn't listen. I know you're still suffering but what will bringing your father here solve? As far as your personal history shows, both your mother and father are dead. Why risk so much?"

"Because, he's playing his games again with my business and my life. I'm no longer the boy he used to push around. It's time he realize whose in charge."

*

The call that he'd been waiting for came around noon. Contact had been made with his father. He sent word that he would be in route to the states and would arrive early the next evening. Andrew was trying very hard not to let the news distract him as the car came upon the charity dinner and the glitz and glamour of the elite that always accompanied these functions.

He stepped from the car with Thomas cleverly blocking the photographers that suddenly swarmed around him. He stepped back to allow Monica room to exit the car freely. He surprised her when he took her hand and helped her to the curb.

They danced most of the evening, talking carelessly as the rest of the guests had their tongue's wagging about Andrew Carter's lady friend. The dinner was delicious and Andrew brought the room to its feet when he donated a check for one million dollars to the evening's charity. Andrew and Monica seemed to forget that they were the focus of so much gossip. With each new song their embraces grew closer. Andrew kept reminding himself of the distance he needed to keep between them. He could never love her, but she was as intoxicating as wine. One waltz led to another, and Thomas watched helplessly from the sidelines.

After they dropped Monica off at her apartment the car became quiet; too quiet. He had tried to keep to his promise concerning Monica but once he held her in his arms, the promise was impossible to keep. "I know that you're upset with me, Thomas. But something inside me tells me it will be different this time."

Thomas looked into the mirror. "How can you be so sure?" he asked.

"I know because it's been nearly twenty years and I haven't once shown any signs of a relapse. And it's in no small part due to you," replied Andrew.

"That's true, but it took me three years to rehabilitate you. I'd hate to see you turn back now. What will you do if the same urge strikes and the same fate meets Monica that met with Elizabeth?"

"It won't." Andrew was quiet for a few seconds. "I'll make sure of that."

*

A new day dawned and Andrew Carter was making his way through his office with renewed energy. Sarah noticed that her boss seemed preoccupied but she said nothing. He flew through the morning's dictation with no effort at all. His morning meeting with his staff had been complete but nonetheless brief. He placed three overseas phone calls in the time it took to place one on the average day.

Sitting behind his desk his thoughts turned to his dinner companion of last evening. Could he miss her already? Would she be free for lunch? A grin came to his face and he picked up the phone. It took a few moments for her to come on the line but when she did it felt as if it had been no time at all. "What are you doing for lunch?"

Monica smiled into the receiver, "Nothing as far as I know, why?" She'd been hoping that he would call all morning. His voice sounded so smooth that it was all she could do to maintain some sense of dignity. She was out of practice when it came to flirting.

"Why don't you come by for a quick bite? I'll have my secretary order something in. I'm pressed for time otherwise I'd take you out." He felt so nervous that he was drumming his pen on his desk.

"Sounds good, but on one condition," she replied.

"Let me guess, you want to ask me more questions?"

"Will that be a problem?" She didn't know where this would lead but the line between professional and personal was blurring. She'd worry later. Right now she only knew she wanted to see him again.

"Absolutely not, you wanted some footage of me in my office anyway. When can I look forward to seeing you?" he asked hoping she would say she'd be right over.

Monica scanned her desk calendar. "How's 12:30 sound?"

"Sounds great, see you then." Once the connection between them broke he buzzed Sarah's desk. "Cancel everything on my schedule from 12:30 on," Andrew said simply. He was happy.

After so many years of dread and bleakness, he was actually happy again.

*

The camera operator was happy with the angle he had, so the tape started rolling and the questions began. "So you're in the import export business is that right? It wasn't so long ago when the mention of those two words brought thoughts of illegal activities, but it's a much more respectable business now isn't it?" Monica asked, her voice once again taking on that professional tone.

Andrew sat with his hands clasped together under his chin. He smiled into the camera. "Yes it is. Any illegal activity is next to impossible to get away with now. I ship materials used to make medical supplies both here and abroad. It's very important. I take the responsibility very seriously," he continued.

Monica smiled. "I'm sure that you do, Mr. Carter."

*

This was what Andrew had been waiting for, the chance to tell his father how much he despised him. He was in the pool swimming laps when Thomas came into view and walked over to the edge. "What is it, Thomas?" he asked as he wiped the water from his eyes.

Thomas's face grew serious. "The plane will be landing in twenty minutes. I'm leaving so I can meet him when he gets off the plane; the fewer people that see him the better."

He jumped from the pool and puddles of water dripped around him as he pulled on his robe. "Then I guess I'd better go get ready," he announced. "I wouldn't want to keep him waiting." Andrew disappeared through the door that would lead back to the main house.

*

The sound of footsteps prepared Andrew for what was about to come next. It had been so long since he heard that voice that shaped and shook his childhood, but still he recognized it the moment it broke the silence in the room. His stomach shifted. Some sounds he could never forget.

"Hello, son. It's been a long time." He stood frozen beside Thomas as if he were unable to move. "Turn around and let me see you."

Andrew turned and slowly faced his father. "Hello, father," he said flatly. "I could say it was good to see you, however hell has a better chance of freezing over," he continued, his expression cold and his eyes filled with nothing but contempt for the man that stood before him. "You're making a nuisance of yourself again I see. Will you never learn that the only reason I allow you to live is hanging by the thinness of a thread?"

His father stood stiffly, his expression mirrored his son's. "I see your attitude hasn't changed. Your mother would be greatly disappointed, Andrew."

His eyes narrowed and Andrew crossed the room to shove his finger into his father's chest. "Don't you ever let mention of my mother cross your lips again!!!" his voice was so full of rage that he could feel the spit shoot through his teeth "Sit down!! I don't intend on letting this reunion take all bloody night."

Reginald Carter wiped the spit from his face with the back of his hand. He straightened his tie and sat down in the chair Andrew pointed too. "Really, Andrew," he said with anger building in his voice, "Still a weakling in every way but with your tongue. Carrying guilt around doesn't make you a martyr, boy, just a fool."

"Elizabeth's death was your fault as much as mine, yet I am the one who suffers," Andrew spoke with anger.

Reginald laughed. "You give me far too much credit, son. It was you with Elizabeth on the ridge that night. And it was you who took her life not I," he replied.

Andrew grabbed his father by the neck and hurled him out of the chair into the fireplace. Contempt drove him and he crossed the room and grabbed him again before he could regain his breath, "You! You are the one who cursed me with the power to do such a thing!!!" His teeth were clinched and hate filled his eyes. "You took from my blood and my flesh was beneath your teeth!!! You made me an animal!!!"

Reginald lay propped up on one arm against the fireplace. "I made you what you were meant to be. But never think that you are different from me, Andrew. Never forget that you are a killer. That you fed on that girl's blood!" he gasped.

"I am nothing like you!" Andrew replied in disgust. "You enjoy what it is that you are. I've spent most of my life trying to escape what I am. What you made me." He looked at Reginald sprawled on the floor with eyes that were absent of any compassion for the person he once adored as a young boy blinded from the truth.

Reginald struggled to get to his feet. "You can protest from the highest mountain that you are not what I am, but you are exactly that! Never doubt that you are the son of a vampire, and a vampire yourself!!" A laugh exploded from his throat and bounded across the room as if he were possessed. "Do you think you are changed because it's been twenty years since you've fed on human blood? Then you have my respect, but never doubt that one day you will feed again, son. And when that happens, only God can save this city you now call your home."

They were inches apart when Andrew spoke in a dangerous whisper. "You cost me what I loved most in my life. I have a chance at that kind of happiness again. I can promise you this, I will never, NEVER become the monster I once was, the monster I worked so hard to contain." He let his words hang in the air. He smiled at Thomas and prepared to walk from the room.

Andrew had just about made it to the door when his father's voice stopped him in his tracks.

"This lady, whom you say that you love, will be your first victim. You know as well as I that we are at our most dangerous when we are aroused in passion." His back remained turned to Andrew while he spoke, his hands behind his back in a superior stance. "However, there are exceptions, like your mother. Are you strong enough to resist? Do you want to take the chance?" he continued.

Andrew shuddered inside. The words sent a feeling of doom through his body. The words were true enough. The bastard, he thought. He wanted so badly to wipe off the smug look that he was sure was on the man's face, but he cleared his throat and swallowed the bile that was almost choking him instead.

"You'll leave here alive tonight only because my mother loved you. You'll return the stock you pirated from my company and crawl back under your rock; you'll keep your nose out of my business, professional and personal life, Reginald, if you want to stay that way."

Andrew walked out of the room and up the staircase to his bedroom. He felt dazed, weakened. Facing his father had taken more out of him then he'd anticipated. After all these years Reginald Carter understood that his son hated him.

The question he wanted answered more than any other, he never got the chance to ask because his father always knew which buttons to push to get a violent reaction from him. Andrew wanted to know why he sent him to America and never arranged for him to return home to Cambridge. Where he could be with his mother when she died, from what he knew was a broken heart. He realized he already knew the answer. Reginald always hated the fact that Andrew's mother supported her son's decision. He wanted to live and die on his own terms, just as she had done. The tragedy supplied Reginald with the perfect excuse to separate mother and son; an act which in the end destroyed them both.

Andrew closed his eyes. He'd faced his first demon, the demon that gave birth to the demon that lived in him. He won the first battle. Could he win the war that his father predicted would erupt inside him very soon?

Chapter 3

Andrew could remember all too well the craving of human blood that once burned in him. Thomas never gave up on his hopes of conditioning Andrew away from the desire for blood. Then finally, after years of hellish nights the taste subsided. He swallowed hard and sweat trickled down Andrew's forehead as he remembered those nights. Nights that at times seemed to swallow him up and spit him out. Nights of endless shaking and dehydration, of chills and head spinning cramps. Night's when death was indeed preferable. Night's when he was more animal than man.

Andrew pulled the blankets tightly around him as a chill swept over him. After so much work to be sane again, to live outside the shadow madness and mayhem, he would not give into the urges of the past. That was his father's world, not his own. He would have a normal life. It was truly the only desire he had yet to acquire.

*

Andrew slept, but nightmares invaded his sleep. And no matter how hard he tried he couldn't chase the monstrous images from his dreams. It was as if Andrew could reach out and touch the scenes playing out in front of him. He saw himself standing in a misty, cold, and very ominous graveyard. He took a step forward and stumbled over something hard and low to the ground. He looked down and focused on the object. A silent cry escaped from his lips, to his horror he was staring at the headstone of his true love Elizabeth.

He tried to run but his feet wouldn't move. Andrew finally heard his own cry, felt it erupt from his lungs, tears filled his eyes...He darted up in his bed. His cold, clammy hands tore through his hair. His body shuddering; tears in his eyes. His breathing, gasps. One thought repeated in his mind......it was only a nightmare...for now.

*

When morning came and Thomas woke Andrew, he was shocked by the man he saw before him. If he hadn't known better, he'd have sworn that Andrew had lost twenty pounds over night. "Master Andrew, you look positively dreadful. Do you feel all right?" he asked with a look of concern.

Andrew laughed softly. "Really, old boy, I'm well aware that I look deplorable. I had a rather cumbersome night," he continued, "I'll be fine once I've had my morning coffee."

Thomas was silent for a moment. "I'll bring it right up." Half way to the door he turned around. "Are you sure that you don't need to rest today?" he asked. He was hoping that he would hear the answer that he wanted, but he knew better.

The warm smile Thomas had grown so accustomed to seeing came across Andrew's face. And he walked over to the old man and placed a hand on his shoulder. "Listen Thomas, I'll be perfectly fine. I just need to freshen up a bit, that's all," Andrew said with a reassuring tone, "Run on, old chap, don't worry so much," he continued.

"Very well," replied Thomas. It was useless to argue.

Once the door to Andrew's room closed, the well rehearsed act that Andrew had mastered fell to the floor. Thomas knew him too well. He could see right through him. He felt terrible, but it was from lack of sleep and nothing more. Andrew knew he had to somehow gain control of the nightmares that had returned the previous night. They would drive him mad otherwise, of that much he was sure. Reginald had worked his magic yet again, thought Andrew. His robe dropped to the rug beneath his feet. At the moment he was thankful that he had no use for a mirror, he knew for certain what it would reflect.

The one bright spot of the day would visit him in the form of Monica Banebridge. And the mere thought of her brought joy to Andrew's heavy heart. She would be his salvation, his anchor. His guardian angel. And he wanted her. Andrew wanted her more than he wanted to breathe. If he could just feel her skin against his, then he was sure it could wipe away the sins of his youth. Every time they looked at each other he felt the pull between them. Andrew knew Monica felt it too.

*

As Andrew walked down the hall towards the stairs, he looked around and realized how many rooms in his home were empty. A wave of old, familiar regret washed over him. He wanted nothing more than to fill the rooms he was passing with children and have a loving wife by his side. Andrew was halfway down the stairs before he could convince himself that those dreams were unreachable. It would be too risky. He never wanted to put his family on the line like his father had done. And the only way to ensure that was to have no family at all.

Thomas met him at the bottom of the staircase with a cordless phone. "It's Hong Kong. They say it very important," he whispered.

He sighed. "It couldn't wait ten more minutes until I'm in the office?" he asked. Andrew glanced at the phone and took it from Thomas. "Yes, what is it?" He listened silently as his eyes glazed over and narrowed. "Oh, he does! Well, you can tell him to take his offer and shove it in the loo!!" He tossed the phone to Thomas in anger. He strode into the living room and began drumming his fingers on the fireplace mantle.

"What's happened, Master Andrew? You seem rattled."

"Reginald thinks he's going to pull a fast one. The bloke thinks he can buy ten percent more stock rather than return what he's already stolen." The tone Andrew used sounded like one of amazement, "He's a cocky bastard."

Thomas was surprised. "What do you think he's after? A hostile takeover?" he asked.

"Nothing that simple, this is just his way of showing me that he can get access to me whenever he chooses too." He turned and looked at Thomas. "He wants me to know that he is still pulling strings in my life," continued Andrew.

"He can certainly prove himself to be quite manipulative when he wants too," offered Thomas with a curious look on his face.

Andrew noticed the look. "Don't fret, Thomas, I've got it all under control. There's nothing that my father could do that I wouldn't be prepared for." Andrew reassured him of that. He slapped him on the back. "I'm going to the office."

Thomas turned and followed him into the hall. "Are you going to see Ms. Banebridge today?"

The elevator doors opened and Andrew stepped inside. He turned around and found Thomas waiting for an answer. "Yes, I am." The doors closed and Andrew smiled.

*

"Good morning ladies," Andrew said as he passed a few women from the legal department on the fifth floor. He was feeling better then he had hoped too after hearing about his father's attempt to worm his slime drenched soul into his businesses. But he was well aware of how Reginald's mind worked and now that he knew what his area of attack would be, he could anticipate every future move he might make.

He was pleased to find his customary cup of coffee on the corner of his desk where Sarah always placed it. As he settled himself into his chair behind his desk, his phone buzzed. He answered it. Sarah had told him that there was someone waiting to see him in the outer office. Andrew quickly thumbed through his desk appointment book. He really didn't care to see anyone right now.

Still Andrew stood and shook the man's hand when he walked into the office. He was sure he'd never met him before. "Is there something I can do for you Mr.—" he had to glance at the business card the man had given to him "—Harper." He offered the man a seat, which he took.

Mr. Harper opened the case he brought with him. "I have something for you, Mr. Carter. It's from your father," he spoke directly.

Andrew face turned grim. "I want nothing from him. So you can take it right back to him." he replied harshly.

"He expected you would say as much, but he's sure you'll change your mind once you know what it is."

"Somehow I doubt it."

"I think you'll want to know what it is as well, Mr. Carter."

"Oh, bloody hell." He dragged in a deep, calming breath, "Just get on with it and then get out."

Mr. Harper opened the case and pulled from it an urn. It was solid gold with an inscription across the base. Andrew recognized it immediately and gripped the desk for balance. It was the urn that he had chosen for his mother's ashes. He hadn't seen it in years. His eyes misted as if he were in a trance.

"What purpose does this serve?" Andrew asked after he cleared his throat. "He wouldn't allow me to have it then, why would he want me to have it now?"

"He simply said you needed it more than he did."

"Your job is finished here—leave—now!"

Mr. Harper was gone and Andrew was shattered. Tears tracked down his cheeks as he looked at what was left of his sweet mother, sitting on the edge of his desk. Seeing this, he remembered just how much he missed her, and how much he loathed Reginald Carter for taking her from him. He reached out, shakily trying to touch it. His fingers barely skimmed it before he pulled them away. What was Reginald trying to accomplish with this? This had to be some game. A strategic move Andrew was certain.

Andrew sat silently behind his desk for what seemed like hours. His eyes were puffy and red from his crying. He couldn't let Sarah see him like this. He coughed and tried to pull himself together. He picked up the phone and dialed for Thomas. It felt like forever before Thomas answered the phone. Once he did Andrew wasted no time with unimportant words. "Come to my office right away," he said quickly.

Thomas knew something was wrong he could hear it in his voice. "I'll be right there," he hung up the phone and went straight to the elevator.

*

Monica was enjoying her first day off in six months. And she was anxious about seeing Andrew later in the afternoon. She could try to fool herself into believing that their relationship was nothing more then a professional one, but in her heart she knew better. There was something happening between them. Under the surface, and it was strong and growing stronger by the day. She was feeling exhilarated and frightened at the same time. In the past she would have never let her heart lead her head. Why was she allowing herself to do something so risky now?

The sweet taste of her French roast felt warm as it rolled over her tongue. Sitting with her legs folded under her, head lying against a large overstuffed chair, puzzling over her sudden attraction to a man she barely knew. She laughed out loud. It wasn't like she'd never seen a man as good looking as Andrew Carter. Hell, she even dated a few of them. But something about him was different. A kind of sweetness so rare in most came to him so easily. It was impossible to resist his charm, impossible to ignore the innate goodness in him.

Monica spent the late morning hours looking over every outfit she owned. Her closets were a disaster. What should she wear? It was an afternoon meeting; she didn't want to appear too eager. After all, this was going to be about business. He wasn't going to throw her on the couch in his office and make love to her. She gasped. Were did that come from? Momentarily floored by her own thoughts, Monica decided on her red business suit. How she felt didn't matter anyway. This was an assignment, nothing more.

It was Monica's mother, Francis, who raised her to be so independent and self-reliant. When her father divorced her mother and moved to Ireland she was just ten years old. And her mother wasted no time trying to prove to her that a woman didn't need a man to feel complete or worthy. So she learned very early on that a life without a man could be both rewarding and enjoyable. Which was why she was still single and alone and unconcerned. Her career had taken the place of a man in her life.

Not that Monica Banebridge had been living the life of a nun over the years. She had had several men in her life, just none that she cared to spent the rest of her life with. And when a relationship didn't work out for whatever reason, she would simply revert back to her mother's motto.

*

Thomas knocked on the door, waited a moment, and then let himself in. He stopped in his tracks when he saw his master's appearance as he sat behind his desk. "Master Andrew, you look as if you've been pummeled. What's the matter?" he asked coming to his master's side. He hadn't seen him look this horrible since he learned of his mother's death.

Andrew straightened himself in his chair. "I feel as much. As if I've been to hell and back," he muttered to himself as much as to Thomas. He pointed to the urn on the edge of his desk. "This arrived, special delivery for me; from Reginald no less."

Thomas couldn't mask his shock, "Your mother's urn." He picked it up and read the inscription. "He swore you would never lay your hands on it. Why do you suppose he changed his mind?"

"More games no doubt," he replied scrubbing his hands over his face. "It's belonged with me from the beginning. The dear soul didn't deserve such poor company while she lived, and I'll always regret leaving her behind. She certainly deserved a better resting place than the viper pit he called a home."

"Maybe this is his way of trying to ease his guilty conscience."

"A man must have a conscience before he can ease the guilt of it."

"What would you like me to do with her remains?"

"Take them to my bedroom." He got to his feet. "Then call and have an exact copy of the urn made into a vase. I want her ashes out of that as soon as possible."

Thomas squeezed Andrew's shoulder, "Right away." And in an

instant he was gone.

The memories of that horrible day he learned of his mother's death returned to torment him. It was the only time since his banishment that he was allowed to return to England. For a mere forty-eight hours. The blatant coldness with which his father treated him would be burned in his mind forever, but it was the pain of loss that brought fresh tears to his eyes now. There was so much that he wanted to say to his mother but he never got the chance. So he held her cold, frail hand, gently kissed her forehead, weeping.

He sat with her for hours in her bedroom. Hating to find her in a coffin and not her bed, he lifted her to lay her on top of her favorite down comforter instead. He cried for hours. He murmured his apologies for not coming in time to say goodbye. And cursed his father's insensitivity over the plans he made for her internment in the family plot. He remembered the argument they'd had over it all too well.

"Father, you know that she hated the very thought of a burial!" Andrew yelled.

"That fear was irrational, Andrew."

"I won't let you take her last wish away from her."

"Isn't it enough I let her go?" Reginald demanded. Am I not allowed even this small concession?"

"It goes against her wishes and I won't permit it."

"Fine," Reginald replied tightly. "But she stays with me, in our home. You had her loyalty all her life. You'll not have her with you for all of yours."

"Keeping us apart in life wasn't enough for you, father? You must continue to punish us even now?"

"You're all that ever mattered to her. I lost her the moment you were gone."

"That's a lie. For some curious reason she loved you, even after you drove me away."

"I loved your mother too, Andrew. I know you find that hard to believe."

*

Andrew decided to make reservations at the French Quarter Inn for two, for an early dinner that evening. It was a bold move considering he hadn't asked Monica if she would join him. But tonight he needed the pleasure of her company, more than she could ever know. She made all the pain disappear. Monica would say yes. He knew it.

He was just finishing work on some of his most important files when his intercom buzzed. With a groan Andrew pushed the button and tried to sound as normal as possible for Sarah's sake. And he let out a sigh of relief to find it was the deli asking what he would like served for his lunch date. He smiled when he looked at the wall clock. Two more hours and she would be there.

It was surprising how much work one could accomplish with both anger and elation as a driving force, Andrew thought, sliding his chair away from his desk and standing to stretch. He glanced at his watch and buzzed for Sarah to come in with her pad and pen for some quick dictation. As always she greeted him with a warm smile and they began their work.

*

Thomas had done what was asked of him. He ordered the new vase as his master requested. But while he went on with the daily household activities he couldn't help but be wary of the storm he felt looming on the horizon. Reginald Carter was up to no good. He was making sure that his son still felt his presence. And it was his responsibility to keep his master safe from the evil clutches of that man. Reginald was planning something, but what? He would never be so careless as to come at Master Andrew head on. He wouldn't be that foolish, thought Thomas.

*

Monica smiled at Sarah when she walked into the reception area of Andrew Carter's office. "I'm here for a twelve thirty appointment with Mr. Carter," she said softly as if not wanting to be overheard.

Sarah smiled in return, noticing that the woman standing over her was nervous. "Yes, Mr. Carter is expecting you. I'll let him know you're here," she replied kindly.

*

He greeted her at the door with a smile as if he'd known her for years. "What, no cameras?" he asked feigning disappointment.

"I could have them here in ten minutes if you'd like," she spoke with the same mocking tone.

"Not necessary." He stepped back and let her through the door and gestured to the chairs and dining table he had brought in for their lunch. "Please have a seat, Monica."

"Thank you, but this doesn't look very professional. What will your staff think?" she asked as she chose the chair on the left side of the table.

Andrew gently pushed her chair closer to the table. "Well, I suppose they will think I fancy having lunch with a very lovely woman." He sat down in the chair on the opposite side of the table. "And they'd be right," he continued with a sheepish grin.

Monica laughed, "I see."

Andrew poured two glasses of wine from the two bottles in the ice bucket.

Monica was puzzled. "Again two bottles of wine?" she asked.

"White wine goes much better with my selection for lunch, but I'm afraid I'm rather spoiled when it comes to my own personal choice of wine. I see no reason why you should have to suffer the effects of my poor habits."

She listened to him describe the ins and outs of his business. But her mind wondered. And soon she steered the conversation from professional to personal. "I'm trying to figure out why you're still one of the most sought after bachelors in the city, any theories?"

Andrew chuckled, "No. Though I'm sure you've heard many on the grapevine. Have you any you'd like to share?"

Chapter 4

Two weeks had passed since the meeting between father and son. Now Andrew stood in front of the fireplace in the living room staring at the vase that now held his mother's ashes. Since the delivery of the "gift," there had been no further contact with Reginald Carter. This was just the way Andrew preferred it to be. He caressed the gold vase as if it held the secrets of his existence in his own private world. A world that he wished he could escape.

He continued on with his work and his life in the manner in which he was used too, pushing thoughts of his father to the recesses of his mind. The past eight days he had seen Monica every night. Good or bad, right or wrong, he was slipping into feelings he had not allowed himself to feel in two decades.

She was a delight in every way. Their conversations were always stimulating, their dancing always intimate, and their growing attraction for each other silently acknowledged between them. They spent hours together talking, getting to know each other. But as far as Andrew was concerned he knew all that he needed to. And Monica was feeling the same. She proved it with every brush of her hand against his.

Last night when they kissed goodnight, instead of their polite kiss on the cheek, she surprised him by turning and gently pressing hers lips to his. It was a moment burned into his very soul. He had no doubts. This was the woman he planned to spend the rest of his life making happy.

Damn the complications Thomas had warned him about over and over again. They couldn't compare to his rising desire for her. His need for her outweighed any possible risk they might face. Andrew would never be tempted to hurt her, the very thought turned his stomach. His father was wrong. Hurting Monica would mean hurting himself. He'd been alone long enough. Andrew could love her. That love inside him now was stronger than any urge he could imagine feeling.

The stomach pains he had been experiencing over the last few days weren't necessarily cause for alarm. Thomas on the other hand saw them as a red flag. Andrew felt they were nothing more than nerves. If things between him and Monica continued on this well, he would soon admit his true feelings to her. He loved her, loved her more than life itself.

As much as Andrew didn't want to go into the office today, he felt that he must. He could accomplish more there then he could at home with Thomas watching him endlessly. There were papers to sign, letters to dictate, calls to return and deals to finalize. He loved his career. Loved knowing that he was helping people all over the world by shipping them badly needed medical supplies. That part of his career was just the tip of the iceberg.

He was a bit nervous knowing the interviews he did with Monica were scheduled to air three weeks earlier than planned. What would people think of him? Not that he really much cared. Now though, it would be difficult to find excuses to see Monica. He would think of something.

*

Thomas waited until his master left for the office before he entered the hidden halls that would lead to the dark sector. The hallway, narrow and long, could seem endless when he felt his age creeping up on him. Within these walls were secrets that only he and his master shared. The dampness made Thomas uneasy, and the stillness made him shudder inside. The clap, clap, of his shoes meeting the concrete floor offered comfort from the dead silence that seemed to own this place.

He had to check the stock. The last thing he needed was to run low on supply. He had a sick feeling that it might be needed very soon. The temperature needed checked. It had to be at a precise temperature of 34 degrees for the maximum effect. Just above freezing, then slowly warmed before the process was completed. If the system were to fail the entire stock would be lost. This was part of everyday life with Master Andrew. His fragile hold on a life meant for mortal men alone was tenuous. And Thomas thought of how much his master longed for normalcy and ached for him inside.

At the end of the hall at the door leading to the main room he put his back into it and slid the steel door open. The temperature dropped noticeably when he stepped into the room. He looked at the large mass of shelves directly before him. To his left, on the wall, he tapped the thermometer. He judged by his clouded breath that the room temperature he read was correct.

He crossed his arms over his chest to hold in his body heat and walked over to tap the first bottle he came to. He was pleased to once again find things in working order. At least this was one area where he had control over his master. He monitored the supply not his master. This was one matter where Master Andrew would not have his way.

In fact Andrew was forbidden to even enter this part of the mansion alone. The temptation to gorge on the supply was too great and they both knew it. Misuse could be as disastrous as a relapse when dealing with the delicate balance of his system.

Thomas decided to return to the mansion. The sound of the door closing behind him reminded him of the closing of cell doors. He thought it an appropriate comparison considering that what was on the other side of the door was his master's only key to a life of freedom. He walked swiftly up the hall to the door that led to the staircase which would lead him back to the main part of the mansion.

*

When his morning tea did not agree with him and his stomach churned, Andrew shrugged it off as anxiousness about the upcoming evening. Tonight was a big night. He was going to have dinner at her place. Much to Andrew's surprise, it was her idea. What does it mean? It means she's crazy for you, you bloody fool, he said to himself. At least that was his hope. It wasn't as if he was an expert on love, but he sure recognized it when he felt it in his heart.

The thought of an evening alone with Monica in her home was more than enough to get his system jumping. So the feeling of illness would pass. But to be sure he sent Sarah out for some antiacid certain that would help. Yes, that would definitely help.

As a boy, when his father would take to his bed ill, his mother would tell him it was because of the long hours that he spent on the road. As he grew older though, he learned the truth. It had nothing to do with his business schedule. He would go into withdrawal when his "feedings" were thrown off of schedule. Andrew remembered seeing his father violently ill at times. Years ago, before his rehabilitation, he too, would become just as ill when he was unable to find blood to quench his thirst.

Andrew would not allow it to happen again. He was stronger, much stronger than Reginald Carter could ever hope to be. He would have to get under control before Thomas saw him. He would jump to all the wrong conclusions and assume that he was having some sort of relapse. And that was simply not true. He closed his eyes and laid his head on his desk. There was no reason to panic.

*

Sarah found him sound asleep when she walked into his office. She was more than a little surprised. She tapped his shoulder until he awakened and opened his eyes. "You really are feeling sick, aren't you?" she asked, knowing that he would never admit it.

Andrew felt better then he had earlier. It took him a moment to focus on Sarah's face. "Yes...I'm just feeling a bit run down. I'll feel much better after I take some of this," he said reaching for the bag she had in her hand.

"Are you sure you don't want me to call Thomas?"

"NO!" he said with more force then he had meant to. "I'm perfectly fine. You know how he worries, why upset him needlessly, right?"

Sarah looked at him for a second. He'd never been so pale before. "Right, I'll be right outside if you need anything." Then she turned and left the office, pulling the door closed behind her.

He drank the thick pink liquid straight from the bottle. It left a sweet after taste in his mouth. He walked into the small adjoining room to the right of his desk and filled a glass with water. He drank it so fast that half of it dribbled off his chin to the floor. He straightened up and splashed some cool water on his face. It was time to get back to work.

Time always moved slowly for Andrew and today of all days was unbearable. His phone buzzed at half past one. "Andrew Carter."

"Hello Drew."

He smiled instantly. "Hello, Monica. How's your afternoon coming along?"

"Too slow for my tastes."

"I agree with you." He wondered if she could sense that he was grinning from ear to ear. "So you're not calling to cancel our plans for the evening?" he continued fearing the answer.

"Absolutely not, I'm looking forward to it. You, on the other hand, might live to regret accepting my invitation. I lack some of the basic cooking skills that you might be used to," she replied jokingly.

Andrew chuckled, "I rather fancy experimental cooking and

dining."

"Then I guess that makes you ready for me, Drew."

*

They chatted for a while and then said their good-bye's until seven thirty that evening. There was no turning back now. It was too late for both of them. Drawn together, a current tugging endlessly, passion and love were having their way. The stomach pain that had been troubling him all morning was suddenly gone. Andrew felt like a new man. And across town Monica was feeling like a new, vibrant woman.

*

Thomas was aware that he would be alone this evening, and he wasn't pleased. This was going too fast for Andrew. If he insisted on going forward with his relationship with Monica Banebridge, then he should at least have the good sense to take it slowly. Thomas was afraid that his master was out to prove a point as well as fulfill his dreams of love. Proving that point to Reginald could end up being the downfall of them all...

*

Andrew was called away from his office to the den by Thomas around two in the afternoon. It was an odd request but the old boy made it sound important. Since it was a slow business day, Andrew felt compelled to find out what was on the man's mind. Although he was fairly sure what it was that he wanted to speak to him about, it was fast becoming an old argument between them. The only thing that allowed Andrew to endure it was the knowledge that Thomas loved him so much.

The usual friendly face that normally greeted him at the elevator was absent. It was obvious that Thomas was angry with him. "I don't know if I should say good afternoon or not, old boy," he said stepping out of the elevator and into the entry hall. "You look a bit put off," he continued, walking past Thomas into the living room.

"How do you expect me to act when you're making a mistake and you refuse to see it?"

Andrew would do his level best to remain calm. He decided that on the way down in the elevator. "Why do you always assume that I cannot make an adult decision? I'm not a boy any longer, Thomas. I have needs."

Thomas shrugged his shoulders. "Oh, please spare me the 'I

have needs' routine. Andrew you're borrowing trouble. More trouble then you may be able to handle. I'm not as young as I once was, I may not be able to save you from yourself this time."

"I don't need you to protect me. I can take care of myself."

"Then you're either blind or a fool. You are not as powerful as you think."

"I haven't once had a relapse, why are you being so pessimistic?" he asked turning around to face him. "Do you want me to be alone the rest of my life? Because you know bloody well it'll be a long, endless life!" he continued, his voice rising in desperation as much as in anger.

"Of course I don't want you to be alone, Master Andrew. I just want you to slow down. You have no idea where this relationship is heading. You can't risk your secrets with her, unless you are sure she is ready to love you without reservation," he replied softly.

"Why must I tell her my secrets at all? I would lose her for sure if she knew the truth. They're my dirty secrets, why should she have to carry them? I can love her and still have my secrets, Thomas. Reginald was able to pull that off with my mother for years before he finally told her."

"You wouldn't do what your father did to your mother. You're not like him, Master Andrew. He placed your mother in an impossible situation by keeping the truth hidden until well after their marriage. Would you do the same to Monica?" Thomas asked, already knowing the answer.

"No." Andrew would never want to do that to Monica. She would never believe the truth, regardless. It didn't matter when he told her. "I have to go," he spoke so low that the words were barely audible.

"I say these things only because I care about you, Master Andrew."

*

The conversation he'd had with Thomas hadn't gone the way he would have preferred but at least it was over. He had lived a life of reserve for long enough. He wanted to love and be loved. To put a smile on her face and receive one in return. Was that so much to ask for? He had to wonder.

Lost in contract revisions it was nearly five o'clock before he looked up from a pile of papers on his desk. He felt exhausted. Given his day, what more could he expect? The only bright spot was Monica's call earlier in the day. She definitely lifted his low spirits. He couldn't ignore that. And nothing would please him more, he realized, than having Monica to come home to at the end of a long day. She would take his mind off the things that hounded him at work. That was his future, a future full of the best kind of hope. Love.

One thought was hanging over him like a dark cloud waiting to drown him with rain. His lies of omission. If Monica ever learned the truth about him, firstly, she most likely wouldn't believe him. And if she did, she would more likely leave him as quickly as she'd come into his life and he couldn't allow that to happen. He wanted to be honest with her. He wanted to do it for their future, and for the memory of his mother. It was what she would have wanted from him, for him to be truly honest with the woman he loved.

Damn this secret. It was eating away at him a little more each day. As much pleasure as he got from being with Monica, without being completely honest with her about himself, they will always have a lie between them. Damn Reginald Carter for putting him in this position in the first bloody place, he thought. Another lie. Reginald Carter, his father, he'd told her, along with the rest of New York, that his father was dead. How would he explain all of the madness? Andrew's head pounded just thinking about it.

*

He spent an hour in his room. Alone. Thomas tried to get him to come downstairs for tea but he refused. So he brought it up and left it outside his door. Andrew wanted some time alone with his thoughts while he dressed for his dinner with Monica. He couldn't decide what to wear. She had told him to dress casual. Should he? Why was he asking such a question of himself anyhow? Why was he so nervous? Again another question.

He brushed his damp black hair straight back, away from his forehead. The process felt relaxing. Next he brushed his teeth, never once regretting not knowing firsthand how he would look when he finished. He would have to take Thomas as his word.

Andrew was relaxed and feeling like his old self when he walked down the stairs two at a time. Thomas had pressed the gray trousers, the royal blue silk shirt and the matching gray vest he wore. The comfort of casual clothes was beginning to grow on him. The clothes make the man, he thought with a chuckle as he reached the bottom of the stairs.

He found Thomas sitting on the couch in the living room. At first glance, the person he saw there looked as old as the various collectors' items around the room. It was very clear that he was troubled.

Andrew came around from behind and sat down beside his loyal friend. "What's the matter, Thomas?" he said while trying to button the cuffs of his shirt. "Come on, tell me what's bothering you," he pressed.

Thomas looked Andrew straight in the eye. "I fear for you," he said simply. "I hope you realize the risk you're taking."

"I've never known you to be so pessimistic." He walked to the bar in the corner of the room. He poured himself a glass of wine and took a drink. "Everything will be fine," he continued.

Thomas looked at the glass in Andrew's hand. "How many glasses of wine have you had today?"

Andrew knew what he was getting at and sighed, "Five, why do you ask?"

"You know why. It's not even seven o'clock yet and you've had five glasses. You know what that could mean."

"It means I'm thirsty, Thomas, nothing more or less then that." He drained his glass and set it on the bar. "I'm tired of all this nagging," he said pointedly.

"You must try to curb your intake of the wine, Master Andrew. It will only increase the cravings."

"You're overly cautious," Andrew argued, glancing at his watch. "I don't want to be late, let's get moving." He crossed the room and walked out.

*

Monica was nervous. Her stomach churned as she remembered feeling like this when she was in high school. It took forever for her to settle on what she would wear. Andrew would dress casually, just like she'd asked him too, but now she was having second thoughts. After all, he wasn't a man who lounged around the house in jeans and a T-shirt, though the prospect of seeing him in them was suddenly very appealing.

She faltered. Maybe they should just go out to dinner. It was a woman's right to change her mind after all. She checked herself in her mirror a dozen times or more. She wanted to look perfect. Why was she so nervous? Dating wasn't anything new for her. Yet she could not remember getting so frazzled over a man. Andrew was different. Special. A total original.

Lipstick. She rolled her eyes and forced herself to get it together. Lipstick. The way things were going she'd be lucky if she made it through the evening without making a complete and utter fool of herself.

*

The drive across town was very quiet, almost somber. If Andrew didn't know better he'd have sworn they were going to a wake. The largeness of the car signified the distance in their opinions about how this evening would turn out. And given the company he was presently keeping, Andrew was surprisingly relaxed and excited. He was finally happy so why couldn't Thomas be happy for him? But he knew the answer. In the back of his head he knew why Thomas could not be happy for him.

Thomas knew better than anyone, even himself, Andrew had to confess, what the past had been and what the future could hold. He wasn't about to let all the "what ifs" ruin this night for him. He'd been patient and he deserved this night more than he could realize. Thomas' worries would not overshadow his enjoyment of it.

Finally Andrew felt the car slow and come to a stop, he lowered the power window and saw Monica's apartment building. His heart jumped to his throat. Any doubts he may have had about whether or not he was doing the right thing, suddenly vanished into thin air.

Thomas cleared his throat to bring his master's attention to him. He knew immediately. The glazed look in his master's eyes confirmed it. Like it or not, Andrew was in love with Monica Banebridge. He took some comfort in knowing that Andrew was, for the first time in such a long time, happy. Happy to love. To exist. To live. So resigned now, Thomas opened the door for what could be a brand new beginning for the man he'd come to love as his son. When that man smiled so warmly at him, stepping from the car, he returned that smile and prayed that God would watch over him.

*

Monica heard the car stop, and froze. Drew was here, finally, he was here. She looked around the apartment that now seemed so small and dull for someone like Andrew Carter. Take a deep breath, she thought, checking herself in the mirror once more. This was it, the point of no return. And much to her surprise she was anxious for the new journey to begin.

The knock at the door made her jump. And for a moment she couldn't even will her legs to move. But as quickly as that feeling came upon her, it disappeared. She pulled the door open and found him standing there with that gentle smile, with the warmth that attracted her to him in the first place. There was a powerful silence hanging in the air, but it spoke volumes for the two of them.

Monica looked at him for what seemed like forever. "Come in, Drew, as usual you're right on time," she said, stepping back from the door to let him inside.

"My mother always told me that it wasn't polite to keep a lady waiting." His grip on the wine bottle he carried tightened when he heard the door close behind him. "Something smells wonderful," he said, looking around the living room, praying his nerves didn't show.

"Don't get too excited, smells can be deceiving." She took the bottle from his tense hands. "I should've known you'd bring your own wine." The smile came easily. "Room temperature or chilled?"

He loosened up and grinned, "Room temperature please. And may I say you look absolutely lovely tonight."

She met his intense stare. "You may and thank you. You look very handsome yourself."

Andrew wondered around the apartment while Monica busied herself with dinner. The size of the place surprised him. It was small but quaint and it spoke of her. Little touches of her were everywhere. He expected as much, the homey feel; the cozy warmth so like her own. Oddly, he felt instantly at ease there. It was obvious that she had simple tastes. It didn't take much to warm her heart. He was impressed by that and he admired it as well. It was a trait that he never seemed to master.

He didn't hear her walk up behind him but he sensed she was there and he smiled. "I envy your ability to live in such a small, comfortable place," he said without turning around.

Monica was surprised by his admission. "Why on earth would you envy me? You have an extraordinary home, Drew, not to mention all of your successes," she replied.

He turned and faced her, "I'm afraid it doesn't mean very much when there's no one to share it with." He touched her cheek, felt the jolt under his fingertips. "Listen to me. Here I am feeling dreadfully sorry for myself when I've got a very beautiful woman to spend the evening with."

Monica saw the shift in his eyes and took his hand. "What's the matter Drew? There's sadness in your eyes," she said softly. Something was bothering him and she wanted nothing more than to make it disappear.

He was silent for a moment. "It's nothing, I'm just dealing with some feelings that I haven't felt in a long time. I guess I'm scared and anxious, and not used to the feelings."

Laying her palm flat against his broad chest, she revealed herself. "I hope your feelings won't scare you off. It's been a while for me too, but I think we should give it a chance, Drew."

*

Dinner was delicious. They danced for hours in candlelight. Swaying to music that filled the air with romance, very little was spoken between them. Neither needed words to convey what they were feeling. He couldn't take his eyes away from hers. She felt completely lost in his eyes as they glided to the music of Johnny Mathis. *Chances are, though I wear a silly grin...the chances are your chances are awfully good!* Monica fell deeper and deeper. And Andrew was already gone.

The light of what would probably be the last fire of the season warmed them as they sat together on the floor talking about nothing and everything. Listening to each other's voices, moving closer inch by inch. So close, their breath caressed their skin. The reflection of the fire danced in the wine at their feet, pooled in her eyes and his. Andrew watched emotion fill them and knew she was feeling the same as him.

Desire licked, danced, and snapped like the crackling of the fire, in him. And from the sensation he felt humming through her at his touch, in her as well. He leaned in, fisted his hand in her hair, drew her smell in and kissed her. Gently first, letting the taste of her, fill him. Then she feathered her fingers over his cheek and took them deeper with an urgency that sent him reeling.

She'd been waiting for him to kiss her all night and never imagined it would be like this. His lips felt like they were made for hers alone. She took his face in her hands, sighed, and fell deeper. The passion burning between them was as fierce and consuming as the fire before them. She pulled him closer, drowning in desire she'd never known. Her hands moving, searching, slowly gliding fingers slipping inside the collar of his shirt. Monica knew exactly what she wanted, him.

He found his control slipping, his need for her burning, driving him. He touched her face, with his fingers and then his lips. She tasted sweet, like nothing he'd ever tasted before. When he reached her neck he felt her pulse trip, quicken to match his own and felt her go weak in his arms. What he wanted more than anything was to make love to her, but fear woke his doubts. He tried to pull away. Pull away before they went too far, before there was no stopping it.

Andrew stopped and with a gasp, pulled away from Monica and slumped against the sofa. "Sorry," he managed. "I didn't want to appear so forward." His voice was raspy. He sucked in a breath. "Please forgive me."

Surprised and jolted she asked, "Drew? Why'd you stop?" she asked in a voice thick and smoky with arousal.

Andrew stood up and smiled. "It's me. I don't want to make any mistakes that could cost us what is happening here," he said softly.

Monica stood up and took his face in her hands. "You think we're rushing?" With a sigh, she dropped her head against his chest. "We've been dancing around our feelings for weeks. If I wasn't ready, I'd have never let it go this far, Drew." As if to prove it, she kissed him.

They looked into each other's eyes and in moments were locked in each other's arms again. It swamped him. His love for her, and before long the clothes Monica had been so nervous about were on the floor beneath her. His shirt soon followed. They made their way back to the bedroom without anymore second guessing. With their passion leading them on desperately, they gave in. It would be a long night.

*

The dim light of the moon spilling through the window cascaded over Monica's sleeping face. And Andrew just stared at her in wonder. He loved her, but could he keep her safe? He came too close and lingered too long and felt the hairs on the back of his neck stand on end. It was just passion, he reasoned. Passion. He could never do anything to her but love her. It was an oath, a promise he'd made to himself while he was making love to her hours ago. He loved her, needed her too much.

He pulled her close to his chest and his heart filled when she rested her hand on his skin. It felt wonderful to finally be this close. He would never take her flesh beneath his teeth. Never. He soon fell asleep, sure of his convictions.

Chapter 5

The morning sun woke Andrew. The intense heat on his face burned his skin as if acid had somehow absorbed into every pore. He rolled over shaking the bed waking Monica. Her hands slid down his back and she pressed her lips between his shoulder blades. But he pulled away. Bounding out of bed and covering his face, moving quickly into the bathroom.

"Drew, what's the matter?" she asked startled.

"Nothing go back to sleep," he replied as he closed the door. He was grateful for having his back to her. His face was burning. The pain was blinding! He turned on the cold water and doused his face before he stopped to take a breath. Andrew never felt such pain before in his life. He'd seen what burns from the sun had done to his father. Andrew moved his fingers slowly over his face trying to feel the damage. His face burned but couldn't feel any difference, for which he was very grateful. "Lucky, boy, very bloody lucky," he whispered.

There was a knock at the door. "Drew, are you all right?"

He slowly turned towards the door. "I'm fine, love. I'll be out in a moment," he managed and sucked in a breath. He had to call Thomas. He had to get out of the apartment and back to the mansion. When he opened the door, he prayed that he still resembled the man she'd seen only hours before.

*

Andrew was pacing a hole in Monica's carpet. Sweat was running off him like water. From now on Monica could stay at the mansion, he would come up with some excuse that she would accept. He couldn't remain in this kind of danger. For chrissake he felt as if he were melting!! Thomas would help him of course. But where the devil was he? He'd all but given up when he heard the knock on the door.

Thomas saw the look of relief on his master's face when he opened the door. He looked like he had been to the gates of hell by the way he was soaked to the bone with sweat. Thomas stepped inside the apartment without saying a word. He looked around in an almost chilling silence. He could sense Andrew's eyes on the back of his head. "It's a lovely place, smaller then I would have guessed, but lovely just the same. Where is she?"

"Breaking news; she had to get to the station."

He turned on his heels, faced his master, and took his face in his hands to survey the damage. The skin was red, and enflamed but it was nothing some salve won't fix. "You're lucky. Seems you're quite capable of finding more trouble than you can handle in a short amount of time."

Andrew took a deep breath and smiled. "Don't start old man, I'm past the point where 'I told you so' would do any good," he said with relief.

"I suppose you are."

"How are we going to get out of here?"

"Through the basement garage while it's still fairly deserted."

*

Behind the dark windows of the Rolls he could relax. He felt totally safe in his car. Here the sun could do him no harm. He ran his fingers over his sore skin, cursing himself and his slip in judgment. He could not afford to take any more risks like last night. Though there were things about last night that were wonderful, it could have all been lost if he'd hadn't acted quickly. Having Monica so close to him was wonderful. Touching her and feeling her next to him meant more than he could have ever imagined.

He smiled, thinking of how much pleasure she'd given him. They made love all night long, that's why he lost track of the time. He surely hadn't intended on staying all night with her. He couldn't allow himself to be so vulnerable again. No matter what comforts might be offered to him.

The streets of New York were crowded and traffic was slowed as a result. But the energy which was so New York still pulsed and it never failed to amaze him. It was a true thrill for him to be among such urgency. In the darkness when the sun set he could be among it, savor it.

Sometimes he missed it, not being able to roam the streets with the sun at his back. But his memory was long and he could escape to those memories at will. And thinking back Andrew remembered a time long ago when he could have walked down the sidewalks of New York City like everyone else.

It had been an extremely dreary day. Very dark and forbidding, but for Andrew it was truly a day that was heaven sent. While everyone he passed was cursing such a shadowy day, he was smiling wide enough for the entire city to see. The average person would never be able to understand the sheer joy that surrounded him. With every step there was elation they could never perceive. It was an experience he remembered with a great fondness, so it was no surprise when he felt a tear fall on his cheek.

Maybe someday he could take Monica on a long walk to Central Park. Andrew counted on something his mother once told him -- 'If a person is a truly good person at heart, then if they wish long enough and hard enough sometimes wishes can be granted and dreams can come true.'

Thomas could see it on his master's face as he glanced in the mirror and frowned. He was off in another time once again. He had that troubled, far away look in his eyes. He understood why his master felt the way he did about Monica Banebridge. He might be an old man but he was not blind. He could see she was very beautiful. He was even willing to admit that she seemed to really care for Andrew Carter the person and not Andrew Carter the legend. But this woman that was loved so deeply had a mountain of pain that she would one day have to face. It was a pain from which no one would be able to save her, no one.

*

The television station was a madhouse. But what normally would have driven Monica out of her mind somehow was having no effect on her at all. Because after all this was no average day, it was the first day after having been so utterly blown away by the passion two people could possibly share. She spent the first two hours of the morning locked inside her office reliving every moment and filing a story here and there. Andrew has been as gentle and loving as she knew he would be.

It was a wonderful night. Andrew had given her the perfect evening. Though his sudden departure from bed this morning had been confusing, she'd never had a more memorable night. It was the persistent knocking at the door that brought her back from her dreamland, "Coming."

Monica rushed to the door and unlocked it.

Mr. Philips looked at her for a moment. "What? Are you locking your door now?" He walked in slowly looking around the office. "Is there something going on in here that your old boss should know about?" he continued with a smile.

Monica smiled and walked back to her chair and sat down. "I

have a lot of work to get caught up on. I didn't want to be disturbed."

He shrugged his shoulders and leaned on the chair across from her desk. "Whatever gets your creative juices flowing."

"What can I do for you, Mr. Philips?"

"Just wanted to let you know that we're airing your interview with Carter on Friday."

"Great." Monica was thrilled but would Andrew feel the same?

"I guess you can give him a heads up if you like."

"I will."

"See you at the staff meeting later on." He walked over to the door.

"See you."

The door closed behind him.

She didn't know what she expected Drew to say. He may not even want to watch it. Most shy people were tough critics on themselves and wouldn't want to suffer through the ordeal of watching them glorify themselves on camera. On the other hand, he may want to watch if for no other reason than obligation.

There was an unexplainable sense of mystery about Andrew Carter. And Monica had to admit she was no closer to uncovering it now then she had been on the day she met him. He seemed so taken with the simplicity of her life. From her cozy apartment to her stash of microwave popcorn, he seemed to delight in it. Odd for such an extremely complex man, but it was also charming. And more than once throughout the evening she caught him staring off into space as if he forgotten she was there. And then this morning instead of letting her drop him off at home, he insisted on staying behind and waiting for Thomas.

*

He was happy to be home and breathed a sigh of relief walking through the door. Thomas immediately disappeared to get him his treatment, tea and paper. Andrew noticed the chill between him and Thomas and knew it was the old man's way of punishing him. It was a ritual he'd been though with Thomas since his childhood. And if he were honest with himself he'd confess that he loved it.

Thomas came into the study a half an hour later with a tray carrying his treatment, wine, tea and crumpets and set it down on the desk. He studied his master's face while he applied the ointment and remained silent throughout. And when he finished he turned and walked out of the room. Andrew stood and groaned, steadying himself against the desk as the door closed sharply.

He stared at the door shaking his head. "It's a little chilly in here." He poured himself tea, something which Thomas normally did for him. But in keeping with the spirit of the punishment such privileges were suspended.

Andrew left the house an hour later without seeing Thomas before hand. He would wait Thomas out. Take his medicine so to speak before he would approach him again. The numbers above the elevator doorway ticked off slowly. More time to feel badly about having treated Thomas with so little respect, he thought, tapping his foot so hard he was sure he was going to produce a hole for his troubles.

The door finally opened and for that, Andrew was profoundly grateful. He moved down the hallway with such swiftness that the people he passed simply stopped and craned their heads to see why he was in such a rush. He did offer quick smiles but not with his usual cheerfulness. He had other things on his mind.

How would he tell Monica that he couldn't stay at her place anymore? Thomas seemed bound and determined to make an example of this situation. He was so bloody dramatic, thought Andrew as he almost ran down a person from the steno pool as he turned into his office. What a wonderful night, he thought. And what a horrible day.

He was in an altercation with his computer when Sarah stuck her head in the door. He looked up from the monitor and softened his face into a smile. "What kind of bad news do you have for me Sarah, that makes you stick your head in to check my mood before you decide whether you want to come in?" he asked pushing himself away from his desk.

"How'd you know?" she asked chagrinned.

"Ten years of reading your body language. Come in and tell me what it is."

"Paris called; they're demanding a meeting, something about a late shipment. What would you like me to tell them?"

"Tell them…" with his sour mood the temptation to tell them to go to hell was hard to curb, "If they want to see me they know where I am, but by the time they board their plane the shipment will have arrived."

"I'll tell them."

This day was proving to be one from hell. Andrew decided that after the third conference call to Paris with him trying to quiet the fears. And more then once during the conversation he found himself wishing that he hadn't renewed their contract. However there were a few good thoughts flowing through his head off and on. The night with Monica was all he was hoping for and everything he wanted it to be. She made him want to be free. He could only ask for so much. They could share more nights again but if she'd seen his face this morning before he got the chance to conceal it, the end would have come before they'd really began.

He had to be more careful in the future. He was risking things he wasn't willing to lose.

His stomach was bothering him again. He knew what it could mean. Knew it last night when he tasted the skin on her neck. The desire had been there. The craving he hadn't felt in so long took root deep in his belly. He couldn't deny that, but he could control it. If Thomas had known about it he most definitely would have taken some rather drastic steps. But he was not his father and would not allow himself such violent pleasures. He did once, but no more.

He wanted to call her. The sound of her voice would ease his pain and reassure him if only for awhile. It would be worth it. If he were a stronger man he'd let her go. Andrew wondered if he was damning her right along with him. Did she love him as much as he loved her? Time would tell him all he needed to know.

Chapter 6

July

The relationship between Andrew and Monica deepened in the two months they had been together. The feelings they shared for each other were serious and all consuming. The heat of summer paled compared to the heat burning between them. Andrew could spend hours, or so he said countless times, just looking into Monica's eyes. But he wasn't alone in feeling the intensity. Monica was also taking on a new side to her personality. Work was no longer the most important thing in her life. It was still a vital part, but Andrew had become more important in a very short amount of time.

They had dinner every evening and then spent the entire night locked away in his bedroom. There were no more nights at Monica's apartment and Monica didn't seem to have a problem with it. She loved being at the mansion, loved feeling like a queen in a castle. As far as Andrew was concerned she was exactly that, his queen. And the mansion was her castle for as long as she wanted.

But the happiness, at least for Andrew, did not come without problems. His stomach had not improved like he had been hoping, and once Thomas knew of the problem he warned him that it was a worrisome sign of things to come. The intensity of the pain was too much for him to deal with alone. So Thomas began to treat his aliments by toying with the strengths of the stock from dark sector below the main house.

A stronger combination, stumbled on by Thomas during one of his all night sessions. Andrew didn't know exactly what it was he was taking because Thomas never allowed him in the dark sector. But it hardly mattered as long as it took away the extreme discomfort dogging him endlessly. A smart man never looked a gift horse in the mouth.

His nights were becoming restless and he no longer slept through till morning. Though he would exhaust himself making love to Monica, while she slept soundly, he laid wide awake and uncomfortable. The night air was tightening its hold on him. Holding as much excitement for him as Monica did. But he would not allow these growing problems to ruin his jubilation with Monica. He held on to hope that his heightened senses and the natural instincts of his kind would quiet, and do so quickly.

And though it wasn't wise, he'd been thinking of asking Monica to move in with him, until the stomach pains and restless nights began to be more prevalent. Besides, it was semantics because she was already practically living there anyway. Some nights when he couldn't sleep he would sit in the chair next to the bed and watch her sleeping peacefully. It gave him strength. Reminding him what he stood to lose if he couldn't control what he loathed inside him. Andrew wouldn't allow himself to worry about what-ifs. There were more good things in his life to hold on to than bad.

So, as was his way, Thomas worried enough for them both. He knew what was wrong with his master even though his master refused to acknowledge it. His blood chilled just thinking about what it could mean in the months ahead, or god forbid, even sooner perhaps. Thomas could only count on the fact that he started the treatment which should cut off any future aliments to come. Master Andrew was strong Thomas knew that. He had seen it time and time again over the years. So why did this time have to be any different. His master could handle it. Or so he hoped.

*

Andrew couldn't help getting excited about the plans he had made for Monica and himself later this evening. He was even including Thomas because he knew he would enjoy it. He called the captain of his yacht and told him to ready it for a midnight cruise. Fine wine, gourmet cuisine, moonlight and basking in her delight and Andrew couldn't wait.

*

It had been six days since he needed a treatment from Thomas. And though it might be foolish, he was proud about that, but now it was time for another one. It would make the pain shooting through his abdomen stop and he could continue his day. When he entered his office he went straight to the phone.

*

Andrew looked terrible when Thomas saw him behind his desk, "Chills?" Thomas asked coming behind the desk and putting his palm against his master's forehead.

"Not so bad, but my stomach is being a...bit difficult," he replied through clenched teeth.

Thomas turned his back to Andrew and set to ease his master's pain. "Here, drink this. This should take the edge off. You must try to relax, give it time to work."

Andrew drank the liquid down. "Thank you, Thomas," he muttered softly.

Thomas smiled and tipped Andrew's head back to check his eyes. He watched his pupils change, clear. "You're welcome, Master Andrew. I'll see you later." And with that Thomas walked over to the door. "Remember, relax and give it a few moments to work." he closed the door behind him.

*

An hour later, Andrew was behind his desk hard at work and happily looking forward to the evening ahead. The projects at the office were coming along nicely, so he was having a great day. He thought about calling Monica, but he knew she was in meetings all day and he didn't want to bother her. She said she would call when she finished.

He called Sarah in for dictation and then he sent for some tea and called the deli across the street and ordered lunch. Andrew was doing a very good job at distracting himself from the craving he'd been having for the last hour. It wasn't a craving by normal standards, no this was something else. He craved...he knew what he craved but admitting it would mean no turning back. The taste of blood. He craved the taste of blood.

Rage erupted and in his anger he shoved himself away from his desk with more strength then he meant too, sending his desk flipping over and his papers scattering everywhere. He let out a wail so guttural that it scared him. Before he could realize what happened Sarah and three others from the outer office came rushing through the door.

"What happened?" Sarah cried in disbelief.

Andrew pulled himself together and stared at the chaos in silence.

"Mr. Carter? What happened?" she repeated, crossing the room.

Andrew looked up at the puzzled faces and tried for levity. "Ah, nothing I just got upset." Pausing, and with a shrug, he dragged his hand through his hair. "Guess I lost my temper."

"You're sure you're okay?" Someone asked, unsure.

"Yes, yes, I'm fine." He raked his hands over his face, annoyed and more than a little frightened at his behavior.

Later, with his desk upright and his papers back in order, he tried to get back to work, pushing what happened to the back of his mind. To actually crave blood made him shudder. There'd been no vagueness in the craving to cling to. He knew what he was craving in a split second. He put his head in his hands and wondered if his sanity was slipping right along with his control.

He wasn't like his father, damnit. The very thought of blood on his lips made him double over in disgust as much pain. His mind swept back to the one time in his life that he followed his urge. Elizabeth. He could remember so clearly his teeth sinking into the soft flesh of her neck. Revulsion made him shiver. She fought him but not for long. Her blood, so sweet, flowed through him. He took his fill and her life was gone. Andrew shook his head to clear the memory. He would not allow it to happen again.

*

When Monica returned to her office she collapsed into her chair and looked at her phone, then her watch. The meeting had gone longer then she'd expected. On a sigh, she picked up the phone and hit the speed dial button marked DC. It rang three times then he picked up.

"Yes?"

"You sound as tired as I feel." She smiled. His voice soothed.

"Well, I thought you'd forgotten about me."

"Nope, just tied up."

"I hope you're not too tired for a surprise."

"Oh really?"

"Yes, really. Up for it, love?" he smiled at the thought of her face when she saw the boat.

"I'm up for anything with you," she replied playfully.

"Good. I'll pick you up at nine."

"That's only two hours to get ready, Drew."

"That's more than enough for you, love. See you then."

*

He felt worn and weary walking out of the elevator and into his hallway. Thomas met him with a glass of wine and a knowing smile. Andrew took a drink and walked into the living room to collapse onto the couch. He put his feet up on the coffee table and let the wine do its work. He felt Thomas watching him. "I'm not dying, old boy, just resting." He opened his eyes and looked at Thomas. "What is it?" he finally asked. Not all together sure he wanted to know.

Thomas sat down beside Andrew. "Master Andrew, Sarah called and told me about what happened today," he said softly.

Andrew thought about lying, but what purpose would it serve. Thomas was the only one who would understand. "I got upset that's all." He shifted on his cushion, closed his eyes again.

"About what? What would make you so angry that you would cause such disarray in your office?"

"If I tell you, you'll overreact," Andrew replied.

"Tell me."

"I had a craving."

"What kind of craving?"

"The kind we pretend doesn't exist."

Thomas sat silently for a while, "It is encouraging that you didn't act on it. You controlled it, right? You didn't hurt yourself did you?" he asked.

He lifted a brow and sighed, "You mean did I cut myself and drink my own? No, I did not."

"Good."

He sat up and rubbed his sore eyes, "I have to go get changed, we're leaving in an hour."

*

Andrew changed into casual clothes and he was sitting on his bed. He felt much better then he had a couple of hours ago. Seeing Monica would take care of the rest. He called his captain to make certain the yacht was ready. Now all he had to do was pick up Monica and take her to the marina. He walked to the window and opened the shutter to look outside. It was almost nine and the sun was down. He walked over to the door, turned out the light, and headed down the hall for the stairs.

Thomas met him at the bottom in his own casual clothes. It wasn't often that he dressed in such a casual way, but he decided he would be out of place in a housecoat and tie on the water. Master Andrew liked him to dress comfortably. "Are you ready to go, Master Andrew?" he asked.

"Yes," he clapped a hand on Thomas' shoulder, "Let's go have some fun."

"Here we go then."

*

Monica was happy to see Andrew when she opened her apartment door. He was standing in the hallway with a huge grin on his face and a dozen roses in his hand. He walked inside and gave her a long kiss. His eyes swept over her. "How are you this evening?" he asked warmly.

Monica loved it when he was close to her so she drew out the embrace as long as she could. She smelled his cologne and felt the flutter in her stomach. "Fine now. Why such a late start to our evening?" she asked inquisitively.

"It's a surprise, Monica."

"Come on, Drew, just give me one hint."

"Nope," he teased, "I'm afraid my lips are sealed."

*

The car ride to the marina was exciting for Monica because she had no idea where she was going. And it was exciting for Andrew and Thomas because they couldn't wait to see the look on her face when she finally saw her surprise. The two of them cuddled in the back seat and fussed over each other the entire ride. Thomas thought he'd had about all he could take when finally Andrew sat up straight and got serious.

"Okay, Monica you have to put this on," Andrew said holding up the blindfold.

"Excuse me?" she asked sarcastically.

"Come on, it's only for a little while." He covered her eyes and kissed the tip of her nose. "You don't want to ruin your own surprise, do you?" he asked sweetly.

"It's low to use your considerable charm against me."

She sat beside Andrew trying to decipher every bump on the road and figure out where Andrew was taking her. Andrew must have anticipated her and had Thomas taking all kinds of alternate routes. Monica had no idea where she was going but she was definitely intrigued by the mystery.

Andrew and Thomas were amused by her expressions as she tried to feel her way to their destination. He found great joy in watching her try to outsmart him. He felt even more attracted to her when she showed her intelligence. He had to admit he liked knowing something she didn't. He was looking out the window when he noticed the marina lights up ahead with a grin.

The car came to a stop and Andrew felt Monica tense up in his arms. When Thomas opened the door he and his master exchanged smiles. Andrew stepped out of the car and turned around to help Monica. After a few seconds of buildup, Andrew removed the blindfold and watched as her eyes filled with amazement. "It gets better, come on."

He took her by the arm and walked her down a small dock. She was looking at all the boats surrounding her when they came to a stop. "Now this is the best part," he whispered softly into her ear.

Monica couldn't believe what she was seeing. In front of her was what she considered to be, the most beautiful yacht she'd ever seen. "Oh, Drew, it's stunning. Is it yours?" she asked without ever taking her eyes away from it.

"Yes. And it's also your surprise, well its part of your surprise anyway. I'm taking us on a cruise in the harbor. Have you ever seen Lady Liberty in the moonlight?" he pulled her close to him and kissed her softly.

"Ah...no." Excitement skittered up her spine. "Really, do you mean it, Drew?" she asked feeling ten years old again and her father was taking her on her first boat ride in Ireland.

"Of course I mean it," he motioned toward the large deck and smiled, "shall we go? I promise it will be an evening you'll never forget."

*

Monica couldn't believe the view from the deck. It was something she couldn't find the words to describe. And the man that gave it to her was something she couldn't describe either. She turned to find Andrew coming across the deck with two glasses of wine and a smile that could light up the harbor. If Monica could have ever dismissed the notion of loving Andrew Carter, she could no longer do it now.

Looking at him with the dim lights of the city surrounding them off in the distance and the moonlight casting him in an almost ethereal glow, she knew that she loved him. Finally she understood that she could love someone without reservation. His eyes told her all she needed to know. And Monica knew that he loved her just as she knew he would never hurt her. She touched his cheek and he smiled, placing his hand on hers. She could have looked into his eyes forever, but Thomas broke the spell when he came to tell them dinner was ready.

Monica didn't quite know what to make of Thomas but she liked him. He was a generous man who cared for Andrew more than Andrew might realize. And it was obvious the feeling was reciprocated. Andrew loved Thomas like a father and he treated him with an affection and honesty that made her love him all the more. It was sweet, she thought, of Andrew to bring Thomas along on the cruise. He seemed to be enjoying himself. She could understand Drew's feelings for Thomas because, though she hadn't known him all that long, she really liked spending time with Thomas too.

The dinner was delicious and the conversation was interesting. Andrew insisted that Thomas tell some of his old stories about England and soon he was headlong into one of his favorites. Monica smiled and watched his facial expressions turn comical explaining things to her. Andrew held her hand the entire time. As he sat back and listened to the same stories he'd heard a million times before. He simply could not remember ever feeling so at peace with himself. He saw them all as being a family, one that could make it through anything together. When he looked across the table at the two people he loved most in this world, it pleased him endlessly that they got on so well.

Sometime after eleven Thomas went below to the game room, while Monica and Andrew danced on the deck with the yacht anchored under the Lady Liberty. He couldn't stop kissing her. Every time he tried he found himself kissing her again. He kissed her lips, her cheeks, and slowly moved down the nape of her neck. She smelled wonderfully inviting and he lingered longer then he should have. In a sudden movement he pulled away from her.

"What's wrong?" Monica asked in surprise, "Why did you pull away?"

He tried to act as if nothing unusual had happened. "Nothing, Love. I thought I heard Thomas call me," he looked down the stairway.

"I didn't hear anything. Are you all right?"

"Yes, of course, but I really must go check down below. Thomas and the chef don't get on so well," he paused, "they'll kill each other if there's a problem. I promise I'll be right back, save my place." Andrew kissed her softly on the cheek and though he wanted to flee he went down the stairs casually.

Once Andrew reached the bottom of the stairs he dropped the act. His legs went out from under him and he went down hard on his knees. He felt it again. The urge. He could almost feel the flesh beneath his teeth puncturing, and the coppery scent of blood. He could almost taste it as Thomas walked in to find him nearly sprawled out on the floor. Their eyes met as the sweat seeped from every pore of Andrew's body. He grabbed hold of the railing and pulled himself to his feet, waving Thomas away when he tried to help.

"It's happened again?" Thomas asked quietly, casting a wary glance up to the top of the stairs to make sure Monica hadn't followed.

"Yes. I guess... I don't know," Andrew replied, wiping the sweat from his eyes.

"Yes you do, but you do not want to face it, Master Andrew."

"There must be something we can do to stop this bloody madness, Thomas. Please do something."

"What would you like me to do?"

"Something. Anything."

He did return to the deck, twenty minutes later and feeling much better. He felt bad about having left Monica alone for so long, but she didn't seem to mind. He apologized profusely though she said it wasn't necessary. They danced. She kissed him. At first he resisted, afraid, but his willpower drained. And before he could think better of it...they were making love.

Chapter 7

Andrew was up early sitting in the chair by his bed when Thomas came in to wake him. He was hoping he'd find him asleep amused by only his dreams. His master didn't look any better today, he noted walking over to place the back of his hand to Andrew's brow. "Good morning, Master Andrew, How are you feeling?"

"Worn out, old boy," Andrew said pushing himself up from the chair, "just bloody worn out." He had the growth of a four day beard on his chin and a red tint to his eyes that revealed their painful condition.

"You didn't sleep at all last night?"

"I wish," he said flatly, shoving his hands deep into the pockets of his robe. "I might be willing to give up my right arm for a night of sleep!"

"I'm increasing your treatments starting today. I know it's not what you want, Master Andrew but it's the only thing I know to do for you." Thomas reasoned when Andrew turned to argue. "It's for your own good."

"I know, Thomas," Andrew replied with the fight dying inside him, knowing Thomas was right, "I know."

*

Monica was totally oblivious to what was happening with Andrew. He had become a master at hiding his problems from her. She was typing her latest story, just as she had been for the past three hours. She had gotten up early before Andrew so she could get a jump on the day. He seemed so tired lately she decided it was best not to wake him. He was a very busy, powerful man with so many things on his mind. She was concerned that he was working too hard. And she was hardly the one to make the suggestion that he slow down considering she was working sixty-five hour weeks herself.

He hadn't been sleeping. Monica knew that. She felt him getting in and out of bed all night, trying not to wake her. Watching her sleep when he couldn't.

The phone was right there. Maybe she should call him, she thought as she finished up the last paragraph. No. She reasoned. He promised to call when he got to the office so she would wait.

Monica went on with her work. The evenings she was spending with Drew were great, though they hadn't left the house since the yacht cruise. She liked spending time with him. It didn't matter what they did. Whether they were doing nothing but sitting in front of the television or working out together in the gym. She didn't care as long as they were together.

She had plenty to keep herself busy today. She had meeting after meeting, as well as covering the arrival of a senator from Wisconsin later in the day. It would have made Monica much happier if this assignment would have been one she volunteered for, but instead it was one she'd been bullied into. It wasn't that she didn't like the senator. Well, okay, she didn't like him. Not his politics or his personality, but she would do the story because she was a professional and that responsibility was ingrained in her.

And to make matters worse the big wigs at the top of the station still wanted something to keep them in the lead for the number one position of most watched broadcast of the nightly news being the goal. The deliverer of the grand solution was to be none other then Monica Banebridge. They expected something to fit the bill by the end of the week. As if she didn't already have enough on her mind. What could she come up with? She had no idea at all. But because she thrived under pressure, she could come up with something.

*

It was after ten o'clock and Andrew still had not dressed for the day. He seemed content enough to remain in his room, in his robe, with his mind closed. Closed, because an open mind right now would do more harm than good and he was smart enough to know it. He felt the darkness becoming a friend to him again. Like something missed and yearned for, it once again tempted him. He ran his tongue along the two sharp teeth that had proved so lethal in the past.

What could he do to keep from causing havoc? He was stronger than the force of evil inside him and all he had to do was keep reminding himself of that. He'd be damned if he'd use his demons as an excuse. Andrew would not give Reginald the satisfaction of being right with his cryptic predictions of the future. He'd fight like hell before he would let that happen.

An hour later Andrew finally dressed, after three cups of tea and one glass of wine he went up to begin a late day at the office.

What he needed was routine and safety. Sarah seemed surprised to see him walk into the reception area outside his office. "Mr. Carter, I wasn't sure you were coming in today."

"I decided I deserved a break. Any morning mail or phone calls I should be aware of?" he asked pleasantly.

"Several calls but no mail, here are the messages."

"Thank you, Sarah. You know where I am if you need me," he said walking into his office and closing the door.

He was happy to see his files arranged neatly on the edge of his desk, just like they were every day. Seeing them gave him a bridge to normality when his world was shifting around under his feet. A tight grip on his vampire instincts was necessary, shaky ground or not. His world was falling apart and he had to put a stop to it before it was too late.

Returning the phone calls took longer than he'd anticipated and by the time he looked at the clock it was after one in the afternoon. He wanted to hear Monica's voice and decided there was no time like the present. He picked up the phone and dialed her direct line. It rang four times before it she answered.

"Hello," answered a tense voice on the other end of the line.

"Monica?"

"Drew," tension eased and she smiled, "you're just coming into the office?"

"I've been here for a little while but I had a lot of calls to return and a crisis to handle. I asked for it though, I should've known better then to wait until lunch time to come in. I wanted to try and catch up on some lost sleep."

"Any luck?"

"No."

"I bet I could send you right into dreamland," she replied coyly.

"You're welcome to try," he said smiling.

"I could wear you out."

"Making an offer?"

"Would you accept? I do love a challenge."

"I aim to please."

*

He sat at his desk with wild images running through his head; crazy thoughts. He imagined himself ripping into the neck flesh of unsuspecting victims, draining their blood from their jugular. He tried to force the evil thoughts from his mind but they would not release their hold on him. Andrew could feel the bile bubbling and rising in his stomach and pushed himself up from his chair. His head was almost on fire, he made it to the sink in time to vomit violently.

When he was through he collapsed to the floor. He was weak, too weak. He wanted to die. This nightmare could not go on much longer. He wasn't as strong as he thought.

Eight thirty came and Andrew was still sitting limply behind his desk. He didn't want to move for fear it would bring on another vomiting spell. He wasn't sure he had the strength it would take to make it over to the sink again. It was best just to stay still. Thomas would come for him soon enough. Right now he needed to save his strength. Had to ready himself to fight the intense battle he was now sure was on the horizon.

Finally after weeks of sleepless nights Andrew felt tired enough to drop off. He was meeting Monica in an hour and at the moment he didn't think he could make it to the door, let alone across town to pick her up. The only solution would be to send Thomas to get her while he stayed behind and pulled himself together.

He looked at the phone and decided it would be too much trouble to pick it up, so he pushed the speaker phone and dialed Thomas. He was still waiting for an answer when he looked up and saw him standing in the doorway.

"Well, don't we look like hell?" he asked coming into the office.

"I've been trying to get you on the phone," Andrew replied while sweat ran off his forehead in streams, "and before you say anything, yes I know I look deplorable." He pinched the bridge of his nose with clammy fingers. "I need you to go fetch Monica and bring her back to the mansion."

"Are you sure you're up for company, Master Andrew?" Thomas asked rolling up his master's sleeve and slipping a needle into his arm.

"Yes, she is exactly what I need." His head was spinning and he thought he was about to vomit again when Thomas tapped him on the shoulder.

"Drink this," Thomas said. "It should take care of the nausea. Shall I leave now?"

"You'd better help me to the house first. I'm too weak to make it alone." Andrew said standing and leaning on Thomas for support.

"Don't worry, Master Andrew, you'll feel like your old self in no time." Thomas replied putting his arm around him and helping him through the door.

*

Andrew was glad to climb into the shower and feel the water caress him. It was soothing and seemed to breathe the life back into him. He closed his eyes and leaned against the back wall of the shower. As Thomas had promised the nausea had lifted and he slowly began feeling more like himself. A surge of energy shot through him like a hot whip cracking across his back and almost causing his feet to slip out from under him.

He decided not to shave because he didn't know if he could trust himself yet. He hadn't done it alone but for a few times and he was afraid that if he cut himself the enticement to do what would come naturally would prove too great to resist. Maybe Monica would find it sexy, he thought as he pulled the silk shirt onto his shoulders, which only a short time ago felt weak and heavy and now felt as if he could carry the entire world on them.

Downstairs Andrew found the dining room set up for a very romantic dinner. Andrew guessed Thomas arranged it when he was still in the shower as he looked around the room in amazement. He walked into the living room and straight to the bar to pour three fingers of scotch. He took a huge gulp and left it rolling around his mouth for a bit. The taste was rich and steadied him. Andrew hoped Thomas returned soon. He wanted to hold Monica.

Twenty minutes passed and then a half an hour. And Andrew was beginning to worry until he heard Monica call to him from the front door. He walked down the hall to the entry way. Monica and Thomas both greeted him with smiles, but it was she who walked into Andrew's arms giving him a long kiss as a proper hello.

"I was getting worried," Andrew said, squeezing her tightly in his arms.

"Sorry, there was a wreck on West Thirty First," Thomas explained putting his hat away in a nearby closet.

"Damned city drivers," he replied simply. Putting his arm around Monica's waist and walking her into the living room. He leaned over and whispered, "Wait until you see what we're having for dinner. Thomas outdid himself this time."

"I can hardly wait." Monica sat down on the couch and pulled Andrew down beside her. "You still look tired, Drew. I thought you rested this morning before going into the office?"

He didn't know how to respond. The treatment helped him feel better but it obviously didn't do much for his appearance. "I did, Love. It's just been a trying day and my stomach was a bit upset earlier." He smiled and cupped her face in his hands, kissing her softly and easing her concern. "But I'm fine now. Besides, I thought you were going to take care of me tonight?"

"Oh, don't worry," she said, nuzzling his neck, "I am."

*

Thomas busied himself in the kitchen with dinner but he couldn't keep from worrying about his master. He looked undeniably drained when he walked into the entryway. And if he noticed so quickly then so would Ms. Banebridge. How could his master explain? He supposed his master would tell her the truth, or at least part of it. That he was feeling under the weather. But if episodes like today continued, he would not be able to keep explaining them away, she would eventually become concerned and then suspicious. And having Monica Banebridge digging around was the last thing they needed.

The reality of the situation was that Andrew Carter was a vampire. Flesh and blood but no longer completely human, like Thomas himself, and different in ways Monica Banebridge could never comprehend. The man she knew and loved would never age or die. While she grows older, he will not. He is frozen in time with a past too dark to understand or forget. But she was what his master wanted, so it had to be. But the darkness from which he had saved Andrew Carter was slowly returning; it always wants to ones who resist the most. The darkness was controlled for now, but how much longer could it continue before it swallowed his master whole?

Thomas hadn't told Andrew, but his eyes were growing darker by the day. His soul cried out for what his body was denying itself. The awesome power was returning and it was only the beginning. The treatment would only satisfy his cravings for so long. And it was his duty to save his master from himself. He'd made that promise years ago to Mother Carter on her deathbed. But he was only one man. Andrew Carter would have to save himself.

The nausea and vomiting were signs of Andrew's rejection of the desire for blood. But soon there might not be any rejection at all. He'd already started becoming restless at night. Had started staring out at the night and began to feel the pull to return. And Thomas knew he had to stop this before it went any further out of control. He could try increasing the treatment strength and thereby its effects. And he could deal with the wine later but only if it proved unavoidable. Leaving such serious thoughts behind, he picked up a tray, and pasting a smile on his face, walked out of the kitchen.

*

Andrew and Monica were talking quietly when Thomas came into the room and told them dinner was ready. So they got up from the couch and followed him into the dining room. Andrew pulled a chair out for Monica and pushed her in but his attention was on Thomas and his distracted movements and it troubled him. "Excuse me, darling, I'll be right back," he said and followed Thomas into the kitchen.

"What's got you so distracted, old boy?" he asked once the door had swung closed behind them.

Thomas' eyes flicked up to meet his briefly before he turned his attention back to finishing off the salads. "What makes you think I'm distracted?"

"Thomas," Andrew said impatiently, "if I was blind and deaf I could still see you're upset about something."

"I'm fine, Master Andrew."

"Rubbish!" he shot back.

"You've better manners than to leave Ms. Banebridge alone," he chided. "Go back to her."

"She's fine," Andrew persisted, "now what's wrong?"

"You have chosen not to discuss it," Thomas said seriously. "But I'm concerned, I think you know why."

"Thomas, I'm fine. For the moment at least, I'm fine."

"Now who's talking rubbish?"

*

He heard the clock striking midnight. And heard it strike every hour since. After three hours of what should have been exhausting sex, Andrew Carter was wide awake. He actually felt exhilarated by it. He paced to the window and opened the shutter, and then the pane. He inhaled deeply and sighed. The night air was humid but pleasantly so. Andrew stared out at the clear night, thinking how wonderful it would be to go for a walk. The simplicity of it blunted the risk which lay in it. It might be just what he needed to fall asleep.

Andrew looked over his shoulder at the woman lying in his bed. Oh, how he loved her. The months they shared together were so fulfilling he treasured them. Each hour, each day was a gift. Soon August would arrive and with it came the chance to ask Monica the question he'd been putting off for weeks now.

He shrugged, coaxing his tense muscles to relax, but the edginess of restlessness won out. So, he slipped out of his robe and into a pair of old jeans. One of the many trickle-down affects of the woman whose quiet, steady breathing was a song to him. She loved him in faded denim and it felt wonderful against his skin. A short walk would do him a world of good and make him tired enough to sleep, he told himself.

Once dressed, he grabbed a pair of running shoes from the closet and slipped out of the room. Now as long as he got out of the house without waking Thomas he'd be home free, he thought. As he tiptoed through the hallway past Thomas' door he felt a pang of guilt but ignored it. He wouldn't realize the danger of his decision until it was too late.

*

Andrew embraced the awkward sense of peace spreading through him. It was different from the peace he found with Monica or the safety he had with Thomas. It ran deeper, felt truer. It had been missing from his life for so long, too long, but it was back now.

He ambled along, finding the city much more relaxing at night. And when he walked into Central Park and found that a few people had the same idea as he did, he smiled.

He walked at a leisurely pace enjoying the chance to be without Thomas' watchful eyes on his every move. He noticed a few people staring, but couldn't decide if it was recognition or paranoia behind their curiosity. So he just kept walking, minding his business, trying to run down the electrical charge driving him.

It brought him to a dead stop, the potent power of the sensation. And what lay behind it was no mystery, the subtle feeling of his teeth somehow growing sharper and the hair on the back on his neck standing on end. And then the rush of dizziness sweeping over him had him steadying himself against a bench. He thought he heard someone asking if he was all right, but he could only manage to shake his head in response. And then, as quickly as the episode hit, the pain and disorientation was gone.

*

Thomas was practically asleep on his feet when he decided he could do no more to help his master until he got some sleep. The climb up the stairs back to the main part of the house seemed endless and exhausting. When he'd reached upstairs, on his way to his room he noticed the light on under the master bedroom door. He continued down the hall and knocked on the door. He opened it when he heard Monica tell him to come in and found her sitting on the edge of the bed.

"Ms. Banebridge, are you all right?" he asked looking around for his master.

"Have you seen Drew? I woke up and he was gone," she said sounding puzzled.

"No Ma'am, I've not," he replied panicked but covering.

"He's probably downstairs. You know he's been having trouble sleeping," Monica continued as she headed past Thomas through the doorway.

"No need to trouble yourself, Ms. Banebridge, I've just come from downstairs, Master Andrew is not there," Thomas said quickly. He was afraid that he already knew where he was and he didn't like it one bit. "Go back to bed, I'll find him and send him up. He most likely couldn't sleep and rather than disturbing you, went up to the office to get some work done. I'll take care of it," he said pleasantly.

Monica smiled sweetly at Thomas, "Thank you, Thomas. And how many times am I going to have to tell you to call me Monica?" she asked over her shoulder.

"I'm afraid you'll have to keep reminding me, Monica. I'm an old man, I forget things easily," he replied with a grin.

*

Andrew was surprised to find Thomas standing at the front door when he walked inside. He couldn't hide his surprise so he didn't even try. "Thomas, what are you doing up at four in the bloody morning?" he asked.

"Waiting for you," he said in a very annoyed tone.

"Well, here I am. Now you can go back to bed."

"Monica woke up a couple of hours ago, looking for you; otherwise I might never have known you were gone."

"Was she worried?" Andrew asked with concern.

"What do you think?"

"I'll go up right now."

Thomas grabbed him hard by the shoulder. "Not before you tell me where you've been!!" he said in a hushed shout.

Andrew was surprised by the show of force. "I went for a walk."

"You damned bloody fool!!!" Thomas continued, "do you realize the risk you have taken?"

"Thomas, what the hell's the matter with you?" Andrew demanded feeling very frightened at the moment.

"Arrogant, reckless fool," he shouted and stormed off.

When the haze lifted and common sense slammed into him, Andrew was terrified. He was more terrified than he had ever been in his life. Just what had he done? Why had he been so reckless? He buried his face in his hands and collapsed on the stairs. He started to shiver when the ache pitted in his stomach flared. What was done was done.

Chapter 8

After he explained his absence, Andrew slept, but only sporadically. Thomas had helped him to the bedroom door but he walked in under his own steam. He didn't want Monica to see him so weak. And as he looked at Monica now, sleeping silently unaware that she was his lifeline, he was thankful. Thankful she didn't question him about his need to go for a walk in the wee hours of the morning. He had no good reason to give her.

The walk tired him; accomplishing all that he wanted, but a long sleep. It was only now becoming clear how stupid he had been to indulge himself. After the confrontation with Thomas, Andrew laid there racking his brain. He reached out and touched Monica's hair. It was so soft and inviting, just as everything about her was soft and inviting.

He wanted to wake her. To show her how very much he needed her and how it was so easy for him to get lost in her. But she slept so peacefully. And then dawn broke, bringing with it a whole new day.

Andrew finally did sleep, he knew that because the next time he opened his eyes he was groggy; and when he rolled over it was Monica who was gone. He sat up and called to her but no answer came. He got up from bed and looked frantically around the room, just as Monica had told him she'd done hours before. And Andrew breathed a sigh of relief when he heard the shower running behind the bathroom door.

He felt plundered with his thoughts foggy and unclear, and his walk only hours before was a hazy memory as if it had taken place years before. He sat down on the edge of the bed and closed his eyes. Andrew was still trying to focus his thoughts when he heard Thomas at the door.

"Come in," Andrew said loudly.

Thomas opened the door and studied his master. "You've slept. I hope well, because it will probably be the last good night's sleep you'll have in a good long while," he said coming inside the room with a tray of tea and crumpets. "I mean really, Master Andrew, how could you do something so foolish?" he scolded quietly, setting a place for the tray.

"Please, Thomas, I have had it up to my bloody eyeballs with your mysterious intimations. Either tell me what the hell you're talking about or shut up!" Andrew shouted. He rubbed his temples trying to relieve the pounding behind his eyes. "I went for a walk to try and relax. I didn't think about the ramifications for god's sake!"

Thomas turned around and looked him in the eye, "Did you really think you could go out there and face the night without a price?" He looked at the bathroom door and dropped his voice to a whisper, "You're a vampire for chrissake! How many people did you pass that you could have very easily killed? Ten..... maybe twenty? Can you sit there and honestly tell me that the urge was not there to do what comes naturally? Master Andrew, your price for tempting fate could be the very thing you are trying to avoid."

Andrew sat listening to Thomas, realizing the wisdom in his words, but he was angry enough to rebel even slightly. "There's no way to undo it."

"Master Andrew, you may not want to hear it, but you have been slowly regressing for some time now. And now that you gone back to the night..." Thomas' voice trailed off in despair.

"I can handle it."

"Unless you can look me in the eye and tell me that being out there had no affect on you, we could have our hands full. Can you?" he asked.

Andrew said nothing, only looked at the old man with a steely gaze filled with the barest hint of resentment.

"That's what I thought."

They fell into a tense silence when the bathroom door opened and Monica walked out into view. "Am I interrupting something?" she asked with her eyes running from one man to the other.

Andrew broke into a convincing smile, "No, Love. We were just discussing a difference in opinion. Thomas doesn't think it's a good idea for me to be walking the streets at such ungodly hours." With an unconcerned shrug he stood up. "I on the other hand think he's being paranoid," he said coming to her side.

"Well, I hate to ruffle feathers by throwing in my two cents, but I agree with Thomas," Monica replied seriously.

Surprise and then pride knitted his brows together. "Wonderful," Andrew muttered.

"Drew, you're a business tycoon whose face is recognizable. And like it or not, fame brings a level of danger with it. You might've been mugged or worse."

"I'm not a defenseless child and I will not be treated like one!!" he snapped, then strode into the bathroom to slam the door behind him.

*

After giving him some time to calm down, Monica found him brooding quietly in the study. Contrite though she was, the woman in her couldn't help but appreciate how sexy he looked; black hair messed and still damp from his shower, eyes hooded under brows slanted with annoyance. And though she walked to him silently, Andrew knew she was there and chose, for the moment, to ignore her. He'd had time to see Thomas and Monica had a point but his pride was as stubborn as could be.

She came around the desk and stood in front of him. And when that proved unsuccessful in winning his attention, she sat herself in his lap. And if she found his passiveness totally alluring, she decided, to keep it to herself. She began running her fingers through his hair and she could see that he was slowly losing his power of resistance.

Realizing she was gaining ground, she whispered into his ear, "Is it really worth all this fuss?" she asked, kissing his neck. "We're only concerned for your safety."

"I won't be bullied," he muttered with little heat.

And then she pulled him into a kiss and he was lost. Lost in passion from the moment she captured his mouth with hers. But it didn't take him long to know that the burning he was feeling was too intense. Danger wound its way through the mounting passion. He was aroused most definitely, but he had been aroused before and never felt his senses kick into overdrive.

His tongue felt thick, as if about to choke him. And his mouth became so dry that it felt unmistakably like paper. Panic crawled up his spine and Andrew felt suffocation hot on its heels. Yet strangely he couldn't stop kissing her. Vaguely, he knew, he didn't want to stop because her neck was sweet; too sweet in fact.

And then kissing her wasn't nearly enough to satisfy him. He knew better but still couldn't stop. The good and the bad sides of him fighting at every turn. Sweat covered ever inch of his body. Get out of here you bloody fool! Before it's too late!! His own voice kept roaring in his head. A burst of effort and Andrew pushed Monica off of him, got to his feet and stumbled to the door.

Before her mind cleared of the hazy passion, Monica found him gone and she was very much alone.

Just outside the door, he collapsed to the floor. He forced himself to sit up and propped his body against the wall for support. Andrew was gasping for breath when Thomas came rushing down the hall.

"What's happened? he demanded, "what has happened?"

Andrew was in the midst of a panic attack and fighting for every breath, "Get...her...out of...here."

Thomas glanced at the door and then back to Andrew. "Is Monica all right?" he asked anxiously, having to keep himself from taking Andrew by the shoulders and shaking him. "Have you harmed her?"

Andrew was sweating and his eyes showed of coldness and death. "No. No. I didn't harm.......her. Just please get her out of here," he pleaded.

"All right Master Andrew, just relax. I'll take care of it. But first we've got to get you on your feet and out of the hall. Come now. Let's get your feet under you," Thomas whispered.

With a worried glance at the door and worried thoughts over the woman on the other side, Thomas got his master on his feet and down the hall to privacy.

*

Thomas walked into the study as casually as he could manage, doing his best not to appear nervous. He noticed the puzzled look on Monica's face immediately. "I'm afraid Master Andrew isn't feeling well at the moment, you may want to return to the bedroom and dress. He'll rejoin you as soon as he takes something to relieve the abdominal pains," he said simply.

Monica was concerned. "Are you sure he'll be all right?" she asked, "should he see a doctor?"

Thomas smiled. "Oh yes, of course he will. He's had theses cramps since he was a boy. I know what to do for him, a doctor won't be necessary, don't worry." He smiled once again and left the room, nervous but grateful he was able to sound unconcerned.

*

He found Andrew lying in the middle of the pantry floor, and was startled. Not by his appearance, but by the low guttural moans escaping from him. He walked slowly to the middle of the room and knelt down beside him. "Master Andrew......Master Andrew let me see you," he whispered softly.

Andrew lay completely still. "Nooooo." His voice was filled with so much anguish and pain that it brought tears to the old man's eyes.

"Please. I cannot help you unless you let me. Look at me. Let me see you."

He was weak but somehow found the strength to roll over and face Thomas. And though he wasn't very alert, he saw clearly enough the horror on the old man's face. "Is it really that awful?" he asked, his words barely audible.

Thomas tried to mask his blunt reaction. In truth, his master's appearance was shocking. Not in a disfiguring, contorted way, but in such a way as to speak volumes about what he was capable of doing. His eyes mirrors of the eyes he once had long, long ago. His pupils were pinpoints showing an aversion to light.

Andrew closed his eyes and felt tears streaming down his face. "So it's true? What they say about the eyes being the mirrors to the soul?" With a loud groan he pushed himself up to a sitting position facing Thomas in the dark safety of the pantry. "I guess there's no purpose in denying the truth any longer, huh, old boy?" Andrew continued, wiping the last of the tears from his eyes, "Father would say real men aren't supposed to cry."

Thomas could sense the shift in his master. He was giving up. It was clear that he did not intend to fight, but just accept the fate dealt to him. "Why are you talking like this, Andrew?" he asked quietly, still sitting on the floor.

A smile came across Andrew's weary face. "You called me Andrew, so it must be hopeless. You only call me that when things are serious." He staggered to his feet and tried to focus his eyes in the dark room.

"I've called you Andrew many times so don't be so dramatic. We both knew that this would happen some day. You've gone two decades without feeding or the desire to do so, and we saw this coming. It's the price you pay for passion. You knew that as well as I," Thomas said.

"Yes, I know. But I thought I was stronger than this bloody curse!"

Thomas stood, grimacing from the pain of his old body. "Not as strong as you think."

"There's no turning back?"

"You haven't fed, so there is always a chance. But you must remain vigilant."

"My eye's hurt."

"I know. I've seen them."

"What do we do now?"

"Anything we have too, to keep you and this blessed city safe."

*

She had dressed and was standing by the window with the shutter open when she heard him come into the room. The brightness of the morning light stabbed through his eyes like knives. He grabbed his head and leaned against the doorway. Monica turned suddenly and was across the room in an instant.

"Close the window!" he cried out as if he were being tortured.

"Oh, god! I'm sorry I forgot." Monica crossed the room and closed the shutter quickly. "How's your stomach?" she asked, joining him on the bottom of the bed.

Andrew eyes were burning as if they were on fire. He opened them, but couldn't see through the tears flooding them. "Better, but my head's killing me," he replied lying back on the bed. "Don't worry I'll be fine in a moment," he continued, trying to sound like he believed it and falling short.

Monica watched him fall asleep. It troubled her deeply to see him fighting whatever it was that was ravaging him. He had the characteristics of a man drowning in the recesses of his mind. And for the first time she found herself wondering about the mental stability of the man lying so obviously exhausted beside her. And then she wondered what she could possibly do to help him; if she could do anything at all.

*

Thomas again found himself receding into the depths of the dark sector. The answer for his master, he knew, could only be found some place in the stock. He only hoped he could find it in time.

Thomas knew he would not be disturbed because he had given his master something to help him sleep. When he was safely inside the room he closed the door tightly behind him and walked between the tall shelves, considering. Running his hand along the many bottles he'd stored there. He updated the stock on a very regular basis so the potency would not be a problem. But finding the right solution to this current problem might be. Thomas knew that for certain.

*

Nightmares tormented Andrew from the recesses of his mind. No matter how he tried, he could not wake to free himself. Instead he was fumbling around in a fog of a dream world knowing things in the real world could be far worse but unable to stem his fear. He heard the voices of all the people who meant the most to him, calling to him, pleading for mercy. And then suddenly those tortured voices turned cruel and haunting.

He found himself in a graveyard. More troubled by the relentless voices then by the evil pictures playing out in front of him, his adrenaline pumped wildly. Visions of violent sex with many potential victims, repulsed him. And seeing the satisfaction of the eventual kill on his face as consuming as the foreplay, was horrific.

Andrew stood outside of himself and watched the women being driven into a hot frenzy. And when they could stand no more, he plunged his teeth deep into their neck. He drained each of them slowly, becoming more and more aroused with each kill.

"No. Noooooo…please god, please," he screamed over and over at the scenes playing out like a movie in front of him. He spun around, trying to find an escape from such horror but there was none. And when his father's voice boomed in his ears he was certain that what was before him was his destiny. Again and again the voice repeated. He put his hands over his ears and screamed to try and smother the merciless voice. "Damn you!" he cried.

An eternity seemed to pass before the madness released him. The evil sights replaced with pleasant pictures of his loving mother. Andrew was confused by her journey into his nightmare, but she offered him the tie to goodness, peace and love. She soothed him. Spoke of her love for him and promised she would never leave him. Her smile soothed his soul, reminding him that, yes, he was worthy of love. And just then the door he'd been searching for opened…and he woke.

Andrew opened his eyes and found himself looking into Monica's loving face. She'd been watching him sleep and he wondered how much she'd heard of his cries. He read something in her eyes, but averted his own troubled, and he feared, evil eyes. But her gaze never left him. He could feel the warmth and love in them, comforting him, driving the cold from his bones.

"Penny for your thoughts," he said, finally realizing that she would stay silent. And the silence troubled him.

"You were having a nightmare. It seemed to take it out of you," she said simply.

"Really? I can't even remember what it was about now," he said getting off the bed, realizing his headache still raged and was worse than ever.

Monica looked at him and her concern ebbed away. "I suppose that's probably best, the way you were carrying on."

Andrew stopped. "Was I making any sense?"

"I don't know. Not really. Mostly just a bunch of mumbles," replied Monica.

Andrew breathed a sigh of relief when Monica left the room to check in at the office. She hadn't been able to make any sense of the dream, but then, he recognized that he couldn't make any sense of it either. He wondered with a groan, how long could he keep this up?

*

Thomas carefully mixed two components of the stock together. With hands which were no longer as steady as they once had been. But he thought, with grim determination, he was doing rather well, considering. If he could come up with something to lessen the symptoms maybe that would be enough to give his master the strength to fight off total relapse. He'd been in the chilling room too long and was cold to the bone. He supposed his chills could be from more than temperature because of what the room held inside, and it was time for a much deserved break.

The old man wanted something to steady himself. He was shaking to the point of nausea. Thomas left the room and made his way back to the main part of the house. His mind racing with so many thoughts that he wasn't sure which thoughts came first anymore. He walked into the kitchen and stopping in front of the stove, he placed his frail hand on the tea kettle, and opened the lid, checking it for water. He turned on the burner and then quickly turned it off.

He wanted something stronger, much stronger. He walked over to the cabinet above the refrigerator and took down the scotch bottle he kept inside. He slowly poured some into a shot glass and drank it down faster then he should have. He coughed and it burned his throat like fire.

Andrew walked into the kitchen; Thomas turned to face him. "What are you doing?" Andrew asked in a disappointing tone. "Is that really necessary?"

Thomas looked embarrassed. "I'm sorry but I needed it to steady myself. Care to join me?"

"Too early for me, old boy," he replied and walked over to the stove and turned on the kettle. "I think I'll start off a little more slowly, thank you." Drinking hard liquor first thing in the morning wasn't his idea of problem solving. It was not that his battle wasn't worthy of such a measure, its just that he had to keep his head clear so he could keep control of his urges.

"That's very smart," Thomas agreed, walking past his master and leaving the room.

Andrew stood there thinking about the disaster that was certain to befall them if he could not resist his desire for blood. The urge was so strong to feed. So overpowering it made his throat ache with the longing of so many years gone by. He swallowed several times before the ache subsided. The shrill whistle of the kettle brought his attention back to where it belongs, to the present, where he was considered just a man, and most importantly, a mortal one. Not just flesh and blood, but human, in spite of the truth.

The tea calmed him, but he could still feel the demons stirring in the pit of his stomach. His self-control was weakening and he had to face it. That was his only chance of stopping the evil inside.

*

Monica was waiting for Andrew when he walked into his study. She greeted him with a loving smile, still oblivious to the danger around her, still innocent to the fate which could claim her. Andrew looked at her for a moment, trying to ignore the sharp stab of guilt. He knew all that she did not, and to tell her would mean losing her.

He knew it was selfish but he needed her with him. He would not harm her. Even if it meant taking the most drastic of measures to ensure it, he would not allow her to fall victim to his madness. He counted on their love to save him. It had too.

Monica noticed the far away look in his eyes, as if he were looking through her to some unknown place. "What's going on with you lately? And don't bother with the usual excuses because they won't work this time," she continued.

"What are you talking about?" he asked as he sat the tray down in front of her. Andrew only hoped he could bluff his way through this time, chalking it up to his moods. "I'm just tired, that's all. You know I've not been sleeping well," he said simply.

"No, it's something else. Now are you going to tell me or am I going to have to beat it out of you?"

He smiled. "Actually, that sounds like it could be fun," he said jokingly.

She didn't smile. "I'm serious, damnit. You and Thomas have been running around here for weeks in some secret code. What? I'm good enough to share your bed but not your problems? Is that it?" she demanded, irritation mounting.

Andrew was more than a little surprised at her tone. "Monica, really you're making too much of all of this. I've never treated you like an object or a sexual toy. Why would you say such a hurtful thing?" He was hurt by her comment; yet, realized that he had been hurting *her* with his silence. The tone of impatience in her voice was a warning. "I love you. Do you doubt that?" he asked.

"Of course not," her face softened and with it, her tone. "But you're keeping something from me Drew. Why aren't you telling me? What's bothering you?"

Andrew searched for something to say, but before he could think of anything believable, he blurted out what he knew was a lie. "Because I don't know what the bloody hell is bothering me!" he confessed, as surprised by his reply as Monica appeared to be. "I'll work it out but I need you to be patient with me a little while longer. Damnit, I rack my fool brain to come up with a solution but it not as easy as I would prefer," he continued.

Monica was caught off guard by Andrew's outburst. She was left not knowing how to respond. They looked at each other for a long time before she finally spoke to him quietly. "I'm sorry. I don't mean to add more pressure. It's just....I know you're hurting, and...I just want to help."

She could see the tears well up in his eyes and no more words were needed for the moment. He just went to her, knelt beside her, and she held him for a very long time. "I just love you," she whispered with tears in her own eyes now, "more than I can ever say."

"I know," he choked. "I love you too."

They made love on the floor tenderly. With a sense of sweet

abandon, he took the risk because sound judgment and willpower deserted him. He melded their bodies and, the romantic in him chose to believe, their souls, exploring the planes and silkiness of her skin and still couldn't get close enough to chase the shadows hovering around them away.

She was so loved, so adored. And Andrew wanted and needed her to know it, to feel it in her heart. And Monica wanted it too and gave herself up to the sensations and pounding needs he woke inside her. Seeking to ease his pain and, in doing that, easing her own.

Desire rose higher, soaring with every quickening breath. They drove each other to the edge of oblivion and clung. With Andrew's moans of pleasure, control, reserve was slipping. His senses clouded with every ragged breath, with Monica's cries urging him on. Never had she been so driven by passion.

His mouth heated her skin with the barest of touches. Madness, pleasure, sensuality collided inside her. Adrift on, prisoner to her senses, taste, touch, smell. The scent of his skin was a wonder in itself. With the curve of her neck so close and his burning lips skimming along her dampened, sweetened skin, he craved.

Instinct and willpower battled, and a thin thread of control tugged him back as he crushed his mouth to hers. Taking her deeper, he thrust himself inside her when she opened for him. Mad with wanting and needing, they found an easy, now familiar rhythm. He sought her cheek, her soft lobe of her ear. And working his way lower and lower still, until he found his mark and felt his fang-like teeth sharp against his lips.........

The desk phone rang. And somewhere conscience found him and he pulled away in time. He pulled himself off of her and covered his face until he was sure he was under control. And still the phone rang endlessly. Monica was laying on her back breathing heavily lost in confusion and fading desire.

Andrew crawled over to the desk and grabbed the receiver with jerky, clumsy movements. "Hello," he croaked breathlessly. "Fine..." he said with his chest still heaving. "Yes, first thing in the morning then. We'll see you then." he hung up the phone and slid up against the desk with his head in his hands.

'I lost complete control! If it hadn't been for the phone call... he should not even allow himself to think the words, but his overcharged mind was spinning out too many horrible possibilities.

And his lovemaking bordered on violent. Andrew dropped his hands and found Monica gazing at him, smiling. She ran her hand through her dampened hair looking as completely satiated as Andrew was mortified.

"You okay?" she asked softly, slowly regaining her composure and the feeling in her body. One closer look at his face answered the question before he could. She lifted a brow, deciding not to force the issue. "Who interrupted us?"

Dragging a steadying breath into his sluggish lungs, Andrew pulled himself together. "The office," he managed. "I've got a meeting first thing in the morning." It took a moment but he finally felt the jangle of nerves unknot his stomach.

"Drew, you were unbelievable," she laughed softly. "I mean, utterly amazing."

But Andrew wasn't laughing. He was shamed. Speechless. He'd had no control over, and no concern for, his behavior only moments before. He'd almost fed. He almost fed on her! The complete control he'd been preaching only days earlier to Thomas vanished only moments ago.

No magic potion would save him now, he feared. He grabbed his robe and pulled it around himself and tied it closed. When he stood up on wobbly legs, he offered only the smallest of smiles to Monica and tried to excuse himself. He had to get out of there. And he had to do it now.

Monica looked up from the floor, "Where are you going?"

"I need to speak to Thomas." Andrew tried to work up a better smile but couldn't quite pull it off.

"Buzz him on the intercom," Monica suggested.

"We've been locked away in here for hours, Love, and you need to get to work." He crouched down and kissed her gently before leaving the room.

Andrew had a look of sheer terror on his face when he ran right into Thomas nearly knocking them both off their feet.

"What's wrong, Master Andrew you look positively hellish?" he asked once he got a good look at his master's face.

"I nearly fed, Thomas!" His voice practically screaming as the full rise of panic hit him.

"Calm down and tell me what's happened," Thomas pleaded, trying to get him to get hold of himself. Several tense seconds passed before Thomas felt some of the stiffness drain from his shoulders.

"I almost fed on Monica!" he shouted in a whisper. "I couldn't control myself!" Andrew blurted out with terror. "What in all that's holy am I going to do now?" he asked, begging for an answer.

"The first thing you're going to do is get hold of yourself and be thankful," Thomas reasoned, taking him by the shoulders. "And you didn't loose control, you had a hold on it, tenuous as it might be, or you would have fed." He waited, and seeing Andrew's eyes calm, continued, "Pull yourself together. If she sees you like this she'll assume you're having a nervous breakdown. And at this point I'm not too bloody sure she'd be wrong. I'll see to her, you go to your room and wait for me there. Go now."

*

Monica heard the knock on the door and knew right away Thomas was on the other side. Even his knocking was formal. "Just a minute," she said, looking around the room at the scattered clothing on the floor. Monica quickly gathered them up, putting them under the desk and jumping into her robe. "Come in."

Thomas stepped inside the room and smiled. "How are you this morning?" he asked doing his best at small talk.

"Fine Thomas," she replied, trying to sound nonchalant. "How are you?"

"Very well, thank you. I'm afraid Master Andrew has been detained and won't be able to see you before you leave for the office. He says he'll call you the moment he's free. I brought your clothes and the car is at your disposal whenever you are ready to leave." Thomas spoke quickly not giving himself the chance to be interrupted.

Disappointment was quickly overtaken by embarrassment. "I'll be ready in a few moments. I'd like to stop by my apartment and pick up some fresh clothes," she said.

Thomas smiled. "Whatever you wish, madam," he answered.

*

Andrew was pacing as he never paced before. So many times he had protested Thomas' negativity about his pursuit of a relationship with Monica. And now, as it turned out, he had been right all along. This relationship could end in disaster for them both. For the first time since he'd known her, Andrew actually breathed a sigh of relief when he heard the heavy door close behind them standing and listening from the upstairs hallway.

The pains in his stomach returned with a vengeance, and along with them came the desire. The craving; the urge for blood. Andrew collapsed and suddenly cried out in indescribable agony. He prayed for a death he knew would never come, and wept at the hell of his life.

"Please.....please...." he groaned holding his stomach sure it was the only way to keep his insides from spilling onto the floor beneath him. Dizzying blackness closed in around him...and he drifted away.

From somewhere, Thomas appeared. If Andrew hadn't known better, he would have thought him to be an angel, but Angels were not for men like him. Angels would never appear to the damned. "Thomas," he moaned.

"Master Andrew where's the pain?" Thomas pleaded, trying to reach him on some level. "Tell me....show me where the pain began."

He ripped the shirt from his master's back, feeling his ridged abdomen. When Andrew screamed, shuddering from the touch, Thomas winced and laid a comforting hand to his wet forehead. This was the worst of all the episodes he'd witnessed from his master. "Hold on." he said, getting to his feet and taking off at a run.

Then Andrew felt a sharp jab in his right arm. Out of the corner of his nearly closed eye he could see Thomas, frantic, at his side. His friend would help him. Almost delirious with pain and fever, and still he knew, could never doubt, the strength of this belief.

The fight to keep his eyes opened was quickly lost. Even fear that it would be a sleep from which he would never wake, couldn't steel his resolve to remain lucid. The overwhelming need for sleep won out. And Thomas was becoming blurred, slipping away. His eyes grew heavier and heavier.

"Sleep now, Master Andrew. Trust me, you'll be alright," Thomas whispered as he stooped over the man he loved as his own.

The last thing Andrew remembered was feeling the old man's feeble hand on his forehead. And then soothing darkness took him away.

*

Thomas stayed by his master's side for hours. When next he looked into Andrew's opened, dazed eyes, it was sometime around nine in the evening. His color was better but he still looked too pale. He was weak and unable to speak until the clock struck ten. "Don't worry, Master Andrew," Thomas reassured him softly. "Just rest and you'll feel better in the morning."

"How long have I been out?" Andrew whispered in a voice as dry as dust. "What time is it?"

Thomas smiled warmly down at the tranquil man in the bed. "You've been asleep for eight, maybe nine hours. It's just after ten p.m.," he replied.

He tried and failed to lift his head... "Monica?"

"I've told her you were called out of town on an unexpected business emergency. She's staying at home tonight because she hates being here without you. She hopes I'm not offended." Thomas replied, giggling in spite of the situation. "I assured her I was not and wished her a good night. Ms. Banebridge is a sweet woman," he added.

Andrew smiled weakly. "Told you," he murmured. And before he could continue he drifted off to sleep.

*

Andrew slept peacefully for most of the night only bothered by what Thomas guessed was dreams. He sat next to the bed unwilling to leave for any extended period of time. He left only long enough to refresh his tea or to prepare another injection. A potent concoction he hoped wouldn't be necessary. An extremely high dosage but given the condition he had found his master in, the level was acceptable to him. It offered the chance for rest and recovery from this latest crisis. But Thomas knew that if things went the way he was expecting these crises would be become more frequent and god help them, more devastating. He sighed, wondering if he was young enough to go through it all again. But for now at least the worst was over.

*

Dawn broke, and with it, Andrew came around from his deep sleep allowing Thomas to begin to wind down for the first time in twelve hours. The jolt from the endless cups of tea through the night was losing its edge and Thomas struggled to keep his eyes open himself. Andrew turned his head, and finding Thomas by his side, before he was able to greet him with a refreshed smile.

His color had finally returned to normal and his eyes looked clearer than they had a dozen hours before. He lifted his head to allow Thomas to slide another pillow under him. Finally, and much to his delight, Andrew's thoughts were clear and focused.

"Well, you look much better this morning," Thomas pronounced, pouring a steaming cup of tea and putting it to his master's lips.

"Thanks to you," he said before taking a small sip. "I certainly feel much better, desperately so, in fact," he continued happily.

"I'm glad to hear it," Thomas said, placing his thumb under Andrew's eye and gently pulling the lower lid down for a better look. Satisfied, he grinned. "You had me worried for awhile."

"I remember this immense pain, far worse than anything I've felt before I'm afraid," Andrew offered, not commenting on Thomas's last words directly.

"I don't doubt it. This episode was extreme by any other comparison."

"No argument here, old boy."

"Finally, no argument," Thomas said lightening the mood. There were things his master would have to be told but it could wait until after breakfast.

It was after breakfast when Thomas grew quiet and then serious. "I have something to tell you Master Andrew that I'm sure you'll find shocking," he began.

"There isn't too much you can say that I would find truly shocking. What is it?" he asked noticing the serious expression on the man's face.

"Yesterday when I found you....I want you to understand that you were dangerously ill. I had to act fast to save you."

"And?" Andrew implored.

"I've had to give you a series of high dosage injections. I had no choice.....I had to inject you with rodent plasma."

"Along with what?" Andrew was growing suspicious.

"Just rodent plasma."

Andrew's mouth fell and disbelief filled his eyes. "My.....do you know what you've done?" he asked still shocked by the revelation.

"Saved you from a fate worse than death," Thomas answered. "You know as well as I that there is no death for you. No release, as you're already dead. What awaited you was what you most fear," he explained simply. "I had no choice." This discussion had been long dreaded, about the choices that may one day await them.

Andrew felt like he'd been kicked in the stomach. "What now?" he asked, accepting the truth. "Never mind I know," he continued in defeat. "Then of course you know what you have to do, don't you?"

Thomas shook his head. "I won't consider it, at least not yet. I'm working on a solution, Master Andrew. It's too early to make that kind of decision," he replied.

"You're avoiding the inevitable."

"I've planned for this. What's happening is only a surprise to you because you refused to see things clearly. It's much sooner than I expected but it's no surprise. Get out of bed, get a shower, and you'll feel like you old self in no time," Thomas said, turning to leave the room.

"You are sure?" Andrew asked doubtfully.

"Take a shower."

*

Thomas was more positive with his master than he actually felt but he knew he was close to an answer. He could stop all this madness if he was given enough time. Master Andrew would go to work today as if nothing unusual occurred. Because his master was a strong-willed man and he could handle himself accordingly. And the injections he'd received the night before should do nicely to quiet his urge, he thought, busying himself among bottles in the dark sector beneath the mansion.

*

Thomas had been right and Andrew was glad for it. He did feel like his old self when he stepped from the steam filled shower. And he was ready to push his new found knowledge of his medicine and what might happen in the future to the very back of his mind; for his own sanity and the productivity of his work day.

He walked into his bedroom and took a deep breath. He grabbed the first suit in his closet and threw the jacket on the bed as he slipped one leg, then the other into his slacks. The silky smoothness of his shirt was familiar and it soothed him. And once his tie was securely around his neck he left, ready to begin his day.

*

Thomas came up to the main part of the house to say good-bye to his master, making sure to sound very upbeat and unworried. And, so, his master left feeling at ease with himself and positive. And then Thomas returned to the dark sector to labor the early part of the day away searching for an answer to the fatal problem facing all of New York.

*

Andrew walked into his office and went straight to his desk. He had tons of work to get caught up on. And it was only a moment before Sarah appeared in the doorway with her usual smile and good humor. He smiled in return and she walked over to the desk.

"Look's like someone played hooky yesterday," she teased as she sat his tea down beside him.

"I was feeling a little out of sorts on the plane, sorry I didn't call in," he replied apologetically.

"No harm done. We're getting pretty good at running things while you're away. How did the trip go?"

"Ah...fine I think. But you know how pessimistic people can be."

"Yes I do," she agreed. "Your morning appointment'll be here in an half an hour."

"Thank you, Sarah."

He busied himself with several projects while he waited for his appointment to arrive. But he couldn't escape the memories of what had happened the day before in his study. Thomas swore everything would be fine, that he'd planned for his return descent to the curse of the damned, but Andrew still couldn't shake the clawing fear. He knew what would happen next. He didn't need to be told. Andrew had to accept the fact that his body needed to feed, and soon.

Files were scattered over his desk, when Sarah interrupted him to show an elderly gentleman with a shuffled gate into the office. At the sound of the door opening, Andrew looked up, gathered his thoughts, and then stood to greet his guest, "Hello, Mr. Niles," he began with a polite smile and an outstretched hand. "It's a pleasure to meet you. What can I do for you?" he asked, and waited until his elderly guest settled himself in the chair Sarah offered him.

Mr. Niles smiled kindly, "Well, Mr. Carter, I am the head of one of the few permanent hospitals in Africa," he paused to clear his throat, "I hate to come to you hat in hand, but my hospital is in desperate need of medical supplies. I was hoping your company might be able to help." He spoke slowly, softly, as if he had given every word weight and thought.

"You've come all this way to ask for medical supplies?"

Andrew was taken aback, why such a long tiresome trip when a faxed request would have sufficed. "I could have looked over your application, made my decision, and shipped all you needed," he answered.

"I understand that, but I felt I should meet with you in person." This time the charmingly wrinkled face broke into a full-blown grin. "Plead my case, face to face, out of respect for all your good works," Mr. Niles said simply.

Andrew was flattered and impressed. "Thank you for your kind words. I'm sure the trip could not have been comfortable for you." The small but sturdy framed man in front of him looked like he had seen easier days. It impressed him that he made it to New York. "I'm sure I can help you, tell me more about your situation," he continued, leaning back in his chair, already certain he'd do everything possible to assist such a selfless act.

*

Monica was thinking about Andrew while sitting at her desk editing news copy. His business trip came up. He hadn't mentioned it. But then she knew this was the life of someone as giving as he was. But what occupied her thoughts most, was the incredible passion he'd swept her up in yesterday.

It was the most unbelievable feeling she'd ever felt. Passion. She'd never needed, or even allowed it in any previous relationship. Too busy, she admitted. Too career-minded, definitely, with no ties to anything important beyond her drive to succeed. But it was different now, and if pressed, she wasn't sure she could say why. Not yet. Was there love? Yes. Could she see a future with a man such as Andrew Carter? Yes again.

Mr. Philips stood in the doorway of her office watching her for awhile when she finally noticed he was there. "Mr. Philips." A chagrinned amusement played over her face and she blushed. "Sorry. My mind's been wandering. Was there something that you wanted?" she asked.

He walked in and sat down in the chair on the other side of her desk. "Just wanted to check, see how your upcoming stories are going. You missed the last few meetings," he began.

Monica smiled. "I know. I've been pretty occupied lately, but I assure you, my exclusive on the city's under-ground raves will be something," she replied.

"Great!" He grinned. "How are things otherwise?"

Monica's eyes changed. "Fine, why?"

Mr. Philips looked puzzled by the shift in her eyes. "I'm a little worried about you, that's all."

"Don't worry about me. I'm great. And even if I weren't, I could take care of myself."

"I hear you and Andrew Carter are involved now." He jerked up a brow and asked carefully. "True?"

"Yes," she said simply.

"He's a bit odd; intense's maybe the word. Maybe you should re-think becoming involved with him, Monica. The man's a hermit, never leaves that mansion unless it's to accept some honor, bask in the mystery he created." Philips shook his head, musing. "Hell, his offices are an extension of his home. Don't you think that's a little weird?" he asked with a fatherly tone.

Monica stamped down on her rising anger, fumbling a bit, surprised at the intensity. "Drew leaves the mansion quite often, actually," she said a little too defensively. "He's a busy man and that leaves little time to walk the streets. Now if you'll excuse me I have work to do," she said sharply. She'd be damned if she'd let her boss in her personal life. She had a father, and his death wasn't an invitation to offer advice.

He felt her anger and cleared his throat. "I'm sorry if I offended you, Monica. I'm just concerned about you."

Monica gave him an icy smile. "There's nothing to be concerned about," she replied, and watched him walk quietly from the room closing the door behind him.

*

Thomas had tried several different ingredients for the new treatment he was working on, but so far he had had no luck making any progress. If he didn't come up with an answer soon it might well be too late for his master. The only other alternative was simply unthinkable. But he had to face the fact that he might not have any other choice.

And Thomas knew precisely who was to blame for the reality both he and his master were faced with... Reginald. He was an evil man driven by the disgusting need and the endless joy of feeding and killing. A man who had decided the cruelest fate he could give his only son was the one his son would loathe more than life. Thomas felt his blood boil, and suddenly all the old man wanted to do was lash out. He couldn't control his anger anymore and had to act on it.

Before he knew what he was doing he drove his fist into the cement wall of the room. But the sudden pain quickly reminded him. He winced, surveying the damage he had done to himself in disbelief. "Damn bloody fool!" he groaned out in pain, scalding himself.

It didn't appear to be broken, though it was bleeding profusely. Thomas wrapped a rag around his knuckles and applied pressure to the wound. Closing his eyes he cursed the pain and the stupidity. He should have known better then to indulge in such a childish act.

Once the bleeding stopped he returned to his work, although at a slower pace then before. He was close to a breakthrough, he could feel it. If there was one thing Thomas had learned over the years, it was how to appease a vampire's fragile system. Whatever the answer, it had to be just right, or it would do nothing but make an already dire situation worse.

*

Three o'clock came and went and Andrew was exhausted. He kept reminding himself that in a couple hours he would be finished and then he could go home. He could have walked out of his office. He knew that. After all, he was the boss. But he didn't want to set a bad example for his employees, especially since he hadn't bothered to show up at all the day before. He rubbed his eyes, trying to clear the double vision he'd been saddled with for the last hour. It seemed to help him regain his thoughts, so he asked Sarah to bring him more tea and continued to work diligently.

A question kept popping up in his head as he worked. Did he want to see Monica tonight? Given what nearly happened last time, Andrew knew it wasn't a good idea, but he needed to see her, because before anything else, he loved her. But could he trust himself anymore? Could he be near her and still keep her safe? Maybe he could control himself this time. He didn't know what made him think that, but he did. Another night without her would be endless, and he couldn't stand the thought of not having her near him.

Thomas would hate the very idea. But right now that didn't matter. Only one person mattered, and it was Monica.

*

Monica was thankful when five o'clock rolled around. She picked up the phone and dialed his number. It rang and rang.

Finally he picked up.

"Andrew Carter."

"You're back!" she exclaimed.

Andrew smiled, feeling all the tension release his body. "Hey, love!"

"How'd your trip go?"

"Uneventful, but promising. Will I see you tonight?" asked Andrew hopefully.

"I thought you'd never ask," she said happily. "I'll meet you at home."

*

Thomas hit the roof when Andrew told him about Monica coming over that night. "You must be kidding!" he exclaimed in a huff. "Are you mad?"

Andrew laughed. "No, I assure you, I'm not mad, just in love," he replied.

"Haven't you learned your lesson?" he demanded.

He opened his mouth to take a swipe at Thomas but realized it was a fair question. And one that he asked himself more than once. "I love her," he replied simply. And through denial he had come to another decision as well. He squared his shoulders and confessed the rest. "I plan to ask for her hand in marriage," he continued. "It might be damn foolish, but I need her."

He watched Thomas, waiting for the storm that was sure to follow.

"What?" Thomas asked looking mortified, hoping he had heard wrong.

Andrew dropped his head and sighed. "Don't look at me that way. We both know what the future holds for me, I've got to grab happiness while I can." He shrugged and sadness came into his eyes. "Do not take this from me. The treatments will work and I will live normally again. Don't ask me to do so alone," Andrew implored of the man he loved.

"It's selfish Andrew. Think of Monica if nothing else." Thomas could see his master had been thinking of little else. "And if you make matters worse with this marriage?"

"If matters become worse.....," Andrew looked at Thomas sadly, "then you know what is to be done," he whispered and left the room.

*

With Monica asleep beside him, Andrew was staring at the ceiling in the darkness of his bedroom. Unable to sleep, his stomach began to ache and his head to throb. But with so many things on his mind he barely noticed the pain. Andrew had done what he planned. He asked her to marry him, and she was overjoyed and eagerly said yes. So now he could cling to his hope for a future of normalcy and shove the nagging fear to the far corners of his mind.

Growing restless, he got up from bed and walked to the window overlooking the street. Looking out at the hot night that was his enemy, he saw, and took some comfort in, the busy street. He recognized the ache, the stab in his gut, and felt the first tinges of longing. A walk would tire him and let him sleep.

In the moonlight, Andrew glanced down at his watch and steeled himself against following through with the urge gripping him so tightly. But reason abandoned him, and the tingling in his stomach spread through him, winning out over right. Just after midnight Andrew went to his dresser and pulled out a jogging suit. A run would be even better than a walk.

He slipped into the pants and pulled on a t-shirt and the jacket. Zipping it, he cast an almost guilty look at Monica, so beautiful in her sleep. He was sure he'd made the right decision in proposing, in making her a part of his life. Noticing the burning in his chest but ignoring it, he smiled at her, picked up his running shoes and quietly left the room.

*

The night air spiked his adrenaline and he felt invigorated by each pull of air he breathed. He started off at an easy pace, building up, finding a rhythm. Breathing deeply, in through the nose out through the mouth, Andrew relaxed, using the excess energy to his advantage, he smoothed out his stride. He covered a lot of ground, easing into the zone where the body felt like a well-honed machine. He passed many people wandering around in the heat, going from club to club. And he couldn't help but envy their freedom.

Then he saw her, alone and running like he was. And brushing wary doubts aside, he quickened his pace, grateful for some company. When she saw him and slowed to allow him to pass, he took a chance. "Mind if I run with you?" he asked with an exhale, already too far down the dangerous road in his head to turn back.

"A woman shouldn't run alone at this time of night."

The woman grinned. Very attractive, she mused and was just enough of a risk taker to shrug off the oddness of the request. "Sure."

So together they ran and only exchanged anonymous small talk between them. Andrew was thrilled to know that his running companion seemed to not know who he was. They'd covered a mile when the first pang rippled through him, the twinge of need. His lips felt too dry. Andrew tried to leave her but she followed, matching his stride. If he'd been thinking more clearly, Andrew would have recognized her words for the come on that they were. But he was too distracted by his fear of knowing what was happening to him.

Andrew tried to calm down and breathe deeper, reign himself in. But his teeth began to ache knowing her neck was a source of relief. He looked around to find they were alone on the running trail. Sweat stung his eyes. His throat ached with craving. It was too late for him to save himself. And she was rattling on and on never noticing the danger sweeping into his eyes. It would be her last mistake...

He lunged, first knocking her off balance, and then to the ground. She didn't have time to react. In a heartbeat he was on top of her, his hand jammed into her mouth to keep her from screaming. The woman struggled, choked, and was overpowered. And as the certainty of her fate began to sink in, fear masked her face. He drove his teeth into her neck and tasted blood again...

Chapter 9

He opened his eyes slowly, feeling outside of his body, removed somehow, and looked around trying to clear the confusion bogging him down. The ground beneath him was cold and he rolled over on his side and found he was under a park bench. Andrew rolled over on his stomach and crawled out from under his shelter.

Stumbling to his feet he focused on his surroundings. Snatches of memory fought through his murky confusion and played through his muddled mind. He was in the park for a run, but why was he under a park bench? He squinted at his watch, dragged his clammy hand around his neck. Nearly five o'clock in the morning. What the hell was happening to him?

Andrew looked for clues, signs of people in the park but given the hour, even Central Park was deserted. There wasn't time to rack his brain for answers. He had to get back to the mansion before sunrise, before anyone woke up and found him gone. There would be time to look for answers later.

He sprinted sluggishly down the running path leading back to the main street of the city. Dragging a hand over his face he felt something crusted on the corners. Andrew looked at the dry matter on his fingers, frowning. It was sticky and unmistakably pungent. His stomach rolled, his throat went to dust as clinging to hope. What the hell had he done?

He ran down the street that would lead back home, with a swirl of questions filling his head. Why did he wake up under a park bench? Unease spread through him when he could not come up with a reason for feeling so dazed. After what seemed like an eternity Andrew found himself outside his home and very nearly dropped to his knees in relief.

He opened the door and slid inside, making sure not to set off the alarm. When the door closed behind him he leaned against it in near jubilation. He took the stairs three at a time and quietly made it down the hall with light step that surprised him. He tiptoed into the master bedroom, being careful not to wake Monica from her sound sleep.

He pushed the door gently into its latch and moved silently to the bathroom. He flipped the switch beside the door and the light blinked on. Turning the handle to the sink, he watched the water run in a stream into the basin. Cupping water in his hands he brought it to his face and splashing to his mouth. When he opened his eyes and stared into the water, his world tilted and he gaped in stunned disbelief. The water turned pink and the coppery scent confirmed his worst fear.

Every nerve in his body snapped to attention. It couldn't be.....no, it's impossible..... He felt his knees go weak underneath him and sank to the floor. Andrew searched for logic in vain. If he'd done what he dreaded he would remember. Wouldn't he? He reached up, groped for, and turned off the light. Bathed in darkness, he shook, muffling a sob in his hands.

*

It was nearly afternoon when Andrew surfaced from his dead sleep. And Thomas rousting him out of bed and hauling him downstairs did nothing to improve his mood. "Do you know how long it's been since I slept?" Andrew demanded while covering his yawn with one hand and rubbing his eyes with the other.

"Master Andrew, you went out again last night."

He heard the accusation in the tone and despite knowing it was him who was in the wrong, Andrew felt hurt. "What, you don't trust me now?"

"Don't bother denying it." Thomas just shook his head. "I know damn well you went out last night after I expressly forbade you." In rising frustration, he began pacing.

Andrew gave in. "I went for a run, but I swear I don't remember leaving, don't remember much else either."

Thomas sighed, "What did you do after your run?"

"I came home."

"You did nothing else?" Thomas eyes narrowed. "Nothing else happened that I should know about?"

He thought of waking up under the park bench. "No."

"You're certain?"

Andrew was becoming annoyed. "Yes."

Monica joined Andrew downstairs for breakfast, but she said nothing about the obvious tension between him and Thomas. They wouldn't speak a word to each other so it was up to her to keep the conversation moving. "Did you sleep okay last night, Drew?" she asked, simply figuring it was the safest topic of discussion. However, when she noticed the looks being exchanged between the two men at the table, she wasn't so sure.

"No, afraid not, love," he replied never allowing his eyes to leave Thomas.

"I'm sorry, babe," she said cupping his cheek. You should have woken me up."

"What on earth for?" Andrew asked, this time with his eyes fixed on Monica, warm and loving. There was no sense in both of us being up all night.

After breakfast Andrew excused himself to dress for the day. He left the table with a kiss for Monica and not so much as a word to Thomas. Monica knew something was going on and she could have questioned Drew about it but decided against it. He and Thomas had their little fights and it usually blew over in a few days.

*

Andrew was pissed off. Not upset, not tense, not angry, pissed off. Thomas had every reason to worry, and given he couldn't remember what had happen last night, well that only made his anger worse. He'd have sworn Thomas could read his mind. There was no way he heard him coming in from his run in the early hours of the morning. Knowing Thomas like he did, he would have called him on it right there.

He tightened the tie around his neck and smoothed out his collar. From on top his dresser he took his cuff links and placed them through the button holes of his shirt sleeves. He brushed his hair and left his room. Adrenaline, fueled by anger, allowed him to go down the stairs three at a time. Until he had a clearer picture of what went on the night before, he would not be interrogated by Thomas.

It was Monica who grabbed him before he could make the elevator. "Are you trying to sneak out of here without saying goodbye?" she asked pulling him into a hug and laughing. "Already tired of me, huh?"

He couldn't help it, she softened him. He smiled and returned the hug. "That will never happen. I've things on my mind and Thomas is in a mood," he said and kissed her to prove it.

"Did you two have a fight?" she asked looking into his worried eyes.

Andrew let the tension drain from his body. "I hate it when we quarrel." He loved the feel of her hands on his face. It calmed him when nothing else would. "Do you know how much I adore you?" he asked in a whisper. Before she could answer he kissed her. Finally pulling away, he smiled warmly at her. "I do love you madly, you know?"

"I know," she said sweetly. "I love you too, madly as your sweet English tongue puts it."

He pushed the elevator button with his free hand. The doors opened and he reluctantly let her go. He walked inside and winked before the doors closed separating them for the day. Andrew couldn't get her out of his thoughts as the floors ticked away above him. He would marry her...and soon.

*

His day was progressing nicely when his personal line rang. Andrew first ignored it, knowing it wouldn't be Monica because she had meetings all morning. After ten irritating rings he gave up, swearing under his breath. "What is it?" he demanded.

Thomas felt taken aback by his master's tone. "It's me. I want to see you down here immediately."

"What is it now, Thomas? I've got work to do." Andrew snapped. If there was one thing he didn't need more of it was Thomas and his sermons. "Just spit it old man."

"I'll give you ten minutes, Master Andrew."

"Bloody hell," Andrew muttered with a roll of his eyes, slamming down the receiver in disgust.

*

Thomas was waiting for Andrew when the elevator doors opened. Andrew stepped into the hallway and without a word headed for the living room. Thomas followed behind him. "What do you want?" Andrew demanded, heading for the bar.

"You lied to me." Thomas spoke in a harsh voice.

"Excuse me?" Andrew faced Thomas, confused.

"You heard me, damnit!"

"About what may I ask?" He turned back to the scotch.

Thomas threw the morning paper at Andrew with such force it slapped his back smartly. "Read the front page."

Andrew turned back, highball in hand. With a knitted brow, he couldn't remember ever having seen Thomas so angry before. He crouched and picked up the paper without a word. He glared at

Thomas before reading the headline:

WOMAN FOUND DEAD IN CENTRAL PARK. POLICE BAFFLED BY SAVAGE ATTACK.

Andrew was stunned. It wasn't a bad dream. Her face formed in his mind. He had seen her...last night.

"Are you responsible?"

"What are you suggesting?" Andrew shouted, but knew his voice betrayed his indignance.

"Read on. The medical examiner says cause of death is severe exsanguination. Tell me the truth!" Thomas screamed.

Andrew remembered slowly, and then sickly, he gasped. He met the woman last night running...The dried substance on his mouth...waking up under the park bench. He walked slowly to the sofa, and feeling dizzy, he sat. "Did I...no. I would remember...Thomas did I...am I responsible for...that woman's death?" he stammered the words, not wanting to believe them.

Thomas softened slightly. "I need you to answer that. What do you remember from last night? You must tell me and you must tell me all of it. I have to know everything."

"I decided to go for a run in the park, and when I got there I ran into her. We ran along the path together...I knew I had to get away from her. I could feel the urge rising..." He shook his head, the grief already closing in. "The next thing I remember is waking up in the park under a bench hours later. If I did this why would I have been so brutal?" he asked quietly. To be responsible for such an unspeakable act was unthinkable. From the look on Thomas' face, he could see the truth.

"My guess would be that she resisted, and you being in the state you were in and needing to overpower her, you fought her...unfortunately you won." Thomas replied, his mind already working on what to do next. "This is far worse than I had anticipated, Master Andrew."

"What will you do?" Andrew asked in horror.

"Anything I have too." He laid his hand on his master's arm in comfort. "You'll continue on with life as normal, but there will be some definite, nonnegotiable changes."

"Whatever it takes, Thomas, do it." Andrew begged.

*

Back at the office, Andrew could not keep his mind on his work. He had killed someone. He wanted to vomit when the weight of the guilt set in. Andrew even entertained the notion of turning himself in to the police, but what would that solve? The woman would still be dead. They might believe he was the killer, but once he started talking about vampires and the need for blood they would consider him crazy, and he would wind up in a padded room.

This madness was his fault of course. He had no one else to blame. Andrew could not, in good conscience, blame even his father. If only he had listened to Thomas in the first place and taken the necessary precautions, none of this would have happened. He sat behind his desk turning pale as thoughts of his carnage played out in his mind. He was now what he never wanted to be.

This was reason enough to call an end to things with Monica. He had proven the relationship could be fatal, but inside he knew he needed her. That was selfish of him but it didn't matter. He needed her more now then ever.

Reginald would love this mess, Andrew thought miserably, trying and failing to accomplish something in his office. He could see that smug face in his mind rubbing it in. The reality that he had become everything he hated was too much to fathom. This thought made his stomach roll and had him shoving out of his chair and making a mad dash to his bathroom sink to vomit.

He could feel himself growing weaker and weaker by the moment. It was well after four. Andrew decided that rather then puke all day in his office, he would go home and puke in his own room. What was he going to tell Monica?

*

Thomas prepared a bath for Andrew within ten minutes of his arrival home. Most of his anger was gone and he was more than willing to help ease his tormented mind by easing his tired body into hot, soothing water. The tension, guilt, and emotional pain seeped out of every pore of his body and relaxation seeped in. He sat with his head against the marble wall, breathing shallow breaths. "Thomas, I've been thinking about this all day, the fact is I'm dangerous, too dangerous. There's no denying it. We have no choice. You know what has to be done."

Thomas wouldn't even consider it. "Absolutely not."

"Thomas-"

"No." Thomas assured. "I can take care of this mess."

"And what about next time?" Andrew asked with half closed eyes.

"There will be no next time."

*

The bath relaxed him but the guilt remained. The woman he'd killed had a loving family who would miss her terribly. With Monica sitting beside him on the couch he listened to her voice of pity, her questions of why. Together they watch her cover the story on the noon news. It made it worse, infinitely so, that his madness touched her, even in this small way.

His conscience hounded him at every turn and it was impossible for him to carry on a conversation with Monica. It didn't help matters that she wanted to talk about it, rehash what he wanted so badly to forget. The instincts of a reporter had their drawbacks. The more she talked, the worse he felt.

The ugly facts ran in his head over and over. I'm a murderer. I killed a defenseless woman......what have I done? It rang in his head like a bell tolling the hours. Yet he covered so well Monica knew nothing of his torment. For Andrew this was a blessing.

When he could take no more of feigned normalcy, he excused himself, claiming he had some business calls to return. But Thomas knew the real reason for his leaving. His master wanted to be alone. With his guilt and his tortured thoughts, he needed to be alone. It was only Monica who believed his lie. Too wrapped up in the story that captivated her, she missed the subtle signs.

Andrew was happy to see her so excited about her work but it saddened him to know that it was by his hand. He paced the study floor searching for peace of mind that eluded him. He wanted to do something for the family he'd destroyed, but what could he do to ease their pain? He learned from the news that they were having tough times thanks to bad investments. Should he send them a check? He was always giving to those who needed it, so why not give to this family?

Andrew liked the idea. Not only would he send money for the family but he would pay for the funeral as well. It was the very least he could do considering. The door opened and he saw Thomas standing in the doorway studying him. "I'm a son of a bastard. Yes old boy, that is what I am," he said quietly.

Thomas frowned sadly. "I know this is terribly hard on you, Master Andrew," he said walking into the room and closing the door. "I wish there were some way I could fix things for you."

Andrew looked at Thomas with barren eyes. "There is, kill me now," he said with conviction. "It's what I deserve. How proud Reginald would be over this, knowing that makes death all the more desirable," he continued with disdain, leaning against his desk. "I've more than earned this fate, Thomas. Save this city and me."

Thomas walked over to the shell of a man and took him firmly by the shoulders. "I cannot kill you. I'm fighting for your life now, even if you are not. What about your plans of marriage and the rest of your dreams?" he asked with a tear in his eye.

Andrew met those painful eyes with his. "My plans and dreams died with that woman last night." He walked away from the desk trying to walk off the ache that would not go away. "I plan to pay for her funeral. It's the very least I can do. Also, first thing in the morning make sure there's a check available for my signature. One hundred thousand dollars will do. I want the husband's burden eased and the children's future secured, if nothing else." Andrew cleared his throat. "Can you handle that?" he asked.

Thomas felt for the man beyond measure, it was written all over his face. The grief and the guilt were clear. "Of course," he agreed. If that's what you want then I'll take care of it," he replied with a sad smile.

"I owe it to them, this family I've damaged forever." Andrew left the study saying no more.

*

His hopes of solitude were dashed when he found Monica sitting on the edge of the bed talking on her cellular phone. "This could be the story of my career.......I know." She met his gaze and smiled. "Listen, I've got to go, I'll talk to you tomorrow. Bye." Monica tossed the phone on the bed. "You look like you lost your best friend." she said.

He put his hands in his pockets and walked to the bed. "As long as I have you I have all I need." He dropped down on the bed and kissed her softly. His face grew serious when he next spoke again. "Is it what you want? To marry me I mean?"

"You're serious?" Monica's laugh faded. "I've never wanted anything more in my life," she replied almost shocked by the question. "Are you having doubts, Drew?"

"Not at all," he said and smiled. "I love you, I have to marry you." And in assuring her, he assured them both. Wrapping his arms around her, Andrew felt some of his pain and fear ease. Monica was lost in her world of planning for the future. And he couldn't quite believe the day would ever come.

*

Later Monica woke and found Andrew asleep beside her. Trouble seemed etched in the fine lines on his face. She touched his cheek and felt overwhelmed by love. What was bothering him? She could feel his restlessness, his preoccupation. Was it work, maybe a failing business deal? She only knew he was pulling away. Loosing him would undo her after having waited so long to open herself up to so much joy.

She wouldn't lose him, she knew beyond doubt that he loved her as much as she loved him. His mood would change and things would be fine. She had to keep telling herself that no matter what.

December 1994

Monica and Andrew were blissfully happy with the dark shadows of murder held off by his positive thoughts. Having known each other six months, they couldn't remember a time when they hadn't loved each other. In ten days they would be bonded for life. Four months had passed since the killing and Andrew was finally sleeping at night and putting it behind him. With Thomas's help, together they had been able to fix the problem of potential relapse, he was never alone outside the confines of the mansion.

*

Thomas hadn't seen such a grin on his master's face in months. Being fitted for his tuxedo had put him in a rare light mood. He was truly at his happiest. "How do I look?" Andrew asked with the grin still cemented on his face.

"You look grand, very dapper," Thomas said with a matching grin of his own. "Are you happy, Master Andrew?"

Andrew laughed. "Old man, I simply can't remember ever being happier in my life," he gleamed. "Everything has fallen into place; the nightmare of the past few months is where it belongs, in the past. This will be a new beginning for me and my soon-to-be wife."

"I'm thrilled for you, Andrew. I really am," Thomas said.

"I love it when you call me by name. I wish it would continue."

"It's not how I was raised."

"I know," Andrew said with a clap on the old man's shoulder. "I'm glad you'll be standing next to me when I marry."

"So am I."

*

Reginald waited anxiously for the cab to come to a halt. It had been weeks since he'd been home to London, and he had much to do. He had plans for his son's future. He smiled as he remembered the joy he took in reading about the murder in New York a few months back; a disaster with his dear son's name all over it. His boy had truly come full circle, and now he was about to take a bride.

Reginald's business would be finished by the wedding day, and he planned to attend. He laughed, picturing Andrew's face when he saw him in among the invited guests. "Oh what fun it shall be," he said smugly, "oh what fun indeed."

*

Monica flew into his arms when Andrew met her at the door. "Hello, Drew did you miss me?" she asked sheepishly.

Andrew could only laugh. "Hell yes, I missed you, love. I was afraid that business trip would never end." He left her go long enough to help her in the door with her bags. Then he kissed her. "This will be the last bloody trip you take until after our honeymoon," he said as he kissed her neck. "I miss you when you're away."

Monica grinned. "I missed you too. Promise you'll come with me next time, then you won't have to miss me."

"That's a promise I can make."

*

Thomas was happy to prepare a special welcome home dinner for the two of them. Monica had been gone for five days and he knew his master missed her. They talked all through dinner and shared kiss after kiss as they talked of their upcoming wedding.

"How's your dress coming along?" Andrew asked, taking another drink of wine. "Will it be ready in time?"

"Don't worry, it's ready. It's so beautiful, Drew," she gushed. When she talked about her gown her eyes lit up.

Andrew smiled, touched her hair. "Of course it's beautiful, look who's wearing it," he whispered. "I love you."

"I love you too."

But as often happened, Andrew's mood grew serious again. "I can't promise you a life without pain, but I can promise to love you through it all and make you as happy as I can," he said with emotion.

"You can't protect me from the sadness in life, Drew. I wouldn't ask you too. There's pain in life so you can appreciate all the pleasure. I just want to be with you. No matter what we face we can face it together," she spoke the words and her heart filled with sorrow for all the pain he had already experienced in his life.

You may never know just how true those words may be, he thought, cupping her face in his hands. Their future was in his hands alone.

Chapter 10

The weather on the morning of the wedding was beautiful and very much appreciated. It was Christmas Eve and snow was falling despite the unusually mild temperature. Andrew was up at the crack of dawn in anticipation of his big day. The ceremony was to begin at six o'clock and he found himself counting down the minutes. The mansion was a whirl of activity with the designer and her staff making some last minute alterations on both the wedding gown and his tuxedo.

*

Monica was as nervous as she could ever remember being in her life. She studied herself in the mirror, watching her mother fuss with her flowers. She wondered how her soon-to-be husband was dealing with his nerves. And then she laughed. Knowing Drew as well as she did, she knew he probably wasn't the least bit nervous. She envied him, his calmness. She wasn't having doubts, just jitters. She was more certain about this decision then any she'd made before.

Life as she knew it would change in drastic measures once she and Andrew became husband and wife. It was hours until the ceremony and Monica wanted to see the man she loved. She glanced at the clock on the wall. Six more hours, she thought as she relaxed on the bed in her hotel.

*

He combed his hair standing in the middle of his suite. With a towel wrapped around his waist, he plotted. He hated this city and its people but he'd waited too long for this opportunity to let it go. Tossing the brush on the bed he went into the bathroom to brush his teeth. He thought of the misery he would bring and Reginald Carter was a happy man.

He hadn't been able to come up with the best way to reveal himself to his new daughter-in-law and his ungrateful son. But he would recognize the best way when it came along. The very thought of the look on Andrew's face made him practically dance with glee. With his teeth, fangs included, nice and clean he went to his closet to pick the perfect suit for such a momentous occasion.

Everything had to be perfect to ensure the proper reaction from his boy. Reginald was sure that Andrew had come up with the death story to explain the absence of a father in his life. It would give him immense pleasure to watch the little prick squirm out of a lie.

While Reginald dressed, he hummed the same melody over and over, "dum dum da dum, dum dum da dum. What a glorious day for a wedding!"

*

"Thomas! Thomas, where are you, old man?" Andrew bellowed from the study.

Thomas rushed into the study out of breath. "Would it be too much to ask that you calm yourself, Master Andrew?" he asked with a look of amused impatience.

"When are the flowers arriving at the gazebo? They'd best not be bloody late. It took forever for me to convince Monica to have the wedding outdoors instead of a church. I don't want her disappointed," Andrew said.

"Relax, everything is moving according to the schedule. And it is not your fault you can't give her the church wedding she wanted. It was a wise decision," Thomas reminded him.

"This bloody curse has to touch even my wedding," he muttered angrily. "Just another thing my father tainted."

Thomas watched his master stew in his hatred. "What purpose does this serve, this need to rehash your contempt for your father?" he asked. "Don't give him the power."

Andrew looked confused. "What the hell does that mean?" he demanded.

Thomas just shook his head. "By allowing yourself to attack your father, you only precipitate more hatred, which will only hurt you, Master Andrew."

"It's the only release I have."

"You'll be married in a few hours, focus on that."

"The one experience Reginald couldn't take from me."

*

The hairdresser finished Monica's hair and smiled at the results in the mirror. "It looks beautiful," Monica said through tears. "Thank you." Turning her head from side to side, she worried, "I hope the snow doesn't ruin it for pictures."

"Don't worry, that's why I'll be there," the woman said with a reassuring smile.

"I just want everything to be perfect for us," Monica said

happily.

She turned away looking out the window to the street and the thin veil of snow falling down... *perfection.* Drew preferred an outdoor service to the formality of a church wedding; that spoke to his uniqueness. It would be charming to leave the gazebo as husband and wife by horse-drawn carriage. To be married in fairy-tale fashion. A wedding in a quaint gazebo was so much more romantic and much more their style. The flurries and flakes would be enchanting. Fresh flowers in December would set the mood. It would be a day they would never forget.

*

As the hour of five approached, Andrew grew tense due to a last minute problem with his tuxedo. "Leave it to me to cause havoc by pulling on an innocent thread." he complained, another impatient glance at his Rolex.

"Calm down, will you? There's time enough in any case." He offered the words in comfort. "And just be thankful the weather holding," he continued, fussing with his tie and cummerbund.

Andrew almost looked thankful then he said, "Imagine Monica's face if her groom has to show up in a jogging suit. Wouldn't that be lovely?" he said cynically, shoving his shaking hands into the pockets of his robe.

"A bit dramatic don't you think?" But Thomas chuckled in spite of himself. "Relax, and I'll see if she's ready."

*

Reginald stared at his pocket watch from the back seat of a limo and smiled. It wouldn't be long now. Soon, he would have the pleasure of wiping that 'holier-than-thou' look from his son's face and replacing it with the fear he's instilled in his son's eyes so many times before. Maybe Andrew would become so enraged at his presence that Andrew would attack him in front of his new bride. Wouldn't that be a lovely way to start their honeymoon? With me rolling around on the ground in mock pain as his wife looks on in horror, he thought as a grin came across his face. "The perfect wedding gift!" he said and broke out in evil-like laughter.

*

Monica was the picture of elegance in her gown. She stood in front of the mirror and was amazed by the beautiful woman looking back at her. Monica wiped the tears from her eyes and smiled. In less than an hour she would have what she most wanted in her life. Drew played heavily through her mind, but never more strongly then at that moment. He promised to make her happy and she knew he would. Knowing that, feeling that, she settled, smiled, and prepared. The butterflies disappeared and warmth took their place.

Their honeymoon was still a mystery to her, but she delighted in Drew's enjoyment in dropping clues. She could hardly wait. Was he taking her someplace warm, or maybe it would be cold and romantic just like the wedding itself. It didn't matter as long as they were together. It would be perfect. She leaned her cheek against the cold glass and sighed. Snow continued to fall as it had all day, but only a dusting remained. How wonderful it will be, she thought. And her smile widened. It would be a gift to spend their first Christmas together, married.

Then guilt overwhelmed her. Poor Thomas, he would be alone for the holidays, how awful! The thought rooted in her mind. There was no way she could truly enjoy herself knowing that Thomas was all alone at the mansion. There had to be some way to make up for the oversight that both she and Drew were obviously guilty of.

The carriage arrived for her at five twenty. A kindly old man helped her into the compartment. When she was comfortable, the old man led the horse-drawn carriage along the street. The air was chilled, though not cold, and the snow still fell with a feverish intent. It refreshed and calmed her, as she leaned back to enjoy the ride.

The wedding party had gone on ahead to the gazebo to make sure everything was just right. It consisted of a few friends from the station and a few business friends of Andrew's. It would have been better if they had some close friends to share the occasion with. They were both so career driven that it allowed little time for forming fast friendships. Still, it would be the perfect event for two such busy people.

*

Monica and Andrew had no idea of the presence that was about to disrupt their lives. The presence had a name........Reginald. One of them knew nothing of his existence. The other knew of it all too well.

*

Andrew was ranting about not being able to find his wool coat and the overall injustice that kept him running late to his own wedding. His missing coat conspired against him. Five thirty came and Thomas draped the found coat around his master's shoulders, and all but shoved him out the door into the awaiting limo. As they moved down the street, Andrew was finally able to relax. He took a handkerchief from his breast pocket and patted his forehead. Even with the chilly temperature and snow, the last few hours had driven him to the boiling point.

Thomas patted Andrew's arm and smiled. They rode along in silence, both thinking their own private thoughts. Andrew thought of nothing but Monica and the deep love he felt for her. Thomas wondered how his master would adjust to having a wife who would be concerned by his every mood and thought. After all, he was a master at keeping secrets, something unacceptable in marriage. But in this marriage secrets would be vital.

*

The wedding march began, and Andrew was drawn to the woman walking slowly over the snow sprinkled grass towards him. And while Thomas beamed with the pride of a groom's father, Andrew felt a tear slide down his cheek. His eyes locked on Monica's, and at once they were one. One hundred guests looked on in happiness. When Andrew reached for her hand he felt it shaking in his own. She smiled warmly and he fell in love all over again.

The judge spoke of love and commitment. He made sure that everyone there knew their role in the couple's lives. He reminded that love and commitment was not always easy and those words hit home for Andrew. Everyone was so taken with the ceremony that no one noticed the unwelcome guest in the back.

The contempt on his face would have been apparent to anyone who looked at him. He refused to hear the words and his abhorrence grew knowing that his son could stand before such a ceremony with such ease. His eyes narrowed and the bile in his stomach rose to the point of nausea. 'What a crock of shit!' he thought.

He focused back on the event in time, to hear his son say 'I do.' Then he spoke all hearts and flowers to his bride, which was enough for Reginald to turn away in disgust. Monica was beautiful he had to admit. And she would be a wonderful addition to their kind if brought into the vampire fold. After the Central Park incident, he was more certain then ever that it was inevitable. He forced himself to listen as she too gushed and spoke of her deep love for his son.

They became husband and wife and shared a long passionate kiss as tears of joy ran down Monica's face. Thomas was crying too, much to his surprise. Andrew pulled away to smile at his wife. The photos were taken, and though Andrew knew they would be useless even that could not pull the smile from his face. He would have an explanation for that later. Pictures could not be taken of their wedding day.

They rode off in the carriage with smiles and waves for the crowd. Each yelling they would see everyone at the reception at the Trump tower ball room in an hour. As the loudness of the crowd grew quiet, Andrew pulled Monica to him and kissed her. "I love you," he whispered.

Monica clung and kissed him back. "Love you too."

Whatever lay ahead of Andrew now, he knew he could face it. That thought preoccupied him for most of the ride. Monica grew quiet, basking, but still gripped his hand tightly. The party would be fun for them both. It would be a chance to celebrate their new life together. And what a life it would be.........

Chapter 11

Christmas arrived and the newlyweds were bright and bubbly. They came downstairs to find a mountain of gifts under the grand pine. Gifts that Andrew had purchased and then forgot in all the excitement, packages sneaked in by Monica while Andrew was at work crowded the tree skirt and overflowed beyond. Like children, Andrew and Monica tore into the presents and prepared to spoil themselves over a sumptuous breakfast.

Thomas came into the living room and smiled. "Good morning newlyweds!" he exclaimed. They turned around and smiled widely at him. "You had quite a busy night," he continued, pouring warmed brandy for them all. "Yet you both look radiant."

"There's too much to do before our flight tonight," Andrew said happily, pulling away from Monica to take the old man's hand in his own. "I'm very glad you were able to be with us last night. It meant the world to me," he said seriously. After a moment, the smile was back on his face.

Thomas felt touched by the words. "I wouldn't have missed it for the world, Master Andrew."

"I've got a surprise for you, old man. It makes Monica and I sad to think of you being here alone while we're on holiday, so we want you to join us on our trip," he said with the same smile brightening.

Thomas was confused. "On your honeymoon?" he asked surprised.

"It would do you well to relax for awhile, you know you deserve it."

"What about your privacy?" he asked.

"You're perfectly capable of finding your own way once we're there. Who knows, you may even find someone to occupy your time. And we'll have plenty of privacy, don't worry about us," Andrew continued convincingly. "What do you say?"

Thomas couldn't believe they wanted to take him along, but it worked to his advantage. His original plan was to follow on a commercial flight and observe his master from a discreet distance. "You're sure?"

Andrew put his arm around Thomas and laughed, "Absolutely!" He winked at Monica and hugged Thomas.

*

Later on, they sat around the living room and talked about the upcoming trip. As hard as Monica tried, no amount of coaxing could get Andrew to tell her where they were going on the honeymoon. She teased and tickled and begged for a clue, but Andrew wouldn't hear of it. When the last gift was given, Thomas set about cleaning up the mess of paper and ribbons. All the while, working out a plan to keep close tabs on his master so as to avoid any more problems.

Andrew was upstairs on the phone when the doorbell rang, so Thomas hurried to greet the visitor who was ringing the bell like there was no tomorrow. He opened the door and felt his heart jump to his throat. He couldn't speak but wanted to say something desperately. He was brushed by and dismissed before he could muster up venom. He shut the door and turned. "What in the name of all that's decent are you doing here?" he exclaimed!

Reginald just laughed in his face. "What? You're not happy to see me?" he laughed again, mocking Thomas.

Thomas' shock gave way to anger. "Why are you here!" he demanded unwilling to take part in this sick game.

"I'm here to meet my new daughter of course."

"You're not welcome here!" Thomas shouted. "Leave now!"

Andrew heard the raised voice of an angry Thomas and was half way down the stairs before he realized who was antagonizing him. "Thomas, what is all the yelling about? You sound..." His gaze swept the foyer coming to fall on his father, stopping him dead in his tracks. "What in the hell are you doing here?" he shouted, looking over his shoulder to make sure Monica wasn't coming at the sound of raised voices. His face contorted in rage. "I told you never to show your face here again!"

"So I guess this means you're not happy to see your old man?" he asked sarcastically. Reginald walked over to Andrew and moved so close that they could feel each other's breath on their faces. "I'm hurt," he continued.

Andrew felt his blood boil beneath his skin. "Bloody damn right I'm not happy to see you! What havoc have you come to unleash now? You can't intimidate me any longer, Reggie," he spat with hatred burning, alive in his eyes.

Reginald's eyes shined too, but with something evil and demonic. "I would like to welcome my daughter to the family," he whispered through clinched teeth. "I'll deal with you later."

Andrew thrust forward knocking the man off balance. "You will never see Monica," he replied with a sneer. "I'll see you dead first! Do I make myself clear?"

"You plan to stop me, do you? You self righteous little shit. You are no threat to me! If I wanted, I could remove you from this earth as easily as I breathe. You would do well to remember that, Andrew."

Andrew placed a strong hand around the man's throat. "Go to her, Thomas," he spoke quietly over his shoulder. His strength was awesome in rage, and he squeezed tightly until he saw Reginald's eyes begin to bulge from their sockets. "Listen to me very carefully. You will leave my home and never return," he said the words slowly so he could be sure the choking man in his grasp understood every word. "If you don't, I will kill you!!!" Andrew spit the last words in Reginald's gasping face. He dropped the man to the floor and watched him grapple for his footing and his breath. "Remember this moment the next time you think I am of very little threat to you. It will do you *well* to remember that."

Reginald rubbed his throbbing throat and glared at him. "I will make you pay. I know all about your little park adventure!" he rasped. "You are exactly what you proclaim not to be! Tell me, was it orgasmic for you when you brought her blood to your lips? Better than sex, wasn't it?"

Andrew's reflexes took over as he felt his hand connect squarely with Reginald's jaw, sending him back to the floor with a thud. "I'll rip your throat out if you don't keep your mouth shut! You would never understand what it's like to genuinely regret an act that is so violent." He leaned down and got in Reginald's face. "But I can promise you, one act I would never regret would be driving you from this earth. Take heed of my words, *father*, I could kill you as easily as you kill every innocent victim you take under your spell with your shallow charm."

Reginald lay on the floor for a long time before he stood to face his son. To his disgust, he found himself frightened. His eyes narrowed, and he tried to act as if he was unscathed. The truth was known, and Andrew smiled almost as devilish as his father smiled before. Reginald backed his way into the corner of the room. "So you think you have won?" he asked struggling to sound, and feel, confident.

Andrew walked slowly to him and stopped. "I have, you pathetic fool, I have. Get out! And if you've any common sense you'll know never to return here," he said easily, knowing he now had the upper hand.

Reginald straightened and started for the door. Then he stopped abruptly and turned around. "What have you told your wife about your father? That I'm dead?" he asked.

"To me you are. The greatest gift I can give my wife is to let her think that," Andrew turned his back to him and waited until he heard the door close. He pulled his hands from his pockets and poured himself a drink from the bar. Victory was sweet. Sweeter than the taste of any blood he could have stolen from a stranger.

*

Thomas joined Andrew in the living room and gave him a glass of wine, removing the brandy snifter from his hand. "You've had enough of this." Your lovely wife is in the shower, totally unaware of the rile that took place under her nose," he said, sitting beside his master on the couch.

Andrew fumed. The nerve of that asshole, to show up on his doorstep the morning after his wedding. He should have killed him when he had the chance. He forced himself to relax and slapped Thomas on the shoulder. "The last thing I want is to have to explain this mess to her. She would never understand, and I could never find the words to make her. Monica deserves so much more."

He shook his head and left the couch to stare out the window. The glare from the sun on the snow stung his eyes, and when he could stand no more he slammed the shutter closed.

"How do you want to handle Reginald? He intends to be a problem," Thomas said studying his master's expression.

"What do you suggest?" Andrew asked at his wits end.

"I don't know. Let's wait and see. I saw the look on his face when he left here. I can honestly tell you, I've never seen that look in all the years I known him," Thomas replied thoughtfully. "It was fear."

*

Monica came downstairs and went to Drew. She was happier than she could remember being. He looked into her eyes and reached out to her. "Did you miss me?" she asked wrapping her arms around his waist.

"Yes." Andrew held her tight. "We've just been waiting to see what you wanted for lunch," he said.

"Anything's fine." Monica looked at Andrew for a moment. "You okay?" she asked.

"I'm fine. Why don't you and Thomas go into the kitchen and decide on lunch," he said releasing her from his arms.

Thomas saved him yet again. "Yes, join me in the kitchen, Madam Monica. There's much to do before the plane leaves," he said standing and offering his arm.

When they were gone Andrew heaved a sigh of relief. Monica could read him like a book. He grew worried and then he grew angry. I'll be damned if I let Reginald destroy my future! I'll see him dead before that happens. With that thought planted in his mind, he went to his study to check on the arrangements for the trip. It had to be perfect for her. He loved her too much for anything less.

*

Over lunch, Monica delighted in telling Andrew how she chose everything herself. Thomas only smiled as he left them alone to enjoy their meal. He had his doubts in the past about how this marriage would work, and maybe, just maybe, he was wrong.

Thomas made his way to the dark sector below and began preparing treatments to take on his master's honeymoon. He was grateful to be accompanying them because he had to keep a close watch on things. The wedding night was a nervous one for Thomas, not knowing if it was safe to let his master engage in lovemaking with his wife was a painful dilemma to wrestle over. He was no fool, of course, he knew that there would be no way of stopping him, but it had troubled him just the same.

The new potency treatment worked well, so far, it troubled Thomas a great deal to intensify the dosage. After the chaos in the park he knew he had no choice. It seemed to allow his master the chance to be at rest from hunger that would easily pull him over the edge. Another positive result, Thomas knew, was the stomach pains subsiding and the nausea had all but disappeared. So Thomas prepared and packed as much as he could fit in the large cooler he had brought down with him. There was no reason to worry, as long as the right amount was given each day. Thomas smiled. All would go well.

*

Eight o'clock arrived. With the luggage packed into the limo's trunk, the three of them drove to the airport. Andrew's private plane was waiting on the tarmac when the car pulled along side. Andrew helped Monica from the car and went to Thomas to help with the luggage. Once the luggage was handled, Andrew, Monica, and Thomas walked up the stairs into the plane. Monica looked around in sheer amazement, while Thomas moved about the plane unimpressed by it. Andrew just watched her eyes light up in appreciation.

He came up behind her and put his hands on her shoulders. "So, you like it?" he whispered.

She turned around and grinned. "Do I like it? I love it, Drew!" she exclaimed.

He laughed. "You don't think it's too boastful? Thomas always says it makes me appear cocky to my business clients."

Thomas laughed as he moved about the large cabin making things more comfortable. "And it does, dear boy."

Monica chuckled, having never seen such pride displayed before. She felt that he deserved as much. Watching him watching her with the excitement of a child only made her love him more. Still, it drove her crazy not knowing where the plane would take them. She tried working on Thomas earlier, hoping he would give in and tell her where her honeymoon would be, but Andrew had sworn him to silence. She made herself at home on the sofa while Andrew went to check in with the pilot. The fabric was emerald velvet and she ran her hand over it slowly.

Watching her from the adjoining room, Thomas understood why his master loved her so deeply. She would liven up the sometimes calm of the large mansion. He knew she might change the person he adored, but with such sweetness that any change could only be for the better. But her need to help at every turn could be disastrous. Though, as he looked at her now, he could see only the promise she held for his master. It was promise that he deserved.

The plane taxied down the runway and they were airborne by nine fifteen, in a clear sky lit by a beautiful moon. Monica's stomach turned with excitement and mystery. Andrew teased, held her hand, and enjoyed watching the wheels turn in her head and her eyes dart to the window now and then. Content and amused, he leaned back on the sofa and relaxed. It was something he hadn't been able to do in hours and it felt wonderful to him. Like a release of all the poison his father had spewed earlier.

"You happy?" he asked quietly when Thomas left to prepare the master suite.

Monica touched his face and kissed him gently. "Yes, so happy I can't even tell you," She feathered her fingers through his hair, and nuzzled, draping herself across his chest "You look like you could sleep for days, tired?"

"Exhausted, are you telling me you're not?" he asked through heavy-lidded eyes.

"I'm too excited to sleep. Rest your eyes a little bit and maybe when you wake up I'll be able to tell you where we're headed," she teased.

"Fat chance, love, but feel free to try," Andrew said through a yawn. He swung his feet up on the sofa, and laying his head in her lap, closed his eyes. It took only moments for him to fall asleep.

*

The flight continued smoothly with Monica trying to figure out their destination for an hour. Andrew was still asleep, and Thomas busied himself in the other room, wanting to give them privacy. The pilot came over the intercom every thirty minutes to update flight progress. Outside over the left wing, Monica watched as clouds formed and then were flown through with ease. And giving in, she tipped her head back and finally slept.

Around midnight, Andrew woke to find Monica staring down at him. He smiled when their eyes met. "Know where we're going yet?" he asked, sitting up and running his fingers through his hair.

"I don't have a clue and the long flight tells me we must be a thousand miles from New York."

"That much you've got right, my love. Don't worry, we'll be arriving shortly but I'm sure we can think of something to occupy our time until then." Andrew touched her nose and pulling himself up from the sofa, reached out for Monica's hand, and pulled her up to him. Together they walked through the plane to the master suite.

Thomas met them just outside the door. "Ah, you're awake. Well, everything is prepared just as you asked, so please, enjoy. I think I'll retire to the guest suite to read." He smiled at them and patted Andrew's back; "Night."

"Good night, Thomas," they said over their shoulders as they walked into the suite. "He's a dear man." Monica said softly collapsing onto the bed while Andrew closed the door and went to her.

Monica's eyes swept the spacious suite. As with everything else, Andrew made sure romance was abounding. Candles, lightly scented of lilac, flickered, and wine was chilling in an ice bucket. "It's so lovely," she murmured. "You're too good to me."

"Not possible," he whispered; his eyes bright, knowing he'd never seen her more beautiful than at this moment. Watching the flames dance, mirroring deep in her eyes, he pulled her against him. "We'll be dining on the finest lobster Maine has to offer."

Monica laughed. "Isn't it off season for lobster?"

Andrew laughed, turned his face into her lush hair, "I pulled some strings."

*

The plane touched down while they slept. Thomas woke them with fresh coffee and the hum of island music outside. Monica leapt from the bed to look out the small window. Andrew just watched her, grinning. Flying around in the giddiness of a child, she practically glowed. Darting from one window to the next, trying to make out anything in the darkness. Dawn was still hours away when they walked off the plane and into a waiting car below.

"We're in the islands," she proclaimed, feeling the salty, tropical breeze caress her.

"The Virgin Islands, specifically."

*

They checked into the largest suite in the hotel. Andrew whisked Monica off her feet and carried her over the threshold, while Thomas and a bellhop carried the luggage in behind them. The suite was the largest she ever seen, decorated with an island flair. They walked around, explored the massive space, and wandered out to the balcony and the moonlit, ocean view. Andrew could see his wife was ecstatic and because of that, so was he.

"You've really out done yourself this time, Master Andrew," Thomas said, excusing himself to get settled in his own room next door.

Chapter 12

Dusk on the beach was beautiful as Monica folded her hand around Andrew's and scuffed her sandals through the sand. The crowds had thinned out, with tourists opting for early dinners, a chance at luck at the slots, or a cruise on the gentle water a mile from shore. Finding a secluded spot near the edge of the beach, they spread a large blanket on the sand and settled in with a basket of fruit, wine, and cheese.

With the water, lapping on shore, clear and glistening, the sky above them darkened, it was breathtakingly stunning. They watched the water's ebb and flow with stolen kisses and tight embraces. Andrew would toy with the gold band on his finger and feel saved. God forgive him, he decided, it was the best decision he ever made.

They ate from the basket Thomas packed for them and talked about the future. And for the first time in so long Andrew wanted to embrace it without the pain, grief and guilt to deaden the joy. He could look on the future with promise and plan. The magic of the island made hope possible. It was easy to get lost in the romance and leave worries behind. With long walks on the beach and long nights of making love, there was room for nothing else.

"Are you having a good time?" Andrew asked, pouring more wine for them.

Monica grinned, lazily propped on her elbows with her eyes turned to the stars, "Wonderful, sweetheart. I don't think I ever want to leave." Her voice was wistful and light.

"Even we have to return to the real world sooner or later," he said, offering her a refilled glass. "The good news is we can return whenever you like. Hell, I'll buy the island and we can use it as our weekend escape." He winked at her gaped expression. "Say the word and it's yours!" he exclaimed, setting their wine aside to joyfully jump off the blanket to pull her into his arms.

Monica laughed loudly. "I don't think that'll be necessary, Drew," she said knowing very well he'd meant every word. "A promise we'll return for our anniversary will do."

"Done," Andrew said squeezing her tightly. "I plan to give you the world," he said, "because that's what you've given to me."

*

Thomas was having no trouble finding things to keep him busy. He always wanted to try snorkeling, and found that he was actually very good at it for his age, or at least that's what the instructor had said. Reading by the pool was relaxing and an indulgence. He was always close if his master needed anything. A week without hovering and time alone was a gift. And knowing his master was doing so well allowed them both to be at ease. The treatments were working with no signs of relapse. He checked on his master several times throughout the night and found him sleeping soundly at his wife's side. So with little to worry about, tropical drinks with little umbrellas and the latest bestseller were a perfect way for Thomas to relax.

*

Parties on the beach were common. The week of the honeymoon they were happening every night. At first they were annoying, but after a few days Andrew and Monica, along with a reluctant Thomas, decided to join in on the fun. Dancing with the sand between their toes and warmed by bonfires, combined with drink and friendly conversations of fellow tourists made for an enjoyable evening.

Thomas struck up a conversation with a charming woman of his age, born and raised in England. She had come with her family as part of a birthday gift. Monica smiled and Andrew marveled at a side of Thomas he'd rarely seen. He wished his old friend luck and a lasting friendship if nothing else.

They continued to dance for hours, locked in each others arms like nothing on earth could separate them. The moonlight was enchanting but it wasn't long before they wanted to slip back to the suite. They drew a lot of attention to themselves. They'd had enough of jokes and drinks and wanted time with each other. Whispers moved along the guests as they were planning their escape. 'Don't they make a lovely couple?'

Monica was resting her head on Andrew's shoulder as they began to make their way through the clusters of people, when it struck with the force of a blow. Clogging the air in his lungs, his grip tightening on Monica's shoulders, his mouth went dry and his knees weak. As his stomach rolled and fluttered and he began to sweat, he slowed and then stopped.

It had been months since he felt like this, and cursed under his breath even as Monica turned to him, concern on her face. So many people, their necks exposed and ready, their blood pumping, enticing him, the strongest craving in his memory seized him. He struggled to keep his composure, trying desperately to make eye contact with Thomas. He stumbled as his knees went to water beneath him, and heard fear in his wife's bellow for Thomas even before he hit the sand.

With his head spinning, Andrew saw the frantic face of his wife above him, felt the cool touch of her palm on his forehead. Too many faces, too much temptation, they had to get away. And then, Thomas was at his side moving all but Monica back a safe distance. The potential annihilation could be considerable if Thomas did not act quickly.

Thomas looked into the changing eyes of his master and moved quickly. "Master Andrew, you've had an allergic reaction. What did you eat at the buffet?"

Monica locked eyes with Thomas. "Thomas do something," she pleaded.

Somehow Andrew squeezed her hand and soothed. "I'm alright.....I just need.....Thomas...help me get up," he mumbled.

"Don't you worry, Madam Monica," Thomas reassured her, "I'll take good care of him but I need to get him to the suite." Using considerable adrenaline he hauled Andrew up into a sitting position and waited until the worst of the dizziness passed and he could get him on his feet. "Up we go."

"Let's go," she snapped, though the worst of the panic was gone.

Thomas assured everyone it was nothing to be concerned about while his master steadied himself against Monica.

Andrew looked at Thomas in a panic, knowing he had to react quickly, but there wasn't much he could do without raising questions. So he said the only thing he could. "Of course, let's be on our way," he said with a warm smile. While Andrew shuffled weak, disoriented, and mortified.

Thomas had planned for this. The syringes were prepared, and to the unknowing eye it would be nothing but a solution to treat for allergic reactions. They rushed into the suite with Monica settling Andrew on the bed and disappearing for the aspirin Andrew needed for his headache. When they were alone Andrew couldn't bluff any longer. "What in bloody hell are you doing, Thomas? You know damn well what I need, how are you going to explain this to her?" he demanded in a loud whisper.

"Relax, the treatment is already prepared, as far as she will know it's a treatment for an allergy," he replied calmly. "Unless you blow it!" he cracked. "Now pull it together," he continued sternly.

Monica came back with a handful of aspirin. "Here, babe, this should take the edge off at least." She handed him two capsules.

He smiled weakly and swallowed them. Another wave of dizziness had him falling back into the night table knocking everything on the floor. "Dammit!" he seethed, grabbing his head in his hand and jerking back against the headboard.

"Drew!" Monica went to his one side while Thomas rolled up his sleeve on the other. "Thomas what are you giving him?" she asked worriedly looking from Drew to the syringe in his hand.

Thomas tried his best to smile. "I'm giving him something for his reaction." Concerned, he watched as he jammed the needle into his master's arm. With every new episode they grew more extreme. Despite the stronger solution they were still occurring. Something wasn't right.

Andrew jerked at the jab in his arm, and Monica grabbed his hand. "Drew, just try and relax," she whispered, smoothing his hair away from his face. Looking over at Thomas she asked, "Will he be all alright?"

Thomas watched as his master calmed and his color returned. "He'll be fine. You two will be able to hit the beach again tomorrow night." It wasn't a lie, just optimistic. "Don't worry, Monica," he replied, meeting his master's clearing gaze. "No harm done."

*

Three hours later Andrew had recovered enough to join Monica in the shower. She was still tense, needing to be reassured, so with a kiss, he sought to prove he was as good as new. He had handled it badly enough, he wouldn't allow her to obsess over it. Repercussions were to be expected given he'd married a woman who knew her own mind, and who now insisted he see a doctor when they returned home. A problem which he would have to side-step later, but for now he wanted to distract, pleasure, pamper her before she questioned anymore.

"I'm planning a surprise for you when we return home," he murmured in her ear before sucking on her lobe. And because he'd accomplished what he set out to do, she didn't have a chance to respond.

Making love was a wonderful distraction, an escape from their ruined evening. Andrew wanted so much to give her that. To wipe away the worry and fear he'd put in her eyes. So he swept her up in a passion which never seemed satisfied.

And feeling her yield, body, mind, and soul, beneath him, arcing up, meeting him need for need, pleasure for pleasure, warm flesh to warm flesh, never failed to humble him. He wanted to stay wrapped in her forever. Wanted to hear her moans, feel her hot breath, and have her molded to him forever. And through the passion, he felt a current of determination steel him. He would free her from his curse, carrying it on his shoulders, and never allow it to touch her again.

The one thing he could offer her without condition was his love. That's all she wanted. And that's all he wanted in return.

*

Lying in bed with his mind hounding him, he held her and hoped that even asleep she would feel his love for her. Why did this have to happen now, on his honeymoon? He would not sleep on this night or many more to come. In her dreams, she shifted away from him, and he felt the void immediately. He ran his hand over her hair and ached with love. She would sleep and because he would not, he left their bed to allow her rest. He left the room after he felt around in the dark, and pulled on his robe.

The living room was black from the clouded moon, but Andrew saw Thomas sitting on the couch, watchful, with an unimpeded view of the bedroom door. And though he didn't need to, he turned on the light. "Taking up the nightshift, old man?" he said, twin parts of annoyance and appreciation warring inside him.

"Knowing you as well as I do, I thought it wise. I figured you'd be restless and edgy. And I was right. So I'm here to keep you company," Thomas said quietly.

Andrew looked at him. "You mean you came to *baby sit* me?" he corrected, crossing the room and sitting down next to Thomas. "Suppose I could have some single malt to smooth out the rough spots?"

In answer, Thomas pushed himself to his feet and went to the bar. "Do you blame me for being cautious?" he asked, taking down two glasses and pouring generous amounts of scotch in both.

"With tonight's fiasco still fresh in my mind?" he asked, considering. "Not one bit."

Coming back and handing his master one of the glasses, he shrugged. "You're going to be fine." He sat, drank.

Despite his heavy mood, Andrew grinned, "Because you say so?"

"Because I won't accept anything less."

*

Two days before they were due back in New York, Monica talked Thomas into joining her for an evening of shopping while Andrew stayed behind to put the finishing touches on a surprise for Monica. Once again she begged for clues, but once again he offered none, just chuckled and pushed them out the door. He was feeling better than he could have hoped after the episode that nearly brought an end to the honeymoon. He wanted to spoil her. And wanting to fulfill every wish before she'd even thought to wish for them; he set out to top even himself.

He showered, decided not to shave, and dressed in a bright floral shirt from one of the shops on the beach. He buckled his sandals, zipped his white slacks, and left the suite with a purpose. Andrew looked at his watch, it was after eight o'clock. Plenty of time to find just what he wanted. The shops on the island stayed opened twenty four hours a day. Monica would be busy for hours. He smiled and set out.

He walked along the sand happy with what was to be his new life, not allowing himself to worry about Reginald's threats and his own spiraling condition. His smile faltered and then disappeared from his face. The long walk did him good and the boutique was just as he remembered, quaint, cluttered, and befitting its name, Diamond in the Rough. A discovery he stumbled upon years before, two miles off the main beach and all but forgotten to the island tourists. He walked up the steps tucking his problems away. It was time to see an old friend, he opened the door and walked inside.

A well-tanned island native looked up, and grinning from ear to ear, walked over and stuck out his hand. "It's so good to see you again, Mr. Andrew."

"It's good to see you too, Nombie. Did you find what I'm looking for?" he asked shaking the man's hand.

"Ah, yes!" Nombie exclaimed. "But it took some finesse on my part." He showed him to the rear of the boutique. "I have it in the back. Please, come, I'll show it to you."

Nombie removed a small bag from the safe in the office, and pulled out a small velvet box. Andrew watched with anticipation as Nombie opened the box carefully. "Well, it's a stunning stone, my friend," he said, very pleased.

"It is beautiful, yes? Just as I promised. Your wife, she'll like it?" Nombie asked with pride.

Andrew smiled. "It's the most perfect ruby I've ever seen," he agreed with a grin. "Flawless, the perfect gem for the perfect wife," he beamed.

Nombie smiled at the approval. "You'll take it back to the states and have it placed in the setting there?" he asked.

"Yes, I'm afraid we're leaving day after tomorrow. Thank you, Nombie, for your fine work," Andrew said, shaking his hand gratefully. He wrote a check for one million dollars and left with the gift of a lifetime in his shirt pocket.

*

The moon was high above him as he made his way along the beach back to the suite, and back to Monica. She would press him for hints of her surprise, and he laughed at the thought. It might take months to finish the ring but the beauty of the stone proved it would be worth the wait.

They would treasure the memories made here. The New Years Eve party on the beach, the midnight cruise, and the long quiet walks with the woman he adored. He would hold this time dear for some time to come.

His jet black hair was soaked from the humidity of the tropical island night. And it settled on his shoulders, weighing him down as he continued on. And then he knew, and the happiness fled. He shivered, becoming frigid in the hot tropical breeze. Andrew stopped to regain his senses, and pulled in a deep breath, waiting for the worst of it to pass, grateful for the deserted beach and privacy. He needed to get back to Thomas while he was clear-minded and strong enough or disaster could strike.

He could feed again. He rubbed his temples and took in deep, sucking breaths to control himself. Andrew could feel himself growing weaker as the sound of voices came closer. Stumbling over to the water's edge, he collapsed on all fours and splashed the salty water in his face. His skin was icy to the touch, and dizziness closed in around him clouding his senses. Andrew steadied himself and rocked back in the sand with his head in his lap.

*

Monica and Thomas walked into the suite calling out to Andrew. They were surprised that he had not returned before them. But Thomas was more than surprised as a coil of dread settled in his gut. Though he had given his master an injection and two glasses of wine before he'd left, he was immediately concerned. Looking at his pocket watch, fear stiffened his spine, it was after ten. Where had he gone? Why would he stay away so long?

Monica wondered aloud about what was keeping him. Although knowing his absence had to do with a surprise for her, excitement edged out concern. "I'm sure he'll be back here very soon, Thomas," she soothed, walking around the suite placing all her packages on the dressers.

"I'm sure you right, Madam," Thomas replied, unconvincingly. They'd stayed away too long. Leaving his master alone, given the last episode, had been reckless, though he'd sworn he was feeling perfectly fine and would not be gone any longer then necessary. Famous last words, he thought as he paced around the suite.

*

Andrew rested with his head in his lap for some time. He didn't know how long he'd been sitting in the sand with the water lapping over his sandals. Too weak to stand, too weak to move, and maybe, he thought ruefully, too weak to breathe. He was struggling to piece together a cohesive plan when he felt a tap on the shoulder. Andrew lifted his head, deciding it felt more like a fifty pound weight.

He turned around and strained to focus his eyes on the figure standing behind him. "Yes?" he asked in a rough, raspy voice.

A man stood over him, a look of concern on his tanned, kind face. "You okay? You need help?" he inquired.

"I'm fine," Andrew said as his vision began to clear. I just need a moment to rest, and you must go now." It was a warning for his safety, as well as the safety of the man standing over him.

"You've been sitting here for more than an hour, sir, and you don't look so good. Hey, let me get the doctor for you," the man insisted. trying to help him to his feet.

"No!!" Andrew bellowed more forcefully than he meant too. He yanked his arm away. The urge was powerful in him now, and it was stronger than it had ever been before. Andrew knew what would happen next if the thoughtful, but stupid, man did not leave at once. "Go now, if you know what's good for you," he pleaded.

But it was too late. Andrew turned on him and saw the blood drain from the man's face. He could feel his fangs prick his lips as he grabbed hold of his prey. Fear overtook the man when he revealed them in the moonlight. "Bloody fool," he spat, shoving him to the ground with a force neither of them expected.

Andrew lunged, pinning the man with his weight, and sinking his teeth into his throbbing jugular before the man could even resist. The fear made it better. The blood flowed faster, and in his greed and madness, he drank his fill.

His victim was helpless. He didn't struggle, though fear glazed his eyes while he lay gasping. Andrew could feel his heartbeat slow, draining him, enticed. Then with a vicious twist of the man's neck Andrew ripped the man's head from his body, splattering blood on the sand beneath them.

*

Thomas had excused himself saying he wanted to retire to bed, but instead he was on the beach hunting his master. Just as he was sure his master was hunting someone at that very moment. He frantically searched, but Andrew was nowhere to be found. Where could he be? He had to find him before...

*

...Thomas saw him, and breaking into a jog, also saw the body at his master's feet. His frantic eyes swept the beach and saw no one thanks to a party further down the beach. He ran quickly to his master, grabbed him by the shoulder and yanked him around. Thomas was surprised to find his fang-like teeth ready to drink again. "What have you done?" He looked at the headless corpse on the sand, then back into the vampire eyes of his master. "Dear god, Andrew, what have you done?"

Andrew only glared at Thomas, knowing who he was and remembering the sanity in which they lived together as a family. He closed his eyes tight and shook his head. His conscience restored with the crazed thrill of the feeding gone. Now it was replaced with horror and regret. When he opened his eyes, they spilled over with tears and the humanity returned. "I don't....know." He fell to the ground and into the face of the dead man that fed him. "I tried Thomas, I swear. I begged him to leave me alone but..."

Thomas yanked him to his feet and steadied him. They looked at each other in pain; in tears; but Thomas was already in problem-solving mode. Damage control was all that mattered now.

"Kill me now, please!" Andrew begged, wanting to drop back to his knees.

Thomas broke, "No!" he cried, "I will not!"

Andrew pulled away in defeat, dragging his hands over his face. "Why do you let this continue!" he shouted. "This will never end, never stop!" he said.

"What will you have me do? Kill you right now and then tell your wife you're gone, vanished, and she's a widow?" he ranted. "I'm this close to finding an answer to this hell. Once you are gone from this earth, Andrew, you're gone forever. Are you ready for that?" he asked, eyes shimmering with fresh tears. "I know I'm not. I know your wife is not. Remember, there's her to consider now."

He made a good argument, and as much as Andrew hated to admit it, Thomas was right. "I thought I could control this curse, and look at me now? How many times will you allow me to do this before you admit I have to be destroyed like the monster I am?" he asked turning to face him now.

"Before you were involved with Madam Monica, all was well. Since then, there has been a price you've had to pay, as I warned you time and time again. If we were still in New York, living alone, I could do what you ask easier than I would now. There are people to answer to now. She loves you, Andrew. So deeply, I think to lose you she'd lose herself. This curse will not win," Thomas whispered pulling himself together. "I will not allow it."

Andrew sat slumped in the sand like a pile of bones. "So, I suffer and now so does everyone who loves me?" he said in disgust. "What a lot I've gotten myself in."

"Tomorrow we will leave and put this behind us."

"And what do I tell Monica?"

"Whatever you must, but we leave before the situation grows worse." Thomas said pulling him up and across the sand. "Now let's get back to her, shall we?" he continued.

"I've got her surprise right here," Andrew said patting his shirt pocket. "But what a terrible price I've paid."

Thomas put his hand on his master's shoulder. "You'll be sick very soon from this feeding. If we're lucky, it will provide us with the perfect excuse to leave."

Andrew grunted. "Some luck, I'm going to become deathly ill but at least we can leave with out arising suspicion," he said with a touch of self-pity.

*

They left the body to the tide. Nature and the sharks would take care of the rest. They made their way down the beach in silence; there were no words that could change what happened. Andrew staggered from exhaustion and grief. He was a monster after all. The drying blood on his collar was all the proof he needed.

Thomas would call and have the plane ready for a predawn takeoff. He needed to put as much distance between his master and this island paradise as possible. He cast a studying gaze at Andrew. His face was drawn and his eyes haunted. And the old man's heart broke for his suffering.

*

It was after midnight when he returned to the suite. But Andrew wasn't surprised to find her waiting for him. He smiled, the great actor, acting. "Hello, love." She came to him and pulled him into her arms. "I'm sorry I'm so late. Your surprise took longer then I expected." He squeezed her tightly, too afraid to let go.

*

Two a.m., the fever hit and he began vomiting violently. The cold sweats and chills came next. Monica phoned Thomas in a panic and he came running. It was worse than he'd been expecting, but he managed to convince her it was a severe case of food poisoning. Thomas phoned the pilot and had the plane fueled for takeoff. At four a.m. they boarded the plane and made Andrew as comfortable as possible. Thirty minutes later they were on the way home. Monica was frantic... and so, too, was Thomas. They had to get back to New York before it was too late.

Chapter 13

The five months following the marriage were a whirlwind, with Andrew slowly recovering from the catastrophe that seized him on the honeymoon. He had gotten back into his old routine at work and in his life. Thomas administered six treatments daily, double the amount given just four short months before and triple the amount given nine months before that.

The components of the treatment changed drastically, but it solved the immediate problem and seemed to work miracles. The syringes now contained sixty percent rodent blood, twenty percent human plasma, and twenty percent chicken blood. It satisfied his desire for feeding, which in the end, whether Thomas liked it or not, was all that mattered.

Thomas waited for news of the body being found washed up on the island, but there was none. So he had been right when he told his master the tide would dispose of the body. His master became hounded by guilt for weeks following the incident, which lead Monica to ask questions, and that only made him feel worse. Both Monica and Andrew were working long hours, so when they did spend time together the last thing they talked about was his being troubled. She knew he would tell her when he was ready to. Until then, she would enjoy being the 'lady of the manor', as Andrew teasingly put it.

They spent weekends deciding on changes Monica wanted to make in the mansion. She had new decorating ideas, and he told her to do whatever she liked. When he decorated, he used his tastes, now that this was her home it should feel like it. Thomas began spending more time below in the dark sector, catching rats and feeding chickens and making sure that they were never low on the serum that allowed his master to live a peaceful life.

Dinner was served every evening at seven and the three of them would gather around the table and talk about the day's events while they ate. Monica adjusted to all the changes quickly, and she loved her new life and the men in it. Andrew was the most wonderful person she'd ever known and Thomas was starting to be the father she desperately missed. Thomas himself couldn't deny the fatherly feeling he now felt for his madam, just like the feelings he'd always had for his master.

Nights still brought a blanket of dread down on both Andrew and Thomas, wondering if the treatments throughout the day would allow for a restful, worry free night. Monica was none the wiser because Andrew had learned how to hide any anxiety he might be feeling. He would lie beside her late in the night and watch her sleep and envy her ability to sleep so peacefully.

But guilt was as much a part of him now as breathing. And memories of what he had done could bring him long nights of despair. It had become routine. Monica would sleep. And he would torture himself by reliving all the horror he was responsible for. And Reginald still played his hand every chance he got, needling him from a distance of thousands of miles. Something had to be done about him. Something effective, something final.

*

Andrew sat behind his desk, detracted by a merger teetering between success and failure. Lack of sleep was wearing on his keen business sense. Still, he managed a smile when he saw Monica in his doorway. She had obviously been watching him for a while, because her smile gave way to a look of concern. "Why so serious, love?" he asked trying to snap out of his somber mood.

She came in and walked behind the desk, sitting down on the corner, she met her husbands' eyes with a level look. "Alright, Drew. I want to know what is going on in that head of yours. I've watched you for weeks, struggling with some…something. I've been patient. Now I need to know."

Andrew watched her for a moment and laughed trying to ease to tension. "I don't know what you mean." He sat up, smoothed his tie. "I'm fine, just working a little too hard," he said, patting her leg and pushing away from the desk to stretch out his legs.

Monica watched him. "Bullshit."

"Such language!" Andrew laughed heartily. "You're overreacting, really."

Her mouth was a thin line. "Okay, I'll guess. You want out of this marriage? You've been diagnosed with a terminal disease? You…" She fell silent when he pulled her into his lap.

"You're not serious?" he asked with a look of amusement.

"What else am I suppose to think?"

"Bloody hell, Monica, I don't know. Please tell me you know I wouldn't keep something so serious to myself."

"What else am I supposed to think, Drew?" she asked

squeezing his hand.

He shook his head. "No, I do not want out of this marriage, you must never think that," he finally said after the shock faded away. "And I've no terminal diseases, just business complications in South America wearing on me. I'll work it out, don't worry."

*

Weeks passed, and though he had to be vague, Andrew tried to be more open with Monica about his troubles but he still ended up telling a lie or two. Honesty was one thing, telling her the truth, the real truth, and loosing her, was quite another. She would have him committed. And if by some chance she did believe him, his life would be over. His perceived openness allowed Monica to relax and that was important to him. As long as she was happy it was one less worry to weigh on him.

The whole truth would never be something she could live with It would send her running away in confusion and disgust, or worse, to the police. His master could never live with himself if he lost her now, and Thomas couldn't live without him.

Thomas sensed his madam becoming more aware of things being kept from her. But work was keeping her too busy to focus on anything unrelated. Andrew kept his wife happy and himself on an even keel. And because it was rare for him to leave the mansion, temptation was snuffed out.

The beginning of June brought another benefit, as Monica and Andrew dressed in their best formal wear and attended the festivities with smiles and enough love between them to fill the room. He couldn't believe it was possible for her to look more beautiful than she did on the night they married, but she did, and he couldn't take his eyes off of her. Monica loved holding on to Andrew's arm as they crossed the ballroom being greeted by the other guests. She thought Drew was the most handsome of all the men there and she loved knowing his heart was hers alone.

Andrew danced until he thought his feet were about to fall off, and then, mercifully, was called up to the podium to speak and presented his annual check and brought a huge cheer from the crowd. They had dinner and made an early exit. Now that he was married the last thing he wanted to do was spend an entire evening with a crowd of overly pretentious people. He had better things to do. They snuggled up to each other in the car as Thomas, grateful he no longer had to attend such activities, drove them home.

*

He watched her come into the bedroom after her shower, and she stopped toweling her hair dry to look at him. "What's going on in that mind of yours?" she asked, throwing the towel on the bed.

He grinned and lifting a brow let her guess the rest. "Did you have a good time tonight?" he came up behind her and ran his fingers through her knotted hair. "I certainly did. Being with the most beautiful woman in New York does wonders for the ego," he whispered as he massaged her shoulders softly.

"I had a great time," she said laughing. "You didn't. I saw daggers in your eyes several times tonight. You looked like you were having a root canal," she teased.

Andrew grunted, "I survived, but I've learned to hate those damn events." He shrugged out of his tuxedo shirt and unzipped his pants. "I loathe being put on display. I wish I could just send the damn checks and skip the rest."

Monica turned and looked at him. "I never knew you hated all the attention," she said.

He kicked off his shoes, stepped out of his pants. "All that pomp and circumstance's a waste of time. It's not me they adore. It's my money."

*

The phone rang at four thirty a.m., waking Andrew from the first sound sleep he had in weeks, annoyed, he grabbed the receiver before it disturbed Monica, "Hello?" The silence on the other end of the line puzzled him. "Is anyone there?" he asked, agitated.

"Good morning, Andrew."

The voice caused a fist to squeeze in his gut. "What the hell do you want now, Reginald?" he demanded, sitting up in bed and swinging his legs out from under the covers to the floor.

"I can't call and see how married life is treating you?" he asked over the hum of the overseas line. "Your wife's making you sloppy. The mess in the islands was dreadfully handled, my boy. She's got you spinning. Should I eliminate the problem?"

His knuckles whitened on the receiver. "You're a very stupid man, Reggie. Come near her and you won't live long enough to regret it."

The silence was broken with his dark laugh. "You don't have it in you," Reginald bated.

Trembling with rage, Andrew's voice took on an edge. "We'll

see."

"Quit hiding behind your wife's skirt and live the life you were meant too."

Andrew stood up, and sucked in a breath, trying to contain his temper. "Go to bloody hell!" He slammed the receiver down and struggled for calm.

Monica was starring at him when he turned to get back in bed. "Drew, who was that?" she asked half asleep.

"No one," he forced a tired smile, "Just a pain in the ass business call. Go back to sleep, love. I didn't mean to wake you. I have to get some papers from the study." He leaned over and kissed her softly.

"You need to sleep, Drew." Monica kissed him back. "Don't be too long."

*

Andrew strode down the long hall and burst into Thomas' room and sent the door slamming into the wall. Thomas bolted up in his bed confused. "Master Andrew, what's wrong?" he asked startled.

"Reginald. He's not going to leave well enough alone. He just called and threatened Monica," he snapped, working into a rant and pacing at the end of bed.

Thomas got out of bed and turned on the light. "What do you want me to do?"

"What do you think?" Andrew replied in disgust. "It's time to rid myself of him."

"Are you certain?" Thomas asked with a raised eyebrow.

Andrew sat down on the edge of the bed and let out a breath trapped in his lungs since the phone call came. "Very," he said.

"Any ideas as how?" Thomas asked.

"I'll leave it to you," Andrew muttered, striding for the door. He stopped suddenly and turned around in the doorway. "As long as it's as painful as possible, do you hear what I say? I want him to scream."

Thomas swallowed the lump in his throat. "Yes, Master Andrew, I hear you," he whispered.

*

Thomas paced inside his room. His master had been pushed to his limit and now there would be no turning back. Reginald Carter had been an abomination as a father. Blackmail and murder were pure evil, but then that was Reginald defined…evil. He went back to bed already forming the outline of a plan in his mind...In a few short hours he would take the first steps in removing Reginald Carter from the earth. He would kill Reginald Carter, destroying him like the demon he became so many years ago, but not before allowing his master a chance at revenge.

Chapter 14

Thomas woke early and immediately set out on the task his master had given him just hours before. This day had been coming for some time and as extreme as it was, Thomas knew what had to be done. It wasn't as if the world would miss Reginald Carter. As hard as he tried to imagine it, he couldn't picture the man having anyone to grieve over him. Few tears would be shed in the end. The question now was how to go about destroying the monster. The monster whose fatal mistake had been threatening his son's wife, and it was the last threat Reginald Carter would ever make.

*

Andrew joined Thomas in the study after he dressed and began discussing the details of what was about to take place. Monica would be asleep for hours yet, so it gave them the chance to talk openly. They stared at each other for a moment in silence, each acknowledging the seriousness of what they were about to do.

"You're certain this is what you want?" Thomas asked again after the silence became too powerful a presence.

"I'm certain. This is the last time that bleedin' fool will torture me. I've given him ample opportunity to leave me alone, he chose to ignore it." He shrugged, having come to embrace this day long ago. His only regret was that Reginald could not die by his hand. A vampire can not kill his maker. And that was a bitter pill. "The fault of his destruction falls at his feet, not mine," he paused, "so what are your plans?"

"Well, given the target, I should think a sneak attack would be prudent. I'm not sure if he is expecting anything or not, but it is best to assume that he is and to be prepared."

"Will you go to the main estate or do it elsewhere?" Andrew began to pace in front of Thomas.

"I'll do it where and when the chance presents itself."

"I have other ideas. I may not be able to destroy the bastard myself but I can and will have the satisfaction of watching him suffer. Bring him here."

Thomas froze. "It makes things easier, but there is Madam Monica to consider," he pointed out. "It may be wiser to do it elsewhere."

"Bring him here," he replied with a grin of triumph. "I think it's time we had some quality time together."

"It may be too risky," Thomas reasoned. "And there's the matter of disposing of the remains."

"Monica's going out of town for a couple days on assignment. She leaves tomorrow morning. We can do right here in the dark sector. And we'll deal with the body when the time comes."

Thomas looked at his master with disapproval. It was pure nonsense what his master was suggesting. But he knew there would be no changing his mind. "It gives me very little time to locate him," he spoke quietly.

"Then get moving. Use the plane or whatever else you need. Just get him here and be quick about it, Thomas." Andrew left the study leaving Thomas to ponder the fallout when his master played his trump card against his father.

*

Monica was busy getting ready for her trip most of the day, but she and Andrew found time to spend together later that evening. His playfulness, warmth and childlike demeanor attracted her. She enjoyed immensely that he seemed more relaxed. He was attentive, charming, and much more himself.

It was easier to be understanding knowing that his stress had nothing to do with them personally. She knew it was business and she was happy to see by his mood that the problem had worked itself out. They lay in bed in each other's arms and talked about how they both worked so much. That would change soon enough since they decided to cut their hours to have more time to spend with each other.

Andrew watched her as she pursed her lips, and knowing the signs knew she was thinking hard about something, determining how to solve it, working every angle. That's one of the things he loved about her. She was a very determined person much like he himself. That's why they made such a good team.

She looked up to find him watching her with a smile. "What are you looking at?" she asked laughing.

"Your wonderful mind at work, you were miles away. You remember the deal, no thinking about anything but each other tonight." He touched the tip of her nose and she smiled. "Though one of the reasons I love you is your mind."

"Sorry, sweetheart. I just can't get my mind off this assignment. It's going to be a tough, I'm not sure I can do it," she said softly, sliding out of Andrew's arms and getting up and going to the dresser.

He shook his head at her. "Like hell! Listen Monica, you can do it and a bloody damn good job too."

She unbuttoned her blouse, chuckling, "My hero. I didn't know I had such a big fan in you, Drew."

He watched her skirt fall to the floor. Caught in the dim light of the bedroom, he was captured by her beauty. She stood watching him. His eyes had gone to smoke skimming up and down her body as she crossed the room to him. He was still humbled by her power to render him defenseless. "Show me," she whispered, running her fingers through his hair with one hand and unbuttoning his shirt with the other.

*

It was late when Andrew heard a soft, insistent rapping on his door. He sat up in bed rubbing his face and trying to focus on the clock on the bedside table. As the rapping grew more insistent he stumbled from bed and crossed the room to the door. Squinting in the harsh light of the hallway, he saw that Thomas looked rushed. "What time is it?" he asked his voice still husky with sleep.

Thomas pulled him into the hallway and closed the door. "It's after three. I've found Reginald, I'm on my way to the airport right now," he whispered.

Andrew became more alert at the mention of his father's name. "Where is he? How long will it take?" he asked.

"I'll be back around four this afternoon. When is Madam Monica leaving?" he asked.

"Ten," Andrew said looking over his shoulder as if the mere mention of her name might bring her into the hall. "She'll be gone by the time you get back, just hurry," he continued. "I've got big plans for Reggie."

*

Monica was up with the sun preparing and getting ready to leave. Andrew woke to find her brooding going over her papers at the desk across the room. He smiled through a yawn, and she looked up in time to see him. "Someone didn't get enough sleep." she said distracted by the work in front of her.

"Whose fault is that?" he asked laughing.

She stopped, looked across the room at her husband, grinning. "Mine, thank you very much. I'd much rather stay here with you and lock ourselves away in this room."

"I know, love, but look at it this way," he said, propping himself on his elbow, "the sooner you go, the sooner you come home," he continued, getting out of bed. "It's what? Two, three days, tops. You'll be back before you can miss me." He walked over, kissed her forehead, and then caressed her cheek. "I'm going to shower, time to join me?"

"Sorry. I've got to get my shit together before I leave for Kennedy," she said covering his hand for a moment with hers.

"Your loss," he quipped, and headed into the bathroom.

Andrew wondered where Thomas was now. It had been over three hours since he left, and he had yet to hear a word from him. Visions of what would happen upon his return went through his head, touching his very core. Reginald would be powerless to save himself and profoundly confused by such a sudden turn of events. He wanted the phone to ring, wanting it over as soon as possible. Wanting this secret he was keeping from his wife, disposed of and quickly.

Knowing the need for dishonesty was crucial didn't make it any more palatable. He had to keep this from Monica. For her own safety as well as his.

The water cascading over his shoulders soothed, and he couldn't help but relax. A few important things had to be taken care of before Thomas returned if everything was to go as expected. The tension was driven from his body through every pore, and he welcomed it. It comforted mind as well as body. He needed to be ready for anything, he needed to be sharp and logical throughout the coming ordeal.

He leaned against the tile wall and closed his eyes as the water pounded him in a rhythmic massage. Like a rainstorm, he embraced it. His mind bombarded him with thoughts of a time long ago in England when he could truly call himself a child from God.

"Andrew! Where are you boy? Come to me at once!" Reginald yelled as the eyes of the disapproving woman, he sometimes called his wife, looked on. "Come on, it's not as if I'll bite you, you know," he continued.

What he didn't know was that the young boy was in the room all along. Hiding behind a corner china cabinet, pretending not to exist and hoping his father would forget that he did, Andrew waited. He stuck his head out and saw the man standing in the middle of the room as if he was waiting for battle. After several deep breaths, he stepped out from his sanctuary, and with all the courage and strength his seven year old spirit could gather, faced the ever present unknown and stood before his father.

"Why do you hide from me, laddy? You look as if I might swallow you whole," Reginald said, trying to sound every bit the nurturing and loving father that he wasn't. "I want to speak to you, Andrew," he continued.

"Yes sir," the young boy replied. Andrew was no fool. Even at seven, he recognized the seldom used, endearing sounding term of laddy for what it was. A tool his father used for manipulative strong-arming, of his father's methods he was not naive.

"I've just seen your marks for the last semester. Three A's... very impressive, Andrew. However, your science grade puzzles me. I spend a great deal of money for your tutorial assistant, and yet you still manage only a B," he paused more for dramatic flair than for pondering his next words. He walked around behind the boy so he could be heard instead of seen.

"I'll try harder next semester, I promise, Father," he replied in defense.

Reginald placed his hands on the small shoulders of his son who tensed up preparing for the worst. "Where have I heard this rubbish before?" he asked, his voice lost the loving tone, replaced with contempt and irritation. The boy looked at his mother, and the fear in his eyes spoke for them both.

His mother broke in. "Reginald! That's enough, leave him be!" she demanded, and stood to face her husband. Andrew was stunned.

Reginald was angered by the interference, and with one movement he sent a strong hand through the air making brutal contact with his son's cheek. It sent him crashing against the wall, bringing the picture above him down on his head cutting him above the right eye. "Damned if a woman will tell me how to deal with my son!" he muttered and stormed from the room.

His mother swept the young Andrew up in her arms, as blood gushed and tears betrayed him and crumbled the front he tried so hard to hide behind.

Andrew slowly returned to reality, and once again heard the water falling around him. He opened his eyes to see Monica standing with the shower door open, looking at him oddly. "Drew,

Drew!" she repeated more firmly.

He closed his eyes and regained his composure.

"Drew!" she insisted, becoming concerned.

"What? I'm sorry, love. Did you say something?" he asked, reaching over and turning off the water, and taking the towel in Monica's hand. He stepped out and dried his face. He walked back into the bedroom with Monica right behind him.

"Didn't you hear me calling you?" she asked, following him around the bed as he tightened the towel around his waist. "I was standing there for five minutes, Drew."

Knowing he frightened her, he turned to her and put her mind at ease. "Forgive me, please." He took her in his arms to sooth her. "I'm just preoccupied with work, just like someone I know."

Reassured, she kissed him. Then she moved away to put the last of her things in her briefcase. "Where's Thomas?" she asked.

"He had to take the day off, something came up," he said, pulling on his pants. "I've arranged for a car to take us to the airport." He stepped into his Italian loafers as he slipped his arm into his shirt.

"To what do I owe the honor?" she asked jokingly, sitting down on the bed beside him. "You hate airport traffic," she reminded him.

He winked. "Ah, but I love you," he said.

"I don't deserve you." She kissed him, running her hand through his wet hair.

*

Andrew's palms were sweating when the driver climbed in the back seat. "You know what you're to do, right?" he asked cautiously.

The man was confused, but he shook his head. "Yes sir. This is all kind of weird. I mean why don't you want to do this, yourself?" he asked.

"Oh, bloody hell! I'm not catholic, okay!" he said exasperated. He didn't have time for the childish antics of a grown man.

The man's eyes narrowed. "What if the priest wants to know what it's for?"

Andrew looked at him for a moment. "Tell him you're superstitious," he shot back. "Now hurry up," he demanded.

*

Reginald regained consciousness to the hum of the engine of

the airplane. Thomas could see him trying desperately to focus on his surroundings. He gripped the back of his head, and moaning, Thomas knew he felt the large knot at the base of his skull. By the look on his face, it was painful. Thomas couldn't help being pleased by the display. A chuckle escaped, and Reginald discovered he was not alone.

*

It was hard to imagine that in a few short hours he would no longer have to worry each time the phone rang. No more surprise visits for the sole purpose of rattling him. Or wondering when the next installment of intimidation might be leveled against him. Andrew prayed the nightmare of a life he had to endure would end, releasing him from its grip. He only hoped that his dear mother would understand what he was about to do, and forgive him.

To rid the world of the person who, by no other definition, was the evil cross he, as his son, had to bear, until now. It was not a simple decision to make, but it was necessary. It was as if the weight of a thousand burdens was about to be lifted.

It hadn't been out of the safe in over six years, but as Andrew held the gun he realized that it fit his hand perfectly. He knew this seemingly meaningless object alone posed no threat, whatsoever. But, combined with the bullet he had safely tucked away in his desk, it would bring the means to Reginald's end. What he found most interesting was how comfortable this weapon now made him feel, when before this moment he loathed the very presence of it in his home.

He walked around the study, his eyes never leaving the gun. Although he knew it wouldn't be him that fired it, he wanted to feel the weight of it. Acknowledging, grim as it was, that he'd wanted to do this from the moment that picture shattered on his head. From the second the blood blurred his vision. Tonight he would finally exact his revenge.

*

The pain in his head was driving him crazy, but at least he knew where he was though, with no help from his host. He stared at Thomas with disgust. "Just what do you think you will gain from this...episode?" he asked trying to sound as annoyed as he felt.

Thomas only smiled. "That, I'm afraid is...how is it these Americans say it? Ah, yes...for me to know and you to find out," he replied with a smirk.

Reginald rolled his eyes and huffed. "How very childish of you, Thomas." He tried to stand, but his feet failed him and he ended up back on his ass. "This isn't a very good way to demonstrate loyalty," he groaned, managing to drop himself in the chair behind him. He ran his hand over his hair trying to groom it. If nothing else, he still had his dignity.

Thomas shrugged. "My loyalties are with Master Andrew, and no one else," he said.

Reginald's eyes went to slits. "I never should have sent you with him all those years ago. You turned him soft," he grumbled.

"Poor judgment on your part, I suppose."

"Wasn't it?" he agreed, rubbing his head and grimacing from the pain. He leaned back in the chair and squeezed his eyes closed.

Thomas enjoyed seeing Reginald in all his well-deserved torment. "What wrong? Headache?" he inquired with a smile.

"You think Andrew's and your secret plan, whatever that might be, is a threat to me? What bloody fools!" But he paid dearly for the outburst, grabbed the back of his head and hissed in pain.

Thomas, finally sick of listening to Reginald whimper, stood up and left the room. He returned a few moments later and tossed a bottle of aspirin in Reginald's lap. "Take those. I hate to see a grown man cry," he said, leaving the room again.

Reginald threw the bottle and it smashed against the window of the plane. "Go to hell!" he shouted, determined to claim some sort of victory, no matter how small.

Thomas continued down the hall, "As you wish. It will be three hours before we're on the ground, and the altitude will do wonders for that headache."

Alone in the entrance room of the plane, Reginald was becoming acquainted with an emotion he wasn't quite familiar with, fear. He was afraid. Of just what, he couldn't be sure, but it surrounded him like an enemy. Andrew didn't have the guts to do any real harm, so all of this must be for show. Yes, he was certain of that, and he could play the game well.

That was just some grand gesture to give the pretense of his son actually being heavy handed. So, having solved the mystery in his own mind, Reginald decided to play along. He couldn't act small or frightened, because Thomas would never buy it. He had to be more subtle.

If he played his cards right, he knew he could turn all of this to his advantage. And that's just what he planned to do. Turn this all around, and grind his pathetic son to dust.

Thomas was watching Reginald's demonic mind at work and wasn't as gullible as Reginald assumed him to be. He was prepared for this. He had learned a long time ago that you had to expect the unexpected when it came to this man. So, he was ready for whatever Reginald had in mind...whatever that might be.

*

Monica picked up the phone in her hotel room and dialed the mansion. Andrew would be working at home today, and she couldn't wait to hear his voice. The line connected, and she counted the rings.

Andrew stood with a needle jammed in his arm and looked over his shoulder when the phone in his study rang. It was the last thing he needed. What he needed was to feed. To satisfy the hunger driving him to the brink. Damn the noise! He strode into the study, and picking up the receiver, tucked it between his shoulder and chin. He ran his tongue over the edges of his teeth before he spoke. "Thomas?" he barked.

Monica was thrown by his tone. "It's me, Drew."

Andrew froze in a panic. He had to pull himself together. "Oh, hey love. Don't mind me, I'm just in a bit of a mood. I miss you. How's the interview going?" he asked hoping he sounded his old self again.

"I'm meeting with his people in an hour."

"I'm sure you'll be great." he took a deep breath and closed his eyes. "Don't worry," he said softly.

"I just can't wait for it to be over," she said.

"Neither can I, when do you think you'll be back?"

"Depends on his mood."

"Good luck," he said softly, finally feeling the injection do its work. "Love you."

"Me too."

*

Andrew was dozing on the chair in the study when he heard a knock on the door. He opened his eyes to find Thomas standing over him. "God, you're white as a sheet! Did you feed?" he asked.

"No," Andrew replied, weakly. "Gave myself an injection, I'll be fine."

"Reginald's downstairs in the dark sector. Care to join me? He's quite pissed over his day being interrupted. And he's throwing attitude like confetti," Thomas quipped, leading Andrew out the door and into the hallway.

"Great. I can't wait to see his face when he sees this," he said, pulling the gun from his pants. "I'm sure he's not expecting it," he said with a grin.

Thomas laughed, "On that point, you are quite right."

Chapter 15

Reginald sat rigidly up against the wall in the small dungeon-like room, his eyes darting from one direction to another, searching for an escape. He couldn't imagine what was in store for him next, but he was determined not to let whatever it was get the better of him. He looked down at his suit and tried, in vain, to make the wrinkles disappear. After assessing the situation, he made it to his feet, but not without consequences. A sharp pain in the base of his skull sent him crumbling to the floor.

With his fingers he felt the back of his head and the large, egg-size knot reminded him of just how limited his resources were at the moment. His animosity was still strong, and he promised himself he would save his strength until the perfect moment came to deal with his son.

*

Andrew followed Thomas down the stairs and into the belly of the mansion. He was surprised by how relaxed he felt. With every step he was taking he came closer to the enviable ending with the man he had to claim as his own. They walked slowly through the dark hallway, neither of them speaking nor uttering a sound. Each kept their own private thoughts, knowing just what part they would play in the destruction of Reginald Carter.

Thomas could feel every hot breath his master exhaled on the back of his neck. Andrew's senses kicked in, and he could feel his father's presence. Smelling him, he reeked of all the cocky smugness so abhorrent to his son's nature. And yet, this didn't make his skin crawl like it had so many times before. Now it enticed him, pulled him in, leaving him wanting to embrace it.

Andrew saw the cement steps ahead of him now. The steps that would bring him face to face with his father. Any second now, he would begin fulfilling his lifelong dream. Thomas took each step slowly. The hallway was so dark for a man of his age, but it was important to keep Reginald disoriented in the inky blackness. Andrew was preparing himself, and following right behind.

Then it happened. The moment he'd been thinking about for too many years to count. Coming face to face with his father, and seeing true fear in his eyes.

For a moment, he stood watching. A beaten man huddled in the corner of a damp, dank cell. His mind spinning, his thoughts scattered. "Hello, Reggie," he said flatly. "I trust the accommodations are to your liking?" he asked as he gestured with his arms.

"What in the hell are you trying to prove?" he shot back. "We both know you're not man enough to do any real damage," he continued, struggling to his feet.

Andrew walked closer and leveled his gaze; those blue bottomless pools were bright with amusement. With only iron bars between them, he grinned. "I'm man enough for the likes of you," he countered, pushing his hand between the bars and shoving his guest back to the floor. "I have big plans for you father, very big indeed."

Reginald looked up from the mucky, concrete floor and glared, his fine Italian suit ruined. "I'm to beg for mercy now?" he asked, sarcastically. He got up, and smoothed his gray hair back in place.

Andrew laughed at the seemingly small man at his feet. "Whatever you like, but it will serve no purpose," he said simply, rubbing his chin in thought. "Did you think you could threaten my wife without consequences?" They stared at each other, but Andrew had the power, and they both knew it.

"You're a coward, Andrew. Even now, you'll only face me with a barrier between us," Reginald taunted.

Andrew spun around and jumped at a visibly surprised Reginald. "I see only one coward here, you fool! And it is the man that would use his sick need for control on his only son, and then make it into a joke for his own amusement," he shouted with vengeance. He was so close to the man's face that he could feel every startled breath he took. "Make no mistake, Reggie, you are the only coward here", he hissed.

Reginald, much to Thomas' delight, was shook by the episode. Sweat began to bead on his forehead, and his breathing became forced and slow. "You won't break me! I won't allow it!" he bellowed, watching Andrew disappear around the corner. "I'm so much stronger than you, you have no idea." His voice was strong, clear, and filled with conviction he no longer felt. They could keep him locked up in the basement of this mansion forever, but he would never give them the satisfaction of knowing they broke his will.

He calmed himself with reassuring thoughts of his powerful mind and with certainty that he knew Andrew, and the way his mind worked. The prig was all bark and no bite. This was all some charade, some feeble attempt to play mind games. He'd been through this before. Men much more powerful than those he now faced had tried to destroy him and failed.

By comparison, this would be a walk in the park. He was a vampire just as his father was, and vampires were immortal, and all powerful; nothing could stop them. Reginald's confidence had restored, and he relaxed. He decided to mock whatever came next. What could happen? After all, he was a vampire.

*

The slow trickle of water could be heard from far down the narrow tunnel. The musty smell was causing Thomas nausea, but he was reasonably distracted by the goings-on in the underground world of the mansion. "You handled him well, Master Andrew," he said proudly.

Andrew looked doubtful. "Ah, I let him get to me, again," he complained, miserably. "Damn him."

"Still, all things considered, you were much calmer than I've ever seen you, where Reginald's concerned." Thomas moved closer to Andrew and placed a warm hand on his shoulder. "Don't downplay the significance of his shaken demeanor," Thomas reminded. "He's afraid of you and what's in store for him. You've got the upper hand, and it's becoming harder for him to hide it."

Andrew shook his head in agreement. "Yes, he's frightened, but when he draws his last breath I want him pissing his pants and jumping at shadows on the walls," he said. "I want him to beg."

"There's not much time. Twenty two hours, the clock is running."

"That's enough time. It has to be. I won't be denied my right to revenge."

*

"Back so soon?" Reginald asked smugly as his son pulled a chair up and sat down inside the cell across from him.

"Miss me, Reggie? I mean it's not everyday a son gets to spend the final hours of his father's life with him," Andrew spoke cryptically, allowing the weight of his words to sink in.

Reginald looked confused by the statement. "What the hell are you trying to say, Andrew?" he asked in a contemptuous tone.

Andrew smiled. "Who's the bigger fool now? This is your last hurrah, Reginald. Take a look around," he waved his arm around the dingy cell, "because this will be the last place you see." He watched Reginald's face, waiting for a reaction.

"You're out of your mind. We both know you can't do anything to me," he said. "No matter how much you want too.

"That's where you are mistaken, Reggie." He walked across the room and leaned against the wall. He was weak and needed to feed, but he wouldn't give Reginald the satisfaction of knowing it. "There are things I've wanted to say to you for so long, I don't know precisely where to begin."

"Alright, I'll go along with your little fantasy, Andrew. What would you like to say to me?"

Andrew looked at him and grinned. "You're pale, Father. How desperately you must want to feed." Remembering the jab tossed in his face not long ago, he tossed it back. "You ache for it, don't you?" he baited.

"As do you, Andrew, I can see it all over your face. It's been too long for you, hasn't it?" he asked.

"I'm not like you, Reginald," Andrew replied defensively.

"You are *just* like me."

"Don't push me."

"Why? What is it that you think you can do to me, Andrew? You don't frighten me," he teased.

"I'll destroy you, but not before you suffer," Andrew replied, walking slowly over to Reginald and crouching down before him.

Reginald grew quiet, sensing true evil in his son for the first time. The look in his eyes mirrored that of his own. "You don't have the stomach for torture," he said, holding on to his arrogant attitude.

"I had a good teacher." He stood and turned and walked to the cell door.

Fear seeped in, and Reginald saw a chance to save himself. Jumping from his chair, he attacked Andrew from behind, and knew it was a mistake when he found himself flying through the air and slamming into the wall. Andrew was on top of him before he could recover.

Surprised by the strength in his son's hands and more

surprised by the lack of strength in his own, Reginald was pummeled like a rag doll. He pushed and scratched at Andrew's face trying to throw him off balance, and for his efforts, his son snapped both his arms like twigs. Reginald cried out in pain as the bones of his arms ripped through his skin.

For an instant, Reginald thought he might pass out, but Andrew had other things on his mind. He picked him up off the ground and slammed him into the wall repeatedly, and Reginald quickly took on the appearance of a bloody heap. Andrew loosened his grip, but only long enough to drive his fist into the man's face before letting the sack of flesh fall to the ground at his feet.

Reginald was a pool of blood and bones on the floor when Andrew stepped back to look at him. "The pain must be blinding, hey Reggie?" he spat out looking down on the mess on the cement floor. "And it's the least you deserve."

*

Thomas watched over his master with a careful eye. It was quite obvious he was weak, but the distraction of having Reginald to deal with kept him focused. "Are you feeling okay?" Thomas asked in a whisper. "You look a bit pale," he continued after no immediate reply came.

Andrew was sweating now and knew there was no reason to hide anything. "Give me a shot to tide me over until he's dealt with. I don't want to look weak in front of him," he said, wiping his face as sweat ran down his chin.

Thomas cast a worried glance at Andrew before he gave in to his request. "Alright, but the two of you are a matching set," he said, standing. "Was that scene necessary?"

Andrew shrugged. "He attacked me and would have done the same to me given the chance," he shot back defensively.

Thomas patted him on the back. "I just don't want you to go too far. You don't have to become him to destroy him." Thomas walked quickly into the corridor and disappeared before Andrew could reply.

"Where's your sidekick?" demanded Reginald when his son appeared out of nowhere. He still lay in a puddle on the floor off to the left of the cell. "I asked a question, dammit!" he exclaimed hotly.

Andrew looked down at his father and stared in disgust. "I heard you, but it is of no concern to you, Father Dear. You see, how you perceive things and how you feel makes no difference. What does make a difference, however, is if you have enough conscience to feel remorse for all the pain you've caused in my life," he said as he gripped the gun under his shirt.

"Listen here, you worthless piece of shit, if you think, even for a moment, that I'm going to beg for mercy, then you're sorely mistaken," Reginald yelled in anger. "I won't give you the satisfaction. Do you hear? I will not!"

"As you wish, but, confession is good for the soul," Andrew said, joking. He threw a jug across the floor and it bounced off Reginald's foot. "There's water in there," he said, pointing to the jug at his father's feet. "Drink some of it."

"Go to hell!"

"You first."

Reginald leveled his gaze on his son and smirked. Blood was crusted on his face, and he was wheezing through broken ribs, yet he smirked, smug, even in the face of impending death. His arms were useless, hanging limply by his sides. "What would your precious mother think about what you're doing to your father?"

"I'm sure she applauding right now. She despised you in the end, Reginald. She felt nothing but contempt and hatred for you. So don't think I'll lose a moment's sleep over how she would feel about you getting exactly what you deserve," he said simply.

"Your soul will be cursed forever if you do this, Andrew. A vampire cannot kill his maker without serious repercussions." If he was begging, he was too caught up in it to notice.

Andrew enjoyed watching the arrogance drain to be replaced with fear, and the ranting of a begging child. It was much more satisfying than he had thought it would be, and he wouldn't trade this feeling for anything in the world. "Ah, Reggie, and you said I couldn't get you to beg," he said, laughing in the man's face.

"I ought to wipe that smug smile off your face!" he muttered, realizing that his attempt to win his son over with common sense failed. He worked his way into a sitting position. "I'm surprised you don't have me chained as if I were a dog!"

"Now that's an idea," Andrew smirked and walked away.

Thomas returned having heard enough of the conversation to draw his own conclusions as to how it might end. He looked at Andrew and winked. "That a boy!" he whispered. He rolled up his master's sleeve and prepared the syringe he removed from his coat pocket.

Reginald watched with interest. "What are you giving him?" he asked. "Some sort of magic potion for his inner demons? How laughable!" he mocked.

*

Eight o'clock came. It had been three hours since Andrew first laid eyes on his father in the dark, dank basement of his mansion, his safe haven from the man he now looked upon. He was feeling more like his old self and growing tired of the constant moaning and groaning from Reginald. It was no longer tolerable for Andrew or Thomas. Reginald now sat in the corner of the cell bound and gagged to ensure the silence that Andrew craved.

But the stare of his father spoke volumes about how the man felt about the treatment he was receiving. He felt certain that if Reginald could loosen the ropes that tied him or spit out the gag that silenced him, he would most likely strike out against him, killing without a second thought. All the more reason to keep him exactly as he was now.

Thomas busied himself with the final preparations for the evening's festivities. Nothing must be forgotten, everything had to be perfect. His master had the most important piece of destruction with him. Having it gave him the sense of control he always deferred to his father in the past. Now, though, it was his turn to play leader in Reginald's sick, twisted little games.

Thomas couldn't begrudge Andrew the pleasure of being the last person his demented father saw before he would be forever damned to hell. It seemed only fair, and he would do whatever he could to make sure that Andrew obtained the satisfaction he so desperately needed to go on with his life. He would look over his shoulder, occasionally, to find his master staring down Reginald with an almost evil grin. Having secret knowledge about what was about to happen to the person he loathed, to the very core of his being, thrilled him.

Andrew felt Thomas touch him on the shoulder, and his eyes softened as he turned his head and faced him. "Is everything ready?" he asked anxiously.

"Yes, Andrew."

Andrew turned his attention back to Reginald and found his rather annoyed expression amusing. He stood up and walked over to him, bent down, grabbed him by the collar, and pulled him up to his feet. Their eyes met with only hatred between them. Andrew dragged Reginald across the cold floor into a room off to the side of the basement. Reginald struggled, but it was to no avail, he was too weak to put up a fight.

Thomas followed right behind, he was quiet, and this seemed to bother Reginald even more. His eyes frantically trying to take in as much of his surroundings as he could, knowing he would never see another place again. Then he was dropped on the floor as if he were a bag of garbage. A cold, rough hand reached down to his face and yanked the cloth from his mouth. His head jerked to one side, and Reginald let out a yelp of pain.

Andrew walked to the doorway and closed the door with a heavy thud. Thomas stood above Reginald with his hands clasped, looking down on him with an air of superiority. Reginald's gaze darted back and forth between the two of them. He couldn't even pretend to know what was about to happen, so he dropped the act and sat quietly on the cold, damp floor beneath them.

He watched as Andrew knelt down in front of him in silence. He was drunk, but, nonetheless, threatening. "Well, Reggie, what do you think?" he asked, looking around the dark room. "Be honest. After all," he straightened up and backed away, "this is the place where you're going to die," he revealed, as his eyes gleamed.

Reginald wasn't laughing anymore, or being smug, or arrogant, or wicked. Instead, he was strangely silent. The cocky demeanor evaporated in the small room he now found himself in. He had no snappy comebacks. "I need to feed," he whispered. "Please, I need...." The solid backhand from Andrew silenced his plea.

"You mistake me with someone who cares! You look like you are in pain, yes, I see that you are. How does it feel to be tortured by your own needs?" Andrew asked as he began to pace in front of Reginald. "I know that feeling well, Father. You instilled it in me long ago. But whatever madness you feel at this moment, it still isn't enough for me. Your need is something you enjoy, something you take immense pleasure in. I am tortured by a need that makes my very skin crawl!" He dropped to the floor, and grabbing a fist full of hair, pulled Reginald's head close to him. "Welcome to my misery." he whispered into his ear. "Not very pretty is it?"

Thomas watched all of this with great pleasure, and he would not hide his joy. One thing did worry him, Andrew was turning into the very monster he despised. In all his anger, he hadn't noticed his eyes changing, his teeth sharpening to fangs like knife points gleaming in the sun, but it hadn't escaped Thomas' attention. He would have to keep a very close eye on his master, because the results could be disastrous otherwise.

Reginald wasn't fairing well either. His skin was white, and his veins easily seen. Still, with whatever strength remained, he begged to feed, begged for blood. He never thought he would beg from Andrew, but he heard himself sounding like a whimpering child. The pain was too much, and he knew he had to face the fact that his son, regardless of how much he hated him, had the upper hand. He held all the cards. He was so weak that he could no longer hold his head upright, but that didn't madden him as much as the gnawing pain in his gut and the pulsating in his throat. He was starving, and he knew it. He would never last if his wretched son had anything to do with it.

Andrew had to fight now to stay focused on his goals, like Reginald, his instincts told him to feed. Only Thomas could keep him focused by feeding him bottles and bottles of wine. Wine that was more blood now than wine, but it kept him calm and lucid, and that was all that mattered.

"Look at him, Thomas," Andrew mocked, contempt in his eyes, and in his heart. "Wallowing in pain like the coward he is, he's hardly worth the time or effort. He's nothing but flesh and bones! Crouching down, he took the bloody face in his hands and waited for the blurry eyes to focus on him. "Not so glib feeling the pain as when you're dolling it out, are you Father?" Laughing heartily, he watched his father suffer. "You're a pitiful piece of shit, not the almighty, but it won't be enough until I say I it is."

Tired, Andrew straightened, and stretched. Gazing down at Reginald, he wondered if the evil inside him would die with the monster that passed it on. He could hope. For the moment, he needed to get away. Some wine, peace, and quiet would strengthen him. Soon he would need all the strength he could get.

*

"If Monica saw me this way, she'd be horrified," Andrew said, nursing his wine and staring at the person withering away in the corner of the room. "She'd run away screaming, and never look back."

Thomas looked at his master, smiling in understanding. "That is why she'll never know of this ordeal. She would never understand why this had to be done. Why it's tolerable for you and I to sit here, watching him, making him suffer indescribable pain, and Madam Monica is too pure of heart to understand. But, you and I do. Don't wallow in guilt, Andrew. It serves no purpose," he explained.

"A necessary evil, Thomas, he deserves this and so much more," he replied quietly.

"I know."

"Give him what he wants," Andrew said, taking another drink from his wineglass.

"Are you sure?" Thomas asked.

"Yes."

Thomas walked over to the small table in the corner of the room and poured another wineglass full, this time with pure blood. He wiped the drips from the edge of the glass and walked over to Reginald. He knew that he was too weak to hold the glass himself. So, after exchanging an uncertain glance with Andrew, he leaned down, cradled the man's head in one hand, and put the glass to his lips with the other. "Drink," he said sharply.

Reginald sipped, but as the liquid slowly revived him, he began to gulp the blood like an animal. He gorged and let blood run from his mouth like a beast after a greedy kill. "Greedy bastard!" Thomas muttered, jumping back from him as blood dripped on his shoes and vest.

Reginald looked better almost immediately, but he was still much too weak to pose any real threat. The veins receded, and his breathing slowed. "Please, more, please!" he gasped.

Andrew chuckled. "Sorry Reggie. My charitable nature only goes so far, I couldn't let you grow weaker, pass out and miss all the upcoming fun. I want you to be fully aware and mindful when the real pain sets in," he said cruelly.

Reginald shook his head. "No, I must have more!" he demanded weakly. He did need more, much more. The act was like giving a starving man only a morsel of food. It was far crueler to give Reginald one small taste of blood, but not enough to satisfy his need. Reginald knew this and so did his son, which is why he allowed it.

Knowing this stoked what little fire remained, and he became belligerent. "Damn you to hell, Andrew! Who is the beast among us now?" he demanded.

"Me?" Andrew asked in mock ignorance. "I'm just giving you a taste of your own medicine, Reggie. A bitter taste isn't it?" he teased.

"All... of...this...because you don't want your wife to know your dirty little...secret. How..." he gulped his breath, "pathetic!" he stammered.

"All of this because I won't be tortured by you any longer, Reginald. I gave you every opportunity to remove yourself from my life on your own, but you refused, continuing instead with your little games. I don't wish to play them anymore. That is what this is about," he explained.

Reginald focused on his son. It was hard, but somehow he managed to find him across the room. "So you're tired of our riles?" he asked sarcastically.

"That, and other things."

"Even when you were a boy, I knew you were a mouse among men. Your mother, bless her soul, bowed to your every whim. I should have beaten more sense into you, maybe then you wouldn't have turned out to be such an utter disappointment," Reginald said weakly.

"It takes such a MAN to abuse a child, whose only mistake was expecting a father's unconditional love. You were the mouse among men, not I, Reggie," Andrew said, disgusted.

"Rubbish, boy. Pure rubbish," he groaned.

"I think I'm through playing with you, Reginald. And your pain, though pleasurable to watch, is enough to satisfy me," he said, pulling the gun from under his shirt and showing it to Reginald. "This is the instrument to your destruction."

Reginald's eyes widened. "A gun? A gun can't hurt me, you fool, and neither can any bullet," he grunted. "So I was right all along. You're no real threat to me," he gloated happily.

Andrew smiled at Thomas, and they grinned at the renewed cockiness of their guest. "Ah, Reggie, this gun will hold this bullet," he said as he demonstrated how they worked, "pure silver and newly blessed by a priest," he continued with a smile and wink.

The smug expression slowly left his face as Reginald became aware they were serious, and this was no longer a joke. "How? YOU could not have gotten a priest to bless a silver bullet!" he stammered.

"How it came about isn't nearly as important as the fact that I did, indeed, get this very bullet blessed, and in doing so signed the declaration of your destruction." He handed the gun to Thomas and smiled, "See you in hell."

Then Thomas aimed at Reginald's chest, pulled the trigger, and Andrew relished the sound.

Chapter 16

The two of them stood over the lifeless body of Reginald Carter. He cursed the life of anyone who knew him. Between them, there was silence. Each had their own private thoughts to deal with, and neither could believe that their actions, had finally come to finality. Andrew felt like he was in shock as he realized that the one person he truly despised on earth could no longer hurt him or threaten his happiness. The silver bullet had done what he himself could not.

For that, Andrew was grateful beyond measure. He took a few deep breaths and relaxed, drinking in his newfound freedom. Thomas wrapped his arm around his master's shoulders and squeezed him. They looked at each other and smiled. Only they could understand the significance of this moment. Only they would know what happened in the dark sector of the mansion only the two of them, alone, could recognize its importance.

They gathered the lifeless body in silence. The only sound was the dripping water down the tunnel behind them. Thirty minutes later, and after several stops to rest, they were a mile into the tunnel. They dropped the body, with a thud, to the wet ground. Andrew was sweating heavily. He wiped his forehead with the back of his hand. His black hair matted to his head. He felt drained and exhausted and ready to take the final step in dealing with his father.

Thomas busied himself thirty yards away before a gapping hole. He moved cautiously, counting out the paces in his head, stopping only to turn up the wicks in the lanterns hanging on the wall. Slowly, methodically, he went about making the final preparations. And, with the low grind of machinery, he ensured Reginald Carter would never be a threat again.

The grave was massive in its depth, narrow in its width, and the only way to dispose of Reginald with certainty. Twenty-eight feet, deep into the hollows of the ground, a burial fit for a monster. With the soft yellow glow illuminating the huge hole, he dropped a stone and listened. Finally, he heard the soft thud, and he smiled. The gateway to hell, where Reginald would burn for eternity, was waiting to reclaim him.

Satisfied, he returned to check on his master, and found Andrew leaning against the wall. Face drawn, slick with sweat though the air was very chilled, he needed rest. "Is it ready?" he asked.

Thomas lit another lantern for a better look at his master's eyes. "Yes," he replied, hanging the light on the nail behind him. "And it's perfect." It disturbed him to see how weak his master looked. "Are you alright?" he asked.

Andrew recognized the tone. "Just tired," he said with a note of irritation.

"It looks like more than that," Thomas replied doubtfully.

Andrew took a deep breath and dropped his head. "Let's just finish this, Thomas," he said with closed eyes.

Thomas watched him for a moment, and finally relented. "Alright, Master Andrew, give me a hand with the body."

"Gladly," he said happily. "What could be more right?" Andrew asked, as they made their way to the hole with Reginald between them. "I hope he's burning in hell as we speak."

"This is a new beginning for you, Master Andrew," Thomas huffed, as he started to feel the weight of Reginald's body taking its toll on him. "It's a chance to reclaim your life, start over, and put your mistakes behind you."

At the hole, Andrew pondered, wished it were so. "It's not so simple. I have blood on my hands." Shaking his head, he walked to the edge and looked down in. "I've become what he always said I would." Turning back to Thomas, sadness filled his eyes. "It's eats at me," he admitted softly, and wondered if it would forever. He just wanted it over with. So he went to Reginald, and dragging his lifeless body, brought him to the edge. "May you forever burn in hell!" he whispered victoriously.

"Let's do this," Thomas said, and came to Andrew's side.

"Absolutely."

Together they put the body into a burlap sack, and Andrew watched Thomas complete the grim task of severing Reginald's head. A long rope of garlic was looped around the torso with a cross for good measure. In silence, they tied the sack and pitched Reginald into the hole. When they heard the dull thud of the sack hitting the bottom, smiles and peace marked the end. Their problems with Reginald were over. Unbeknownst to the two of them, more remained.

Thomas turned to Andrew, and winked. "He'll be encased in ten feet of cement; the rest of the hole will be filled with eighteen feet of dirt and clay." He went to the machine and pushed the trowel over the opening of the hole. "Here we go," he continued, and they watched as the cement poured.

*

It was four o'clock in the morning before Andrew was back in the mansion on his way to bed. He was exhausted, but the hum of exhilaration assured that he would not sleep. His father was gone, driven from the earth, and he witnessed it. Would the grip of his curse now loosen its hold on him? Collapsing on the bed, he could only pray that it would. Wide awake, he lay in his bed, lonely for his wife but thankful she wasn't there to hold him.

How could she ever understand what he had done? He killed his father, while she, adoring her own, would do anything to have him back. Her father had been the true meaning of the word. He loved his child more than life itself, and he was gone. If he could have traded his father for hers, he would have, but why wish for the impossible.

It wasn't guilt that he was feeling. Guilt was an emotion that didn't exist where his father was concerned. But keeping this secret from Monica would be difficult for him. If there was guilt it was because he hated to lie to her. So he consoled himself by believing a lie of omission, for the greater good, was acceptable. Even, dare he think it, right.

Andrew rolled on his side, and though his body was limp with fatigue, sleep would not come. Frustrated, he sat up, covering his face with his hands. When he put his feet on the floor, the sensation hit him, rippling and already too powerful for him to control. The now familiar feeling of nausea swept over him, a blanket of fear was pressing in around him while his head filled with pressure enough to explode his eyes from their sockets. Gripping both sides of his head, he held his breath hoping the siege would release him and disappear before swallowing him whole.

But Andrew was pulled under, and could neither stop nor control it. The aching in his throat returned, and he was at his demon's mercy. Lost to it, he fell to his knees, and clamped closed his eyes to the pain. "Have to feed...need to...feed," he cried between ragged breaths. And then, a surge of energy brought him to his feet, and with reason gone, he went back into the night.

*

He moved with the fluid grace of a predator, letting his instincts lead him, knowing time was of the essence. The sun would rise soon so he had to move quickly, or it would be too late. He headed for the park, already tasting the warm blood flowing over his tongue. He knew someone would be there. Be them beggar, hoodlum, or blue-collar worker finishing a late shift, he would find them. Allowing him to satisfy his hunger, allowing the most hated part of himself to do what came so naturally. His tongue throbbed and his teeth ached, his throat burned. He needed to do this, he had no choice. At that moment, the sane side of his conscience was in battle with the animalistic side, and loosing. A war of great consequence was waging wildly in his brain. Still, his hunt continued.

Andrew entered the park and only a few feet inside, he heard quiet voices ahead further down the path. He walked quickly, letting the lull of voices entrance him. Adrenaline pumping, nearing a fevered pitch, he saw them just ahead. They noticed him approaching, and pretended they didn't, given the lateness of the hour. Reaching them, Andrew wasted no time, and soon the quiet night burst with snuffed out screams of fright and horror.

Clasping his hands over both the man and woman's mouths simultaneously, he silenced them. His brute strength was used for knocking their heads together to disorient. Then he drove his teeth deep into the man's jugular, draining him as the woman's horrified eyes went blank, and she slipped to the ground unconscious. Andrew would remember the woman's fearful gaze, and be haunted. What was good in him would be tormented with the memory for the rest of his days. But instinct was stronger than will when he sank his fangs in her neck and felt her blood coursing through him, reviving him. The war in his head and heart was over now...evil had won.

*

Unfortunately for Andrew, he remembered the horrific details of what happened only hours before. As he sat at the breakfast table under Thomas' watchful eye, he knew there was no need to confess what he had done. He could see the pain in the old man's eyes, and it mirrored his own. Thomas didn't need the details that now stabbed at his conscience, the repugnance was written all over his face. Thomas knew rehashing it wouldn't change anything, and there would be no easing his master's guilt.

So, Andrew sat long after breakfast was over, and well into the noon hour, torturing himself with his memories. It was, he knew, the least he deserved. Misery loves company, after all. So lost in misery, he replayed every vicious detail as penance for his sins.

That was how Thomas found him, hours later, eyes dull, brow pinched, hands folded together and pressed to his lips as if sobs were threatening. Without a word, he sat down across from Andrew to console him with his silence. Andrew's eyes filled, and he shook his head in grief and pain.

He never felt pain so great before, or one that was so consuming. So much for the hope that with his father gone, the destruction and the reckless killing he was responsible for would end. Andrew finally understood that the vampire in him would never allow for him to be tamed.

"I am so dreadfully sorry, Andrew," Thomas said with heartfelt emotion. "This is my fault," he continued. "I should've never left you alone."

Andrew's eyes never left the table, or the pattern he was trying so hard to memorize. "Please, Thomas," he muttered wearily. "Was it you out there?" he mumbled. A tear fell, and a groan escaped him. "Was it you who attacked two innocent people like an animal?" he raged out loud.

"It is a curse, Andrew. It doesn't leave you with a choice of right or wrong. It's a hallow need, and a powerful one. Over which, I might remind you, you have no control and were never meant to."

"Go tell that to my victims, Thomas."

"I'm almost there, Andrew," Thomas said hopefully. "I know the new formula is within my reach. Trust me, please."

Andrew looked at him in doubt. "The magic potion," he cracked, and a sad smile appeared. "Maybe we should have loaded the gun with two bullets. One for Reggie, and the other for me."

"Be patient."

"And how many more innocent people will die while I sit around this damned mansion being patient?" he exclaimed.

*

Lost somewhere in the fog of his mind, he was taking refuge in his office when his phone buzzed, Andrew sat, not moving. He didn't want the intrusion of real life, or of business. He stared at it but made no move to answer it. And yet, still it buzzed and buzzed until annoyance won out over indifference. He reached it and picked up before he could change his mind, "Yes?"

"Hey, babe!" Monica said, cheerfully.

At the sound of her voice, his mind and mood shifted gears, and his tone softened, "Hello, love." Wincing at the wrench in his heart, he slid his chair back to prop his feet on his desk. "When do you land?" he asked.

"How's thirty minutes sound?" she asked.

"Wonderful," he said, finally feeling some hope and incentive to pull himself together. Her love would soothe and tether him to the inherent goodness in him. His love would keep her safe. "How'd the interview go?"

Monica sighed, remembering the intensity in the ex-senator's eyes as she delicately asked him about his relationship with a known call-girl. "Well, his baby brother's top dog at the IRS, so, I get the feeling there's a tax audit in my future."

Her lightness and humor had him chuckling, something he was sure he'd never do again. "It's hell getting caught with your pants down."

"You sound tired," she murmured, slipping out of her heels, and leaning against the plush cushions at her back, closed her eyes. "You're not sleeping again, what's wrong?"

Andrew swallowed the lump in his throat before he could answer. "Nothing for you to worry about," he lied.

"It comes with being a wife."

"I'm handling it," he said and meant it, hearing her voice might have made everything bearable. "With red tape and primitive conditions, complications aren't uncommon."

"So you've been too busy to miss me?" Monica laughed, and he loved hearing her laugh. "You can make it up to me."

"Any suggestions," he teased, and then turned serious. "Hurry home, sweetheart. I love you."

Chapter 17

He stared at the phone for a long time. She would be home very soon, and he needed to pull himself together. He knew how he was feeling. Drawn, weary, and tormented. He was a man who felt so deeply, and it would show on his face. And because she knew him, and loved him, so well, she would see it. He had to forget the monstrous things he had done, and be the husband she deserved, and the man she loved.

He scratched at his cheek, and rubbed his fingers over the bristle of two-day stubble. Needing a shower and a shave, he pushed himself to his feet and strode out the door. When he arrived home, he told Thomas to ready a pot of tea while he went to his room to change.

Alone again, Andrew went through the motions of normalcy. He mechanically removed his clothes, ducked under the icy-cold spray to clear the scattered thoughts from his brain, and then dried off, again forgoing razor and shaving cream. In a silk, royal blue shirt and black slacks, he looked, and nearly felt, like himself. Skimming his fingers over the smooth coral buttons, he wondered if he could pull it off.

When he saw his hands trembling he clasped them together and lowered himself to the edge of the bed. He watched his knuckles whiten from his vice-like grip. Fingers more likely to tap a computer keyboard or shuffle papers, to have a cigar resting between them, or fine crystal against them, were being used in violence, to bring death.

Two more people robbed of their lives and not for some noble cause, nothing noble at all. Two people who, no doubt, had families that at this very moment grieved for their loss. Would he ever be able to look at his hands and not see blood on them?

*

Andrew focused his emotions, he could not change what was done, and torturing himself would accomplish nothing. He left the bedroom and walked down the hallway trying to will himself to forget along the way. Andrew went down the stairs slowly, reaching the bottom as the door closed down the hall. When he heard Monica's voice, the smile came easily. It encompassed him as he walked towards her voice.

Andrew appeared, grinning. "Ah, there's life in the house again."

At the sound of his voice, she turned. His vivid green eyes, laughing, his hair damp, tousled; her favorite shirt open at the collar, he was a sight for sore eyes. She leapt into his arms. "I really hate going away without you, Drew. I miss you too much."

Tightly wrapping his arms around her, he buried his face in her hair. This was what he needed. To remind him of what he was fighting for. "You've spoiled me too, darling." Andrew said pulling away to kiss her. "I toss and turn without you next to me," he murmured, keeping her close as they strolled to the couch.

"Yes, but it wasn't worth all the trouble. You couldn't accuse the man of running off at the mouth," she said.

Thomas came into the room, smiling. "It's nice to have you home, Madam," he said, putting a tray on the coffee table.

Monica smiled at Thomas. "It's good to be home," she said, leaning up and kissing him on the cheek.

Thomas flinched, and then smiled. "Ah, yes...here's the tea and scones," he continued.

Andrew chuckled. "Relax, old man, she's already taken."

Monica slapped Andrew's arm. "Don't tease him, Drew. I didn't mean to startle you, Thomas."

"That's quite alright, Madam. Don't be offended, you just took me by surprise. I'll be in the kitchen if you need anything," he said, and then he left the room.

"I didn't mean to scare him, Drew. I just think the world of him and I did miss his fussing over me," she said, laying her head on his chest.

Andrew wrapped his arms around her. "He's never had anyone but me to show him affection before, give him some time to get used to it. Don't worry, sweetheart, he's fine. He's a strict, proper man raised quite differently from your warm, affectionate upbringing."

"That's a shame."

"Yes, but that's how it is. He's very fond of you. It won't be long, he'll think of you as a daughter, and hover over you as he does me." He sat up and poured them some tea.

"So, what kept the two of you so busy while I was gone?" she asked, as he handed her a cup.

Andrew paused, took a sip of his tea, and smiled. "Just annoying business matters I should have dealt with but kept putting off," he said, sitting back on the couch.

Monica laughed and lifted her legs into Andrew's lap. "Sounds like we both had loads of fun."

Settling back, tea in one hand and his wife's calve resting in the other, his only response was a sigh.

*

Monica was soaking in the bathtub while Andrew stayed downstairs on the couch in the living room, finishing off his second pot of tea, flipping through the channels on television. His first mistake was lingering on CNN. He knew it the moment he saw the reporter's face. Recognizing the scenery at the man's back, confirmed the sickening feeling in his gut.

Listening to the subdued, monotone voice speak of the bodies found in Central Park just after dawn was enough to have the tea abandoned for four fingers of scotch. The police had no leads and refused to comment on the similarity between this case and the attack and murder in the park months before. The longer he listened, the more he drank. Lost in his guilt and his need for a self dealt punishment, Andrew drank the first highball and wasted no time pouring a second.

His body, his vampire being, was growing accustom to the fresh human blood he had indulged in. His instincts were deriving pleasure from the hunt and the kill, and the reward of blood. Andrew could feel it with every breath he took. He was losing the battle of remaining more human than vampire. His judgment was impaired, and his morals were descending into an abyss from which he might never be able to retrieve them. He was powerless to stop it.

He would carry the weight of the deaths of four people, forever. Disgusted with himself and the public's morbid sense of curiosity, he shut off the TV and hurled the remote across the room to crash into the mantle of the fireplace. Damned if he would allow it to happen again, he decided, his mouth set into a grim line, and a steely glint in his eyes to pin Thomas with when he hurried into the room.

If it had to be a battle to regain control of the hunger that grabbed hold and twisted him in its grip, then so be it, he mused.

He refused to be at the mercy of this goddamn curse, until he could no longer distinguish between the sane and the insane, and would blindly follow his natural instincts. His conscience, he reasoned, would be his savior. Reminders of the evil deeds already done should be weapon enough.

His stomach pain, more frequent now, could and would be dealt with. More treatments, more wine, more willpower. Andrew stood up and tossed back the last of his scotch, saying nothing as Thomas brought the remote back to the coffee table, looking at him with apprehension.

He was the richest man in the world, but he could not buy his freedom from a curse that was not his own. So, if he could not buy his freedom, then he would fight for it. Andrew walked over to the window across the room. The sun was setting. He opened the shutters and looked out at the city that, for years, had been his sanctuary, at times, and his prison at others.

This was his fate, to live in this city forever, and never have death claim him. To live eternally, and watch the woman he loves grow old and die. And still, he would live, gaining his years in age falsely. While all those he loved disappeared. Andrew never felt more alone.

He leaned his head against the glass and remembered something his mother had told him right after his father had given him the family 'gift.' She'd taken him aside in his bedroom and looked into his eyes.

"What your father has done is wrong, but you are only as evil as your intentions. Remember this, and he will have lost in his attempt to make you like himself."

Her words offered little comfort now in the harsh light of reality. Looking out towards the harbor, he saw the tip of Lady Liberty and closed his eyes. Thousands of lights in the city and he was still trapped in a darkness no one else could ever know. Andrew knew he would kill again. For all his mental boasting and steeled determination, in that instant he knew it was a certainty even he could not outrun.

While the New York police searched the city for what the papers called a 'perverted madman', they would never know that the man they were searching so relentlessly for was the city's most respected citizen, businessman Andrew Carter. The story that could make his wife's career, unbeknownst to her, would start right in her own home. Andrew's mind was racing, and thoughts of his beloved mother offered him no peace. He clutched the curtains on both sides of the window and clenched his teeth.

He thought he might explode from frustration and depression, but when he was just about to break he felt a comforting warmth take hold, and a state of grace and calm surrounded him. He could feel her. His mother was right beside him, and tears came to his eyes even as peace filled his heart. His mother was there to comfort him in death as she had in life, just as she promised.

*

Thomas found Andrew sitting in the corner of the room in a chair that was almost never used. The chair was his mother's and sitting in it made him feel close to her. He walked over to him and watched him for a moment. Heavy, dark thoughts were occupying his master's mind. And it was time to put a stop to it.

"Master Andrew, Madam Monica would like you to join her upstairs," he said softly, watching his master carefully. "Go and join her, and I'll ring when dinner is ready," he continued.

Andrew inhaled a breath and released it slowly before he acknowledged Thomas' presence. He looked up with a puzzled look and ran his hands through his hair, a nervous habit, which revealed a troubled man. "I'm not feeling well, Thomas. Can you give me a treatment before I go up?" he asked, sounding more like a boy then a man.

Thomas looked into his eyes and frowned. "Wait here a moment." He disappeared only to return a minute later with a syringe in his left hand and a glass half-full of a thick red liquid, in his right. "Roll up your sleeve, Master Andrew, and drink this slowly," he instructed.

Andrew did as he was told and closed his eyes to relax. The liquid warmed him, staving out the cold. He was so warm that he did not feel the prick of the needle in his right arm. "Thank you, Thomas," he whispered.

"You'll feel better shortly," Thomas said, rolling down his master's sleeve and buttoning it at the wrist. "Your color's better already." Ever watchful, he pulled down his master's lower lids, and grunted his approval. "Now you better get up there to her before she comes looking for you."

"Okay," Andrew said, pushing himself up from the chair. He walked slowly out of the room with Thomas following him, watching him walk down the hall, around the corner, and up the stairs.

*

Andrew walked into the bedroom and unbuttoned his shirt. The stomach pain was manageable; he would feel better soon. "I hear my presence is requested," he called into the bathroom.

"Absolutely," she answered when she saw him appear shirtless in the doorway. "Are you joining me?" she asked

"Of course. Thomas'll ring when dinner's ready. Besides," he continued, his pants falling to the floor, "I've been waiting for this all day."

*

An hour later, after having made love, they lay content in bed. Wrapped in each other's arms, they relaxed. They were enjoying being with each other where they could discover each other all over again. The ringing of the phone awakened them from their sleep and made Andrew fumble around in the dark to answer it.

"Yes, Thomas?" All right, what time is it? We'll be down in fifteen minutes," he said in a raspy voice. He hung up the phone, leaned over, and kissed his wife's shoulder. "Dinner's ready," he whispered in her ear. "Up, up."

She smiled but moaned. "What time is it?"

Andrew sat up and put his feet on the floor. "Nine."

Monica rolled over and squinted as Andrew turned on the bedside lamp. "Nine? I take it we're having a late dinner?" she asked as she pulled herself up in bed.

"Thomas knew we wanted some time alone, he's a smart man. So he decided a late dinner would be more appropriate," he said, lying back on the bed with his head in her lap.

Monica kissed him softly. "I knew I was crazy about him. He's so intuitive."

"Come on, let's not keep him waiting. He's made something special for you," he said. They got dressed, and walked arm and arm downstairs and into the dining room.

*

Dinner consisted of lobster with salad and a fruit cobbler desert. The conversation was light, and happy. Thomas was relieved to see his master feeling better, and his madam so happy to be home. This was a family. Although not without its problems, it was something to be proud of all the same. Every family had its own secrets from the outside world, and sometimes even from the world within the family.

*

Just before midnight, the halls of the mansion were quiet and the walls blind to what was about to happen inside them. Andrew was safely tucked away in his bed, no doubt celebrating his first night of restful sleep in ages, with Monica right beside him. Thomas however, walked the floor of the sector below the mansion with anxiety, thoughts driving him forward when it was sleep that he needed most.

The answer was somewhere in the bottles he was staring holes through, and he had to find it. More important than anything was offering his master some peace of mind by making sure that he would not kill again. *Guilt* was more difficult to deal with than the act itself. And it was *guilt* that was smothering his master. It had to stop.

Thomas desperately wanted to sleep, but the need to set his master free from the damned existence he endured was of the utmost importance. He poured from one bottle to the next searching and searching for the perfect amount of each ingredient, but it was difficult for someone of his age. His aged hands proved rusty for such a task, and frustration angered him more often than not. Minutes turned into hours, and he was left baffled by the mystery in front of him.

The walls of the small, dank, dark room seemed to close in on him after a time, and pressure filled the small space allowing him very little room to breathe. How many nights had he spent in this place working endlessly toward the desired result? So many he couldn't count them all, and still he had nothing concrete to show for it. Nothing with which he could go to his master and say that his problems are solved, and no more innocent people need to die.

He sat down on a small bench in the corner of the room and exhaled, feeling beaten and useless. He looked at his wrinkled hands with disdain and covered his face to rub his tired eyes. He wiped his forehead from the heat that seemed to come from nowhere. His gray hair soaked through with sweat. However, he knew he must continue. His master was counting on him.

He checked in the storage area to assure that he had enough supplies to conduct the experiments without running out. The rodent plasma was available to Thomas in large amounts. The human plasma as well as the blood was below normal stock, but he would update the stock in the morning, so he did not need to worry about that. He might stumble onto something with these experiments and he might not, but he would lose nothing from trying. They stood to gain so much if luck was on their side. So, with a deep, determined breath, Thomas went to work, saying a prayer that something positive would come from the long night of work that lay ahead of him.

*

The brightness of the summer morning awakened Monica, but to her surprise Andrew still lay sleeping beside her. She thought it odd at first that he would still be sound asleep. It was usually the other way around. Monica looked at him, and kissed him gently on the mouth not wanting to wake him. She got out of bed quietly and went to shower, she had the day off, and she planned to enjoy it. The shops in Manhattan were waiting for her and her credit cards. The water was running, lavender scented the steamy air, and Andrew still slept.

He finally awakened with Monica standing over him with a smile on her face. "I was getting ready to call in the reserves. Plan to stay in bed all day?" she joked, bending down and kissing him.

Andrew smiled and accepted the morning greeting from his wife. "Can't a man sleep in with his wife without being nagged?" he laughed.

"Of course, but your wife has been up for an hour while you've been tucked in bed sleeping the day away," she said, walking over to the table and pouring a glass of water. "Thomas has breakfast waiting."

Andrew felt sluggish when he stood up from bed, but he brushed it off as the result of over sleeping. "So we shouldn't keep him waiting?" he asked, pulling on his robe.

"I don't think so, besides he looks a little pale. How long has it been since he's seen a doctor?" she asked, concerned.

Andrew couldn't answer the question. He knew that if Thomas was pale it was only because he'd spent the night working on a more powerful treatment for him, and he would allow his health to suffer in exchange. Whether Andrew liked it or not.

Chapter 18

Weeks later, after the horror Andrew had inflicted on the innocent of New York City had lessened, he allowed himself to return to work. Monica was beginning to worry about him. He supposed it did him good to get back into the swing of things. But it didn't absolve him of his sins.

The texture of his silky, jet-black hair had taken on a new appearance. He ran his hand through it and noticed its rich fullness. Andrew pinched the bridge of his nose. No doubt, his hair was just another sign that the internal war beating down inside of him was having a greater effect on him than he first realized. He inhaled deeply and blew it out between his teeth, pushing himself away from the desk, he stood and walked to the sink in the small room off his large office.

He gripped the sides so hard he thought he had seen indentations in the shape of his hands in the marble. The war inside his head between conscience and instinct was still raging with force, pervading his every thought. He reminded himself of this over and over as he removed from his shirt pocket the receipt of, yet, two more anonymous cash donations to cover the expenses of two more innocent victim's funerals.

As he put his hands over his face, he couldn't be sure that he hadn't aged in the weeks following the latest calamity he could claim as his own. With his fingertips he felt what he thought was the unmistakable trace of wrinkles around his troubled eyes. In a fleeting moment, he chuckled at the fantasy he was unsuccessfully trying to delve into.

His neck felt stiff as he reached around to rub it, "Damn, this life," he whispered, leaving the room and getting back to his work.

*

With the clicking of her high heels on the marble floor of the news room, Monica commanded a certain amount of respect. She walked with an air of confidence that few of her colleagues believed genuine. Thanks to her now award-winning interview with Andrew Carter, the man she now proudly called her husband, Monica Carter was on the fast track. With a face recognizable nationwide, high profile politicians and celebrities wanted to talk to her. But, even the most seasoned in the media could not have been prepared for the madness responsible for the station humming with a frenetic charge.

She still found it hard to believe as she watched footage from their Carmel, California affiliate over and over again. The smoke and flames were thick, giving the quaint little Oceanside community the look of a war torn third world country. Huge plumes of black smoke filled the sky, obscuring the sun, and leaving the entire town in the inky blackness of night. If she doubted such tragedy could happen, she only needed to hear the unmistakable screaming of the wounded for proof. The bombing had happened.

At nine am west coast time, just an hour ago, a twelve-story building filled with predominantly women and children, was all but blown off the map in the heart of Carmel, California. Her head spun over how best to cover such a horrific event without sensationalism, and her heart broke over the countless dead, many of them infants and young children. It was still unclear who was responsible. Be it one man or one hundred the results were the same—carnage. WNYC had broken in to regular programming with a live feed through their affiliate six minutes after it happened.

Monica hurried into her office with her thousand different thoughts racing. Ugly images from the scene flashed in her mind. Her secretary followed her in and said, "Your husband's on line two, Monica. Sounds like he's having a great day, not a care in the world. He must not know yet."

She sat down behind her desk and tried to pull herself together. She picked up the phone and hit line two, "Drew."

Andrew knew instantly that something was wrong when he heard her voice. "Hi, sweetheart, what's wrong?"

"Drew, haven't you heard the news?"

He stiffened, jolting up in his chair. "I've been bogged down with meetings all morning. What's happened?"

"Turn on your television."

Standing, he rummaged through papers until he found the remote. "What channel?" He pushed the power button.

"Doesn't matter." Already the tension was needling between her eyes. She began massaging it away with two fingertips.

Hearing an exact echo of what she was hearing in her own office, she heard him gasp, and she closed her eyes.

"Dear god!" he whispered, dropping back into his chair. "What the hell happened?"

"It's pure evil," Monica said. "I won't be home tonight. I'm taking the station's plane to Carmel in thirty minutes," she explained, trying to prepare herself for loosing the buffer, slim though it made be, of distance. "Philips and the network want me live for the evening news."

"Of course they do, you're the best reporter they've got," he said, his eyes locked on the screen across the room. "You need anything?"

"Actually, they're in desperate need of medical personnel and supplies, maybe you could..."

Andrew cut her off, already jotting notes down. "Say no more, I make the call right now, my California branch can handle it. We did a lot of good with the riots, anything else?"

"Thomas is taking care of it, babe. I'll miss you."

"You'll be too busy to miss me. Be careful, love."

"I will, don't worry. Love you."

"Love you too."

*

Andrew stayed glued to his television for the remainder of the afternoon. He directed his California branch to lend all assistance possible concerning the Carmel situation. For this, he didn't have to sit back helplessly. Considering his vast resources, he could make a real difference, and he planned to do more. The exhausted face of a firefighter filled the screen smeared with greasy soot slicked by sweat, and heat, and pain. The camera pulled back, revealing his misery. In his arms, he was carrying the small body of a child pulled from the building.

Medics rushed over and took the boy, laying him on the ground. The camera angle was tight on the medic's backs, but a tiny, bloodied hand lay limp on the ground. Andrew closed his eyes to the scene that sickened him. Thoughts of the child and the countless others trapped in the ruins, and of the sick mind that brought about such destruction, filled his mind.

People would walk by, come in, and ask if he'd heard the news. He would answer by pointing to his television, because his voice would fail him if he were to try to speak. Andrew tried to direct his attention back to his work but he kept being drawn back to the scenes in Carmel. Finally, he turned the television off, escaping the pain and ugliness as the people of California never would be able to do.

*

Andrew walked out of his office, down the hallway, and into the elevator so he could go back to the mansion. He made plans to join Monica in Carmel first thing in the morning. He wanted to be on hand personally to make sure everything that could be done was being done. He'd also rounded up four doctors to accompany him, to relieve those already there, and exhausted.

If he could have done more, he would have but for the moment, as the elevator slowly dropped floor by floor, nothing more could be done. He looked at his watch and found it was past six. The day slipped away from him without him being aware of it. He loosened his tie and closed his eyes, feeling the elevator come to a stop. He heard the doors open and sensed Thomas standing in front of him before he opened his eyes. "What a bleedin' awful day."

Thomas nodded his head in agreement, "Yes, I know. How about a glass of wine, Master Andrew? You look tired."

"Sounds good to me," he said "I am tired beyond description."

*

A cab was the quickest way to the bomb site. Long after it pulled away, she stood transfixed by the mayhem. The obliterated remains of the best Women's and Children medical facilities in the United States lay in a heap in front of her. The devastation made Monica sick to her stomach. It rolled and pitched from the smell of explosives and death in the air, and from the sight of misery in the eyes of the rescuers who passed by her.

However, it was time to do her job, to put a human face on the pain, and responsibly and compassionately bring such ugliness into the country's living rooms. She found a mark and motioned the cameraman to set up. Automatically, she checked her hair and makeup in her compact, took the mic her tech handed her. Then noticing a firefighter off by himself, she approached him slowly.

He looked over his shoulder when she tapped him. He saw her, and saw the mic, too. His face hardened with contempt. "I'm through with interviews, lady. You see what's going on here? These people need help."

Monica understood his disdain and offered a sympathetic smile. "I'm not here for ratings. I have a job to do. It's my responsibility to see an accurate report informs the public about what's happened here. What about the people across the country who have family out here?"

He let her words sink in. "I'm Mike, how can I help?"

Monica smiled, and offered her hand, "If you could answer a few questions for me on camera, I'd be grateful."

"Sure."

"Okay Dave," she gestured to the cameraman. "Let's do it."

*

Andrew was in bed reclining against the headboard, shirtless, and the remote resting on his stomach. Ten thirty, and he was in bed for the night. Monica's final live report from Caramel had been heartbreaking, body bags filling by the dozen, rubble still burning, people unaccounted for, as bright orange flames lit up the night sky. He was so proud of her, and of her professionalism, but he could see how affected she was by the chaos around her.

She called moments after finishing, and after assuring her that she did wonderfully, he told her he would see her tomorrow. Her surprise gave way to relief. She told him her stay in California was indefinite. It would make it easier to deal with everything with Drew at her side.

Now he was alone without even her voice to keep him company. He would sleep. A stronger potency of injections, and a new, thicker wine would ensure it. He looked at the door knowing it was locked from the outside, and he was grateful. He was a prisoner until the new treatments took hold. Although, there were no stomach pains to worry about, and no dry mouth wearing on him, he was still nervous. It had to be this way. To assure his safety and the safety of innocent people, Thomas, at Andrew's urging, would keep him under lock and key.

*

Monica walked through the lobby of her hotel not sure she wasn't already asleep on her feet, according to her wristwatch, which was blacken from all the smoke she had to walk through. She was covered with all the filth from the bomb scene. Knowing she would feel better after a hot shower and soft bed, that was all that was on her mind, walking into a crowded elevator, and wedging her tired body against the back wall. Her head filled with pictures of the terrible things she'd witnessed at the scene. It would be a long time before she would be able to erase the grim memories from her mind.

Monica opened her eyes when she heard the bell above her. The elevator had stopped at her floor. She walked into the hallway, and ambled down the plush carpet. She slipped her card key inside the lock, opened the door, and went inside, shutting the world outside her suite. Flipping on the lights, she checked the air conditioning and continued left through to another, equally large room. Off to the right was another doorway. Inside that room there was a spacious bedroom, but the bathroom beyond was all she had on her mind now. She kicked off her heels, sighed, and headed for the bath she promised herself.

With the luxurious sound of the running bath, she walked back into the living room wrapped in a thick over-sized towel. After making sure the door was securely locked, she went in search for a room service menu, and then went back to the steamy bathroom calling to her tired muscles. Hanging on the backside of the door, inside a clear, thin plastic bag, she found a robe she was sure would feel like heaven against her skin.

The bubble bath she had found on the counter beside the sink filled the air with a pleasant floral scent. With a pleasant hum, Monica let the towel fall to the floor at her feet. She'd had a miserable day. She slipped a testing toe into the water, before deciding it was perfect and, stepping into the hot, velvety, bubbly water. With a moan of sheer pleasure, she eased down into the tub, with bubbles enveloping her, she stretched out her legs and sighed. She'd been dreaming of this all day.

*

Thomas was up at five a.m. taking care of last minute details for their trip to California. Though he thought his master's heart was in the right place, he was less than thrilled with his decision to make the trip. As long as he'd known him, Andrew had always taken care of important matters in person. He was a strong believer in the hands on approach. Thomas always respected him for it, but going made him nervous. His master wouldn't be able to do any more there then he could at home. It wasn't as if he could go to the site and direct the situation himself.

Concern about what affect the change of environments would have on his master, heightened. He hadn't been on a trip since his honeymoon, and he remembered all too well the disaster that occurred. Monitoring him there at the mansion was one thing. Monitoring him in California, amidst all the chaos, was something else entirely.

However, Thomas was no a fool. He knew better than to try to change his master's mind. And compared to the pain and suffering going on in that poor city, the risks Andrew Carter would be taking seemed small to his master's stubborn way of thinking. So, putting his reservations about the trip aside, Thomas prepared the injections to take along with them. He hoped with them along, the only tragedy his master would face would be one not of his own making.

*

Andrew rolled over sluggishly, slamming his palm into the alarm presently driving spikes through his head. For a moment, he listened to the silence. Then opening his eyes, he sat up in bed, squinting at the clock. It was five thirty in the morning. He got up, put on his robe, and made his way in the dark to the bathroom. The cold water revived him, and then he walked back into the bedroom and switched on the light.

He was thankful he packed his luggage the night before, now all he needed to do was get dressed and get to the airport. He picked up the phone and buzzed Thomas to call the pilot and make sure the plane was ready and the catered breakfast he'd ordered for his guests had arrived. The cars he'd sent for the doctors were picking each of them up and bringing them to the plane. Andrew hung up the phone, pleased everything was going like clockwork. He smiled and looked at his watch. At this rate, they'd be in the air by seven o'clock.

They were in the air by seven and the pilot promised a smooth, swift flight. Once the altitude leveled off, and the seat belt sign went out, they moved about the large cabin enjoying the catered breakfast provided. All the while, Andrew exchanged glances with a clearly, troubled Thomas. But, his concerns were directed elsewhere; with Monica, and in Carmel, California.

*

Monica moved around her suite with a hurried purpose and a cellular phone crammed to her ear. "I've got to be back down there in ten minutes for a live feed back to New York, Ronny. So you'd better think of some way to get me there," she directed, not giving an inch. "I mean, we're all pressed for time right now, so deal. You want to be the one who calls Philips and tell him we can't give him a live report because traffic's hell?"

She alternated between taking drinks of scalding coffee and bites of a stale muffin, while she listened to yet another excuse. "Listen, Ronny. Get your ass in a car, any car. Steal one if you have too, but get your sorry ass over here!" Slamming shut the phone, Monica felt like a real hard ass. Drew would be proud, she thought, leaving her room for the lobby. Ronny arrived in minutes.

Monica was in the passenger seat drumming her fingers impatiently. "Can't you make this thing move any faster?" she demanded. "My cameraman's waiting to go live in three minutes!"

"We're almost there," Ronny complained, toying with the idea of booting her ass out onto the freeway.

She made it with seconds to spare. Dave rolled his eyes, and throwing her a mic, pointed to her and counted down. "Four, three, two, one," he signaled her.

"This is Monica Carter live from the remains of the Kensington Women and Children's Medical Clinic. Behind me, you'll see the devastation is clear. The bodies of women and children are still being removed from the rubble. It's a sad sight to witness, Mitch. We will be here for the entire day bringing you, and the country, more news as it becomes available. For now, I'm Monica Carter, in Carmel, California. Back to you, Mitch."

She let out a sigh of relief when Dave said they were clear. She handed him the microphone, angry. "That was too close."

Dave laughed. "Yeah, let's not do that again, okay?"

Monica smiled. "You can say that again."

Monica moved out of the path of rescuers and watched as Fire and Rescue carried another body out of the dirt and debris. With grim, grimy faces, they carried the body to the coroner's area. Monica wiped a tear from her cheek. Another victim claimed by madness. Suddenly, she wanted Drew's arms to comfort her. But she would have to wait awhile longer. His arrival couldn't be soon enough.

She turned her face up to the humid sky, wishing for a ponytail for her hair. Only eight o'clock in the morning and it was already seventy-three degrees and climbing. It would be another day in oppressive heat with little hope of finding any survivors.

At least the police were running down a lead about the person, or persons, responsible. Rumor had it, a despondent ex-husband of a patient, angered by her refusal for reconciliation, planted the bomb for revenge. With a borrowed cap from the Red Cross, Monica tucked her hair up off her neck, and shaking her head sadly, walked off to see if she could lend a hand.

*

Andrew was waiting for her at the hotel when she came back after her mid day report. The look on her face when she walked into the suite and saw him was enough to tell him she needed him. He crossed the room and pulled her into his arms. "I'm here now," he whispered, pressing his lips to her cheek. The tired look on her face, the sadness in her vivid green eyes, had him gathering her close again.

Monica squeezed him so tight she thought her arms might numb. "I'm so glad you're here."

"Me too." He drew away, walking her to the couch to get her off her feet. "The doctors went directly to the site. They're a cheery lot, let me tell you, but they're top notch trauma specialists." He continued, sitting her down, and then sitting next to her.

"You're a hero, Drew. The people at Carter Enterprises have been wonderful. And the supplies are so badly needed." Monica said, snuggling close, and lifting her aching feet into his lap. "Drew, I'll tell you, seeing all the loss is a nightmare. And it's endless."

Andrew began kneading her arches, as she rested her cheek against him. "Close your eyes, love," he murmured, lulling her with the massage and his soothing voice.

She let herself drift, and let the ugly images of her morning go. The warmth she felt in such a strong, yet, gentle touch was comfort enough. "I'm glad you're here."

"I wouldn't want to be anywhere else."

"It's going to take a long time for this city to recover, Drew. What kind of diseased mind would orchestrate such evil?"

Though, he knew she didn't expect an answer from him, he considered the question. Someone as kind as she wouldn't comprehend that evil existed everywhere, sometimes where you least expect it. Andrew held her tight, listening as her breathing deepened, and she slept.

*

Later, Andrew watched her come out of the bathroom unbuttoning her blouse, listened to the water running for a bath. "The catnap helped." He leaned back on the bed on his elbows and inhaled deeply, relaxing every tense muscle in his body. "A hot bath will do the rest."

Pulling on her robe, she walked over to the bed, "I'm not the only one who's exhausted." She put out her hand and Andrew took it. "There's room enough for two in there," Monica said, pulling him up from the bed.

"Oh?" Andrew laughed, as she tugged him to his feet, already pulling his shirt over his head. "Lead the way."

*

The bath relaxed them almost to the point of unconsciousness. So, with their skin still heated and soft from their long soak, they lounged, dozing, in the huge, canopied bed on a raised platform with three steps, in the middle of the master bedroom. Covered with deep, dark colors of burgundy and forest green in the pattern of checks with two large pillows under their heads for comfort.

It was in this swell of opulence Andrew awakened three hours later, and alone. Finding a note on Monica's pillow, he rubbed the sleep out of his eyes and read her quickly scrawled lines. She'd gone to oversee final edits for the tape that would accompany her evening report. So, for the moment he was alone, he mused, and considered calling Thomas to come for tea.

He walked down the hall into the living room, hands shoved deep into the pockets of his robe. Walking over to the large window, which offered a view of the harbor off in the distance, he peaked through a slat of the pulled blind, and thought about a late dinner on the water. When he took a deep breath he could smell the smoke from the bombsight through the glass. He closed his eyes and smoothed the damp hair off his forehead, feeling a bead of perspiration trickle down his back.

He knew the signs well now. The profuse sweating was just the beginning. The treatment from half a dozen hours before was loosing its potency. Thomas needed to administer another injection, now, before the symptoms grew worse. Andrew held his hands out in front of him to study them. To his relief they were steady.

He put his hands on his waist and backed away from the window, heading for the phone. Once Thomas was called, Andrew had nothing to do but wait. The bar across the room looked inviting. So, he set about making himself a drink, poured himself a scotch, added two splashes of water, tossed in a couple cubes of ice, and swirled it around before he drained half the glass with one gulp. Restless now, Andrew paced. There were hours between him and the freedom of night. For now, he would have to be content inside the suite.

At the knock on the door, he sat down on the sofa and shrugged out of his robe. Resting his arm on the arm cushion of the sofa, he heard the door open, then close. Thomas crossed to him and crouched down; opening the case, he sat at his feet. In silence, he prepared the syringe, set it aside, poured a glass warmed wine, now more than fifty percent human blood, and gave it to his master. While Andrew drank slowly, Thomas gave him the injection.

The affect was immediate. The profuse sweating ceased, the restlessness eased, when he finished the wine, he slumped back on the sofa, put his legs up, and exhaled. The crisis averted, the painful symptoms relieved before leaving him weak and fumbling for an explanation.

An hour later, Andrew still sat on the sofa, having never moved a muscle. Letting the treatment do its work so he would be refreshed when Monica returned was essential. Thomas had left the room to check in with the office at Andrew's request. While he rested, he watched the evening news, waiting for Monica's report, with an ear out for word from home about the investigation into the Central Park killings. The emotional aftermath of the bombing, and the guilt, never far from his conscience, of his own sins, worked him into a morose, dour mood.

Too much death, Andrew mused, leaning forward and putting his feet on the deep, plush carpet, and squeezing it between his toes. Some were his responsibility. Most were the responsibility of someone unknown. But, he would do everything he could to assist in the recovery of this city from tragedy, while doing whatever was necessary to keep from adding to the tragedy of his own making. He rested his elbows on his knees and redirected his thoughts to a wonderful candlelight dinner on the water, and the company of his lovely wife.

*

Andrew lay down beside Monica at ten minutes past five in

the morning. He'd slept restfully when they'd gone to bed just before one. But, for the last thirty minutes he walked the suite. Too many heartbreaking images crowding his mind for sleep to return. When she'd asked him to come with her to the bomb site for the late news report, he went gladly. He found the devastation was absolute. With word that morning that the structures of the neighboring buildings were badly damaged, it was more bad news the city did not need.

But, the evening began on a better note. Dinner on the water had been romantic and eased the tension knotting in Monica's shoulders. She relaxed, enjoyed her meal, chatted with him, and laughed. That it had been the escape for her he'd planned it to be, pleased him.

So, with those happy thoughts he closed his eyes to sleep. When the alarm next woke Andrew, he rolled over on his side, eyes still closed, feeling rested. When he opened his eyes, reality rudely set in, realizing he wasn't at home in his own bed as he had been in his dreams. With the haze of dreaming gone, he looked around remembering—the suite in California…the bombing…the deaths.

He rolled onto his back relieved to find Monica sitting on the edge of the bed with her back turned to him. She'd knocked the alarm to the floor when she upended her purse in search of lipstick, he guessed. Reaching down, she yanked the cord from the wall and silenced the alarm.

It was then he heard the soft drone of voices from the TV, the volume low so as not disturb him. Tuning into voices, he heard what Monica had known since the sunrise ringing of her cell phone. Confirmation the bombing had been the climax in the worst case of domestic abuse in the city's history.

He pressed his palms against his eyes and yawned. "What time is it?" he asked. The sound of his voice made Monica jump.

"Early," Monica looked over her shoulder, and smiled. "I was hoping to get out of here without waking you up." She leaned down and kissed him, "It's almost seven."

Andrew slid himself up against the backboard of the bed. "Jesus," he muttered, and with a lift of his chin had her looking back to the TV. "When'd they make an arrest?" Another yawn escaped him.

"Four thirty this morning. I've got to get down to the police station for the press conference." She sat up, and adjusted the pins in her hair. "What do you have planned for today?" she asked, striding to the closet and pulling the suit jacket, which matched the slim skirt she wore, off its hanger.

Andrew folded his arms across his chest and watched her put dainty pearls in her lobes. "I'm planning to go by my offices here to find out how our coordination with the rescue teams is going." Fully awake now, he got out of bed and went to button a button she missed at the back of her neck, and give her a squeeze from behind. Monica turned in his arms, and touched his cheek with her fingertips. He pressed his lips to her cheek and whispered, "You look beautiful."

"I've got to go, I'll see you later." She gave him a long kiss goodbye. "Bye."

Andrew watched her leaving the room, confident stride, all business. He was a very lucky man to have such a wonderful woman in his life. He thought of the countless men made widowers by the last violent act of a man unable to let go, and ill-timed doctor's visits. He was lucky to have her, lucky to love her, and lucky she loved him just as much.

*

Andrew and Thomas had dinner together in his suite, without Monica, that evening due to some late breaking development concerning the bombing. After having another version of the same old argument, the two of them ate in silence. Andrew didn't see the harm in taking Monica for a stroll to the beach when she returned to the suite, but Thomas saw the harm clearly. So, they sat with so much tension between them it nearly breathed.

"I'm looking out for your safety, Master Andrew," Thomas repeated for he thought the fifteenth time.

"The treatments having been working marvelously, I've been feeling fine," he said convincingly.

"Oh, is that so? So, then tell me, why didn't you sleep through the night last night?"

Andrew became angry and shot back a bit too loudly, "If you'd have seen the misery I did, you wouldn't sleep either. Why must every insignificant problem I have mean something dark and sinister?" he demanded.

Thomas was quiet for a moment, taken aback by the tone. "Very recent history demands it, Andrew. And if you stop acting like a spoiled child for a moment and consider the consequences, you might see I'm bloody right."

When he was certain the weight of his words sank in, he threw his napkin on the table, stood up and stormed off.

*

Thomas was fuming. He'd never been so angry with Andrew. He walked down the hall to his room. His master had the attitude of an impossible child. If Thomas were twenty years younger he would have used his fists to beat sense back into him. He slammed his door behind him, never wanting a drink more than he did right now.

*

Andrew checked his watch through blurred vision. He'd been sitting alone at a table in the hotel bar for hours. With Monica off working and his recent row with Thomas, he decided there was no reason to rush back to his hotel suite. No, he thought, wallowing a bit, it was much more productive to sit in an alcoholic haze. He waved to the waitress who'd been serving him both highballs of scotch and suggestive, 'I'm up for anything' looks all night. He motioned her over and she seemed disappointed when he only wanted another drink. He smiled, missing completely, her offense as she sauntered off to get his drink.

Resting his head on the palm of his hand, he knew he was drunk. Sitting there alone in the dark bar with only neon signs to hold his attention, in his rumpled shirt, and his sour, pitiful expression. His usually well kempt hair disheveled by the nervous raking of his fingers, and to complete the perfect picture of a billionaire, cocky, self-righteous soul, a pair of glassy baby blues. Finishing off the last of his drink, he gained his feet slowly. He swayed, tilted, but only for a moment, and made his way out into the lobby of the hotel. He so badly needed to clear his head, he turned for the doors.

Staggering out into the street he hailed a cab and promptly collapsed into the back seat. One look at his surroundings and he grimaced, he wasn't in his limo any longer, instead he was at the mercy of public transportation. With the order to be driven some place where a person could clear his head, the cab began moving with the heavy flow of traffic.

Ten minutes and twenty-five dollars later, Andrew was dropped in an area more suitable to the quiet contemplation he desired. And the cabby earned himself a seventy-five dollar tip. It had nothing to do with his driving but more to do with Andrew having nothing smaller than a hundred dollar bill on him.

Andrew moved with the gait of a man immersed in alcohol, but he wasn't as drunk as he'd hoped to be. He slowly began walking with what passerbys would assume was the weight of the world on his shoulders, never knowing just how right they were. His stomach had been churning for almost a half an hour. If he had used whatever brain cells were not pickled, he would have gone up to the suite and waited the pain and hunger out.

But, being here in the quiet of the night was what he sought. As if he had to prove something to himself and to Thomas. Who, if he knew what the man he'd come to love as a son was doing, would be having a stroke right now. Still ignoring what good sense he had, Andrew continued on his path of destruction.

Passing many people along his way, certain he had control over his urges, the sly instrument of false security flourished, and he thought himself infallible. After all, he hadn't laid a finger on the people he'd been walking among. Mind-over-matter. They walked past, unaware of the threat he posed to them. And though Andrew Carter was known, and recognized on television, he was rarely recognized in person. He moved along, receiving not so much as a second look.

With his tie swaying easily in a sticky breeze, he loosened it and opened the collar of his shirt to breathe. And then, unaware of his quickening pace, Andrew strode on, attuned to nothing but the rising pressure in his throat, and the screaming whoosh unrelenting in his head. Sweat chilled his skin as he felt the muscles tighten in his body, one by one. A fire was blazing inside him but he kept moving. Unsure of where to go, of what to do, he sucked in a breath, grappling for control.

He prayed for solitude, knowing if he were alone with no one to make his unwilling victim, then he could harm none. Sweat streamed down his neck and trickled down his back. A stiffening pain was grinding in his stomach with wicked abandon. And then, Andrew stopped, grabbed his head in agony. He staggered away trying to block out the voices thundering in his head.

Someone grabbed him to steady him, and he lashed out without hesitation. He plunged into the throat of one while grabbing another and silencing the screams of horror. Throwing his first victim to the ground dead, he turned on the other with animal like viciousness. The man struggled, enticing Andrew to drink more quickly, more greedily than ever before.

As the man barely clung to life, his neck snapped with a brutal jerk. The lifeless body fell to the ground at his feet. He seized the two remaining hysterical companions trying to flee. But Andrew surprised them, and himself, by taking to the air and landing directly in their path, cutting off their only escape.

Soon, and with precision, two more bodies fell to the warm ground. With blood drying in his mouth, Andrew, charged by the bounty of his feeding, then returned, oblivious, to the hotel. He felt no remorse, no guilt over what he had done. That would come later, when the hum of power abated.

*

Time and history were good teachers for Andrew. He awakened to the new day with Monica curled against him in blissful sleep, and the weight of conscience settling in. Ignoring all the lessons taught in the past, four more people had paid for his mistake. If he had any cause to doubt what had happened, the faint taste of blood reminded him. When the tears came, filling his eyes, he let them fall.

He slid out from under Monica, sat up in bed, and cupped his hands over his face in misery. Why hadn't he just come back to the hotel last night? Why did he insist on that walk to clear his head? He knew only evil could come from placing himself in that position, but he did it anyway. Now more blood was on his hands.

Thomas would be livid when he learned of the mess he had created. Regret nearly choked him. He should have heeded Thomas' warning instead of insisting he was able to take care of himself. Foolish men commit foolish mistakes.

On his feet, Andrew pulled on his robe and went into the living room, dreading what he had to do next. He picked up the phone and dialed Thomas' number. It rang three times, and then finally he heard Thomas say, "Hello."

Andrew closed his eyes and forced the words out of his mouth. "Thomas, I need to see you."

The line was quiet for a moment. "I'll be right there."

"No," he said too quickly. "Downstairs, ten minutes."

"Fine."

With the call over, Andrew still clutched the receiver in his hand, listening to the hum of the dial tone in his ear. He was afraid of facing Thomas and telling him the truth. But, he had no choice. The bodies would be found soon, if they hadn't been already, then it would hit the news and the papers. Then, Thomas would know the truth anyway. It was better to prepare him. It was the right thing to do.

*

Thomas found Andrew sitting in the lobby in a V-neck sweater, a pair of Dockers, and brown loafers. A careless way to dress for a man so insistent on looking his best. It was a red flag, a warning. But, it was the utterly lost expression on his master's face that sent Thomas' heart plunging to his feet. He walked over to his master warily, stopping in front of Andrew and looking down at him in gaped apprehension, as he sat on the couch his head in his hands. "What's happened?"

Andrew opened his eyes and Thomas's shoes where the first thing he saw. "You'd better sit down." He was rubbing his hands together nervously. Almost feeling the skin peeling away from them, he watched Thomas sit next to him, preparing for the worst, and decided to get it over with. "It happened again last night," he whispered the words thinking it would blunt their meaning.

"What?" Thomas asked, as if not knowing what he was talking about.

"What in bloody hell do you think?" Andrew's whispered anger flaring.

Thomas looked at him impatiently. Taking a deep breath, he rubbed his temples and asked, "How many?"

Andrew closed his eyes again trying to erase the mental images from his mind. "I'm not sure. Three, maybe four."

Thomas shook his head. "Lovely. Where?" he whispered, the wheels in his head turning in search of a solution.

"I can't remember."

Thomas rolled his eyes, "Even better. Well, we'll know soon enough." He stood up and walked away, obviously disgusted with his master and his actions.

Andrew watched him go, and he buried his head in his hands. Trying to numb the pain over what he did and by the cold way Thomas treated him. His eyes were stinging, despite staying well away from the early sunlight peeking through the lobby's windows. He deserved far worse than this simple, although intense, discomfort. It was nothing compared to what those people had suffered at his hands.

Thomas was pissed and justifiably so. What more could happen, Andrew wondered, sitting back on the couch and watching more potential victims pass by? Now this city would have to deal with two mad men. One who bombed the medical center, and the other lurking in shadows of the night. He would have loved to distance himself, but he couldn't crawl out of his own skin.

He sat in the lobby until the sun's heat through the window across the room became too intense for even Andrew, in his self-torturing state, to handle. With worry lines etched deep in his brow and pinching the corners of his eyes, he ducked inside an elevator and lowered his head to hide the condition of his eyes from the others inside. Listening to the bell chime for every floor, he counted off the floors impatiently. Arriving on the penthouse floor, he stepped out of the elevator, guilty and ashamed.

He was just about to put his key in the door when it opened from the inside and Monica was smiling at him. He covered his surprise well. While cursing himself for leaving his sunglasses behind, he watched her face for any sign of strangeness when she met his eyes with hers but her smile remained and she stepped back to let him in.

He embraced her, pressed his cheek to hers, grateful she saw nothing of the monster inside him. They spent the hours until noon, wisely, in each other's arms. But as Andrew held Monica, torment raged. Behind the eyes, which looked so lovingly at his wife, grief thrived, eating him alive. If his soul were alive, it would have died then. She lay with her head on his chest, her breath on his skin, giving him the strength he lacked to fight for his life and for their life together. Appreciating that, he held her tighter.

Shutting out everything and everyone, inside the quiet room with shades drawn, he refused to dwell. To not worry about what might happen in the future or what had already happened would be a bequest denied to him. For now, he would just be with Monica and shut the demons inside away. So far away they could never find their way back to the light of day.

But, Andrew knew better. It was only by some miracle he'd been able to control his passion for his wife without hurting her. He was grateful for that and hoped his control would sustain and keep Monica safe.

Monica had to be back at the bombsight for a midday report so Andrew concentrated on the things he could control, such as delivery of medical supplies and other sorely needed necessities like water and food. Things that were tangible. He watched her dress while giving orders over the phone to his staff. As he lay in bed with nothing but a sheet to cover him, she knew he was following her every move, even while he took care of business.

She could feel his eyes on her and desire welling up inside as he hung up the phone, but willpower won out. "If you keep looking at me that way, I'll never get out of here."

"There're worse ways to spend a day."

"Drew," was all she said, leaning across the sheet and giving him a long, deep kiss goodbye.

*

Somewhere between two and three o'clock Andrew dragged himself out of bed and forced himself to get dressed. He had plenty to do to keep busy while Monica was doing her job. As he tied the tie hanging limply around his neck, there was a knock at the door. He crossed the floor in three long strides and opened it. He wasn't surprised to see Thomas on the other side. He was expecting him to show up sooner or later with the exact look of disapproval he was currently wearing on his aged face.

Thomas said nothing as he pushed his way past Andrew and into the room. They exchanged heated looks with each other before Andrew finally braved speaking to him. He was quite clearly in an elevated stage of agitation. "We've got to get going, Thomas," he said, sliding the knot of his tie up to his neck. "I know you're angry with me right now, but you're no angrier with me than I am with myself."

"I'm beyond angry, Master Andrew," he corrected with an icy tone. "Angry would be a tremendous understatement. If you would've listened to me last night, I wouldn't have to run around covering your ass," he spat, throwing the morning addition of the city paper at him. "Do you see the kinds of headlines you're making now? Not another article about the shining example you are for the rest of the corporate world, no, nothing like that. You made the news because you're bloody arrogant."

Andrew let Thomas finish his tirade, and then he opened the paper to look at the front page. His eyes narrowed and the hair on the nape of his neck stood on end. He was expecting graphic details, but nothing like what he was seeing. There it was, in bright vivid color, the sins of which he was guilty smacking him in the face. "We were expecting this, Thomas. Have you come to say I told you so?"

"Far be it from me, Master Andrew. What do you have planned for us today?" he asked annoyed by the general acceptance his master was exhibiting.

Andrew ignored the tone in Thomas' voice. "Making sure there are enough medical supplies to last the rescue teams. Fretting about the terrible mistakes I made last night won't erase them, so don't look at me like that," he said noticing the stare he was receiving from Thomas. "I know better than anyone what happened. I don't need your sour mood to remind me."

Thomas watched Andrew as he put on his jacket. "We need to go home, and the sooner the better. What if someone saw you or worse yet, recognized you? It won't be long before someone starts putting two and two together, and then we'll be dealing with a fine mess."

"My conscience is heavy enough, old man, I don't need you trying to make it worse. Monica wants to go home together. And her assignment isn't over," he said plainly, opening the door and walking out of the room.

Thomas followed him into the hall and closed the door behind him. "Going out there last night like you did, you were asking for trouble."

They walked down the hall to the elevators without speaking further. There was nothing more to say. Only preparation for possible fallout remained, but waiting would be agonizing. In the deserted garage Thomas opened the back door to the limo and stepped aside allowing Andrew to get inside. Thomas slammed the door and walked around to the other side, sighed, got inside, and tried to calm himself for the drive.

The streets were crowded and the afternoon heat stifling. What was more uncomfortable was the heady silence stretching between Thomas and his master. Looking at all the people on the sidewalks, he wished for wisdom enough to see his master through this. More than once, he glanced at the dark sullen figure sitting low in the seat behind him. He could have said something to him, make some attempt at small talk, but he decided against it. What, he thought, would that solve?

Thomas had dealt with the tempers Andrew could throw before. Experience taught him that there was no reasoning with his master when he was in one of his moods. Therefore, he felt it best to remain quiet. Though he had to admit, the thought of kicking the very stuffing out of his master held a certain appeal.

Their car ride ended pulling into the garage under his company offices. Stepping out of the limo, Andrew buttoned his coat and straightened his tie on his way to the elevator, and to his offices above. Thomas was on his heels, quietly problem solving, the wheels turning in his mind.

*

As dusk set in, Monica was happy to look over her shoulder and see the limo pull up behind her to the left of the chaos. She smiled when she saw Andrew get out of the back and looked up at the emerging stars, praying this night would find more survivors of the blast. She wrapped her arms around him when he came to her with a sad smile on his face.

"It's hard to remember that just days ago, this was a thriving city, isn't it?" she asked as his eyes locked on what remained standing across the street. "It has an eerie look to it under these stars, but they still hope to find more survivors."

Andrew's gaze shifted back to Monica, "How many confirmed dead so far?"

"Thirty six dead, twenty wounded. The rescuers say there's still eleven unaccounted for."

They held hands and watched as a body was dragged from the rumble. The mangled boy and the faces of the approaching doctors pinched with grief silenced everyone. When later, rescuers pulled a woman free, thinking she was dead; the body suddenly began jerking in the arms of the soot-covered rescuers. Her scream brought cheers of joy as the grim looks from the doctors changed and they began frantically working to stabilize her.

Needing to feel useful, Andrew rolled up his sleeves and pitched in. Helping to clear rubble or offer cold water to the firefighters humbled him. Monica watched him with pride. Thomas watched him knowing the debt he was trying to repay. Together they witnessed him, in the thick of it, smoke and soot smearing his face, hunched over to catch his breath, a tear escaping his eye.

*

Andrew spent the rest of the night working and helping

whenever and wherever he could. The light blue denim shirt he wore was rolled up at the sleeves and covered with dirt and soot. His face was smudged with grease from his left cheek up across his nose to above his right eye. His blue eyes were even more brilliant against the dark grease around them. Monica watched him, as did Thomas, in amazement. She, because of the seemingly personal interest he was taking in the rescue effort, he because he knew the drive behind it. He was trying to make up for the trouble he caused the night before. But, it still would not protect him or hold back the madness he was struggling against.

It was there, far below the surface, rooted inside his master, danger festering to be released. Even though he wasn't committing these violent acts with free will, they were, nonetheless, more frequent and with far more vicious fervor. And, as a result, so too were many innocent people dying. It would be up to him to end the spiral of violence, up to him to save his master from himself.

By eleven that night, Andrew was on his knees in exhaustion. Taking a much deserved break, he collapsed beside Monica who was changed, reading copy, and ready to go on the late news. Soaked with sweat and covered in dirt and dust, she never ceased in finding him irresistible, so she smiled. "It's nice to see there are still men like you," she said, watching him laying back on his arms on the ground next to her chair with his eyes closed.

Opening one eye to look at her, then sitting up, he asked, "Men like me?"

"Wealthy and famous, but that doesn't keep you from getting your hands dirty, or from putting your money where your mouth is." Grinning at his embarrassment, she turned back to her copy, "And he's modest too."

"Don't give me too much credit, love," he said. "Anyone without ice in their veins and the means would want to help any way they could," he said simply.

She cupped his cheek and slid out of her chair. "Give me ten minutes then we can go."

When she returned, he was flat on his back asleep. Hands laced behind his head, knees bent, the treads of his boots sunk in the mud. She was tempted to leave him as he was. Sleep for him was always elusive, but she crouched down instead, skimming her fingers along his cheek.

He woke easily and let her help him to his feet. He took her hand and started for the limo until she slowed, then stopped, "What is it?"

"Dave just updated me on some local news. Some people were killed in one of the parks last night," she said.

He was struck breathless, "That's frightening."

Monica began walking again and Andrew followed on leaden legs. He had hoped that with everything going on, this bit of news would go unnoticed by her and he wouldn't be forced to lie. "As if this city doesn't have enough to deal with, now some sick-o takes advantage of the situation and mutilates people. Dave said it was pretty bad too, looks like someone drained their blood for...well, no one knows for what, but their guessing it's cult related," she continued, unaware how pale Andrew became with every word.

He might have passed out, if not for sheer power of will. Her description and the contempt in her voice scared him. He thought himself to be a monster and now his own wife was confirming it. With the hair on the back of his neck standing up, they reached the car and he opened the door. She got in with him following right behind trying to look unaffected.

"At least there is some good news anyway," she continued, breaking Andrew out of his fog.

"What's that?" he asked as the engine purred and they went on their way.

"The police found a witness who might've seen it happen."

Andrew felt all the blood rush to his head, tasted the bile gushing to his throat. He wanted to throw up but bent forward and put his head between his knees instead.

"Drew!" she exclaimed, leaning down, her hand protectively on his neck. "Are you okay?"

Andrew pulled in one breath and then another. Pull it together! His mind screamed as he sat up. "What? Ah, yes I'm fine," he managed, but his face, dripping with perspiration, betrayed him. "What about a witness?" he asked praying he heard her wrong.

Monica wiped his forehead and gently pushed his head down to drape a towel over the back of his neck she'd wet with cold water from the mini bar. "There now, I knew you pushed yourself too hard. Just take it easy."

Andrew lifted his head and managed a smile. "I'm just tired and hungry, that's all," he lied.

The fact that his carefully constructed world was falling apart was no reason to panic, he thought cynically. If what she said was true, he was exposed. His very existence was threatened. If someone had seen him...he couldn't even finish the thought. Dread bloomed in his chest, tightening it painfully. His skin turned to ice. He had never felt so cold in his life.

Chapter 19

They arrived back at the hotel and Andrew took Thomas aside to tell him about the latest development, when Monica left them to soak in a hot bath. Both knew the other had plenty to sort through in his mind, what more needed to be said? Thomas watched Andrew and saw all the signs as he tried to busy himself at the bar. His master was about to break and there wasn't time for it now.

When he finally decided on scotch and water, he joined Thomas on the sofa while Thomas tried to calm him. "Maybe you should drink something from the private stock," he suggested, taking the glass from Andrew.

"I'd rather not. Besides, I think we're beyond that."

Thomas held the glass, stood, and crossed the room. Dumping the scotch into the small sink behind the bar, Thomas insisted, "I'm afraid it's necessary, Andrew." He removed a wine bottle from the small cooler behind the bar and filled another glass with the thick red liquid. "It's better safe then sorry at this point."

Andrew put his head in his hands, "Thomas, how much worse can it get?"

Thomas grunted, "Don't ask."

Andrew straightened himself, when Thomas sat down and gave him the glass. Miserable, he relented and took a small drink, cringing as the thick liquid went down his throat. "So, what do we do now?"

Thomas was quiet for a moment, considering. "Nothing," he advised, "At least not until we find out what we're dealing with."

Andrew let the shock wash over him. "Thomas, they have a witness for chrissake. And you just want to sit here and wait for them to come and cart me off?"

"We're not sure what this witness knows, if he knows anything at all."

"And if the police show up before that?"

Thomas frowned. "Then we'll deal with it, Andrew."

"This couldn't get any worse, we should leave"..."now."

"Calm down. Do I need to remind you what happens when you act without thinking?"

Andrew leaned back hard on the sofa with a resigned sigh. "I hate the position I've put us all in."

"I hadn't anticipated this, Andrew. You'll have to give me a while to sort out a plan. If we need a plan at all," Thomas said in his own defense.

"I don't mean to pressure you, Thomas, I just want to know what's going to happen before it actually does. It makes me feel like I have some control over the situation, that's all."

"It's alright. Have I ever let anything happen to you?" he asked, trying to lighten the dark mood in the room.

Andrew smiled, "No, but I don't make things easy on you, do I?"

The old man gave him a rueful smile, "Hardly."

"One step at a time?"

"Yes, Andrew," he slapped him comfortingly, "One step at a time."

*

Thomas moved among the dozen or so reporters inside the police station trying like hell to blend in. He wasn't the cloak and dagger type, yet, here he stood in the place he least wanted to be, wearing dark sunglasses and a fedora, pretending to be something he was not. But, he loved the stubborn fool he'd been with since his boyhood. So like it or not, this was something that had to be done.

He had to assess the damage his master caused. Luckily, the place was crawling with press and Thomas was able to move about unfettered, and put his ear to the ground for information. For the moment, he would listen closely and fade into the background. He would find out what he needed too sooner or later.

*

After milling around the open office doors of the police station for over two hours, Thomas heard the beginning of a conversation that grabbed his interest and earned his full attention.

Captain William A. Casey listened intensely to every word the man across his desk had to say, intimidating the man without a word. The way any man towering in a six-foot three, solidly built frame, in his mid forties, blonde hair and mustache, and a no nonsense attitude, who rumor-had-it could punch a Buick and walk away the winner, could. "So, do we have a witness in the park or not?" he asked in a tone suggesting he couldn't care less one way or another.

"Yep, and one that says he can give us a description of the suspect."

"A description?"

"Yep."

"Well, Daniels, what are you waiting for? Go get a sketch artist and get to work. I've got enough on my plate with this bombing mess. I don't need this headache too."

"I'm on it."

"No," he barked, pulling on his mustache. "If you were on it, you wouldn't be here. This bastard drained the blood from four people for some sick cult thing, murdered them, I mean ripping into their necks and killing them. I want this sonofabitch. Understand?"

"Yes sir," Daniels said, practically running out of the room.

Thomas swallowed hard at the description of the case. It was definitely Andrew's little after hours blood bath they were talking about. They had no idea what they were getting in to, they had the reasoning behind the attack so wrong. If they were led to his master, their theory would be shot to hell. One look at Andrew Carter the billionaire, do-gooder of the country, and they would dig deep into something darker behind the attacks.

This witness could be the end of Andrew Carter. Thomas had to think of a solution. He waited around the station until the man driven out of the office returned an hour later with a thick sheet of sketch paper in his hands. He moved closer to the door and leaned against the doorframe and turned his head towards the door.

Captain Casey stared at the composite drawing. "So this is our man?" he asked, focusing in on the eyes. "Get into the system. See if this sketch could match them; check MO's and rap sheets. I want this guy, soon rather than later."

Daniels shook his head in agreement. "I'm already on it! Did some checking and came across a picture that's damn close. He reminds me of billionaire tycoon, Andrew Carter."

Casey glanced at Daniels, humored him. "Yeah, I suppose, through the eyes."

"And he's in town," Daniels continued.

"You're serious?" Casey rolled his eyes and stood up behind his desk. "Jesus, so's his wife. He showed up with doctors and medical supplies. Hell, last night he was up to his shins in debris, lending a hand. Half the men in this city fit this description, and I'm not laying my ass on the line just so it can be handed back to me by the mayor. Guys like Carter don't go around cult killing, it musses up their manicures." He shook his head. "Work the sheets, the system, but get me a suspect, a serious suspect, Daniels."

Thomas' mouth was dry and he could hardly swallow. He saw the sketch on the corner of the desk and knew he was looking at a very close likeness of his master. He made his way through the maze of desks shutting out all the loud talking and profanity from thugs, and walked out the door.

Out on the street he stopped to be sure he wasn't being followed or attracting attention. He took off the hat and sunglasses, and took a deep breath. He had told his master not to worry. However, there was plenty of reason to worry now. He ran up the sidewalk and hailed a cab. He had to get back to the hotel and tell Master Andrew.

*

Daniels thought about the question for a minute. "The witness can place the man in this sketch, in the park, at the time of the murders. If it happens it is Andrew Carter, so be it."

"You really want this guy to be him don't you, Daniels?" he asked, amazed.

"I want whoever's responsible for these murders. I don't care if it's him, but I'll admit I'd love to knock him down a few pegs."

Casey leaned on the edge of his desk and folded his arms across his chest. "What's your problem with Carter?" he asked, interested in the answer.

Daniels shook his head. "I don't think he's as pristine as his image makes him out to be, that's all I'm saying, Captain."

Casey walked around his desk and poured himself a cup of stale coffee. "Follow the evidence, Daniels. Be objective, you can't just decide it's Carter and that's that." He sniffed the coffee and grimaced, but drank it anyway. "It's my ass that'll have the commissioner's foot up it. And if that happens, my foot'll be up yours."

"Can I bring him in for questioning?"

Captain Casey took a deep breath. "Show the witness several photos along with a photo of Carter, mix them up, and don't make it easy. If he identifies Carter, then we'll go see him and ask some questions, understand?" he asked, making sure his meaning was understood.

When Daniels disappeared down the hall, Casey rested his head in his hands. The last thing he needed was a hotshot like Daniels looking to make his career with one publicity-grabbing case. The press would have a field day if they got wind of the sainted Andrew Carter and the park murders being mentioned in the same breath. No, that was exactly what he didn't need. Daniels was way off base. Casey shook his head. No, this was the work of some sick, twisted little bastard, not an upper-crust gentleman who was a champion of the people.

*

Andrew heard the knocking first, so he got up from the couch, where he and Monica had been relaxing between trips to the site, and walked over and opened the door. He found himself looking into Thomas' genuinely terrified face. Having looked into his face so many times in his life and found understanding, comfort, reason, and wisdom, it was disconcerting to see such a degree of fear looking back.

Andrew swallowed the lump in his throat and whispered, "So it's bad news then?" He knew the answer before he asked the question. The expression on Thomas' face said it all.

Thomas walked inside and closed the door behind him. "Where's Madam Monica?" he whispered.

Andrew gestured with his head trying to stem the rise of panic from the pit of his stomach, "In the living room." He took deep breaths, clasped his hands round his neck, and closed his eyes. "What are our options?" he asked, already pleading for a miracle.

Thomas stepped closer and spoke so softly he could barely hear himself. "I can tell you their witness gave them a description that is almost the bloody mirror image of you. They even recognize how much the man described looks like you, but there's real doubt about it."

Andrew paled and his breath backed up in his lungs. "Christ," he whispered sharply, "And...?"

Thomas shrugged his shoulders, "And I don't know. We've got to play things carefully until we know what's going on. I should think, before long, the police will arrive to question you. When that happens, you'll be polite and very helpful."

Andrew was mortified at the suggestion. "Thomas, you know I can't handle this. My conscience will get the better of me. This is a disaster!" he said louder than he meant to, bringing Monica out of the living room.

"What's a disaster?"

Andrew spun around to face her. He tried to speak, but was silenced by his fear. Thomas turned to Monica, smiled, and said, "One of his business ventures fell through." He put his arm around Monica's shoulder and walked with her back into the living room. "It's a trifle messy and I'm afraid Master Andrew is in a terrible spot at the moment," he continued as they crossed the room to sit on the sofa. "He's a little cross."

Monica's face changed from curiosity to concern. "How bad is it?"

Thomas patted her hand and winked, "It's a problem but nothing we can't handle."

Monica took Thomas by the hand, "Is there anything I can do?"

"I'm afraid not," Thomas said warmly.

Monica looked at her watch. "I've got to call the station," she said, getting up from the sofa and walking into the hall that led to the bedroom.

*

Andrew stood in the doorway listening to the explanation Thomas dreamed up on the spot. Listening to the soft murmur of his wife's voice carrying down the hall, he shoved his hands into his pockets and walked over to sit down next to Thomas. "She doesn't deserve these lies," he muttered, the inner turmoil plain on his face.

Thomas slapped his master on the shoulder. "She doesn't deserve the truth either," he reminded him.

"My stomach is killing me."

"It's time for another treatment."

"I had one three hours ago, Thomas."

"And now it's time for another one, Andrew. We must do whatever is necessary to keep you under control. Things are bad enough already, he said, as he went to the bar and filled another glass full of the thick red liquid that turned Andrew's stomach.

Then he removed a syringe from the small black case he carried in his jacket so it was available on a second's notice. "I know you hate this and so do I, but right now my concern is not your comfort as much as it is your safety," he said, handing

Andrew the glass. "Now hold still. This is going to pinch."

*

Monica had been called away to the site despite it being her day off. This left Thomas and Andrew with the time they so desperately needed to prepare a believable story if it became necessary. If the facts would seal Andrew's fate, then fiction would protect him. If facts would put Andrew behind bars, fiction, clever fiction at that, would remove all suspicion.

The important thing was for Andrew to appear relaxed, and to tell as much of the truth as possible. He was fighting a serious case of nervousness but if need be, would rise to the occasion. His guilty conscience would do little to help him gather the strength needed to give the performance of his life. Andrew didn't have to be reminded of everything he stood to lose if he wavered. Innocence or guilt didn't matter nearly as much as his conviction to save himself.

*

Daniels walked through the station with an air of superiority. His broad smile gave him the appearance of a carnival clown. It was going to be one of those days when he loved being a cop. All the other shit that went along with it, that made him from day to day want to quit and change careers, were ignored. Today it would be erased if only for a little while. He knocked on the Captain's door and stuck his head in.

Casey thought he looked like the cat that ate the canary. "Have something to tell me?" he asked with a burrowed brow.

"We have positive ID. He identified Andrew Carter."

"He's sure?"

"As sure as he can be, says it was dark but that the picture of Carter looked like the guy," Daniels said almost elated.

"Let's go talk to the man," Casey said, as he walked past Daniels and out of his office.

*

Casey and Daniels walked into the lobby of Andrew Carter's hotel complaining about not making enough in a month to stay there one night. They went to the front desk and asked to see Andrew Carter. The desk clerk said they would have to be announced, and he buzzed the suite.

Thomas answered the phone and after a moment said, "Send them up."

He hung up the phone, "They're here." Silence filled the room.

Chapter 20

Thomas busied himself in the serving area of the kitchen. Andrew did his best to appear casual and polite to the two police officers he faced in the living room of the suite. He offered a seat to each of the men. They gratefully accepted, but all Andrew could be grateful for was Monica's absence. He sat opposite them on the smaller love seat and smiled as warmly as he could manage. "How is it I can help you, gentlemen?" he asked, and his mouth went dry with the last word.

Captain Casey smiled in return, "We've just got a few questions we'd like to ask you. I'm sure we can clear things up quickly with your input."

Leaning back on the love seat, Andrew seemed relaxed and confused about what he could possibly tell them. It was an act worth the academy award, and it was snowing his visitors very effectively. His eyes held many secrets but they were his and his alone. There was no need to divulge anymore than necessary to guests, "Go right ahead."

Casey exchanged looks with Daniels, who at the moment looked like he was getting ready to score the winning touchdown in the game. "Great. Mr. Carter, I'm sure you've heard, by now, about the killings in the park two nights ago?"

"Yes, of course," charm came with great effort, "Simply dreadful."

Andrew reached into his pant's pocket and pulled out a checkbook. "Have you come to solicit a reward for information from me?"

Both Casey and Daniels seemed floored by the question, "Ah, no that's not what..."

Andrew sat up and opened his pen. "I'd be happy to do it. I mean, it's very sad, indeed, when people wait for monetary gain before they do what is morally right, but whatever helps," he said as he began filling out a blank check. "How's twenty five thousand to start?" he asked, looking up from the check. He knew this was not what they had come for but by the expressions on their faces, it was doing the job of throwing them off their rhythm.

Casey recovered enough to speak, "Mr. Carter, that's very generous of you but that's not what we meant." He waited until he had Carter's full attention. "I'd like to know if you were in Serenity Park two nights ago."

Thomas was listening in the doorway of the kitchen, waiting for the right time to enter with the coffee he'd promised when they arrived. He was interested in how his master would answer the question, so he waited.

"I went for a walk two nights ago, but as to where I ended up, specifically, that I cannot tell you," Andrew said, ripping the check from the booklet and laying it on the coffee table in front of him. He crossed his legs and felt a trickle of sweat roll between his shoulder blades down his back.

Daniels eyes narrowed. "Serenity Park's on the upper-east side of the city. Was your walk in the vicinity?" he offered this information to jolt him and Andrew recognized it.

"I couldn't say for sure, I'm not familiar with Carmel. This is where the killings took place? Serenity Park? I suppose it's possible I passed through."

Before they could answer, Thomas came into the room with a tray filled with coffee and scones. He noticed the silence and stopped in his tracks. "Am I interrupting? Oh, forgive me, I'll just set this down right here and you may help yourself." Andrew found his act amusing.

Andrew looked at him through a half smile and said, "That's alright, Thomas. I'm sure Captain Casey and his friend don't mind."

Captain Casey smiled widely as he looked at Thomas, it was a welcomed interruption, because he had missed lunch and was starving. Daniels clearly annoyed by the friend remark, accepted a cup of coffee with a look that could kill.

Once Thomas was gone, the questions continued, "What time did you arrive at the park, Mr. Carter?"

Andrew scratched his chin and thought a moment. "It was rather late I'm sure. About two, two thirty in the morning. I'd forgotten my watch so it's hard for me to remember, but it was around two when I left the restaurant and it was about a ten minute drive I suppose," he replied, thoughtfully.

Daniels couldn't wait to get his two cents into the conversation, "You make a habit of going for a stroll that late?" he asked smugly.

Andrew resented his tone more than the question itself. "I sometimes have trouble sleeping so I like to walk to tire myself."

Casey cleared his throat and sent Daniels a warning with his hard glare. "You mentioned a restaurant."

"Yes, right here in the hotel downstairs."

"Were you alone?"

"Yes."

Daniels eyes narrowed, "The entire time?"

Andrew was growing more and more impatient. "Yes, that's right. Captain Casey, this is sounding more and more like I'm being accused of something here."

Captain Casey grabbed Daniels arm and silenced him. "Well, the fact is we've got a witness that can place you in the park near the victims just prior to the attack," he said almost in a defensive tone.

Andrew crossed his arms over his chest and eyed the two men with an offense, "I am being accused of something. Yes, I was in the park and may have seen or been in the proximity of those poor unfortunate people, but I don't remember seeing them, nor them seeing me. It is a rather large park, I'm sure they were in the vicinity of just about everyone in the park at one time or another."

"When'd you leave the park, Mr. Carter?" Daniels asked. He could smell that the rich boy across from him knew more than he was telling and he wanted more than anything to catch him in a lie.

Andrew cleared his throat and sighed, "Not long, I was passing through."

Captain Casey wrote something in his notepad and asked, "Did you speak to anyone?"

"Not that I recall."

Casey scratched his chin, and referred to his notes, "Just a few more questions, Mr. Carter. Do you think you're easily recognizable?"

"People recognize me all the time. I try to be as inconspicuous as possible when being out in public for obvious reasons."

"Oh, I don't know, you seem pretty at home in the limelight to me," Daniels cracked, hoping to put him off balance. He was feeling lucky so he let him have it with both barrels.

Andrew stood up and glared down at Daniels, who at the moment looked a bit concerned as to what he might do. "I think

I've been more than helpful," he said. "So, if there's nothing else, I've business to attend to!"

"I think you're right." Captain Casey stood and nodded at Daniels. "I apologize for Officer Daniels. We'll be in touch if we need anything further," he said, pushing Daniels across the room to the doorway.

Andrew followed them out and opened the door. "If you need to see me again feel free, just don't bring this ass with you again. Take the check and offer the reward. Find the killers, Captain," he said, closed the door, and all but collapsed against it. He opened his eyes to find Thomas smiling from the end of the hall.

"Bravo, Master Andrew. Bravo."

Chapter 21

Monica was still in edits when she called Andrew to tell him there was no way she could make it for dinner. Andrew, still rattled by the visit from Captain Casey and his stooge, understood. "I understand, love," he said softly.

Monica recognized his tone. "You sound tired," she said as she pushed the rewind button on the computer in the mobile unit truck.

Andrew rubbed his eyes and took a deep breath. "Yes, but otherwise, I'm fine. Don't worry about me." He was worrying enough for both of them. The perfect world he built for them might be falling down around them, but that was for him to carry, not her. Knowing he was lying to her ate at him, but he couldn't do anything about it.

"But I do worry about you. Maybe you should see a doctor."

"You're overreacting to fatigue and hunger. I'm fine, sweetheart." Another lie, he thought and ignored that they were coming so easily now. "It's nothing that can't be handled with some vitamin B-12 injections, so relax."

Monica wanted to argue, wanted to protest his constant need to downplay her concern for his health, but someone yelled at her from the background. "I've got to get back, honey. I'll try not to be here all night," she said before sending a kiss over the line.

Andrew smiled, "Try hard. I sleep better with you beside me."

He hung up the phone worrying that the house of cards he and Thomas had so carefully constructed was about to come tumbling down. He was all alone in the living room of the suite but Thomas hovered somewhere near by. Nothing ever again would be as simple as the conversation he'd just had with Monica. The police were not what concerned him the most. What concerned him most was his increasing need to feed on humans like his father had done so happily before him.

It was the excitement and the thrill of the kill. Seeing the fear in their eyes as he drained them of their life's blood aroused him. The fight, the line between good and evil was becoming more blurred with every kill. Soon, even Thomas, even his need for a normal life with the woman he loves might not be able to keep him from going over the edge.

His thoughts cleared and he looked up to find Thomas before him with a worried look on his face. "Your thoughts must be awfully dark if I'm to go by the look on your face. You handled the police well, Andrew. There's nothing more for us to do but wait and see what happens next," Thomas said simply in his proper English attitude.

Andrew watched him in amusement. "My Thomas, you're certainly dealing with this bloody disaster much better than I, I'm afraid," he said wrapping his arm around Thomas' shoulder.

"I'll agree things are a bit desperate at the moment, but let's not jump ahead of ourselves," he continued.

"Now that's where you and I disagree, old man. I think that's exactly what we should be doing. We should be making plans instead of sitting around here hoping for the best."

Thomas watched his master carefully as they walked into the kitchen. "I think you might be going to extremes here. They just questioned you, leave now and they'll wonder why," he warned. He planted both hands on his master's shoulders and said, "You'll make them question your reasons for leaving."

Andrew thought about this for a moment. "We can tell them I have business to attend to. That's understandable, even to them."

Thomas let his hands drop to his side. "What about Madam Monica?"

"She'll be thrilled, she thinks I need to rest, and to maybe see a doctor. We'll tell her I'm heading home to take it easy, and leave. I need distance from the authorities to get my head together."

Thomas saw the desperation in his master's eyes, and although he didn't like the timing, he relented. "I'll make the arrangements."

*

The day remaining was filled with uncertainty and tension. Andrew tried to relax, distracting himself with new shipments heading to the site. He should never have come to this city, needed or not. Too many problems faced him now and they could all very well destroy him.

Thomas interrupted his thoughts again when he walked in the room. "I wanted to let you know we can leave whenever you're ready."

Andrew turned around. "Thank you, Thomas. I think I'll wait

for Monica to return. I need to see her before we go," he said thoughtfully.

Thomas nodded. "As you wish," he replied.

"You think I am wrong in leaving, don't you?" he asked, walking over to Thomas.

"Your timing's off, but it's not my decision, Andrew."

"Everything I've worked for these past years is crumbling in my hands, and I'm frightened, Thomas. We managed to keep the monster at bay for so long, I suppose I grew complacent. And, look what's happened. I've made so many wrong choices and I'll live with them, but Monica's the one right choice I've made, and I can't allow this to touch her. Your tricks and potions aren't enough, Thomas. I have become the one thing I've always feared most."

Thomas could say nothing in argument because what his master said was true. "All is not lost, Master Andrew."

Andrew rolled his eyes. "Like bloody hell!"

Thomas laughed, and this surprised Andrew. "You're surprised by my laughter?"

Andrew ambled towards the window to greet the moon. The night was calling to him but he shut it out. "You have to face facts, Thomas. I'm no longer controllable. My father's gone now." He dropped his head and sighed. "I should know the peace I've been cheated out of my whole life, but even damned, he's gotten what he wanted. So maybe it's time for me to join him."

Thomas shook his head quickly. "I will not discuss this, Andrew," he whispered.

"But we must discuss it, Thomas." Andrew turned away from the window to look him in the eye. "I've abided your wishes for too long. I'm out of control. Look around you. Look at all that's happened because I can no longer quiet my urges. There was a time when the good in me could overpower my natural instincts, but no more.

"I take the lives of good people, Thomas. I attack them and drink from them as if they were a means to an end, my own private fountains and it is wrong! I don't discriminate, I could put the poor, or the homeless, out of their misery, and it would still be wrong!" He was yelling now and Thomas could do nothing but let him. "I am a killer! And no matter how innocent my intentions might be, when it's over and the body is at my feet; no matter where the fault lies, I am nothing but a vicious killer!" He strode from the room leaving Thomas struggling to find some words of hope. But there were none.

*

Hours passed with silence between Andrew and Thomas. Thomas excused himself to pack his master's clothes and to take refuge in the master bedroom. Andrew was alone in the living room brooding. It was late and Andrew longed for his wife. He could find hope in her presence, even though he knew he needed time away to protect her. He needed time to think clearly and without emotions that could keep him from making the right choices. He changed into his robe and then he returned to wait for her.

Thomas entered the room with a look of confusion and a shirt gripped in his hands.

Andrew leaned his head back and relaxed. "What's wrong?" he asked.

"This shirt has blood on it," he said flatly, holding out the rumpled piece of clothing.

Andrew sat up and looked at it. "What? Where?"

"On the collar."

"You're mistaken, Thomas," he said bolting to his feet to see for himself.

"See for yourself," he said, tossing the shirt at Andrew.

Andrew looked at the collar and saw it, "Shit! How could I be so stupid?"

"I'll take care of it, Master Andrew," Thomas said, taking the shirt and leaving the room.

*

The door to the suite opened at four o'clock in the morning and Monica was surprised to find her husband waiting in the living room. She went to him, wrapped her arms around his waist, and pulled him to her. "You didn't have to wait up for me, Drew," she said kissing him softly.

He smiled and pulled her into a long kiss that took her breath away. "I couldn't wait to see you. And, I've also got some news," he said dropping onto the sofa.

Monica yawned and stretched her tired muscles. "Good news or bad?" she asked.

Andrew saw the happiness drain from her face. He leaned over and took her face in his hands. "You decide. I have to return home," he said chuckling.

Monica tensed, her hands coming up to cover his. "You're sick, aren't you?"

"No," he assured her with a wink, and then turned her around to massage her tired muscles. "Things are a bit crazed at the office and I must return before chaos ensues."

Relief flooded through her as Andrew's worked the knots from her shoulders. But restlessness took root and she pulled away and went to the window to look out at the city below. "Can you come back when it's settled?"

Andrew joined her at the window and eased her back against him, wrapping his arms around her from behind. "I'll try, but things are quieting down here. You'll probably be home before I have a chance to return."

She smiled. "I hope so."

*

Thomas and Andrew boarded the plane moments before dawn, with Andrew retiring to the master suite. The shades were pulled on windows in anticipation of his arrival, so he lay down on the bed, protected in the darkness, to rest his eyes. They had begun to bother him, and with his stomach in knots and his throat on fire, he felt and looked horrible. Three treatments and several glasses of warmed human blood did nothing to ease his discomfort.

He'd grown accustomed to the warmth of human blood straight from the jugular vein; there was no substitute that was its equal. His thoughts were as painful as anything he was feeling physically, but he could do nothing to quiet them. He thought of the last kiss he shared with Monica and tried to accept that he might never kiss her again. The walls were closing in on him, when he at last fell into a much needed, but troubled sleep.

*

Touchdown at the airport in New York was both a blessing and a curse. It was raining and dark as dusk when they taxied to a stop. A blessing very much needed, considering the curse. A dozen reporters were waiting at the bottom of the stairs. And off course, he looked like hell. His eyes were dull, his hair untidy from sleep, he was pale, weak, and not the gregarious, affable charmer these reporters were used too at all. After all, he was known for his health-conscious attitude and his robust figure, but at the moment he looked frail and unwell.

*

On the ground, Andrew answered a few questions before escaping. When asked about his being pale and looking tired, he answered with the truth. He wasn't feeling well and he had returned home to tend to some business matters and to rest. They let him go without much of a struggle and he was grateful to them and said as much. The car was waiting, he got into the back seat, and Thomas whisked him away.

Riding through the streets of Manhattan, Andrew felt himself growing weaker by the moment. He buzzed Thomas to step on it, and within minutes they were outside the canvassed entryway to the mansion. Thomas helped Andrew from the car and into the mansion, and then up the stairs and into his bed.

Thomas checked his eyes and felt for fever. "I'll be right back, Master Andrew," he said in a soft, soothing voice.

He was barely conscious when Thomas returned and ice cold to the touch. Quickly, Thomas removed his master's clothing and covered him with warm blankets from the closet. Thomas had never seen him so pale before. His master was weakening. The morning's treatments offered no relief and he felt utterly helpless.

The first slivers of panic sent Thomas hurrying to the dark sector. Desperate measures were needed. Without concern for consequences, he retrieved six bottles of human blood from stock and took them up to the master bedroom. The first bottle he administered through IV drip. He prayed as the needle slid into the neck of his master and the blood began its work. Now there was nothing left to do but wait.

Two hours passed with Andrew in a deep sleep and Thomas by his side. His color improved but he was still too weak. Other things were happening as well. Monica called to check in but didn't want to wake him if he was finally sleeping. Captain Casey had phoned informing him that he was coming to New York to ask Andrew some more questions. There was new information that needed addressing.

Thomas managed to put him off for a few days, saying his master was ill and could not receive visitors at the moment. Captain Casey agreed to wait, but Thomas knew from his tone, the man wasn't convinced his master was ill. Thomas only hoped three days would be enough time to get his master back on his feet.

Andrew woke up early in the morning after twenty-seven hours of unconsciousness. Still weak and lethargic, he managed to mumble a request for water and Thomas gave in. Within seconds of swallowing the sip, he was out again. Thomas laid a cold compress on Andrew's forehead and checked the IV line that was feeding his master the human blood he so desperately needed before going back to his reading.

His color was improving but Andrew sleeping so deeply worried Thomas. He rarely left his master's side. Once he saw his master was resting comfortably, he left the room to attend to some urgent matters downstairs.

The cleaners were coming to pick up the laundry, and with it, the only piece of evidence linking his master to murder. As a man used to respecting the law, this illegal act weighed heavily on his conscious. But, Thomas had to protect his master, at any and all costs.

The laundry room was to the left of the kitchen, and Thomas went through the door separating them like a man on a mission. He'd taken the option of hiding the evidence in plain sight. Tangled in with the soiled and dirty laundry from California was a crucial connection between his master and the murders there. Quickly, he went through the clothes on the floor until he found what he was looking for. As he held the shirt in his hands, it was hard to believe the danger it held, that a simple shirt could be capable of destroying someone's life. But, it held that power, like it or not.

The blood was barely noticeable, just a small smear on the right side of the collar. A spot really, nothing much at all until you considered the weight it would carry in an investigation. He'd learned a lot in all his years among the dead, and the shrewd wheels of experience were turning. He should destroy it, now. Before more questions were asked. Before their cleaner remembered six weeks down the road, when the smell of fame and money got the better of him, the blood he'd removed from a suspects clothing.

If Captain Casey was coming this far for questions, he had a damn good reason, and no doubt, an ulterior motive. He'd have connected the dots by now too; the similar killings here in New York for one, and only God knew what else. If a search warrant came into play, they had to be ready. Thirty minutes later Thomas went to the dark sector with the shirt, a bottle of bourbon, and a box of matches.

With the problem solved, and the potential evidence reduced to ash, Thomas was back at his master's bedside in time to hang the third bag of blood in the series of five running to the IV. He adjusted the feed on the line and checked the needle in his master's throat. Then, he sat down in the chair at the foot of the bed, and settled in on the fifth chapter of his book for the long haul.

Ten pages later, Andrew moved his head and called for Thomas. He was beside him taking his hand in his own in an instant. "There, there, lad, I'm here," he whispered, ringing cool water from a cloth for Andrew's head.

Then the moment Thomas had been waiting for finally arrived. His master opened his eyes. Thomas was smiling. "How are you feeling?"

He found it impossible to focus so he closed his eyes for a minute and opened them again slowly. "I've felt better, old man," he rasped and began coughing violently.

Thomas held a glass of water to his mouth and tipped some down his throat. "Easy now." When the coughing stopped, Thomas lowered his master's head back down to the pillow. "You're very weak, but your color is improving and you're body's warming."

Andrew turned his head to look at Thomas, "I'm in trouble."

Thomas smiled. "Not anymore, Master Andrew."

Andrew tried to pull himself up in bed and collapsed for his trouble. "Oh, I feel just bloody wonderful," he muttered weakly. "What's happening?"

"Captain Casey is coming to New York."

He closed his eyes, groaning, "When?"

"Tomorrow afternoon."

"What does he want now?" He was becoming more alert now and he didn't care for the dose of reality he was being exposed to.

Thomas let out a breath and walked across the room to the closed window. Not a drop of natural light made it through the thick curtains. Lamps at the sides of the bed lit the room. "He has a few more questions for you."

"I've got nothing to say to him. I already answered his damned questions, Thomas. Did you tell him I am ill, and that I'm not accepting visitors?" Even weakened, his voice became harsh.

Thomas walked over, placed a reassuring palm to his cheek. "It wasn't a request. Calm down or I'll sedate you. You must rest. You'll need your wits about you when he arrives."

Andrew raised himself on his elbows and sent the room spinning around him. Still he had the mind to yell, "Thomas, what in bloody hell are you thinking?"

Thomas raised his hand to calm his master as he saw the color begin to drain from his face. "I'm thinking that if I said no, he'd show up in an official capacity."

Andrew lowered his head and closed his eyes. He could feel the vomit churning in the pit of his stomach. "Well this is still my home and if I don't want him in it, then in it he shall not be!" he yelled louder than he wanted too and felt as if a nail had been driven into his skull.

Thomas sat down on the bed and patted his hand. "Screaming like a raving lunatic isn't going to solve anything, and you need your rest."

"I'm fine. I'm feeling much more like my old self."

Thomas chuckled and said, "That's because I'm feeding you whole blood through an IV."

"There really is no use in fighting it anymore, is there?"

"Right now it's important that we get you on your feet again."

"It's time to let me go," Andrew said seriously.

Thomas avoided Andrew's eyes and said, "It's not important now, just rest." He couldn't discuss this with him. Letting him go was impossible for Thomas to consider, and even more so to admit to. Andrew accepted this option much sooner and without regret, leaving Thomas alone in his uncertainty. He wasn't ready to let him go.

"We both know what this means," Andrew continued when Thomas turned to face him again, holding up the IV line. "This means I have regressed fully to the other side. There are no more magic potions that will fix me, Thomas."

Thomas heard every word but he still denied them. "One day at a time, Andrew, one problem at a time. I need time and your trust."

Andrew felt for the man fighting to keep him. "Take care of me and you take care of all the problems."

Thomas slammed his fist into the nightstand. "I don't have to listen to this!" he shouted, striding for the door and leaving the room, slamming the door behind him.

Chapter 22

Silence filled the room and it was enough to drive what little peace remained from Andrew's mind. He'd upset Thomas and he'd not meant to. But knowing that did not change anything, Thomas was hurting and he was alone.

The walls started closing in around him and he felt the familiar uneasiness return to smother him in his weakened state. Thomas needed to face the reality of the situation and deal with it, whether he liked it or not. Things were out of control and nothing could regain it. Andrew didn't have the strength to guide events down the correct path.

His tightly guarded world was unraveling around him, and then there was Monica. What about her? She loved him blindly, and he had accepted that and lived with the guilt brought on by it, but no more. Once the truth was out, she would be in more pain than anyone deserved in a lifetime, and he would be the cause.

He would have to look into her eyes and see the pain and that would be worse than anything the law could do to him. Minutes ticked away to hours. It was enough time to think of all the happiness he and Monica had shared and about how dangerously close they were coming to losing it.

Captain Casey wasn't about to let this drop, so what could he do? He couldn't kill him outright. That would only bring about more suspicion. Not to mention it would be wrong as hell. But Andrew no longer had the luxury of obeying his conscience.

It was time to save his ass. He sat up in bed and collected himself. Closing his eyes, he prayed for the room to stop spinning. Moments later, not only had the room stopped its swirling dance, but his stomach finally had a bottom. Edgy, and hating being confined to bed, he put his feet on the floor and slowly pushed himself off the bed.

It felt strange standing, as if the legs he was standing on were wooden, but he managed it. He looked himself over and found the body he was in, foreign and unrecognizable. Then he realized he was tethered to his bed by the IV. Disgusted, he pulled the needle from his neck and reached for his robe. He tightened the belt around his waist and stumbled to the door for spite. Andrew was weaker than he thought on his feet so it was a moment before he opened the door and moved, trembling, into the hall.

He gripped the banister with his hand and started down the staircase. Each step brought him closer to his goal and he was never as happy to reach the bottom then he was at that moment. He placed his unsure footing on firm ground. "Thomas? Thomas, where are you? You're still not pouting over our little disagreement, are you?"

"You mean the one where you want me to kill you?" Thomas asked, appearing out of nowhere. "What the devil are you doing out of bed?" Annoyed, he went to steady his master before he ended up flat on his face.

Andrew looked at him and grinned. "I'm already dead, old man. Think of it as a mere technicality," he said with a chuckle, hoping it would lighten the mood. It did not.

Thomas sneered at his master, "You know damn good and well what I mean, Andrew."

The smile disappeared from Andrew's face. "Yes, Thomas, I do," he admitted.

Thomas walked with Andrew into the living room and over to the sofa. He looked as if his feet were about to go out from under him. "What the hell are you doing to yourself? You need the IV and the entire series of the treatment. Especially in the condition you are in," he grumbled half under his breath but loud enough to be heard.

Andrew let out a deep breath. It took him a moment to answer. His head was pounding. Thomas was right this was not a smart move. He felt as if a truck had hit him. "You know what they say, if the mountain won't come to…" He suddenly felt a rush of vampire instincts run through him and it sent chills up his spine. It hadn't been the first time he felt them during this episode but it was the first time they didn't sicken him as they should have. This time they felt, dare he even think the word, natural.

When Andrew and Thomas both realized that they were solving nothing with their constant bickering, it was Andrew who decided to cry uncle and admit defeat. He didn't have the strength to fight anymore. The argument ended and he returned to his bed. He needed peace and quiet and a shield from Thomas' wounded eyes. When he helped Andrew back to bed, there was a silence that spoke more than either of them ever could.

Tucked safely back in his bed, with Thomas brooding

downstairs, the atmosphere Andrew had been yearning for finally settled around him. Like a blanket blocking out a stiff wind, many thoughts flowed in and out of his mind. He found it hard to keep them straight in his head. Hooked up to the IV, he floated. Each thought bringing him another step closer to the edge of the invisible cliff he had himself perched on for years.

It was as if he was trapped with no means of escape. He didn't want to face the fact that what kept him living so freely for so many years wasn't genius as much as it was blind luck; blind luck that was now at an all time low. He rested his head on his down pillow and closed his eyes. The pain in his head was no match for the torment that ripped at his heart.

So much emotional pain coursed through his body that even his endless years on this earth could not provide him with enough time to right the wrongs he has committed. Nothing would truly undo the damage of so long ago when with his first look at the world through his vampire eyes and did the unthinkable. He took her in his arms, in all her innocence as she looked at him with her trusting eyes, eyes filled with nothing but love for him, and did the unforgivable. Sank his teeth into her throat and drank from her.

Taking her blood, and with it, her life. Filling his life with all the guilt and madness one person could handle.

Andrew could remember that time as clearly as if it were all happening right in front of him again. A vampire never forgets the instant he passes through the veil between mortal and immortal. And while all memories of being human remain precious, like treasures hidden away for safe keeping, it's the memory of entry into living death, and that one alone, which burns brighter than all the rest.

Of all Andrew's sins, he counted his first as the most damning and unforgivable. He took her trust and used it against her. He stood over her when he finished with her and watched her life ebb away.

Andrew watched with horror. The horror in her eyes as she realized she was dying. The horror knowing it was at the hands of the man she loved the most in the world. And, it was with her final breath that she ruined him with the question he could not answer then, nor in all the years since.

"Why?"

Now as this memory played itself out in his mind, he remained grateful. That her death had come swiftly, that he'd had the presence of mind in his state to pray for her soul, and though it was futile, his own.

Dark memories were coming at him full force now. The walls pressed in closer around him. The air thickened and became stiff. Andrew felt like he was breathing through a straw. His skin grew clammy and his head pounded out a merciless rhythm in his temples.

Then, just when he thought he was about to pass out and be spared any more torture, her spirit appeared at the foot of the bed. Andrew blinked, hoping that he saw her but knowing that he was mistaken. He was asleep and this was a dream. It had to be. But, she was right there in front of him. He was seeing her again—her beautiful, fair, raven hair falling to her hips.

She was as enchanting as he remembered. Although, there was an ethereal, golden glow about her now that he supposed came from heaven. He gaped at her in disbelief, his eyes filling. It truly was Elizabeth that he was seeing.

No matter how tightly Andrew closed his eyes, when he opened them she was there. Watching him, smiling at him, words failed him. He watched as her smile brightened, Elizabeth was enjoying his temporary loss of speech.

She moved and came around the left side of the bed, she wasn't walking but instead she was hovering. Terrified in one breath, exhilarated in the next, he tried to back away. She saw the fear in his eyes and laughed. The sound surprised them both. Her laugh still sounded like he remembered. An easy, infectious lilt that sent chills up his spine. He hadn't heard her laugh in so long, and God, how he had missed it.

They stared at each other in silence at first. Elizabeth could see that her presence troubled and perhaps frightened him, and that wasn't what she had intended. Andrew shivered as if he was chilled. Wanting to ease his fears, she spoke to him. "Don't be frightened, Andrew. I mean you no harm." She spoke with sincerity and compassion but he was still uncertain.

Her voice was as sweet as he remembered, soft like velvet. He felt sweat running down his neck. "Are you really here, Elizabeth?" he asked clearing his throat. "Or have I finally lost my mind?"

She smiled softly at him. "I'm here. It's not your imagination or your mind playing tricks on you. You're sane, or as sane as you ever were. I'm here to help you, Andrew."

"Help me?" he was puzzled.

"Yes, Andrew."

Andrew was amazed and confused. "Why would you want to help me...." his voice trailed off, "after what I did to you?" He wanted to know why. He needed to know why.

"Because you're a good man, Andrew. I also know your intentions were honest, and are still. You didn't mean to hurt me."

Andrew shook his head. "How do you know of my intentions, then or now? I've done horrible things. Things that have damned me forever," he said in disgust.

"And you've done many good deeds as well, Andrew. I've come here to make sure you know that. And, that I've forgiven you, I did long ago. You need to release yourself from your guilt and move on."

"How can you possibly say that to me?" He was stunned by the compassion given to him freely.

"It's what's keeping you from living, isn't it?"

"Simple guilt is not the only thing haunting me, I can promise you of that. I've done terrible things to many innocent people, whose only crime was being in the wrong place at the wrong time."

Elizabeth reached down and touched his arm. "I know what you've done, but I also know the man here with me now. What you did was wrong, but it was also unintentional. In your heart you know that is true," she reminded him.

Andrew felt the warmth of her touch and shivered. He laughed at her words. "Good man or not, I am a killer. And what is worse is I don't know how to stop," he said angrily.

"I have to go now. But remember, Andrew, you are only as evil as your intentions."

The air stopped dead in his lungs. "My mother used to tell me that. Where did you hear that, Elizabeth?"

She smiled again as she moved away, "From your mother. She sends her love to you, Andrew, now and always."

"You've seen my mother?" he asked as tears welled up in his eyes. "I miss her terribly."

She smiled. "I see her all the time. We both know that you have within you the power to regain control of your life again."

And with those final words, Elizabeth disappeared as mysteriously as she arrived.

Andrew was alone again, with his thoughts, and with his fears.

*

The bitterness and resentment Thomas felt for Reginald Carter, at that very moment, never burned brighter. It consumed him. He worked with him for ten years prior to the birth of Andrew and during those years, he could always sense that something wasn't right but he could never put his finger on it. The early years with Andrew in childhood, there were things happening in the cities of England and these events left the police baffled.

Reginald was often away on business and it wasn't until many years later that Thomas realized that Reginald's business brought on those strange happenings. And as he thought about it now, he wished he could have seen it all more clearly and stopped the evil from continuing. Maybe there wouldn't be such fall-out now.

With the police set to arrive tomorrow, Thomas had no idea where events would take them, so he resigned himself to waiting. Patience had never been one of his strongest points, not when it came to his master. But, he grappled for it now because it was needed. Maybe the only thing they had going for them was his master's physical decline, Thomas thought as he finished preparing Andrew's tray.

His heart ached as he walked through the kitchen door and into the dining room, through the living room, the hall, and up the stairs. He was tired but passed it off as he reached the top of the stairs. What he needed was a good night's sleep but he was smart enough to know he wasn't going to get it this night or maybe the next. There wasn't time for sleep. This thought alone made him even more exhausted.

Thomas knocked lightly on the door hoping to find his master sleeping. His hopes fell when he heard his master say, "Come in." He opened the door, balancing the tray with one hand while he closed the door behind him with the other.

"You look as if you've seen a ghost," Thomas said once he got a good look at him. "Are you feeling worse?" he asked, setting the tray down on the nightstand next to the bed. "You don't feel warm," he said, feeling his forehead with the palm of his hand.

Andrew's hair was wet and his robe was a fresh one from the closet. He had taken a shower to help his nerves. It isn't every day he gets a visit from his dead lover. He was convinced he was bordering on lunacy. "You wouldn't believe me if I told you," he whispered up at Thomas, unsure if he believed it himself.

Thomas watched his master carefully. "Try me," he said suspiciously.

Andrew scratched his cheek and laughed. His eyes looked off somewhere far away. He was not in the room. He was somewhere else, somewhere dark. "While you were downstairs I had a visitor," He shrugged, "It was quite amazing really."

Thomas was confused. "What are you talking about? If you had a visitor, I would have known," he said, certain that his master had had a dream and mistaken it for reality.

"Not that kind of visitor, old man," he said shaking his head in disbelief.

Thomas studied Andrew's expression. "Is there some other kind? Did they fly up here on wings?"

"That's exactly what I'm saying, Thomas." Andrew looked him in the eye. "It was Elizabeth. She came to me."

Pity and sympathy filled the old man's eyes. There was still so much guilt and pain in his master. "Elizabeth is dead, Andrew," Thomas said, checking the IV, swabbing Andrew's neck in preparation for injecting the needle. He wasn't getting enough blood and he was hallucinating. "I'm putting the IV back in. You need to finish the treatment."

Andrew was shaking his head again. "I'm not crazy. I know damn and bloody well what I saw, Thomas!" he said defensively.

"Alright," he replied, but slid the needle into his neck anyway. "What did she want?"

"She said she came to forgive me."

With a lift of his grey brow, he adjusted the feed on the line, "And did she?"

"I suppose so but I don't feel any different about it."

Thomas patted his master's arm. "It's time to move past all that. You can't change it," he said warmly.

Andrew took a deep breath. "That's what she said."

"Then perhaps you should listen to her," Thomas said, setting the tray on Andrew's lap.

*

Sometime after midnight Andrew awakened. The pain in his throat returned to remind him he was not the human he pretended to be. So he lay there while his throat ached and his mind spun in his head. He needed to feed and not from some tube running in his throat. Andrew was more vampire than man now, and there could be no denying it. No matter how much he wanted to.

He was what his father had made him and there was no changing that. No amount of Thomas' remedies would end the pain he was feeling. And even if the problem were solved, it would only be temporary. A year here, five years there, only to return stronger the next time and there would be a next time. As sure as the sun rose every morning and set every night. Forever is a very long time for a vampire.

The phone rang an hour later. Andrew picked it up, thankful for something more to do than stare out at the night from his bed. The voice was music to his ears and calm to his heart. "Monica, it's good to hear your voice, Love."

She was exhausted but hearing his voice picked her right up. "It's good to hear yours too. I'm sorry to wake you, but I needed to hear your voice."

"I wasn't sleeping," he said with a husky voice. "I can't sleep without you here. How's things going? Do you need anything?"

"No, I'm wrapping up here tomorrow afternoon. Can you send the plane for me?" Monica said with a deep breath. "I can't wait to get home. I can't wait to sleep eight hours in a row for that matter."

Andrew sat up and smiled, "Absolutely. Is everything alright, Love?" he asked with concern. He could hear it in the timbre of her voice.

Monica wiped the tear from her cheek and gripped the receiver tighter in her hand. "Yes," she lied. "Everything's fine, I'm just tired." It was the first time she'd ever lied to him, but she didn't want to talk about it over the phone.

His smile was gone, and the nagging feeling remained. He knew her too well. Something was wrong and he wished more than anything that he could hold her. "You're sure?"

Her eyes filled up with tears as she strained to keep her voice even. "I don't want you to worry, Drew. I just need some sleep."

Andrew rested his head against his pillow, "Get some sleep then. I'll see you tomorrow night." But he knew it wasn't tiredness he was sensing, but pain. "I love you, Monica."

She closed her eyes and felt herself shaking, "I love you too," she whispered and hung up the phone.

*

Morning returned and with it so too the feeling of uneasiness that settled on him the day before. It almost suffocated Andrew now as he lay in bed trying to find the strength to face the day. Not only did he have to tolerate being probed by Captain Casey, yet again, but also, and more importantly he had to worry about what was going on with Monica. She'd be home tonight and see him in this condition and that would only make things that much more complicated.

Thomas sent the plane off early that morning and he too worried about how Andrew's condition would affect Monica. She would most certainly want to know why she wasn't called, and he would have to come up with a good reason. But the issue that lay most heavily on his mind was their impending visitor for the day, Captain Casey. It did work to their advantage that Andrew was still bedridden and looked about as sick as a person could.

If things got out of hand, Thomas could use it as an excuse to end the questioning. Other than that, there was very little to be hopeful about as far as Thomas was concerned.

Andrew sat up and put his feet on the floor. He steadied himself on the edge of the bed and forced himself to his feet. His head felt like a paperweight and left him feeling sluggish. He closed his eyes and took a deep breath. He was hoping he would feel like his old self after Thomas came and administered the last of the five treatments. Thomas had warned him that he would not feel the effects until he'd received all five pints of blood. So now, all he had to do was wait.

*

After breakfast and a shower, Andrew dressed in a clean robe, and climbed back into bed with Thomas as his shadow, insisting on helping him. He was afraid his master would fall and hit his head in his weakened state. And, they needed to discuss a few things before Captain Casey arrived.

Thomas could see Andrew was nervous, though he tried to hide it. "Just relax, Master Andrew, I'm sure he just wants to clear up a few things with you," he said, hoping he sounded convincing to Andrew, if not himself. "What will be will be."

Andrew looked at Thomas with disbelief and laughed darkly, "Who're you trying to bullshit?"

"Okay," Thomas smirked, fluffing the pillows behind his

master's head and back. "You're right, but you have to be relaxed and calm when he arrives or he'll be suspicious," Thomas replied, sitting in the chair next to the bed.

"He's already suspicious, Thomas. Do you think he'd waste his time coming here otherwise?" Andrew said with his voice filled with tension. "I'm just bloody grateful you got that shirt out of here when you did."

"There's nothing to justify granting Casey a search warrant," Thomas replied trying to allay Andrew's concerns.

"Why come this far without one?"

"We'll know soon enough."

"Besides, as concerned as I am about that, I'm concerned about something else even more," Andrew continued, allowing some of the edge to his voice to disappear.

Thomas smoothed his master's blankets, trying to make him more comfortable. "I know you're worried about Madam Monica, but you'll just have to wait for her to arrive to put your mind at ease. It's very important that you stay focused. It's crucial actually," he insisted.

"Yes, yes, Thomas."

"Might I suggest you get some rest before our guest arrives?" Thomas wondered aloud, walking to the door.

"You might suggest it but it won't work. I've got too much on my mind to sleep. Besides, it will work to our advantage if I look as badly as I feel," he joked.

Thomas laughed. "It might at that," he said, pulling the door closed behind him.

*

Monica was a wreck waiting for the editing on the final report. Her thoughts wandered, her heart ached. Work, no matter its importance, was the last thing on her mind. So much devastation around her, she looked at the ruins of the clinic, tense, hands fisting and releasing at her sides.

Most of the rubble was hauled away and being stored as evidence. Most of the bodies were recovered too. And she had dealt with it all professionally. But now, there was devastation within her as well and she was at a loss as to how to pick up the pieces and move forward.

It wasn't fair, she'd been telling herself over the last two days. It did nothing to ease the pain, nothing to lessen the loss. She knew what was keeping her from picking up the phone and calling Drew. He deserved to hear it face to face. So, she could comfort him, and he could comfort her.

This wasn't a business deal, it was personal and it affected them both. This would surely devastate him as it had her. How would he handle it? And, how could she help him when she couldn't make sense of it herself?

The plane would have her back in New York by midnight and she could go home with Drew and feel his arms around her. Maybe then, she could pull herself together, she thought. But, when he saw her, one look, and he would know. Monica took out her compact, and in the mirror, surveyed the damage. The bags under her eyes were subtle but telling.

Telling of the last two sleepless nights, the sadness she felt with every breath. Oh yes, her husband would know. And he would want to fix it for her. Then she would tell him. But she had to make sure she wouldn't go to pieces. Monica had to be strong, for herself as well as for Drew.

At least she had the flight to let it sink in. And they would survive it. As long as they had each other, they could survive anything. It would take time, of course it would, but they would survive it.

*

At one fifteen that afternoon, the doorbell rang and a feeling similar to being struck by lightning washed through Thomas as he walked to the door. He opened it with a smile. As expected, Captain Casey stood on the other side with a smile just as bright and just as false as the one that greeted him. "Good afternoon, Captain Casey, please come in," Thomas said, as he stepped back to let him in.

Captain Casey nodded his head and walked in. "I've read about this place, but I guess you have to see it to believe it, huh?" he asked, looking around in wonder. "Does this entire building belong to Mr. Carter?"

Thomas smiled. "Yes, his offices are on the top three floors," he replied politely.

"This is a lot of space," Captain Casey said, craning his head to look past Thomas.

Thomas still had a plastic smile in place. "Master Carter requires it. He likes his space."

Captain Casey straightened his suit jacket and rocked back on his heels. He could think of nothing more to say for the sake of polite conversation. He stayed silent while a dozen private thoughts went through his head.

Thomas enjoyed watching him make a complete fool of himself. Standing in front of him with that 'you don't have a clue about what I'm thinking' look on his face, he wanted to get this over with as soon as possible. "Would you care for something to drink or would you prefer I go and tell Master Carter that you've arrived?" Thomas asked, determined to move things along.

"I'll pass on the drink, but thanks. Just let him know I'm here."

"Very well." Thomas started up the staircase. "I'll only be a moment."

"No problem," Casey replied.

*

Thomas knocked on Andrew's door and went in without waiting for a reply. "He's here, it's show time," he said softly. At least he hadn't lied outright, Andrew had been napping and he looked like hell.

Andrew pulled himself up in the bed with some assistance and propped himself against the headboard. His eyes were red and his color was worse than it had been an hour earlier. "I feel like bloody hell. When can I have the rest of the treatment?"

Thomas fluffed the pillows behind Andrew and straightened the covers. "As soon as our guest leaves. Here's some of the private stock, it's pure so go easy when you drink it," he said, handing him a black coffee cup.

*

Thomas returned for Captain Casey after a few moments and found him wandering through the living room. "Come with me, Master Carter will see you now."

The staircase seemed enormous to Casey as he walked up the stairs behind an individual he didn't know but had already decided he didn't like. But at the moment he was only interested in what Andrew Carter had to say. He guessed Carter would be helpful in the least helpful way possible.

It had been Daniels who went to the commissioner and pushed for this visit, not him. His heart just wasn't in it. Because what did they really have to support suspicion of the great Andrew Carter?

Daniels had a bee in his bonnet and was pushing to be the commissioner's lapdog. Daniels was a little pissed off to be left behind on this trip.

Casey would have loved to send the young over-achiever in his place, but the commissioner had over ruled him. The problem was Daniels was too pushy for his own good and made more enemies then friends. With no one he could use as a sounding board at the end of the day when things got tough at work.

This left Casey with two options. Put up with tight-ass remarks or drum him out of the force. But as much as it pained him to admit it, Daniels was a good cop. And an even better cop at a distance, in someone else's daily orbit. As he was reaching the end of the upstairs hallway, he was happy to have made the trip without him.

Just when he was sure that he couldn't lift his feet for another step, they reached a closed mahogany door. Thomas gave him a second to straighten his coat again, and then he knocked. "It's me, Master Andrew."

"Come in," a small, tired voice said through the door.

Thomas opened the door and the game began. "Master Andrew, Captain Casey," he said as he ushered Casey through the doorway.

Andrew smiled sleepily. "Yes, of course, please come in and make yourself comfortable, Captain. Take a seat," he said softly.

His eyes swept the large, airy room. Rich wood, deep blues and creams for colors, a sofa, and fireplace. Money to burn, he thought, and chose the chair nearest to the bed. "Nice room," he said making eye contact with his host for the first time since he came in the room.

"Thank you. My wife and I like it a great deal."

"Where is Mrs. Carter?"

"Still on assignment in California. I'm afraid Mr. Philips keeps her pretty busy. The bombing was awful, but she's wrapping up her story as we speak," Andrew said, as he rested his head on his pillow.

"Well, I'm sure she'd like to be here—with you so sick and everything—anyway," Casey said as he took a pen and notebook from his jacket pocket.

Andrew took a drink from the coffee cup in his shaky hand. "I'm sure you're right, but I hope to have turned the corner by the time she returns."

"You don't want her to worry?"

"She's got enough on her mind right now. And this isn't the first time I've had one of these episodes, and it probably won't be the last I'm afraid."

"I've read up on you a little and your health problems. Sorry it takes so much out of you."

"I've grown used to these bouts. I'll be back on my feet in a couple of days. Care for something to drink? Thomas will be happy to get you whatever you like."

Casey looked at Thomas, who was standing directly behind and to the left of his chair. "I'd appreciate a cola if you have it," he said, in an attempt to get some private time with Carter.

Thomas smiled. "I'm sure I can come up with one," he said. He nodded to Andrew and left the room.

Andrew watched the man in the chair across from him. The man who came so far to make his life more difficult, and he hated him. For all the pressure he was bringing to his life and for all the naive, preconceived notions he was so obviously harboring towards him. Andrew was disgusted just by Casey's existence in the world. A world they were destined to share.

What disgusted him more, however, was that he was sitting there propped up by pillows and willpower, with the most artificial grin on his face. And, sadly, the man was swallowing it whole. He took another sip from the mug that was still in his hand, letting the thick warm nectar slide over his tongue and down his throat.

"You've come a long way just to ask me a few questions, Captain Casey. Please, tell me how I can help you?" he asked with false sincerity. He studied the man's eyes with a hard stare.

Casey began feeling uncomfortable under his host's penetrating stare. He squirmed in his chair, crossed his legs, and refocused. "I wanted to clear up a few things, Mr. Carter. Namely, the killings here in Central Park."

He rubbed his chin thoughtfully, for the benefit of his guest. He wasn't actually giving any thought to the question at all. He shrugged, "What does one have to do with the other," replied Andrew.

"That's right around the corner from here, isn't it?" He wrote down every word. "Were you walking on those nights too?"

"What're you implying?"

Casey look confused, he referred to his notes, "Nothing. But considering the nearly identical aspects in both the California and New York cases, you could see why we want to eliminate even the slightest common denominator?"

Andrew took a labored breath. He wondered where the hell Thomas had run off to and what was taking him so long. "This common denominator you speak of, is me?"

Casey's eyes narrowed. "Just crossing my T's and dotting my I's, Mr. Carter. Getting back to your walk, you weren't concerned? I mean, the late hour, in a place secluded by trees, off away from high traffic areas. You've got the look of a guy not strapped for cash. You live in a city like mine the parks become a dangerous place by midnight."

Andrew thought a moment and said, "Well, I'd had a good deal to drink, I suppose my judgment was off. However, I'm capable of protecting myself, Captain. I was trying to tire myself so I could sleep. The bombing had been horrendous and there was so much to be done to help. I was exhausted. I was shaken by the amount of devastation. I needed to walk it off."

"Yes, it is terrible. The loss and pain the city and its people have had to suffer," Casey agreed, already thinking ahead to the next question. He was laying the ground work.

"Anything else?"

"Just a few more things," he continued, pulling on his chin. "You say you're capable of protecting yourself and I'm sure that's true, you're a big guy." He filed that information away for the moment. "You don't go out much, a man of your obvious wealth and resources would choose to remain a recluse. Why?"

"You disappoint me, Captain. You say you've read all about me. I should think you'd know all about my medical history," he replied snidely. "And I go out often. I just use my car when I do. I'm a private person, yes, but I have to be in my position. And as I said, there are health reasons involved."

"Yes, I've read about your skin allergies," Casey shifted gears, preparing to set a trap. "And I guess a private man would expect to find plenty of privacy in a park at such late hour. A man fitting your description was seen talking with the two of the victims, do you recall that?"

Andrew shook his head. He had to be careful, very careful. "I'm afraid I don't, but I'm sure if I came across them I would have spoken to them. I was raised to be a polite person, to be courteous. I'm sure I exchanged pleasantries and nothing more," he said. He crossed his arms over his chest, quickly growing tired of questions designed to incriminate him.

Captain Casey studied his notes again. He looked up to find Thomas standing beside him, tray in hand with a cola and a glass of crushed ice on it. "Thank you," he said, taking both the glass and the cola off the tray.

Thomas smiled and tipped his head, "Certainly."

Casey took a gulp of the soda, sighed rubbed his mouth and pondered. "We, that is to say, the investigating officers, discovered a hair on one of the victim's clothing. It matches yours," he said slowly, getting to his feet.

Chapter 23

Casey waited. He searched Carter's face for some breach in his composure. Some tell-tale sign that would give him away, but he didn't flinch. Perhaps my instincts are right, he thought, and Andrew Carter was innocent.

But Andrew was in shock and hoped he covered well. He caught sight of Thomas out of the corner of his eye and prayed his face was as unreadable. Captain Casey dropped the bombshell, and his heart leapt into his throat. "Excuse me?"

And there it was, Casey decided. The abject look of confusion in the man's eyes, or was it terror? Or simply the result of his sickness? It didn't matter. He played his card and would have to see it through. "In color and length," he replied, shifting his weight from one foot to the other. "The hair in evidence matches your color and length."

Thomas released the breath he held in his lungs and waited for his master's next move. Color and length in and of itself was hardly proof of anything. It was a test. And he prayed his master could sense this and respond accordingly.

"This is what you've based your trip on?" Andrew wondered aloud. "I'm fairly certain there are others in your city with black short hair."

Casey smiled, lowered himself back into the chair. His opinion of this man's guilt or innocence would be strongly affected by this man's next response. "Of course there is, Mr. Carter. What would you say if I asked you to provide the LAPD with a hair sample for comparison?"

"I'd say the next conversation you're going to be having is with my attorney," Andrew said flatly. "Good day, Captain Casey."

*

He was looking guiltier by the second and he knew it. Andrew's headache had returned without mercy. Monica would arrive home within the next couple of hours. So, he laid his head against the pillow and closed his eyes to rest as the last of the fourth bag of blood pumped into his veins.

There were several things going through his mind. He couldn't go to prison. It wouldn't kill him, but it would expose him. He would waste away without his treatments and death would never release him from the torture. And, there was Monica to consider. What would she say to him when the truth came out? What would she do without him? His stomach filled with knots just thinking about how she would react. Andrew's thoughts began to mix and he was finding it hard to concentrate. His eyes grew heavy, his thoughts grew dim and faded into the background.

*

Thomas was busy downstairs in the living room when the phone rang. He put down his dust cloth and walked over to the bar, and picked up the phone. "Hello," he said.

The static on the line meant that it was long distance. "Is this the Carter residence?" asked a very Irish and very unfamiliar voice.

"It is. May I ask who's calling?"

"My name is Douglas O'Neal. May I please speak to Mrs. Carter?"

Thomas wrote the name down on a pad beside the phone. "I'm afraid Madam Carter is away on business, can I ask what this is about, Sir?"

"I'm sorry, that's confidential. Can you tell me when she's returning?"

"Sometime this evening, can I take a message?"

"Please tell her that Douglas O'Neal phoned and that I'll try back later."

Thomas wondered what this was about but didn't question the man further. "Yes, I'll see that she gets the message as soon as she returns." When he hung up the phone, a sinking feeling fluttered in the pit of his stomach. "Now who might that be?" he asked himself.

*

The rain falling outside as the plane made its way across the night sky matched Monica's mood as she struggled to make herself comfortable. She had hoped to feel better by now but tears spilled over and she wondered if she would ever feel whole again. She was about to arrive home and crush her husband with news that a week before she never would have expected to receive. Wishing couldn't change reality, though she would have traded anything if it only could. What could she say to him to make it hurt less and how could she help feeling that she failed him?

Monica clasped her hands together and put them in her lap, trying to calm herself. She couldn't face Drew like this, or she would go to pieces in his arms and everything would come out wrong. Days ago, she'd been given the assignment of a lifetime and couldn't wait to get started. Now the story of a lifetime was complete and just when she should have been the happiest she'd ever been in her life, she couldn't remember ever feeling this much pain in her life.

*

Casey wasn't returning to California like he'd said. Instead, he was making himself right at home in a hotel room at the Peabody across town from the Carter building. Andrew Carter had bulked at a simple request. Would an innocent man have anything to fear? Twenty five years on the job had him seeing a red flag.

He laid his tired body across the bed and took a long, deep breath. Sleep tempted him but he had to check in at the station. Sitting up on the bed, he picked up the phone. It rang three times before it was answered, and the voice on the other end was very familiar. "Mayor Banes," he said in a honey dipped voice. "I wasn't expecting you to answer my phone."

"More like prayed I wouldn't, I'm sure. What the hell are you doing in New York City, Captain? Aren't I keeping you busy enough around here?"

"You keep me plenty busy, Sir. I'm following a lead in the park killings. The commissioner green-lighted it," he said in his own defense.

"I know all about your lead, Captain, and you're wasting time. There're leads here that are getting colder by the minute."

Casey smoothed the crease in his forehead. His boss' boss was a real jackass. "I think there might be something to this Carter connection of Daniels, Sir."

"You didn't seem to think so a week ago. What changed your mind?"

"His hair sample matched, Sir, we're just waiting on the DNA to confirm it."

"You mean the sample Daniels obtained without Carter's knowledge? And, by the way, D.A. Abrams loved that. He didn't have a warrant or Mrs. Carter's permission to search their suite after he checked out. His attorney will get it tossed. Let me make this simple for you, you have nothing but circumstantial evidence.

Right at this moment you've got nothing that links him physically to the murders themselves. I, for one, am not going to put my ass in a sling trying to convict one of the most respected businessmen in the country unless the D.A.'s damn sure he can win it."

"The DNA will confirm he's our guy. If he's made one mistake, he's made others. We'll dig deeper. And what about the witness description? It's a dead ringer for Carter."

"Shaky at best, Captain, and if the DNA matches, great. Until then, get your tail on the next plane back here, you understand?"

"I can't get a flight back till morning." That was a lie, but at least this way he buys himself a few more hours.

"I'll see you in your office when you get back."

"Great, see you then."

Casey dropped back onto the bed in disgust. He hated that arrogant jerk he had to take his orders from. They never saw eye to eye on anything. But what burned his ass was that the mayor was right about the evidence. The hair could be tossed by a clever enough attorney. They needed more than they had before they made their move.

*

The plane taxied down the runway with Monica's heart stopping the same instant. When the pilot came on the intercom to tell her Thomas and Andrew had come to greet her, she had to fight the licks of panic in her throat. She felt herself go cold when the door opened and the stairs moved up to the plane. In seconds, Monica would see Drew, and unless she pulled herself together, she would have no control over how to tell him the news.

*

Thomas looked at his master and frowned. "You should have stayed in bed, Andrew. You look positively frightful."

Andrew knew he looked a bit worse for wear but Thomas, he was sure, was overreacting. "I'll admit I've looked better but you must admit I've also looked much worse."

"So true, indeed. How are you feeling? And please tell me the truth."

"Actually, I'm feeling much better. That IV's doing the trick, old man. When do I get the last bag?" he asked.

"Tomorrow morning in your office," Thomas met Andrew's eyes in the mirror. "And I think I'm going to add one more bag to the cycle, just for good measure."

Andrew's concern transformed his face. "Is that necessary?"

"Better safe than sorry," he said, opening his door. "Here she comes."

*

Monica measured each step carefully as she made her way down the metal steps. Each step made her heart skip a beat. She saw him step out of the car and look up at her. With his wonderful smile full of love greeting her, she felt safe. She smiled back but it was forced and more difficult than she thought it would be.

He looked so striking in the moonlight, she thought, so happy. And knowing she was about to change all that made her heart ache. Sick to her stomach, she watched him coming to the bottom of the steps to meet her. For a moment, as her heels touched the pavement and his hand reached for hers, she thought her legs would give way underneath her.

Andrew gathered her close and picked her up in his arms. Hugging her tightly, swinging her around in midair. "Hello, Love!" He kissed her quick. "I missed you terribly," he said with a laugh of delight.

She turned her face into his neck. "I missed you, too," she murmured, pulling away just enough to see his face. Monica held back the tears and smiled, her act was Oscar caliber, "You're a sight for sore eyes, Drew." She pulled him close. "I love you," she whispered.

If he felt anything strange in her embrace, he didn't mention it. "I love you too." He tightened his arms around her again. "Let's go home, shall we?"

After she hugged Thomas and they were inside the car, she laid her head on Drew's shoulder and fell into silence. She could gladly stay there forever.

*

They rode in silence back to the mansion. It only took a moment before Andrew sensed something was troubling her. And for once he actually was sorry his vampire instinct of reading thoughts was never mastered. Reginald had been a master at reading the minds of his victims, people in general, and most especially his family. For Andrew that trait was difficult to learn and easily forgotten.

He was thankful about being spared another way of manipulating people. But at the moment, it would have come in very handy. She didn't want to talk, she wanted only to be held, and though it cost him, he obliged her in silence. Andrew didn't push her to tell him anything. She would tell him when she was ready. He tightened his arm around her, pulling her closer to him and gently kissed her forehead.

*

Once home, Thomas excused himself to go brew a fresh pot of tea, and Andrew took Monica into the den for privacy. His problems forgotten, his wife's distress was his only concern now. Something she didn't want to share was eating her alive. She stepped ahead of him and went into the den, he followed, and closed the door. He looked at her until she finally looked away.

He started to go to her but stopped half way across the room when he saw the tears in her eyes. Monica had started to cry and it caught him off guard. "What is it, Love?" he asked, wanting so much to comfort her but feeling it was the last thing she needed or wanted now. "You're scaring me."

She looked at him, her eyes filled with fresh tears. "I don't mean to," she managed. "I just don't know how to do this."

Finally, he went to her, pulling her chin up to him, he said softly, "Just tell me. I can take anything but seeing you this unhappy, Monica."

She felt his every breath, but the words wouldn't come. "I don't want to hurt you, Drew."

Andrew held his breath. "What're you talking about? Why would you hurt me?" He didn't like where this conversation was heading and now he was powerless to stop it.

"I never would," she insisted, "Not intentionally." She used her shaky hands to wipe away tears. "I have something to tell you, and I know it will be painful."

"Tell me," he said stiffly. "It can't be any worse than what I'm already thinking, just bloody tell me," he sounded more irritated then he wanted to.

Monica said nothing for the longest time and Andrew turned away in frustration. Telling him would be a nightmare, but not telling him would be worse. She watched him drop into a chair and knew she couldn't wait any longer. "I wanted to tell you, at the right time, in the right way."

"Are you having an affair?"

The pain on her face gave way to a brittle laugh. "You think

I'm leaving you?" Monica went to him and dropped to her knees. "You must be crazy if you think I'd ever want to leave you, Drew." She closed her eyes and gathered her strength. "I'm not having an affair. I went to the doctor while I was in California because I was feeling so lousy," she said, putting her hand on his knee. "He ran tests to rule out everything you can imagine."

"What's wrong?" Fear seized him. "What's the matter?"

She watched his face when she said the words. "I can't have children, Drew." The words hung in the air between them. She watched his face fill with bewilderment and heard a gasp escape from his throat.

"I don't know what to—what did the doctor say, exactly?"

"That I have too much scar tissue in my fallopian tubes," she said with tears in her eyes.

"He's certain?" Andrew felt like he'd been kicked in the stomach.

Monica touched his cheek. "Yes, he ran the test twice."

He felt like a heel. Sitting there seeing the pain on her face. Christ he felt her pain. What she didn't know was he could not have children either. Not in any normal way. He should have told her long ago but he was hoping to explain it to her later when they were considering having a baby.

It seemed like the cruelest reality possible that now she couldn't have a baby. He felt worse for her because he'd had so long to get used to the fact that he could never become a father. Now the woman he loved most couldn't be a mother. It was a cruel irony.

The silence grew before Andrew found words to comfort her. "I'm sorry, Love. I know you wanted a child, so did I."

Monica pulled herself up onto his lap and hugged him. She kissed his neck and whispered, "We can get through this together right?"

Andrew squeezed her. "Of course we can. This is a terrible loss but it doesn't have to be the end of the world," he assured her.

"I'm sorry, Drew." And she held him tighter.

"Me too, Love," he murmured, feeling her warm tears wetting his neck, he sighed. "Me too."

*

When they walked into the living room, Thomas had the tea setting on the coffee table beside a tray loaded with pastries and muffins, but he was nowhere to be found. "Thomas thinks of everything," Monica said, sitting down on the sofa. "But really, I couldn't eat a thing."

Andrew smiled a half-hearted smile. "You must be tired, would you like a bath instead?" he asked.

"No thanks. Just hold me."

"My pleasure."

*

Thomas came down from straightening up the bedroom so it looked as it did when his madam left. He saw them asleep on the sofa, and for a brief moment found himself smiling at them. His master needed to get some rest and from the looks of it, so did his madam. He quietly took the trays back to the kitchen, and when he returned he gently tugged at his master's arm to wake him.

"Master Andrew, wake up, Master Andrew," he whispered. It took a few seconds but finally Andrew opened his eyes to find Thomas standing over him. "Come on now, it's time the two of you get off to bed," he continued.

"Alright, Thomas, is the room straightened up?" he asked quietly.

"Yes, don't worry."

"That seems to be all I can do at the moment," Andrew said, rubbing Monica's shoulder.

He picked her up in his arms, cradling her as if she were a child; she was surely as innocent as one. He carried her through the room, into the hallway and up the stairs. When he reached the top and started down the hall, a wave of guilt rushed over him, and it startled him. He reached the door to the bedroom just in time. Pushing open the door, he crossed the room and laid her on the bed. She didn't stir, so he covered her and went into the bathroom.

He steadied himself against the sink and in the dim lighting he could see his hands shaking before him. He couldn't decide what hurt him more. Not being able to bring a child of his own into the world, or somewhere deep inside him being almost thankful because of it. Andrew knew that Monica would probably never fully recover from the loss.

Suddenly the words escaped from him, "So be it."

*

He filled his glass again and allowed the thick nectar to remain rolling around on his tongue before swallowing it. It tasted good.

Better than he wanted it too, but it calmed him, allowing him to think more clearly and reason with his inner demons. Andrew rested his head on the back of his chair and let out a deep breath. Damn the treatments for not working, damn the fates that took motherhood from Monica, damn his evil ways which were sure to be his downfall.

He heard the door open behind him but he didn't turn to see who it was because he already knew. The footsteps came across the room and stopped directly behind him in front of his desk. "Thomas, you should be sleeping, it's after one in the morning," he said quietly.

"I could say the same to you, Master Andrew," Thomas replied, coming around the desk.

"I'm afraid that's bloody impossible, old man. I'm restless and we both know what that could bring about."

"At least you had the good sense to stay in the house. We don't need any more complications to deal with right now," Thomas said, lifting the bottle on the edge of the desk and smelling it. He looked at his master and smiled.

Andrew looked away. "Precisely why I'm being a good little boy and staying in here with my bottle," he snorted.

Thomas leaned on the desk. He raised an eyebrow and said, "I see we're in a mood."

Andrew turned his head and looked at Thomas, "Bloody damn right!"

*

The ringing of his phone woke Captain Casey from his precious sleep. He rolled onto his side and felt around in the dark for the phone. He grabbed for the receiver and dropped it. Muttering, he yanked it up to the bed by the cord. "What!" he barked.

"Sorry to wake you, sir," Daniels said apologetically. "The lab just called. They found something interesting."

Casey rubbed his eyes, sat up, and turned on the light. "Well?" he asked.

"Some of the blood they found on the victims wasn't their own."

"Interesting," he replied, coming more fully awake.

"It was O positive," Daniels paused for dramatic effect, "The same blood type as Andrew Carter."

Casey opened his eyes wide, swinging his legs out of the bed and putting his feet on the plush carpeting of the hotel room floor. "That's all the probable cause we need, Daniels. Get the commissioner on the phone. Tell him what's going on, I want a warrant to search Carter's home and business as soon as possible. And I want the green light to bring him in for questioning," he ordered. He wasn't thrilled with the prospect of going head to head with Mr. Carter, or his high priced attorney, but he had to do his job.

"I'll get him on the phone right now," Daniels said. "You know if the DNA from his hair's a match, we've got him."

"That'll never make it into evidence, Daniels. It was obtained without Carter's consent and without a court order. We need more. Talk to the commissioner, I'll be waiting." Casey hung up the phone with his gut telling him he was on to something. This was it. His mouth had gone bone dry. Andrew Carter might actually be a murderer. He stood up and shuffled into the bathroom to get a glass of water.

*

Casey picked the phone up on the first ring and was surprised to hear the commissioner's voice on the other end of the phone. "Sir, I hadn't meant for you to call, I didn't want to disturb you," he apologized.

"Listen, I've worked it out with the NYPD brass. The search warrant will be at your room first thing in the morning. Their not happy we're looking into Carter as a suspect. He's a fuckin' saint far as their concerned. So make sure your P's and Q's are in order. This blood match is good, but a positive I.D. in a lineup to go along with it would be better. If we get DNA that puts him at the scene of the crime, it'll be Christmas and my birthday rolled into one. However, until then we tread lightly. Don't screw up! Be respectful and discreet. If it's him, I don't want to lose him on a technicality," the commissioner warned.

Casey took a deep breath. "Yes sir. I'll bring him in first thing in the morning."

*

Andrew and Thomas returned to their rooms just after four a.m. Both of them wondered what more could go wrong. They were unaware that life as they knew it would never be the same again.

Chapter 24

Casey was out of the shower and wrapping a towel around his waist when the knock at the door startled him. Enough to make him risk knocking himself out cold from the spill he nearly took on the wet floor. He threw a towel on his dripping hair and went to the door. Muttering, he opened it to a uniform cop from the NYPD who was holding an envelope.

He thanked him, and reminded him it was confidential, no leaks to the press. He couldn't have been clearer. A smile covered his face opening the envelope. Daniels would be sorry he missed this moment. It was the warrant to search Andrew Carter's building. Casey pushed the door closed with one hand, while he dropped the towel to the floor with the other. This should prove to be a very interesting day.

A cord of anger was coiling in his chest. He hated being made a fool, but Carter had used his charm and made him one, like it or not. By convincing Casey he was innocent, he'd suckered him, and Casey's pride was a powerful foe. But the evidence was mounting, circumstantial or not that said otherwise.

And further investigation would strengthen the case against Carter. The fact that Daniels had been right made his pulse pound in his temple. A cop lived and died by his instincts and his had failed him. Andrew Carter might look the part of a man too educated, too kind, and one above reproach, but more and more he was looking like a cold-blooded murderer.

He put it back into the envelope, tossed it on the bed, and went to get dressed. He thought about slapping the cuffs onto Carter's wrists, and cringed. When news of the arrest hit the press, all hell would break loose. He didn't look forward to it. The cameras, the reporters, the salacious innuendos created when the facts weren't lurid enough.

As he holstered his weapon, Casey thought about how he should approach Andrew Carter. He certainly wouldn't throw his hands in the air and accompany him to the police station in delight. However, he would come without a scene. Men like Carter didn't cause scenes. No, he wouldn't bluster and puff up his chest, he'd leave it to his attorney to do the grandstanding. It would be a pain in the ass, because no one likes being dragged off under a cloud of suspicion. But he felt better reminding himself that he was just doing his job.

Carter, however, wouldn't see it that way. And who could blame him? He was one of the most respected men in the country. But Casey's gut told him if he got him in a lineup, he could nail him. They had to make sure their shit was together. Arresting the sainted Andrew Carter on some crocked up charge would be a nightmare.

Yeah, that would be a blast. The press would be so far up his ass they'd be able to count his fillings.

Casey turned off the light and walked out of the bathroom. In a navy blue suit and polished loafers, he looked professional. He crossed the room and shoved the warrant in his jacket pocket. He was dreading the press involvement but knew there would be no way to prevent it.

It was suppose to remain confidential until they officially charged Carter, but society being what it was; odds were better than even that it would leak to the press. It was human nature to secretly enjoy the problems of the famous. There would be some rat photographer from the one of the rags hanging around waiting to score a million dollar picture of Carter in handcuffs.

Casey opened the door and nearly plowed into the cabbie he called. "Jesus," he muttered. He got in the passenger side of the cab and cursed. In moments he was on the streets of New York making a bee line for his backup, and Andrew Carter.

*

Andrew had been in his office for only a few minutes before his phone started ringing. It seemed everyone wanted to talk to him about something important. He found it amazing that things could get so out of hand in his absence.

He'd been away from the office for months at a time before and things never got this screwed up. Sarah was so happy to see him she ran up and gave him a hug. She'd never done that in all the years she'd worked for him.

He should have checked in more often, but it wasn't as if he didn't have his hands full. So, he smiled and reassured everyone that he was back now and he would handle everything. Then he disappeared into his office and set about putting things back in order.

An hour passed and Andrew was beginning to see the bottom

of his desk, when Sarah came walking briskly into the room. "Phone call for you on line three," she said, turning to leave.

"Wait a minute," he said, as he picked up the phone. He motioned for her to take a seat. "Yes, what is it?" he asked, annoyed that the office was in so much chaos. "Come to my office in an hour. I have to go," he snapped and slammed down the phone.

Sarah watched him, waiting for him to bark an order at her so she could leave. "Is there something you needed, Mr. Carter?" she asked when he remained silent.

He rubbed his forehead and sighed. "Yes, perhaps you can tell me why the hell things are such a mess around here?"

Sarah was silent.

"Well?" he demanded. "Where the bloody hell's Winston?"

Sarah shifted in the chair. "He isn't here?"

Andrew's eyes narrowed. "What do you mean, he isn't here?"

"He quit," she said.

"He what?"

"Quit," she repeated.

He was shocked. "Why in hell did he do that?" he demanded.

Sarah knew the anger would come sooner or later. "He said his doctor told him to get into another line of work, something less stressful. We tried to reach you in California but with all the confusion we couldn't get through to you," she defended.

Andrew laid his head in his hands. "So what you're telling me is this place has been running without any proper supervision concerning all our pending deals. Is that right?" he asked in disbelief.

"We've been holding things together rather well I'd say."

"I wouldn't," Andrew snapped, and then felt awful for taking his mood out on her. "Well, it's nothing so terrible that it can't be corrected. I'm sorry to snap at you, Sarah. It's been a trying week."

"I thought you were coming in as soon as you got back from California?"

"That was my intention, but I picked up a virus in California and for the past few days I've been flat on my back in bed."

"Are you feeling better?" she asked with concern.

"Yes, much. Send Bradley in here. He just got promoted."

"Will do," Sarah said smiling.

*

Captain Casey made it across town in record time. He was in a cab and at the mercy of the old man behind the wheel. And though he spoke almost no English, he did get him where he wanted to go, so Casey paid the fare and walked up to the huge doorway. He looked around; the building really was quite enormous. He knocked three times.

A moment later Thomas was surprised to see this particular visitor at his door. "Why, Captain Casey. I thought you went back to California?" he asked, trying to seem unaffected.

Casey smiled. "Well, some new information's come to light and changed my plans."

"And this new information brings you back here?" Thomas asked, stepping back from the door.

"Small world," he said, with a glance over his shoulder to the NYPD patrol car pulling to the curb. "May I come in?" he asked while the elderly man's piercing gaze cut from him to the car and the three uniformed officers getting out of the car. His eyes shifted back to Casey before he stepped back to let him in. "Thanks," he replied, coming inside with footsteps approaching from behind.

"What's the meaning of this?" Thomas demanded of Casey, though his eyes stayed on the plainclothes detective as he walked up to the door. When he recognized him from countless fundraisers he and his master attended, he saw the discomfort on his face as well.

"I'll explain everything to Mr. Carter," Casey replied as the backup he'd requested crossed the threshold. "Shall we go up to see him?"

"No," Thomas replied shortly. When Casey's narrowed his eyes in surprise, he continued. "He's in the office. We've been away as you know; it was time he got back to the business at hand."

"I'm glad he's feeling better. Then he'll have no problem coming downtown for a little chat," Casey surmised, tucking his hands in his pockets. "Did Mrs. Carter return home safely?" he asked sitting down on the sofa.

Thomas turned his attention to the others. "Lieutenant Pillar, it's always nice to see you." He stuck out his hand. "What brings you here?" he asked.

Shaking hands, Lt. Pillar flicked an annoyed glance to Casey. "I'm sorry, Thomas," he offered. "Seems Captain Casey has secured a search warrant for the mansion. I've been ordered to execute that warrant and conduct the search."

"On what grounds? Searching for what?"

"He can't divulge specifics," Casey interjected.

Fixing Casey with an icy look, Thomas responded, "Master Andrew has rights, Captain."

The uniformed officers looked nervously to the Lieutenant, who wanted to diffuse the rising hostility. "He does," Pillar agreed. "Suffice it to say, we're looking for evidence in the Central Park killings. I'll tell you and Mr. Carter what I told my Captain, and what he told the Commissioner. I think this is horse shit, but I'll do my job and we'll be out of your hair in no time."

"Will you call your boss and have him come down or should I just pop up to his office and talk to him there."

"I'll take care of it," Thomas snapped, heading for the phone on the hallway table. "Right after I phone his attorney."

When he picked up the phone, he saw Monica coming down the stairs. He had to think fast, so he hung up the phone and struggled to appear unconcerned while the bottom fell out of their lives. Thomas watched his madam studying the men in confusion as she continued down the staircase. "Ah...Madam Monica...." He had to tell the truth or he'd be caught in a lie. "This is Captain Casey," he began, on his way to the stairs. "He's a California police detective. He's here to speak with Master Andrew. And, this is Lieutenant Pillar with the NYPD. I'm afraid there's been some confusion."

As she reached the bottom her smile faltered while she studied the rather serious men with Thomas and the officers by the door. "Gentlemen," she offered her hand to them both, but didn't miss the tension between them. "Andrew's in the office, is there something I can do to help?"

Casey studied her as she had him, and she was as beautiful in person as she was on television, "It's good to meet you, Mrs. Carter." Shaking her hand, he replied, "Your husband can clear this up in no time."

Monica smiled, her mind already trying to read between the lines. "You're a long way from home."

"Yes." Casey looked over her shoulder and eyed one very stressed out servant. "I'm hoping my visit will be brief," he replied slightly amused.

"Thomas will get Drew, while we all make ourselves comfortable in the living room." She tried to ignore the slivers of worry tingling through her, "Shall we?"

*

Thomas walked back down the hall to his master's office with a dire sense of emergency on his face. He passed everyone he came across in silence. He pushed through the door to his master's office without as much as a word to Sarah.

Andrew was surprised when he looked up from his files and saw Thomas standing in the doorway. The old man's face said it all. "You look horrified. What's the matter?" he asked, getting up from his chair and coming around the desk.

Thomas took a deep breath and spoke directly. "Casey's downstairs with his sidekick and Lt. Pillar's with him and Madam Monica-"

The sudden fear sent a chilled sensation along the back of his neck. "He didn't return to California last night?"

"No, he didn't."

"For chrissake, what's he want now?"

Thomas' face went white. "He wants you, Master Andrew, to accompany him downtown and shrug off his search warrant for the mansion."

"A search warrant." There wasn't time to give into the panic that was choking him. His wife would be confused, or worse, frightened. He had to get to her, reassure her. But first, he had to cover his ass. "What about the dark sector?"

"I've engaged the false wall, Master Andrew."

"Can he do this?" he asked in disbelief. "Come in here and invade my privacy without cause?"

"I'm no lawyer, but there can be no warrant issued without cause proven to a judge."

"Does Monica know why he's here?" he demanded.

"Not unless he's telling her right now. Come on, we better get down there," he replied, taking his master by the shoulder. "You can call Steven when we get there." Thomas moved with authority, ready to take control.

"Steven's out of town."

"Randolph then," Thomas said. "But listen to me Andrew, we've no idea what the authorities have against you, so don't go off half cocked. Keep your mouth shut until we know what we're dealing with."

"Who the hell does this man think he is?" Andrew asked grabbing his coat.

"At the moment," Thomas said, pushing him through the door, "He's your worst nightmare."

Chapter 25

The walk to the elevator had never been longer or more difficult to achieve. With each step, he felt the gravity of the situation close in around him, crushing his chest, shattering his lungs, and robbing him of every breath.

The whirl of activity around him, as he made his way through the hallways, seemed faint, distant. The deals being made on the phone, the fingers flying over computer keyboards became unimportant. What petrified him most at the moment was Monica alone with Casey. Andrew didn't want her to hear any of this madness from him. If she had to know, it was his responsibility to tell her.

When the doors closed and they were safely inside the elevator, Andrew couldn't contain his composure any longer. Sweat ran down his neck as if he'd come in out of the rain. "What do we do now?" he asked, as he watched the floors tick by slowly. "I cannot go to jail, Thomas, for all sorts of obvious reasons, not the least of which being I'll never survive in that kind of environment," he said with an air of desperation.

"I know that Master Andrew. But you will have to go with him, at least for the moment."

Andrew turned white. "Are you out of your bleedin' mind?"

Thomas pushed the emergency stop button, bringing the elevator to a halt in between floors. He placed his hands on Andrew's shoulders. "Listen to me, Andrew, we have our hands full enough without having him wrestle you to the ground and drag your stubborn ass out the door!" he said harshly. He took a deep breath to calm himself and when he regained his restraint he continued, "Compliance will work in your favor. An innocent man has nothing to hide. And let's not forget Monica. The quieter you allow this to happen; the better it will be for everyone, especially her."

"So you have some sort of plan to handle this then?" Andrew asked hopefully.

"I've been preparing for this for awhile now, I knew it would come to a head sooner or later. I would've liked a few more days for the pieces to fall into place more smoothly." He hit the button again and they began lurching downward.

*

Andrew followed Thomas out of the elevator and they walked into the living room together. She had served them tea and was making small talk about the decor of the room. It was obvious to Andrew that Monica had no clue who Casey was and what he represented for the two of them. She didn't know this was the man that would forever alter their lives.

Thomas cleared his throat and everyone turned. Casey smiled, set his cup on the table, and got up from the couch. "Well Mr. Carter, I've got a warrant for you," he said politely.

Andrew remained calm and shook Casey's hand. Casey watched Carter closely before he continued. "Lt. Pillar of the NYPD, who I'm told you know quite well, will conduct the search of the Mansion. In the mean time, I'm afraid you'll have to come with me," he said.

"Is that so?" Andrew knew the prick was enjoying this. He would have loved to wipe that smart-ass smile off his face but why add assaulting a police officer to the charges?

"Yes, afraid so, I've got questions that need answers, and you'll want to answer them undistracted. So, let's clear out and these guys can do their job." Captain Casey turned and looked at his gracious hostess. "In a more structured setting, Mrs. Carter. Don't worry."

Andrew needed to explain this to Monica, if he could that is. He could see the look of confusion on her face, the worry beginning to cloud her eyes. She really had no idea what was coming. And, he didn't want an audience when he broke her heart. "I'll need a moment with my wife, Captain."

Casey felt for the guy's wife. It was clear she had no idea about her husband's late night activities. He sure would love to hear the line of shit this rich dude was about to feed her, but he decided to be kind. "Sure, no problem," he said, about to follow Thomas out of the room.

Andrew went to Monica and hugged her. "You're too kind, Captain." Monica could only stare at Andrew as Thomas showed the captain out of the room.

Monica looked into Andrew's tired eyes and had never seen them so troubled. He pulled closed the pocket doors to give them privacy. "Come sit with me, Love," he said softly. He loosened his tie and shirt collar and walked with her to the couch. He wasn't sure where he should begin. He'd known somewhere deep inside himself that it would come to this. Knowing that his secret, however much he wanted to keep it separate, would have to be revealed to her. But knowing didn't make this moment any easier.

Monica touched his cheek. She supposed business could get competitive, even ugly at times, so he'd crossed the line, stepped on a few toes. It happens. "What's going on, Drew," she whispered.

He smiled and his eyes grew moist, surprising them both. "I don't know how to soften this," he said, wringing his hands, trying to rid himself of the imaginary shackles he felt tightening around his wrists.

"Just say it," she took his hands to still them.

"Captain Casey's come to take me in for questioning, Monica," he mumbled. He lower his head in shame, he couldn't look at her.

She squeezed his hands. "That's crazy, Drew," she said, "Concerning what?"

"In connection with murder."

She felt like she'd been kicked in the stomach. "What?"

He was shocked at the ease with which the word came spilling from him. "The charge is murder," he repeated.

Monica was stunned into silence. After a deep breath, she managed to find her voice. "This is insane."

"Regardless, it's happening. And he's got a search warrant as well."

She took a deep breath. "Murder? Who?" The reporter in her was coming out at the worst possible time.

Andrew was staring at the carpet on the floor in front of him. He could not believe he was having this conversation, and he hadn't even gotten to the betrayal that would kill her love for him forever. He felt broken and as old as the histories of his kind in the passages he read as a boy...hundreds of years old. Of course, he thought he was reading a simple work of fiction matching his father's own sick sense of humor. He felt every year due to come to him descending.

"Andrew?" Monica watched him drift away. He was as stunned by all this as she was.

Her voice allowed him to focus again. "Ah, it has to do with that mess in California," he answered flatly, emotions threatening to rip him apart. He sucked in a breath and ran his hand over her hair.

Monica watched him shifting uncomfortably beside her. She could feel the fear emanating from him like the heat from a raging fire. "Not the bombing?" she asked horrified.

Andrew eyes snapped to hers. "Good God, no!" He stood up and went to the bar, "Those poor unfortunate people in that park." He shoved his hands deep into his pockets.

"Those people who were attacked and killed?"

"Yes."

Monica raised an eyebrow; the reporter in her was surfacing again. "But those people were mutilated viciously. How can they think you're responsible?" she asked.

"I'm sure they have their reasons. Because of that, I have to go downtown and answer questions and Lieutenant Pillar and his men have to do a search of the mansion."

Monica went to him and wrapped her arms around him. "It's all a misunderstanding, Drew," she said calmly.

It wasn't a misunderstanding at all. It was true and Andrew knew it. And now he had to tell her. He opened his mouth, "I..." The knock on the door and the voice from behind it broke his confidence. "I'll be right out!" he said loudly. He hugged Monica tightly. "I'll take care of this, Love. Let them do what they have to do. And please try not to worry."

She didn't want to let him go. "Should I call Randy?"

He pulled out of her embrace. "I'm sure Thomas has already taken care of it." He ran his hand through his hair.

"I want to come with you, Drew."

He shook his head. "Absolutely not." He wrapped her in his arms and held her tightly.

"Drew…"

He cut her off, and framing her face in his hands, his gaze swept over every inch of her. The mossy green of her eyes, her blond hair, lush, long, and easily twined around his fingers. He wanted to burn her into his memory, needed to, if he was going to get through whatever lay ahead. "No arguments now. Stay here. I can't be worried about you, I have too many other things to be concerned with right now."

"All I want is to make sure they treat you fairly."

He smiled in spite of the catastrophe before them. "You're a reporter and a damn good one, but a lawyer you are not. That reminds me, when this hits the news we'll be in the middle of media hell."

Monica was terrified. "Drew, I'm the news media. Mr. Philips is going to want an exclusive."

Thomas slid open the door and Casey came in breaking the intensity of the moment. They broke away from their quiet understanding, their eyes locked to each other. "We have to go. I've been more than generous," he said.

Andrew took Monica by the hand and looked at the pompous son-of-a-bitch. "Oh yes, Captain Casey, you've been a real prince."

"Be nice or you'll hurt my feelings. Come along nicely, Mr. Carter and I won't cuff you."

Andrew laughed. "Are you serious?" he asked.

Casey with his ever-present smile said, "Its procedure to advice you of your rights."

"I feel much better knowing that, Captain."

*

"Andrew Carter, you have the right to remain silent..."

He heard these words before and he still remembered every word.

"...held against you in a court of law..."

Andrew felt the need to throw up.

"...If you cannot afford one, one will be provided for you..."

He felt helpless and doomed and his wife could do nothing but watch him. He needed to tell her more but there wasn't time. He heard himself mumble, "Yes."

With his bicep in the grip of Casey, Andrew made himself look away from his wife. "Thomas, did you get in touch with Randolph?" he asked, being led through the hallway to the door.

"Yes, Master Andrew. He'll meet you down at the station," he said quickly.

Monica followed them to the door and Andrew turned and smiled weakly at her. "I love you. Don't worry, I'll be in good hands with Randolph."

Lt. Pillar stood off to the side and watched this idiocy play out in front of him. He hated that he had to be a part of this. Andrew Carter was a 'class A' guy with a strong sense of right and wrong. Whether contributing to the police benevolent fund or underwriting the purchase of bullet-proof vests for every cop in the NYPD, Carter had been there for this city. "I'm sorry about this, Mr. Carter," he apologized. "You have my word we'll be as unobtrusive as we can be. And be out of your wife's way as soon as possible."

"Thank you, Lieutenant," Andrew said looking at Pillar.

Monica touched his face and tried to smile. "Mr. Philips will call, he'll want an inside scoop."

"Tell him I said to go to hell," he said and leaned over to kiss her one last time.

Chapter 26

Monica watched as her home and her privacy was invaded. She tried, in vain, to occupy her time finishing up the last minute details of a story she was working on, but her mind wandered. When the news of Andrew's arrest leaked to the press, a feeding frenzy would erupt. And it would be leaked to the press as sure as she was breathing right now. And it would be leaked in time for the evening news. She knew how her business worked. How it thrived on misery and pain, and how if this happened before she knew him, she'd be right there in the thick of it.

If she were the person she had been two years ago, she would have been the first one to shove a microphone in Andrew Carter's face. When she was of the opinion that the 'bigger they are the harder they fall' syndrome. Now though, it was as different as night and day. She had no desire to be the reporter to beat all reporters and be the first to break the news to the world.

Now she knew the real Andrew Carter. The man she fell in love with, the man who didn't possess an unkind or destructive bone in his body. It was impossible for her husband to be capable of such unspeakable acts.

The press would shoot from the hip. Monica knew that all too well. Especially those of the tabloid variety, they would lead the public into a feeding frenzy. What drove them and everyone else like them, was the almighty ratings. Numbers. It was all about numbers to them, their blood, and reason for living. So what could she do to protect him? Nothing in the grand scheme of things. In the end, if she tried covering this story, it would be considered a snow job because she was screwing the suspect in question. God bless the USA.

*

It was almost choking him—the thought that this was indeed the end for Andrew Carter, billionaire mogul. As the car turned onto the street where the police station was located, he thought he might throw up. But just when Andrew was certain he could taste the bile of his stomach in his throat, the car stopped.

He wouldn't give this cop the satisfaction of seeing him loose control. He was still a man, damnit!

Casey got out of the car and opened the back door. Taking

Andrew by the arm, he said, "Let's get you inside."

Andrew looked at him coldly and considered resisting but thought better of it. What purpose would it serve? His image would be destroyed the second the media found out, so why make it worse on himself? In his conscience, he felt he deserved whatever he got. He was guilty after all.

The walk up the side steps of the station seemed endless but he managed it with dignity. All the dignity a guilty man could muster. What would his mother say right now if she were alive? Wherever she was, wherever good people like her go when they leave this earth, she'd tell him to be strong.

*

The station was in chaos with Andrew looking every part the misguided, defeated man he felt like. Captain Casey took Andrew directly to an interrogation room and guided him into a chair behind a large table. "Is there anything I can get you, Mr. Carter? Coffee, tea?" he asked while he began riffling through some files he picked up, on his way into the room.

Andrew never felt such contempt for anyone except his father. This guy didn't even belong to this department yet he walks in and acts as if he runs the place. "My lawyer," he replied.

"Okay," he said, "but don't say I didn't offer. I'll go see if your attorney's arrived yet." He left the room and another uniformed officer came in for supervision and closed the door.

It didn't take long for Andrew to feel the walls closing in tighter around him. He'd rather be dead than be in this room, he thought. What must Monica be thinking? That she married a psychotic killer? He didn't want her to be hurt, but no matter how things turned out now, she would be. He would have to live with it for all eternity, and that was not a pleasant thought.

*

Randolph was the first one through the door when it flew open and slammed up against the wall. "Don't say another word, Andrew," he said, putting his briefcase on the table next to his client.

Casey closed the door. "He hasn't said anything yet, Mr. King, I assure you."

"But it's not from your lack of trying, is it, Captain?"

"Hey!" He put his hand up in an innocent posture. "I resent that. I'm just doing my job here," Casey said sharply, slapping a file down on the table. "Can we get started?"

Randolph put his hand on Andrew's shoulder and sat down next to him. Andrew said nothing only nodded. "Why not, this shouldn't take long."

Casey leaned against the wall and smoothed out the creases in his forehead. He knew this would be about as much fun as getting his teeth drilled. If ever there were two men more willing to bend over backwards, he'd like to meet them, he thought sarcastically. Maybe he should have brought Daniels with him. He would really enjoy this.

*

Thomas knew what he had to do if Mr. King failed to get his master released on bail, or better, cleared of all charges. It was dangerous for him as well as countless others but desperate times called for desperate measures. The plan would be tricky and useless if Andrew couldn't get out of jail. In all of his sixty some odd years, he'd never been called on to do anything quite so massive. But, he had to do it for his master. For the man he loved as a son. There was no room for error. Lives were at stake, his, Andrew's, and too many more to count.

*

"I'm aware of what you're calling evidence, Captain. However, I need some time alone with my client," Randolph said, glaring out over the top of his glasses.

Casey clasped his hands behind his neck tightly. "I thought you said there was nothing to hide?" he asked Andrew, becoming frustrated.

"I won't have you using your street-thug tactics on my client. You're trying to ride him into confessing, and I assure you that won't happen, Captain. He's not a common punk off the street. I want to hear his side on things."

"Fine," Casey said through clinched teeth and narrowed eyes. "I'll be outside when you're ready to continue, gentlemen." He walked out of the room angry at the smugness of the two men. Slamming the door behind him, he went to get a cup of coffee.

Andrew looked at Randolph now that they were alone. "What kind of trouble am I in?"

"Depends," Randolph pushed his glasses higher on his nose. "I've just scanned the file, but they've got a hair sample from you that's a match to one found on one of the victims, DNA results pending. But, that'll be inadmissible because they obtained the sample through nefarious means. Your blood type was found at the scene." He shook his head. "Did you do this?" Randolph asked, not certain he wanted to know the answer.

Andrew said nothing at first. "There are things going on you're not aware of, Randolph," he said, agitated.

He tossed his glasses on the table and took a deep breath. "Make me aware then. Your ass is in a sling."

Andrew had no clue where to begin. "You know about my past and everything that happened in England?"

"Only what you've told me, which isn't much."

"I did not intentionally set out to hurt those people. It was out of my control."

Randolph closed his eyes, shaking his head he said, "Christ, Andrew, are you saying that you killed those people in California?"

Andrew didn't want to admit it out loud. "Yes."

*

The phone didn't ring and Monica was slowly going out of her mind. It had been hours since Andrew left and still she heard nothing. The police left after searching the house from top to bottom, and they left empty handed. Thomas was off somewhere attending to what he said was some emergency business for Carter Industries. Every so often, he would come into the living room to check on her and she found that endearing. He was a sweet man.

She directed her every thought to her husband. He was all she could think about. To accuse him of such a crime was laughable in her mind. She was married to him for goodness sake. If he had a violent side to him, she would know, wouldn't she? And then, it happened, Monica allowed the one thought to enter her consciousness that she'd been pushing away all night.

Could her husband be responsible for the murders of innocent people? Ashamed at even considering such a question, Monica willed her thoughts into another, more positive, direction…if she could find one.

*

The three of them sat looking at each other in silence. It had been four and a half hours and still Andrew would admit to nothing even remotely incriminating. Which did not surprise Captain Casey, he expected as much. But it was becoming frustrating, this stonewalling, for everyone. No one was willing to stop it, to take the first step. Time crawled and the stuffy little room was anything but comfortable. Andrew had long ago removed his tie and jacket, rolled up the cuffs of his shirt, and tried not to break under the pressure. But the stress was catching up with him. And the dull ache in his throat returned.

He wasn't sure which scared him more, being locked up in a cell or loosing control and acting out. Taking hold of someone by the neck and feeding the hunger he was beginning to feel. He would have to be stronger than the monster inside him. "How much longer do we have to do this, Captain?" Andrew wanted to know. "I've got nothing to say because I've done nothing wrong."

Randolph was just about to ask the same question. With a sigh, he dropped his glasses and laced his fingers together. "If you're planning to book my client, Captain, get on with it," he added in accord.

Casey was tired of all this bullshit himself, but something was there, beneath the surface, and he was betting the next round of questions would shake Carter up.

"Just a few more questions, Mr. Carter," he began after a yawn. "Do you make it a habit to pay the funeral expenses of perfect strangers?" he asked watching Carter's reaction.

For his part, Andrew hoped he didn't look as shocked as he felt. He watched, while Casey spread out computer printouts and copies of receipts, his mind working out how to respond. He'd taken careful steps to insure that no one would trace the payments back to him, and yet here was proof coming back to bite him in the ass. "What are you talking about?" he asked innocently.

"I'm talking about this computer printout," he said, sliding it across the table so Andrew could see it. "Look familiar? I have to admit, I wasn't crazy about Lt. Pillar's attitude towards you, but he's true to his word. He did his job and found that in your study. And after a couple of hours of hard work by some of the uniforms out there, it's all starting to fall into place."

Andrew could feel the eyes of his attorney, who knew nothing whatsoever about this, burning into him. "I make donations all the time to various charities, what the money is used for is entirely up to the heads of those charitable trusts."

Captain Casey shook his head and smiled, "That's true, but these amounts are peanuts compared to what you normally give to any charity, Mr. Carter." He slid off the edge of the rickety table, and tugging his tie loose, ambled across the tiny room. "You had them locked up tighter than a drum—like you were hiding them—odd for simple charitable donations."

Andrew was livid and he could no longer contain his anger. "Hiding them? Why would I, when I've nothing to hide? And I fail to see how my confidential files fall into the scope of this investigation, Captain."

Casey lifted a brow, he had touched a nerve. So the man wasn't unflappable after all, he thought. "It's called probable cause, Mr. Carter."

"What makes you think that money went for funerals?" Randolph interjected.

"Because the cashier checks in question weren't made out to charitable organizations." His eyes flicked to Carter. "They were made payable to the funeral homes dealing with the arrangements, and this is the weird part, with specific instructions to cover the expenses of the victims. I talked with the family of the victims and they were beside themselves. When it came time to pay the bill, they were told it had been taken care of. The receipts had the name of the benefactor responsible. Conaire, Inc." Casey waited a beat, gauging Carter's reaction. "Sound familiar?"

Andrew knew exactly what Conaire, Inc. was because he owned it. It was supposed to be buried in so much red tape that it would be impossible to determine ownership, but that theory had just been shot to hell. "Yes. I own Conaire, Inc. It was one of my very first acquisitions," he replied.

"So, can you explain why your business picked up the tab on the Teal's and Rourke's funeral expenses?"

"My companies help with donations and charitable causes, Captain. And each company has its own CEO, who makes donations at their discretion."

"But it's your money, Mr. Carter," Casey pointed out, circling the table. "Your funds, so your permission would be required. These CEO's aren't required to clear those decisions with you? Come on!"

Andrew felt his control slip, he reined it back. "I have a board that handles that."

Casey tapped a pencil and cleared his throat. "That's a lot of money to spend without your direct knowledge. Your signature is on the checks."

Andrew took a drink of his cold coffee. "I don't consider anything under two million dollars to be a lot of money, Captain, and I don't always pay attention to what I'm signing. As to whether it's a lot of money, well, that's *your* opinion. What we're talking about here, isn't even a drop in the bucket."

Casey hoped to keep his chin from bouncing off the table. "Must be nice," Casey sat back down on the edge of the table, inches from Carter. "We found a hair on Mr. Teal that matches yours. We found blood, independent of the victims, on one of the victims, O positive. That's your blood type. You don't recall seeing the victims in the park, but the hair proves you not only saw them but had personal contact with them."

Randolph cut in before Andrew could speak. "Captain we'll discuss the legality of the hair sample at a later date, in front of a judge most likely."

Casey stood up and stretched, he was so tired he could sleep for a week. He switched gears. "I'd like you to come with me," he said taking his jacket from the back of the chair.

Andrew's breath caught in his throat.

"Where?" Randolph demanded, "My client's been here for seven hours, Captain. Patience is dwindling."

"I realize this is tiresome, Mr. King," Casey said in a condescending tone, "He says he's got nothing to hide so I want him to participate in a lineup. If our eye witness doesn't ID him, he's free to go, for the moment."

"My client's been helpful, now he's done."

Andrew looked at Randolph in sheer fear and snapped, "I'll do it!"

"Andrew—," Randolph snapped back, grabbing his arm.

Casey slapped him on the shoulder. "Good," he interrupted. "I'll be right back."

When the door was closed and they were alone, client and attorney, Andrew began to hyperventilate. The pain shot through him like a hot poker. He felt everything that made him who he was slipping away from him.

"What in the hell are you doing," Randolph demanded?

Andrew stood up and took Randolph by the arm. "Listen, we are in a no-win situation here, if I refuse to take part in a police lineup, it'll only add to their suspicions and make a bad situation worse," he said calmly.

"And if you're picked out of this lineup, you're dead," Randolph argued. "They'll lock you up and throw away the key! Andrew, I'm not a cut throat. I'm in business and contract law. Steve is your man, not me. You need someone who can smell blood and move in for the kill," Randolph advised.

"There's no time," Andrew replied.

"I'll make time."

*

The clock in the kitchen read nine p.m. and Thomas was beginning to worry. Something had gone wrong, he could feel it. And now, he was feeling the pressure himself. Across the street sat an unmarked police car with policemen and surveillance equipment watching every move inside the mansion. But there was too much to do to let prying eyes stop him. The plans he was making would just be harder to carry out.

His master was never accomplished when it came to handling stress. His temper was quick, and in this situation, it would only antagonize the police. He could make matters worse for himself, just by loosing control and saying the wrong thing.

*

"Just follow the yellow line—," Casey said to the men. All of whom were nervous because, sure as they were standing there, they were all guilty of some crime. Whether they were guilty of the one in question did not matter. "—and lean against the wall when you come to the end of the line, gentlemen."

Andrew kept his head held high as he followed the yellow line. His hope was to blend with his surroundings and become a chameleon of sorts. However, as he got a look at the men around him, his hopes faded. He would stick out like a sore thumb in this crowd. The pain in his stomach was searing and the aching in his throat was unrelenting.

With all the available blood around him, he couldn't help being tempted. The yellow line ended and Andrew found himself in a small narrow hall with a door at each end. He was second in line of eight men leaning against the wall. Waiting, dreading what might come next. Each standing straight as if they had a stick shoved in their backs, their eyes front and unblinking.

When the bright fluorescent lights above them flickered on, Andrew noticed a huge mirror directly in front of him. He knew the witness was behind it, holding his future in their hands. This witness, this man or woman, had the power to destroy him. He waited, almost sensing their eyes burning into him.

The madness in this world had to be stopped and maybe this person felt like speaking out against the violence around them and their city. This offered him little comfort when he heard a voice come through the speaker and say, "Number one step forward, please." And so it began.

*

Captain Casey stood quietly behind the witness and waited for some response. This was important, the commissioner flew in with the witness himself, and now he was breathing down his neck...literally. He was standing right beside him.

"Number two, step forward, please."

Andrew stepped forward with his hands down at his sides. He looked straight ahead and prayed.

Casey watched the expression on the witness' face as they looked into the face of Andrew Carter and so far there were no signs of recognition. Having his boss there made him nervous but there was little he could do about it. This was important to him as well. The people of California were up in arms about the savage attack that claimed the lives of their residents. They were looking to the mayor and police commissioner, the men they had elected to solve the putrid crime, to deliver.

They were under pressure from all sides. That meant Casey, the man directly in charge of the police department homicide unit, was also under pressure. But, they had to be sure before they ruined a man's life. Especially when the man in question was Andrew Carter.

The witness interrupted Casey's thoughts. "That's him. Number two. That's the man I saw in the park in California. Do you know who that is? That's Andrew Carter."

"And he's the man you saw?" Casey asked cautiously.

"I think so."

"You think so?" the Commissioner asked. "We need more than 'I think so' to book this man."

"It's him, it's him."

Casey took a deep breath. "And you wouldn't be saying this just because he's well known, a celebrity?" he asked. His gut was telling him to be careful with this.

"No way, it was him I saw, looked like hell too, dazed almost, I thought he was drunk."

"Fine," Casey replied. He pressed the intercom button and released the lineup. "Thanks, Todd," he said, waving to the police officer who was filing the men out of the room.

The witness was led out of the room and the commissioner shifted his penetrating eyes to Casey who said, "So I guess we book him then."

"Get this ball rolling, Captain."

"Yes, sir."

*

Andrew was sitting in the interrogation room when Casey came in the room. "Where's your attorney?" he asked looking around the room.

"Why? Do I need him?" Andrew asked.

"Yep, I'm booking you for the murders of Mr. and Mrs. Teal and the Rourkes, Mr. Carter."

Andrew went blank. It shouldn't have come as a surprise to him but it did. He was guilty. He did do it, so, of course the witness would identify him. "I need to make a phone call," he said quickly.

"Don't blame you at all, could be a long night for everyone."

Chapter 27

The lingering smell of dampness and mildew started Andrew's stomach churning as soon as he was placed in the holding cell. Captain Casey had brought him to lockup after he was booked. He still had ink on his fingertips to remind him of the indignity of the experience. He was stunned by how much could change in twenty-four hours. So, here he sat as the hour grew later, on the edge of what he could only assume was to be his bed for the night.

Randolph was still waiting for Steve so they could prepare for his arraignment. Andrew knew only one thing; he could not be locked up over night. It was impossible.

Everything was spinning too far out of control, and what pained him the most at the moment was there was nothing he could do about it. He thought about Monica and how she was handling this mess. He was sure it had hit the press by now. She would learn that he was being held like the animal he knew himself to be, but from whom his wife had been carefully shielded.

He told Steve Hardy to get in touch with Thomas and give him the news before he heard it from anywhere else. It was important Monica hear it from him rather than from some news bite. Thomas would know what to do when he learned the news. Andrew could only hope there was still a chance for him.

Andrew gripped the edge of the mattress and swayed back and forth on the cot. He looked around the cell in disbelief and horror. This was to be his punishment. To be caged like his father. He could never allow it to happen, couldn't allow himself to be kept away from his beloved wife. Away from his life, such as it was.

He could feel the sweat soaking through from his scalp to his hair and dripping onto the blanket underneath him. He swallowed hard several times to keep the bile from rising in his throat. While the faces of the people he killed danced in front of him. No matter how hard he tried they grew closer and closer to him. His screams were caught in his throat. He could not give voice to the fear squeezing his sanity from him.

Andrew jerked himself off the cot and slid along the wall to put some distance between himself and his tormentors. His hands and face were slick with sweat, and the heat escaping from his body was more intense than anything he had ever felt before. They would not be pushed aside. They loomed closer and closer until Andrew was sure they would move through him. He could go nowhere. He had backed himself into a corner.

"Please...I'm sorry...I didn't mean to...hurt you," he pleaded. Was this what it would be like if he was imprisoned? Would these ghosts haunt him forever? He shook his head vehemently. "No! Leave me be!"

"What's the matter with you, buddy?" a short, portly police officer asked from behind a desk on the other side of the room. "Hey, what's going on?" he asked, walking quickly over to the cell.

Andrew heard nothing but the voices of the ghosts that had come to drive him mad. Like a child, he was hunched down in the corner, curled up in fright. He clamped his eyes shut so tightly he brought tears to them. And, before he knew what happened blackness closed in all around him...

*

Monica was sitting alone in the living room when Thomas came in with a tray of tea and muffins. A wealth of sympathy overcame him when he saw her. She was sitting with her knees drawn up to her chest and her face stained with the tears she'd been crying for the past hour, from the moment they found out the latest from Andrew's attorney. "Madam, I've brought you some tea and muffins. Please can I pour you a cup?" he asked, looking down at her in the dark room. The only light came from the fireplace across the room.

She said nothing, only shook her head.

"It's late Madam, you must eat something or Master Andrew would never forgive me."

"I can't eat...with him...in that...*place*, Thomas." Her face was drawn and her eyes were puffy. When Thomas sat beside her, she grabbed his hand. "We have to get him out of there. He isn't capable of such evil. This is so wrong," she said, her voice gaining heat as anger overtook grief.

"Steven's doing everything he can for him. I'm sure he'll have him home in no time," Thomas said with a smile, trying to reassure her and himself.

Thomas left her alone when she promised to eat something before he returned. There was a lot to do and only a short time in which to do it. Bail would be granted and his master would return home. And from there everything would move rather quickly.

He made his way down to the dark sector and opened the door. As always, he checked the temperature gauge. It was perfect. He moved fast, pulling bottles from the holes two at a time and placing them in the coolers he brought down earlier in the day. If things went as planned, there would be no chance to rebuild the stock. It was essential he have as much on hand as possible. Two bottles...four bottles...six bottles...

*

The clanging of his cell door awakened Andrew. Through heavy-lidded eyes, he managed to focus on a man standing over his cot with an easy smile on his face. "What...where...," he stammered.

The man placed his hand on Andrew's shoulder. "Easy does it, you fainted a little while ago. Just try to relax; I'm checking your vitals. Don't worry, I'm a nurse."

"Where's my attorney?" Andrew asked, becoming more alert.

"I imagine he's trying to arrange bail for you," he replied. "He's before the judge as we speak. You were invited to attend but I guess your body had other plans, so the hearing went on without you," he said with a chuckle.

Andrew felt disoriented but didn't miss this stab at humor. "You're a bloody hoot."

"Nah, just trying to lighten the mood."

Andrew's head was pounding but he decided to sit up anyway. He grimaced as a sharp pain shot through his head. "I don't mean to sound ungrateful but when the hell can I get out of here?" he asked.

"That's up to the judge, I'm just here to make sure you're okay physically and you seem to be just that, better than my equipment in fact. Can't get a reading on your pressure or hear a discernable heartbeat," he said, tapping his blood pressure cuff a second time. "Are you under the care of a physician?"

"My pressure is often low and my personal physician is aware of it, yes," Andrew replied, resting his head on his hand. "What I really need is to be home with my wife."

"And I'm sure you will be very soon," the nurse said, standing. "In the meantime, get some rest and get in touch with your doctor first chance you get."

*

Monica relaxed in the one place where she and Andrew spent their most precious time together, their bedroom. She roamed the house for comfort but couldn't quiet her confusion or fear. And in this lovely room lay the link to Andrew she needed so badly.

The man who loved her changed her life. She closed her eyes and wrapped her arms around her middle wishing they were his instead. She calmed herself by picturing his face in her mind, but fear lingered in the background. What could possibly lead anyone to think her husband was a cold and devious killer? It wasn't possible. He was too gentle.

She walked the room to keep from shaking, and then sat down in front of the fire when chills moved through her. In the gathering quiet, she slipped into a comfortable daze. The man who held her here by firelight, who loved her so tenderly, couldn't be capable of such brutality. In this room the world outside could never intrude. Yet it was intruding now. Even as memories bathed her in his scent and touch, the ugliness pressed into her soul.

Drew was not an animal. And it would take an animal to commit those crimes. He would have to be vicious. That wasn't the man she knew, not the man she married. That animal couldn't be the man who stole her breath every time he came into the room. Drew was not a monster.

Before midnight, she woke in front of the fire, her head resting on her arms as she lay sprawled out on the carpet. Monica almost called out for Andrew before she remembered she was alone. Stretching, she looked around the room and it was empty. And yet, Thomas was still trying to take care of her. There was food on a tray, still warm, waiting for her on the footstool at the end of the bed.

Wanting to mollify Thomas, Monica took a deep breath, sat in front of the tray, and began picking over the food. A meal of all her favorite foods, but it failed to appeal to her. She picked up the fork and began eating anyway. Too busy her hands and her mind, she ate, but she didn't taste the food.

*

Thomas spent the last hour on a satellite phone in the study. But even as he continued on with last minute details of an alternative he hoped to avoid, he worried and waited for the phone to ring. They'd been through this once before, it hadn't been pretty, and love had been at the root of it then. When his master met

Monica and once more fell in love, his master had come full circle. Love was the root of it again.

It should have been easy for him to harbor resentment towards her, for the upheaval in life since then, but he could not. He could not only understand his master's deep love for her, but also felt a bit of it for her himself. He couldn't undo the past and he wasn't sure he wanted too. Because since Monica Banebridge came into their lives, they had been happier, more fulfilled men somehow. Even now he couldn't see taking that away from his master or himself.

It had been a lonely life before her. So how could he wish for the return of that life? It was without many problems, true. But there was sadness in it that he wouldn't want his master to feel again. No, he would do whatever was needed to see that didn't happen…or die trying.

*

Andrew sat up on the bed when he heard the door to his cell being opened. He watched as Steve Hardy walked into the cell. "Well? When do I get out of this hole, Steve?" he asked anxiously.

"Bail's set at three million dollars," he replied. "I'm arranging the paperwork right now. You should be home within the hour, Andrew."

"Thank God!" he exclaimed in relief.

"The bail's outrageous, but given your resources you're a high flight risk," he explained.

Andrew was eager to leave and growing more so by the minute. "I don't care about the money, Steven; I just want to go home. Monica must be going out of her mind by now."

"I understand," he said, sitting down on the bed. "Listen, Andrew, I haven't had a chance to go over the entire case yet, but what I've seen so far and from what Mr. King has told me, we've got a lot of work to do on your defense. The 'up a creek without a paddle kind of work', pal."

"I don't want to think about that right now."

"The sooner the better, Andrew, trust me."

"Look, we'll talk about it this afternoon."

"Sounds like a plan," Steve agreed. "I'm going to go light a fire under these guys. I'll be back," he said, motioning to the guard. "Sit tight."

Andrew paced around the cell. Circumstances had spun too far out of control. And now there was only time to react. There wasn't time to weigh the pros and cons. His own weaknesses had backed him into a corner. And he was scared out of his mind. Soon he would have nowhere to turn, no escape available to him. Once events were set in motion, there would be no turning back. But his most painful regret wasn't for himself, but for his wife. The truth would devastate her but the time for lies was over now. Her only mistake was loving him, and she was about to pay a terrible price.

*

When the phone finally rang, Monica flinched. She felt too charged to sleep and could not face getting into bed alone. As she heard Andrew's voice calling to say he was on his way home, she could hope it was over and they could get on with their lives. It was almost two in the morning and he should be arriving any minute. She couldn't wait to hold him. She nearly wept, and decided to wait in the bedroom for him. When she came face to face with Andrew and fell apart, she didn't want an audience.

During the past twelve hours, she felt like she aged thirty years. One look in the mirror proved those hours had taken their toll. With a groan, she whirled away. She looked as beaten down as she felt.

*

Andrew let out a sigh when they turned the corner and started down his street. He'd never been so happy to see the street he'd lived on for almost two decades now. As they slowed to a stop in front of the mansion, his thoughts turned to the woman waiting for him inside. Despite the drudgery of the hours spent being grilled, the threat of confinement and the end of his freedom, a smile reshaped his face. "God, it's good to be home," he said, sitting up in the seat for a better view.

Steve saw the look of contentment on Andrew's face and laughed. "I'm sure it is. Just don't forget, I'll be coming by this afternoon to discuss strategy."

"I need some time with Monica," he said. "Come round at four."

With an eye out for lurking paparazzi he pulled into the first available parking space and shut off the car. "It looks quiet. So let's get you inside before the press hounds back at the police station realize we duped them."

*

Thomas pulled the door open before Andrew had a chance to turn the key in the lock. They stood in the doorway looking at each other for a moment before they embraced. Showing such overt displays of affection was something they rarely did, but under these circumstances, it was completely appropriate. Steve eased them through the doorway and closed the door. He didn't want to take the chance of any well-hidden photographer snapping candid pictures for a six figure payday.

"It's very good to see you, Andrew."

"It's good to see you too, old man," Andrew replied, smiling. He looked past Thomas into the living room and his smile faded. "Where is she?"

Thomas noticed the worried expression on his master's face and said, "It's nothing to be concerned about, she decided to wait for you upstairs. She's a bit...worked up over the events of the day."

"I imagine she is," Steve added, putting his hand on Andrew's shoulder. "I think I'll let you get upstairs to your wife, I'll see you later this afternoon then," he continued.

Andrew looked up the staircase, anxious and distracted. "Fine, Steve, just phone before you come 'round." And, without another word he started up the stairs.

"Certainly." Steve watched him disappear at the top of the stairs. When he was sure Andrew was out of earshot he turned to Thomas, "I'm sure you have questions so let's go into the living room."

Thomas shook his head. "Yes, let's do that."

*

He placed his hand on the door and felt a lump rise up in his throat. What was he going to say to her? He put his hand on the knob and turned it slowly. When he pushed open the door, she was there waiting. His whole reason for living was coming towards him. Her fear and tension rolled into him in waves, her tears bringing tears of his own.

Andrew let her rush into his arms, let her burrow into him. He lifted her, stepped inside, and closed the door behind them. He let her lips caress his throat, feeling removed from the stresses outside these walls. Her arms wrapped around him and there was such warmth in her embrace.

He felt so much love for this woman—in this instant it

overwhelmed him. He could no longer discern where he ended and she began, such was the power of emotion between them. He could feel every beat of her heart against his chest. "I...I'm so glad you waited up. I need you Monica. I've never needed you more," he whispered, his voice thick with emotion.

"I'm right here, Drew." She kissed him and brought his face close to hers. "Tell me what happened. What did they put you through?"

"Nothing too terrible." His eyes were closed and he just wanted to feel her breath on his face. "We have to talk," he continued, pulling away and walking them over to the fireplace.

She felt her heart drop. "Talk about what, Drew?"

He lowered himself onto the carpet and brought her into his lap. "I've got something to tell you that I should have told you long before now."

"If it's more bad news, I've had my fill. I just want to be with you right now, Drew. Can't we talk about it later? It's almost three in the morning."

She looked exhausted and after so much time keeping her in the dark, he didn't see how a few more hours could hurt. He shrugged his shoulders and drew her close to him, "Whatever you want. We'll sit awhile and try to unwind."

She snuggled into his arms and laid her head on his chest. "Just tell me one thing," she said, looking up at him.

He glanced down and smiled at her, "What's that?"

"That this is a terrible mistake."

He evaded. Tomorrow was soon enough for truth. "Don't worry about it."

*

"I still think this is our best option to keep Andrew safe," Thomas insisted after Steve spent the last half hour telling him about the case, and what defense—if any—he could offer Andrew.

"I'm not listening to this, Thomas. I mean I hear you. I hear every word, but officially, I haven't heard a thing. I still think it sounds a little extreme. Guilty men have been found not guilty before. It happens all the time. Maybe you should have more faith in my ability as a top notch defense attorney," Steve replied, crossing his legs on the coffee table in front of him.

"Please," Thomas scolded. "Now is not the time to be sensitive. I have every confidence in your ability to defend

Andrew, but you know damn well he can't stand trial. Besides Andrew and myself there are only two living people who know what Andrew truly is, his doctor is one, and you're the other, Steve. Do I really have to go over what he is capable of doing, of what he's already done?" Thomas said pacing in front of the fireplace.

"No, I remember all too well what he has done and what he can do when pushed into a corner. Frankly, I don't know why you just didn't call me first when all this happened today. I mean why did you bother calling Randolph? What can he do for you under the circumstances?"

"Andrew thought you were out of town and time was of the essence, Mr. Hardy." Thomas snapped.

"All right, no need to get your britches in a knot, Thomas. And don't call me Mr. Hardy, that's my father. All I'm saying is Randolph is a very intelligent lawyer. If you're in a bind in business, he's your man. But he's not honed to the little tricks criminal lawyers can use to minimize damage. He allowed questions to be asked and answered that I—knowing what we're up against here—never would have tolerated." Steve grimaced. "And don't get me started on the lineup."

"I know," Thomas snapped, knowing he'd made a miscalculation. "But I couldn't let him go to the police station without legal representation, now could I?"

"You should have beeped me." He shook his head over the ramifications of Thomas' haste. "I didn't even know what was going on until Randolph called me three hours later," Steve said, standing up and stretching. He yawned, dead on his feet. Jetlag was winning out over adrenaline.

"There wasn't time."

Steve walked out of the living room into the hallway. "Well, just give me twenty four hours to see where we stand legally. That's all I ask," he said, opening the door. "And don't open the door without asking who it is. There's going to be reporters camped outside here any time now. And the news vans won't be far behind," he tossed the warning over his shoulder as he started down the covered entranceway.

"The phone's already ringing off the hook."

"Wonderful," Steve replied sarcastically, as he disappeared at the end of the entranceway.

*

A light tapping at the bedroom door awakened Andrew. He opened his eyes and squinted at the clock on the night stand. It was just past four thirty in the morning. He groped around at the bottom of the bed for his robe. He had been wrapped around Monica for solace as much as warmth.

He fumbled for the door and yanked it open. In the dim light of the hallway, he saw Thomas standing on the other side of the door. "What is it, Thomas?" Andrew asked through a yawn.

"Everything's ready at a moments notice, I have everything under control. Steve left a short while ago and he wants us to give him twenty four hours to work on things, before we make any decisions."

"Twenty four hours? Fine, he's got them, but no more. Get some sleep, Thomas. I'll discuss it with him when he drops round today. I want to get back to bed before Monica realizes I gone. This is all set in motion as a last resort, do you understand?" Andrew asked.

"I understand, Master Andrew."

When Thomas left, Andrew closed the door and made himself comfortable in the chair opposite of the window next to the bookshelves. He felt too wired to sleep, even though that was what he needed most. This day was going to be hell. He needed to be sharp, clearheaded. Any missteps could ruin him. His entire future rested on the decisions he made. And they were decisions he would have to live with forever.

Chapter 28

When he next woke he found himself in the chair in front of the fireplace. He couldn't remember trading one chair for the other, but it wasn't hard to imagine walking the room relentlessly in the hopes he might expel some of nervous energy that kept him awake. It was early and he opened the door to find the hall was still washed in the golden light of early morning.

He closed the door and crossed to his side of the bed. The clock on the nightstand read six forty-five while across the bed Monica was finally asleep. For more than an hour after they'd made love, she'd tossed and turned, her murmurs growing to pleas, as she tried to outrun the nightmares he'd brought to her. So, he left her—finally peaceful—and went to prepare for the day. There was no more time for worry. That time had come and gone. There was only time for action.

A shower did little to root out the pressure welling up in his chest, or ease the anxiety knotted in his shoulders, but it cleared his head and sharpened his senses. At the sink, he tightened the towel around his waist and let out a deep breath. He was tired. His body and his mind were exhausted. Living life as a mortal was draining the strength from him. He could feel it coming out every pore.

The special lighting he had installed six months earlier, finally allowed him to see something he'd never seen before, himself. As haggard as he looked, he felt more like the mortal he was supposed to be than the monster lurking beneath. It was because of his own insecurities that he hadn't seen himself before now. The ones planted by his father at such an early age. The ones, which allowed him to believe he was what he pretended to be. But to look himself in the eye and see the curse alive there, see the truth of his fate, was too hard.

So much went though his mind as he stood there. He had errands to take care of this morning so this was not the time for self reflection. Before Monica could wake up and ask where he was going, he needed to slip out. Before Steve showed up to discuss his case, he needed to return. One errand was something he should have done a long time ago but his monumental guilt kept him from doing so. This was no time for procrastination. Today was the day to get it done.

He was brushing his teeth when the intercom buzzed. He spit out the toothpaste and answered, "Good morning, Thomas." He smiled wide to get a look at all of his freshly gleaming teeth. "Checking up on me are you?"

"I wanted to know what you want for breakfast, Master Andrew. I buzzed into the bedroom first but no one answered," he said sounding concerned.

"It's nothing to worry about, old man, she's just very tired—it was a long night," Andrew said, taking his robe down off the door and pulling it on.

"Yes, it certainly was that. So what will you be having?"

"Some coffee and a muffin."

"Coffee?"

"Yes, Thomas. I would like some coffee this morning."

"All right. When will you be down?"

"Five minutes."

*

He walked quietly into the bedroom and over to the closet. He took a pair of slacks from a hanger and slipped them on. He zipped them and took a white shirt and cardigan from the closet as well. He stepped into his loafers and left the room. He walked down the hall buttoning his shirt as he went. He went down the stairs slowly, pulling the cardigan on over his shirt on the way. He looked at his watch. It was seven fifteen, he would be able to eat his breakfast and be out the door by seven thirty. However, getting past Thomas would not be as easy.

Thomas greeted Andrew warmly when he walked into the kitchen. "Good morning!" he said cheerfully.

Andrew stopped and looked oddly at Thomas. "And why are you so cheerful?"

"The glass isn't half empty, it's half full, remember?"

Andrew shook his head and walked over to the cabinets. "I'll be jiggered, you've finally lost your mind, have you?" he opened the door and took down a mug from the shelf.

Thomas laughed. "I assure you, I'm quite sane. I just prefer looking at the positive side of things," he replied lightheartedly.

"Really? Now I have to think that you've gone completely mad," Andrew said, filling his cup with coffee and taking a sip.

"Everything's well in hand," Thomas reminded him in an upbeat tone. "We have our options, don't forget."

"Yes, we do have our options. But none fill me with relief, Thomas. Frankly, I see it as a lose-lose situation." Andrew took another long drink of his coffee.

"Just try to relax."

"Easy for you to say," Andrew said with a frown. He went to the counter and chose a muffin and then took a large bite. He washed it down with the last of his coffee and set the cup in the sink. He turned and said, "I'll be back shortly." Then he went through the door without another word.

Thomas was right behind him. "You're not going anywhere," he stammered, surprised.

He lifted a brow at the tone, but kept moving. "Don't get excited, I've got some things to take care of, that's all," Andrew said as he went to the closet and took out his coat.

Thomas stood silent and then, "Well, I'll go with you," he said quickly.

"No," Andrew replied, laying his hand on the old man's shoulder. "Not this time. I've had Juan bring my car around from the garage. This is something I have to do alone." He pulled his coat on and walked to the door. "I won't be long, and don't fret so, Thomas, I'll be fine. I'm a big boy. Leave Monica sleep as long as she likes. See you soon."

"But Andrew, the sun is up," called Thomas, but it was too late. His master was gone.

*

It had been years since Andrew had driven his Viper sports car. Needing time alone—and privacy—he decided this was as good a time as any to change that. It was a beautiful machine and a nod to his male ego when he bought it on a whim four years ago. It was simply a toy he purchased because he could afford to do so.

He opened the door dropped down into the leather seat. The smell of leather was stimulating and coaxed a smile from him. Lifting his other leg inside, he pulled the door shut and shoved the key into the ignition.

When the engine roared to life, his smile grew in spite of his heavy mood. This car made him feel like a stud. The original windows and windshield had been replaced with special black tinted windows. They blocked out every ray of sunlight and permitted a form of independent transportation without fear for Andrew. For him it was in the most literal sense, freedom.

He drove off as the first news van pulled up across the street. His timing accidentally perfect, he escaped the beginning of what was sure to be an onslaught of media sharks thirsty from the scent of blood. Traffic was light, given the hour, and he laughed as he drove completely undetected. He slowed when he turned the corner. He hadn't been back to his destination in such a long time. It had been easier to avoid it and move on. Now he had no choice. It was the right thing to do.

His mother would have been proud of him, a simple fact that quieted his doubts. And it was that as much as his conscience that was driving him. And, it was right. This risk he was taking. A penance deserved. And one he was willing to pay.

Andrew began to fidget as his destination grew nearer to him. He was nervous and unable to control his panicked thoughts. But it was important that he relax and allay the panic. He could not appear the least bit unstable when he arrived. It was important that he get what he was coming for, he could accept nothing less. He turned the last corner, and there at the end of the street it stood majestically in the brightening sunshine.

The breath caught in his throat as he took it in. It was beautiful but his conscience never allowed him to appreciate it before. Andrew backed the car into the space right in front and shut off the engine. He wiped the sweat from his forehead with the back of his hand and closed his eyes so he could steady his breathing.

Pulling an umbrella from behind the seat, Andrew opened the door. From behind the sunglasses that wrapped around his eyes, he saw the sun moving behind a cloud. If he was to make it inside safely, he had to go now. With the door open, he opened the large umbrella and pushed himself out of the car. Moving quickly he made it to the sidewalk and ran up the steps three at a time. And then the door was in front of him, a gateway to the forbidden.

New York's largest Catholic cathedral, and all he had to do was step inside. A sanctuary awaited him. Or Hell would open up and swallow him whole. He would have to trust. He would have to take a leap of faith.

Andrew could feel intense heat underneath his skin. He had to get inside before he was reduced to ash. He yanked open the door and darted inside. Out of breath and in pain, he'd been burnt by the sunlight. He looked at the damaged, burned flesh on his wrist and hissed in pain.

He sucked air into his lungs waiting for his skin to cool. When he heard someone behind him, he reacted as if under threat. Spinning around rather unsteadily, he saw a priest approaching him. He was an old man with kind eyes. He reminded Andrew of Thomas. And he chose to see that as a sign.

The priest smiled and tipped his head. "Can I be helpin' ya, my son?" he asked, his Irish accent so crisp it sounded like he just stepped off the island.

He relaxed and trusted in the ease he felt in this man's presence. "Thank you, Father," Andrew said with a smile. "Could you hear my confession?" he asked, deciding to wander farther into the heart of the church. The old priest at his side as the two of them walked down the aisle toward the alter, the crucifix high above on the wall beyond, the holy water, and all the other symbols he as a vampire should oppose.

"So you'll be needin' the confessional then?" the priest asked as he clasped his hands behind his back as they made their way to the front of the church.

Andrew shook his head, forcing himself on. There was serenity here if he allowed himself to be touched by it. "I'd rather speak to you face to face, Father," he replied, cradling his wounded hand gingerly.

"All right then. Well, I suppose I should be tellin' ya, I'm Father John Patrick and this grand church is my charge. Now, how can I be of help to ya, Son?" He asked, giving a sweeping gesture to a front pew with his hand.

Andrew dropped down into the pew and blew out a breath. "I'd shake your hand, Father Patrick, but I seem to be unable to do that at the moment."

The humor lighting the priest's eyes dimmed as he sat down next to Andrew and touched his arm. "You're hurt. Perhaps it's a doctor you need instead of a priest?" he said in a more serious tone.

As Andrew began sweating, he couldn't say if it was because of physical pain or the hypocrisy of thinking he belonged in this holy place. The beautifully ornate pews smelled of polish, the hymnals shined in the candlelight. He didn't know where to begin but knew he had to begin somewhere. "I'll be fine. I committed many sins, Father and guilt weights heavily on me."

"Aye," Father Patrick smiled. "And it weighs heaviest on your heart."

"These sins I've committed are unforgivable. I haven't the impudence to ask for absolution, but I must clear my conscience."

"God forgives all, my son," The priest said, kindly. "That is, if you are truly repentant."

"I assure you, I am, but that doesn't change what I've done."

Father Patrick studied the troubled man next to him and saw the torment within. "It is not me you need to be assurin', my son."

Andrew leaned back and closed his eyes again. Taking the comfort he felt underneath his anxiety. His hand felt like it was on fire, but he wouldn't focus on it. "Is it God then?"

"It's not such a task," the priest said. "It's simple, ya see. God knows your heart, Andrew," and then he smiled, "Inside and out."

"I didn't tell you my name." Andrew inhaled deeply. "You know who I am, Father?" he asked, straightening himself.

When Father Patrick laughed, his bushy white brows danced. "Yes, my son, I know who you are. Your good works and charitable nature has placed you high on my prayer list."

For a moment, he questioned why he was there. Why burden this man of God with his atrocities? But he needed to, regardless of what happened after he left this place, he needed to purge himself. "Everything I tell you is held in the sanctity of the confessional, right?"

"Of course, my son."

"God will never forgive me."

"If yer repentant he will. He is a loving God."

If ever he could unburden himself it would be now in this place he thought. "I've taken lives, Father Patrick, many lives."

The priest was stunned. For an instant, he could only gape unblinkingly at the man whose reputation defied such an admission. But he did seem tortured, the truth was in his eyes.

"I am sorrier for these sins than I can ever express, Father Patrick."

Silence followed, each of them thinking their own thoughts. Andrew fearing it may have been a mistake to tell this priest of his sins. He deserved to burn in hell for all eternity and deserved nothing in the way of absolution. While Father Patrick was still surprised by the weight of the confession, he knew it was in his calling to offer loving support without judgment.

When finally the quiet between them was broken, the priest

wanted to understand.

"So what I've been readin' in the mornin' paper is true?" Father Patrick inquired, looking into the man's eyes for the answer because it was there that a man harbored all his secrets.

"Yes, it is true," Andrew laughed a chuckle that grew into a roaring chortle. Father Patrick looked at him in bewilderment. "Forgive me, Father, I mean no disrespect," Andrew said, trying to regain his composure. "It's just that I am used to the press for my business accomplishments but this, this kind of scrutiny is something else entirely."

"I see."

"No." Andrew shook his head. "I'm afraid you don't. At least not the whole picture anyway. I still have much to tell you, Father."

Father Patrick turned to face Andrew in the pew. "Go on then," he said simply.

Andrew chose his next words very carefully. "I don't want you thinking I'm some raving lunatic who spends his evenings chasing down innocent people." His eyes, intense, bore into the kind eyes watching him. "It is far more complicated than that I promise you. There's evil in me, Father. I must do it to survive. I have animal instincts, animalistic needs. I suppose that's closer to the truth, Father. And I have worked diligently over the years to control them, and up until recently, I've done very well."

Father Patrick held up his hand to stop him and saw the pleading in his eyes. "I'm afraid I don't understand, my son. In what sense are you an animal?" Father Patrick asked, his soft green eyes showing both confusion and compassion.

"I feed off of other people, Father. I require the one substance to live that only they can give me."

The old man's eyes narrowed. "What substance is that, my son?"

"Blood."

Father Patrick opened his mouth to speak but words failed him. "Did ya say blood, Lad? Human blood?" Father Patrick finally managed to say.

"Yes, that is what I said, Father," Andrew replied, watching him carefully. Did he think Andrew was crazy? Was he afraid? The last thing he wanted to do was cause the old man's heart to fail.

And then the priest knew. In the center of his heart, God spoke to him. "You're different from any other man I have ever met. However, this need of yours is not the reason, my son. Your soul is dead, it is."

"Not anymore, Father Patrick I found someone who gives it life."

In Andrew Carter he sensed no evil. "Do you have faith in God, my son?"

"I did once," Andrew admitted. "But that was many years ago. I have no right to have faith in God, Father. A man has to be human to have that right. And I haven't been that in too many years to count."

Father Patrick shook his head. "No, my son, as long as you're havin' life in your body, there is still hope."

"I have never wanted life more, but I can't bring myself to hope," Andrew exclaimed.

"I've seen many things, Andrew," Father Patrick explained. "The grace of God, and the corruption of the devil."

"I cannot be saved, Father." A wave of panic gripped him. "I tried to tell myself I came because it was the moral thing to do. But that's not entirely true, I came for forgiveness," he muttered, raking his good hand through his hair. "For God's forgiveness and mercy, but my soul is out of his hands. I am here in front of you, breathing, talking, but I'm a dead man. A dead man desperately clinging to life! I am an animal. I am undead, a child of the evil you are sworn to wage war against…I walk the earth as one of you. But I am a vampire."

Father Patrick was silent as he digested what this man had told him. He had seen much evil in his life, many demons from hell. He surprised Andrew when he stood and placed both of his strong hands on both sides of his face and looked into his eyes. "I have seen many otherwise unbelievable things in my life as a priest. I have exercised demons from the souls of God's children. This is not too hard for me to believe. One only has to be lookin' into your eyes to see that you are tellin' the truth," he said, seriously.

"You don't think I'm mad?" Andrew said in amazement, placing his hands over the hands that warmed his cheeks. "I know what I did was wrong, hard as I tried I could not stop it."

"I can only offer you this in comfort. May God bless you for your courage."

Chapter 29

He arrived back home just after nine in the morning. He parked the car in the garage and took the garage elevator straight to his office. Andrew wasn't sure what to expect when the elevator door opened. The story was all over the radio so Andrew was certain everyone in the office knew he was suspect in the murders in California and here in New York. His wrist was throbbing and the pain had him teetering on the point of delusion. Father Patrick treated the vicious burn with ointment and wrapped it in a bandage for him before he left the church, but it did little to help.

The floors moved by slowly and he took slow, even breaths.

The elevator stopped on the sixth floor, the doors opened and he stepped through them into the reception area. Everyone continued on with his or her work but he could feel their stares as he made his way to his office. He was happy to find Sarah at her desk typing up reports as though nothing unusual had taken place. He waited a moment and spoke to her, "Good Morning, Sarah." He smiled at her, searching her face for any hint of fear or disgust. "How are things this morning?" he continued, walking over to her desk.

Sarah smiled warmly at him. "Better than things are going for you, I expect."

His words were caught in his throat. "Would you do me a favor and call all the principles into the conference room for a meeting?"

"Sure. When's the meeting?" Sarah asked as she picked the phone.

"Nine thirty. Tell them not to keep me waiting. I've got plenty of things to deal with today," Andrew replied, walking to his door.

Sarah turned in her chair. "For what it's worth, I know you didn't do what they're accusing you of, Mr. Carter."

Andrew stopped and turned in the doorway. He smiled at Sarah. "Thank you for your faith in me."

*

He closed the door behind him and let out a sigh. This was going to be tough. Having all the men he has known for years looking at him with suspicion. Sitting down behind his desk though, he didn't have time to worry about the things he could not change.

Other things needed his total attention right now. He had to make arrangements for Carter Industries in his absence, should worse come to worse. No matter what his problems were, there was no reason to let the people he employed suffer. They all had families to support and he had to remember that.

He typed his password into the computer. He wanted to see where he stood financially. The police would soon freeze his assets if they hadn't already done so. He had to talk to Mr. King to make sure his company would be able to function under the freeze. He waited for the information to come up on the screen and as he had suspected, his personal bank account had been frozen. That didn't worry him, he maintained Swiss accounts for just such an occasion. The good news was that his company assets seemed to be fine for the moment.

Andrew took a deep breath and lowered his head into his hands. He was tired and worried about so many things over which he had no control, and he hated it. He hated the weakness in it. But this was his karma, his fate, and he would be damned if he would drag more innocent people down with him.

*

Thomas was frantic and growing more so by the moment. He couldn't be sure where his master was but he had some idea. The only thing he was certain of, outside with the sun up there was no place for his master. This was a bad time for him to be experimenting with tolerance to the sun. When he left, he'd said as little as possible about what his errands were or why he had to go alone.

Thomas knew him so well, it wasn't an impossible task to figure out where he had gone and why. He'd been pushed past the breaking point with his arrest. With his conscience weighing heavily on him over the last year, his guilt was smothering him so he would go to the one place he had sworn to never go again. Self-punishment, Thomas knew. Andrew hadn't been inside a church since his mother's death.

He had gone to pray for her soul and for forgiveness for being a less than perfect son to her. Andrew's pain had to be great to go back. And knowing this, Thomas felt the pain in his own heart. When would his master be allowed peace?

The final stages of the plan were taken care of in the early hours of the morning before Andrew awakened. Now it was just a matter of time. Such drastic measures would need to be taken once it was blatantly clear they could no longer remain in this city.

It didn't matter how things turned out legally. From the day this investigation started, a shadow had been cast on Andrew Carter. He would be looked on with a certain degree, no matter how small or insignificant, of suspicion forever. Thomas had said as much to Andrew but he didn't need to. It was an unspoken understanding between the two of them. The only one truly in the dark was Monica. How they would begin to explain this to her, he had no idea. Neither he nor Andrew could avoid telling her any longer. The time had come.

*

Andrew stood up at the head of the conference table to greet his board members as they came, one by one, into the conference room. Each wearing their own plastic expression and shaking his hand as he offered it to them. It occurred to Andrew as each of them took their usual seats around the table that over the years he'd come to regard these men as, if not friends then at least business confidants. It was uncomfortable now to see them all looking at him with such uncertainty. He took his seat and nervously began shuffling papers around in front of him. He looked up to find everyone eyes on him expectantly.

Andrew broke from their stares, looked down at the papers in front of him, and cleared his throat. "First, let me begin by saying that I know you all are aware of my legal difficulties, and there is absolutely no need for any of you to feel uneasy. Secondly, and more importantly, there are some serious business decisions that have to be addressed by those of us in this room, and the sooner we deal with them the better I should think. Don't you agree?" he said, waiting for a response.

They nodded their heads in agreement.

"Fine then." Andrew opened the file under his left hand and scanned it quickly. "I'm going to be away from the office a great deal more often until this whole situation is cleared up. I hope I can trust you all to deal with the day to day business operations in my absence."

He clasped his hands together and placed them on the table in front of him. With his penetrating gaze, he looked each man in the eye. "Any questions before I continue?"

"I have a question, Mr. Carter," a short, solid, bearded man said, from the far end of the table.

Andrew smiled politely. "Go ahead then, Larry."

"How long do you expect to be tied up with your legal problems?"

"Hopefully not that long, but you needn't worry, I'll be keeping a close eye on things."

"I have no doubt."

"Good. Anything else?" He looked around the table waiting for other comments. Nothing more was said so Andrew shuffled through the papers in front of him until he found the ones he needed. "We have a lot of ground to cover in a short period of time. The most pressing issue is the vacant seat on the board, any thoughts gentlemen?"

"I suppose we should fill it," Mr. Gains offered up, sarcastically.

Pushing his glasses onto his nose Andrew let out a deep breath. He was growing impatient with Larry Gains, it was obvious that he already had him tried and convicted. He could see it in his eyes. "No shit," he replied, crisply. Andrew surprised himself, and if the expressions on the men's faces were any indication, he'd surprised them too.

Larry Gains cleared his throat. "It wasn't my intention to upset you, Andrew," he said innocently.

"Only my friends call me Andrew, Mr. Gains. And you're no friend of mine," Andrew said evenly, trying to keep his temper in check. "To continue, it is absolutely vital the seat be filled immediately. I was hoping to deal with it after the first of the year, but given what's going on now, I want to resolve the situation right away. No matter what happens concerning my legal matters, I will vote as I always do during my absences, via proxy. A vacant seat will send up a red flag to anyone looking to find a weakness and use it in an attempt for a takeover."

Mr. Roark, a graying, somewhat overweight, but otherwise intelligent man, cleared his throat and said, "What about Larry Davidson?"

Andrew rubbed his temples. The headache he'd developed on the drive over was returning. "Larry Davidson? He's a good man, he'd be perfect. And right at home on the board."

"He's been anxious to do something since he retired and with his wife recently passing away, it might be the perfect distraction for him." Mr. Roark added when he saw Andrew's interest piqued.

"Well, let's get a hold of him and make him an offer—today, in fact. Don't waste any time. Make it an offer he's too smart to refuse," Andrew said with a smile.

"I think six figures should impress him enough."

"Just make it in the high six figures. I want this settled as soon as possible," Andrew insisted, tossing the papers aside and picking up another file.

"We're very close to locking up the deal for the medical companies in Germany," Mr. Gains said with his usual plastic smile and matching charm.

"Excellent. I've wanted those companies for five years, about time something starts going my way."

An hour later the meeting was over and Andrew was sitting behind his desk lost in thought over how many things were about to change. His head was pounding and his stomach was churning. That was to be expected, Thomas had warned him. He looked at his watch, he'd stayed longer then he wanted too. He had to get home.

*

Andrew walked into the kitchen and found Monica standing in front of the sink looking outside through the blind she opened on the window. He could tell by her posture that she was tense. For a time, he stood there in silence cursing himself. What had he done to this woman he loved more than anything? Knowing he caused her pain was more then he could stomach. And knowing he would have to cause her more still before the day was through, tore at his heart.

He went to her and put his hands on her shoulders. "Where are you, Love?" He kissed her temple from behind. "You're a million miles away," he said, pulling her back against him.

Turning, she wrapped her arms around him. "I was on our beach. I wish we could go back there and forget all about this mess," she said, wistfully.

"I know this is tough, Love, but I promise all this will be over soon."

"You wouldn't be the first innocent man convicted and sent to prison."

Andrew squeezed her tightly and kissed her cheek. "Such

dreary thoughts in that head of yours," he whispered.

Monica cupped his face. "Your hair's getting longer than I've ever seen," she said, wanting to change the subject to something mundane. Turning his head from side to side, she took his hand and felt the bandage. She looked down and gasped. "What happened to your hand, Drew?"

He watched concern flood her eyes and tried not to flinch when she pulled it near for a closer look. "I'm clumsy, that's all," he said, kissing her quickly on the mouth. "Don't worry, I'm fine."

She unwrapped the bandage and winced at the grisly burn. "This needs to be seen by a doctor. It's a bad burn, Sweetheart."

"Thomas will see to it," he assured her, and feathered kisses along her jaw line. "Now, don't fret."

"Where were you off to so early this morning?"

"I had a few errands to run and I had to stop in for a meeting at the office. Why? Miss me?" he teased.

"I always miss you when you're not with me."

"I will be with you for the entire day. That is, if you don't mind sharing me with my lawyer."

"If I have too," she whined, playfully.

"You are such a trooper." He tweaked her nose and stepped out of the embrace. I need to get ready for Steven. I hope he's got some good news. Heaven knows I've gotten enough bad news to last a couple lifetimes."

Monica became concerned. "Something more has happened?"

"For starters, all of our personal assets have been frozen, and to make matters all the more difficult, the members of my board aren't exactly brimming with confidence over my arrest. Some are ready to revolt."

"Is it really that bad?"

"It's getting there."

"When's Steven arriving?"

"He'll be here in time for lunch, which reminds me, I need to speak to Thomas about the menu. Where is he anyway?"

"He's off somewhere. I haven't seen much of him."

"I better go hunt him up."

*

Thomas was busy in the dark sector. His nerves frayed and he was at his wits end with Andrew taking off without him. What could he have been thinking? Taking off with the sun up and blazing. It was as if his master had a death wish. Thomas knew all these problems were taking their toll on him, but he still needed to curb his reckless impulses. Now was the time to live with the consequences of all his misguided actions. All he could hope was that Andrew came home soon and more importantly, that no harm had come to him.

Thomas finished packing the last of the vials into the cooler at his feet, fearing his master's choices. Perhaps he would flee and never return. It would prove most calamitous if he made such a fateful decision. What a disaster it would be if he did choose to disappear without so much as a word to anyone. Imaging the horror entailed in trying to explain all that had transpired from the time his madam met Andrew until this very moment. He could barely stomach the thought.

There were contents in this room today, contents which were invaluable to his master. Thomas couldn't keep his eyes from wandering to the far corner and locking on the large refrigerating system storing them. Knowing what was inside was truly making him ill. The contents would play the most important role in a plan, but that didn't mean he had to like it.

This room was the lifeline to his master's existence. But it never struck him before that a space so small and dank could hold such importance. For Andrew not to have access to it, to be locked up in some cell, to be driven completely mad by the absolute need of its contents and yet be denied, was beyond Thomas' comprehension. The cruelty would be immeasurable. He shook off the last of these nagging thoughts and prepared to leave the room and return upstairs. Where he was sure Monica was searching for him by now.

Under no circumstances could she be allowed to find this room or what it held inside. Too many questions would be asked before his master was prepared to answer them.

*

Andrew nearly knocked Thomas down the stairs when he opened the door. "Good Lord, Thomas! You gave me quite a start, old man," he said, grabbing hold of his shoulders to steady him.

"Nice to see you made it back in one piece." Thomas said shortly, pushing his way past Andrew and walking away in the direction of the living room.

Andrew couldn't help chuckling, following after Thomas like

a boy who'd been scolded by his father. "Come on Thomas, don't be cross with me. No harm has come to me," he said in his own defense.

Thomas grunted as he continued into the living room. He marched past the sofa and spun around on his heels. With a look of total arrogance he said, "I can think of several occasions when that was anything but true."

Andrew covered his mouth to stifle the laugh rising in his throat. He couldn't help being amused when Thomas admonished him in an effort to let his hurt feeling be known. "That is true, old man," he agreed. "But I had some things to take care of and I didn't see any reason to drag you along."

"Poppycock!" Thomas snorted.

That was it. He couldn't hold it in any longer. Andrew was roaring with laughter before Thomas even could finish his dignified expression. "Oh, Thomas, you haven't said that to me since childhood! You always did know how to cheer me up."

"It wasn't meant to be amusing, Andrew," he said sternly.

Andrew smiled and looked at Thomas. "Sorry, I just wanted to tell you to fix something light for lunch. Steve will be here at noon."

"Yes, I know. He phoned while you were out. I had no idea what to tell him. Why do you insist on placing yourself in danger?"

"You know very well where I was going and why, so don't pretend otherwise." His gaze met Thomas' angry eyes and watched understanding blunt the anger. "And I'm back now and nothing bad happened to me," Andrew said, simply.

When he went to and lifted his master's damaged hand, he said, "Nothing but a severely burnt hand." Thomas shook his head in dismay. "Get upstairs. This needs to be tended."

Andrew nodded. "Thanks, old man," he replied with affection.

*

Steven Hardy rang the doorbell at precisely twelve noon. Thomas showed him into the living room where Andrew was anxiously waiting. He crossed the room and shook his client's hand. "Where's your lovely wife?" he asked with a smile.

"She received an overseas call a few minutes ago. We're to begin without her," Andrew said, showing his guest to the sofa. "Would you like something to drink?"

"A martini would be great."

When Thomas left, Steve put his briefcase on the coffee table and opened it. "How are you?"

"I've had better days, Steven."

"I guess you know then, that your personal assets have been frozen?"

"Oh yes," Andrew replied, ruefully. "That news smacked me in the face earlier this morning. But I'll have all I need with my diverted funds." Andrew gratefully took the glass of wine Thomas brought him and took a long drink.

Steven nodded his appreciation to Thomas as his martini was put in front of him. He opened a file from his briefcase and pulled his glasses from his breast pocket. He got straight to the point. "You don't make it easy do you?" he asked but didn't wait for an answer. "Your options are few, Andrew. The evidence against you in California is circumstantial but compelling. And once they get the DNA results on the hair you'll be in serious trouble."

"I thought the hair's inadmissible."

"Yes and no," Steve said, glancing at Andrew over the tops of his glasses. "Because they obtained your sample without your knowledge or proper consent I could argue it's fruit of a poisonous tree and I might get it tossed. However, the prosecution could argue permission wasn't required because your expectation of privacy was unreasonable given housekeeping's and the hotel staff's access. Or, and this is their stronger argument, that since the hair was retrieved from the bed clothing and that bed clothing is property of the hotel, if permission was needed at all, it was the hotel management's to give, not yours."

"You can't be serious?"

Steve shrugged and took off his glasses, "I said it was a strong argument, not necessarily a winnable one," he paused, his expression sobering, "But win or lose on that, they've got blood evidence on the victims. And it gets worse, Andrew. California's been a bug up the NYPD's ass about connecting their murders to the killings here. So under orders from the prosecutor's office, you're now being actively investigated in the Central Park killings as well. And they won't make the same mistakes. They'll be here with a court order to draw your blood for comparison and to obtain a hair sample before day's end. Combine that with the eyewitness California's got, and there's a case even without the hair that was illegally obtained."

"So, it's only a matter of time before they show up here with warrants and court orders. And admissible DNA will be the last nail in the coffin for me. No pun intended."

"I'll go to the wall for you Andrew."

"I have no defense, Steven. I am guilty. It's karma."

"Not unless you want me to go into a courtroom and say you're not culpable because you have this tiny problem of being a blood sucking vampire," Steve offered sarcastically.

Andrew smiled smartly. "Very cute."

"You have other options?" Steven asked with a raised eyebrow and a glance to the hall to ensure privacy.

"Yes."

"My advice would be to use one of them."

"And you're certain about this?" Andrew wanted to be sure he understood. It had to be crystal clear.

Steve shook his head, pushed himself off the sofa, and took a deep breath. "Look, we can go into court and call the legality of the hair sample into question, but the blood evidence alone will bury you. I'm good Andrew, but I'm not that good. And there's the documented proof that you paid for the funerals," he said.

"What difference does that make?" Andrew protested. "If anything, it should make me a caring man."

Steve laughed and took a sip from his martini. "The DA will use that Andrew. He'll paint a picture of a man so tormented by his guilt, he would do anything to ease his troubled mind. Play the 'where there's smoke, there's fire' card for the jury."

"So in your professional opinion, I'm screwed!" Andrew exclaimed, pushing himself out of his chair and shoving his hands in his pockets in frustration.

"I understand your frustration, Andrew. And I'm giving you the best advice I can. There's no guarantee one way or the other." Steve came to his side and put his hand on his shoulder. "Just be damn sure you want to risk your freedom. You won't be able to handle prison, Andrew. You're not cut out for a place like that, especially a man with your particular weaknesses. Without your daily treatments, it would be hell on earth for you and dangerous," he continued.

Andrew's attention was on the floor. How much he loved the Japanese rug he stood on. Monica brought it home as a gift when she'd been in Japan for an interview. It still enchanted him. "It seems such a drastic step."

"You always knew it might come to this one day, Andrew. Life in prison would be much worse. Are you ready for that?"

"What am I going to tell Monica?" Andrew asked, meeting Steve's eyes.

"Anything you have too." Steve finished the last of his drink in one gulp. Wiping his lips with his napkin and said, "Or the truth is always an option. She'll think you're crazy, I know I sure as hell did. But she loves you and maybe that'll be enough."

*

Monica walked into the living room smiling. The brave face was for her husband. She didn't want him to know just how terrified she was. Even when found innocent, his reputation would never fully recover from the scandal building all around them.

Monica saw Andrew before he noticed her, and couldn't miss the tension in his jaw, the bleakness in his eyes. "I'm sorry my call went on and on. Lunch will be ready in twenty minutes," her voice rushed on. She took Andrew's hand and pulled him down next to her on the sofa. "How do things look, Steve?"

He offered a quick smile. "I think we have things well in hand."

*

Lunch was a nice distraction with no one wanting to discuss the elephant in the room. Andrew was quiet, pensive and unable to coax his appetite, just as Monica was unable to coax her's. He picked at his salmon and salad while she picked over her's. Who could eat and socialize now? With so much unknown, with her husband facing such a threat?

*

After lunch they were all back in the living room taking care of last minute details with Steve, when Monica found her thoughts occupied by the silent distance of Andrew. He was occupied by his own thoughts, only giving Steve half answers and grunts when he was spoken too. But he had a tight grip on her hand, so tight it was going numb. So Monica placed her other hand over his, rubbing it lightly to allow his grip to relax.

"You understand everything I've explained to both of you? Either of you have any more questions?" Steve asked. He gathered up the papers spread over the table. He looked over at Andrew and frowned, taking off his glasses he added, "Andrew, try not to worry. Have a little faith."

"Faith, right." Andrew repeated the word but he did not believe faith alone would save him. The relaxed smile from lunch was gone. He was too busy accepting what had to be. "I know you have another meeting Steve, so I won't keep you any longer," he continued. He stood and embraced him, the show of affection surprised Monica but she was touched at the display.

Steve pulled away from Andrew and laughed. "I'll call you after I talk to the D.A."

"Thanks."

*

Monica was still sitting on the sofa when Andrew came back into the living room. He walked Steve to the door and was surprised to find she was still waiting there when he returned. He went to the bar and poured another glass of wine. "Can I fix you something, love?"

"Not right now," she said, watching him carefully. "You know, you don't have to keep the stiff upper lip for me, sweetheart."

He shot her a grin over his shoulder before he came and sat down next to her. "I'm determined to get through this without falling apart," he said with confidence. "I'll be fine."

Monica leaned up and put her arms around his neck. "I think you're worn out, you didn't sleep last night. You tossed and turned most of the night."

He gave her a guilty look and sighed. "I was hoping I didn't disturb you, I'm sorry. The last twenty-four hours have been hell. I wish this didn't have to touch you," he said. His voice held sadness even while he tipped her face up for a kiss.

"What touches you, touches me, Drew. I don't need you to protect me." She blew out a breath because the edge she heard in her voice wasn't intentional. But he'd been quiet, dealing with his fears on his own, in his head. "I want to help you. Let me," she said with conviction.

Hearing those words, and the pain behind them, cut through him like a knife. "You do help me." He wanted to say more but couldn't. He knew he deserved what was coming, but she was an innocent victim, guilty of nothing but loving the wrong man. "Your handling the press is invaluable to me. I'm used to handling crisis alone. I don't mean to shut you out. You know that, don't you?"

She kissed his cheek. "Sure. I'll be in the office trying to deal with all the fall out," she said, standing and kissing him again. He watched as she disappeared through the doorway.

*

Monica walked into her office and pushed the door closed behind her. She loved this office and was thrilled when Andrew not only built it for her but also designed it himself. Unfortunately she didn't spend as much time in it as she would have liked, but it did provide her with an excuse to spend fewer hours at the studio because she could do most of her off-air work at home.

Wandering around the office she took in the spirit of the place. Because Andrew knew her so well, he designed it to her tastes perfectly. The cherry wood desk was oversized just like the one in his office except he chose oak for his own. And there was a bay window in the left wall which offered a view of Thomas' herb garden below. When she pulled the blinds open and looked outside the sun winked in to warm her face.

Monica sat down in the large leather chair and pulled herself up to the desk. It was covered with files and papers, all research for her next story. She groaned as she started going through the chaos trying to arrange some sort of order. In the back of her mind was the last conversation she'd had with Mr. Philips. He wanted her to talk to Andrew to get his side of the story out, on WNYC of course.

But getting the inside scoop on a story she now found herself living was making her ill while it made her boss salivate. The potential for a ratings explosion made him forget his ethics and sink to a low usually reserved for the tabloids. He glossed over the conflict of interest issue and argued there was no one better for this story than the woman on the inside. That she would care more about the truth then anyone else. But the last thing she wanted to be where her husband was concerned, was a reporter. So let some other network dig for the scoop. She would not put her husband under a microscope and dissect him for ratings or anything else.

Turning her head from side to side to release the tension burrowed deep into the base of her skull, she tried to prevent the headache that was threatening. When that failed, she rested her chin in her palm and considered resting her eyes. It wasn't just Andrew's legal problems adding pressure, she mused. The over sea's call she received earlier wasn't work related at all. The call had come from Ireland. It was Dr. O'Neal checking to see how she was feeling.

She told him she felt just as she had the day he told her she could never become pregnant—destroyed. She cursed the damned IUD she used in college. If she had waited for Andrew, they could've had a child by now...she couldn't know how wrong she was, or how ironic it was that in the end—at least where Andrew was concerned—it made no difference.

*

Thomas was in the master bedroom dusting when Andrew found him and they exchanged a knowing look. "Are all the arrangements taken care of?" Andrew asked, leaning against the doorframe.

"Yes, I've seen to everything," Thomas replied as he continued to dust the mantle of the fireplace.

"How're we financially?"

"I transferred two billion dollars to several bank accounts several months ago."

"That much?" Andrew lifted a brow and studied Thomas. "And I never realized it."

Thomas chuckled. "That's because you really have no concept of monetary worth. Do you have any idea what you made last year alone?"

"Not really," Andrew said truthfully. He didn't place much value on money. "You always think ahead, Thomas. You've always taken such good care of me. In so many ways I'm like a child, needing you to watch over me and protect me. Whatever would I do without you?"

"Sometime in the not too far off future, you may have to find out. I'm not as young as I use to be. I'll soon be sixty three and unlike you, I can't live forever." Thomas looked into his eyes and smiled. "But, let's not dwell on that. I plan to be here for you for many more years to come, Andrew," he promised.

"I don't know how to tell Monica."

"You'll find a way because you have too. To get her to go along with the plan, Andrew, you'll have to be honest. Tell her the truth. It will be hard, but it must be done if you want to keep her."

Andrew wished it was that simple. "I'll lose her the minute the words leave my mouth, Thomas."

"You'll lose her if you stay silent. Give her a chance to make up her own mind."

"I love her."

"So then, what other choice do you have? After all this time, she deserves the truth. She loves you, don't underestimate that."

*

Monica was able to get a lot accomplished. She filed most of her research and was looking through her desk for her address book when she heard a knock at the door. "Come in," she said, still rummaging around in her desk. She looked up to find Andrew standing in the doorway. "Hey. Did you talk to Thomas? He was looking for you."

He came in and closed the door. "Yes," he said with his back to her. "He's upstairs tidying up a bit," he continued. He turned around and found her watching him strangely.

"You feeling better?" she said with an uneasy sensation taking hold of her stomach. She tried to ignore it.

"I guess I'm just tired." He walked over to the desk and smiled at her. "It's time we had that talk."

"Alright," she said quietly.

Sitting down in the chair directly in front of the desk, he waited while Monica pushed her work aside. "I'm not sure where to start," he said, clasping his hands together to keep them from shaking.

Monica recognized his body language and mistook it as anxiety over his legal situation. "Well then, just start at the beginning."

He tried to find a place from which to begin his story, knowing that once he did, there would be no turning back. Seeing her right in front of him with those trusting eyes, he was finding it difficult to say anything—especially the words that would change them both forever.

Monica's smile disappeared and she angled her chin. His eyes were pulling her in. "You're scaring me, Drew. Just tell me what's making you so miserable," she pleaded.

Andrew could see he was only making it worse by stalling. So, with a deep breath he began. "I should have told you this a long time ago when we met, but it didn't seem necessary. Then I fell in love with you so I avoided the issue. I couldn't risk losing you, so I said nothing."

He knew he had her full attention by the expression on her face. Her eyes never wavered, and in them, he could see confusion gathering, but more than that, he could see the love. "I see now how wrong I was to keep it from you," he sighed and fought the urge to abandon the conversation.

She felt his anxiety and swallowed hard. And then, something shifted inside her, and the chill that moved through her had her crossing her arms over her chest. "Go on." She didn't know what his confession would be, but knew it wasn't going to be easy to hear.

Knowing her so well, Andrew saw the steely resolve in her eyes and admired her for it. "Hindsight being what it is, I should have been honest with you, Love." He pushed himself forward to meet her steady gaze. "But I convinced myself it wasn't important. It was all in the past and we all have secrets in our pasts, don't we?"

The air in the room seemed to thicken, Monica inhaled a strangled breath and pushed back the building fear. "I suppose so," she said softly.

"Anyway," he stopped, raked his hand through his hair, and closed his eyes to gather his courage. "If I would have known what would happen..." He trailed off, shifting in the chair, then pushed on. "I'm unlike any man you've ever known before, Monica. I have differences you're not aware of because I haven't wanted you to see them. But I have innate goodness in me; my mother always said that of me." Fear propelled him to his feet and had him pacing in front of the desk.

Monica watched him and wished she hadn't been so persistent in wanting to know everything that her husband was feeling. She felt pain. His, and her own. And knew some things were better left unknown. Tucking her hair behind her ear, she was sensing she was about to suffer regret for the rest of her life.

"I never wanted it," Andrew continued. "And I didn't ask for it, it was just thrust upon me. My father and I had rows about my not wanting the gift and his insistence that I accept it." He dropped back into the chair, and reaching across the desktop, clutched his wife's cold hand. "In the end though, I really had no choice. The son of a bitch got his way just like he always did..."

Monica was stunned to hear the harshness in his voice. She'd always thought the two of them were very close. This was a side of

305

Drew she had never seen. "Wait," she interrupted him. "I'm confused, Drew. I don't understand what your father has to do with this. What's this all about?"

Andrew laughed heartily. "My father has everything to do with it. He was a monster, but it's more than that. If it were just that it would be easy but there is so much more to the story." He slumped back in the chair and closed his eyes for a moment.

"In England my father was feared. All through my childhood, people would turn and walk the other way when they saw him coming. He frightened people. I thought it was our wealth that frightened them but I was wrong. It was the power he had, and what he would do with it when he had a mind to, that frightened them. And God help me, it frightened me too. It got so bad; the only peace I knew was when he was away on business. When he would come home after a business trip I never knew what he was about to do from one minute to the next. No matter what it turned out to be, good or bad, he'd drag me along for the ride."

Monica heard him speaking with such hatred, and it scared her. She hadn't known he was capable of it. She was frozen, compelled to stay and listen even while part of her wanted to run from the room. No matter how difficult it was to hear she had to stay.

"Mother, bless her soul, did her best to make it all easier to take. And, I suppose, if I am to be totally truthful, I'd admit that he loved her in his own way. And she adored him, was able to look past all his faults and excuse the greatest part of them. Something I could never learn to do. Even as a young lad, I held him responsible for the evil he unleashed, and I still hold him responsible to this day. I lied to you when I told you my parents were killed in a plane crash. Although my mother—God rest her soul—is dead, and has been for many years now, my father was alive and well until a little more than a year ago."

"Why lie about it?" Then her mind shifted gears, "You hated him?"

"Yes. I know your father was a good and decent man, that he was loving and treated you like a precious gift—but not everyone has that. My father was an animal. He used to strike me as a boy and belittle me whenever he got the chance. Any loving part of him was offered to my mother. Reginald was gentle and caring with her, treating her like a queen. That was one of the few things we agreed on."

"And there were times when he could be a loving father but they were rare. Any love and acceptance I received came from mother. But when I turned twenty-nine something changed in him. He began treating me more kindly and speaking to me more warmly then he had in years." He shook his head ruefully, shifting in the chair. "I should have been expecting it, seen it coming. He and I went for a walk one evening; mother had stayed behind to tend to some arrangements for my thirtieth birthday party. We walked on the grounds of the estate and when he suggested we go out by the moors I thought nothing of it. And that would be the last mistake I would make."

"What happened?" she whispered with a tear running down her cheek.

Andrew leaned back in the chair and tried to still his shaking hands. He cleared his throat and continued, "He fell farther and farther behind me the nearer we got to the moors. I was telling him about the cricket game that I had that afternoon, and before I realized what was happening, he'd grabbed me and yanked me around to face him. I saw the look in his eyes then. And I've seen it in my own eyes many times since." Tears filled his eyes. "He was too strong for me. Before I could stop him, he lunged at me and sank his teeth into my neck."

"Oh my God!" Monica cried. Horror drew her to her feet and around the desk. "Why would he do such a thing as attack his own son?" she demanded.

"It was his gift to me."

Monica dropped to the floor in front of him. With his reply, she leaned back, shaking her head in disbelief, "His *what* to you?"

Andrew could see the horror on her face and wiping his cheeks with the back of his hand, he continued, "Gift. That was his gift to me, or so he said. I can still remember lying there on the cold ground and feeling the blood seeping from my neck," he said.

"That's sick," she cupped his cheek. "Did you report him to the authorities?" she asked, wanting to comfort and soothe.

"It would have done no good."

"I don't understand."

"Do you remember telling me about the story you did on the occult several years back?"

"Yes, what about it?"

"My father practiced. He was a vampire."

*

Thomas had been keeping himself busy around the mansion. Almost an hour passed since Andrew had gone into Monica's office. He couldn't help wondering how things were going. He worked the feather duster with wild abandon and decided that since Madam Monica hadn't come running out of the room screaming, things couldn't be going all that badly. Of course, it could mean something else entirely, like maybe his master had chickened out and decided not to tell her. Thomas certainly didn't envy his master's position. His wife was about to think him completely mad.

On the other hand, maybe he did tell her and she was calling for the padded wagon to take him to the mental ward. And in her place, Thomas could see how he might make the decision. But he wasn't above admitting an urge to go in the office to end his curiosity, but a stronger thread of respect prevailed. If ever two people needed privacy, it was his master and madam.

If his madam took the truth well and didn't go off half cocked, there would be hope that they would be able to start again with a clean slate. Thomas hoped her love was stronger than the betrayal she was bound to feel. And that she would understand that it was for her safety as well as his that he kept the truth from her. But, when the utter shock wore off and confusion evolved into anger, it would be his master who would have to accept her cutting temper, her slings and arrows.

Thomas hoped she had enough love for forgiveness because Andrew could never survive what he was about to face without her. If she loved him, and Thomas knew that she did, then she would see in her heart that the good in him far outweighed the bad, and give him a second chance. If not, his master would have to gather strength enough to say good-bye.

Thomas checked the time, took the cell phone from his vest pocket, and dialed the number he'd been forced to memorize because no one must ever know that the number existed. It rang four times before someone picked up the other end. "Is everything ready?" he asked, getting straight to the point. These people were paid, and paid well, to do certain jobs without detection.

He didn't know their names and they didn't know his. Their faces were unknown to him as was his to them, which was just the way everyone wanted it. "Excellent. I'll be in touch." The line went dead.

*

Monica was struck speechless. She had to think she heard him wrong. She had too. She hadn't heard him say that his father was a vampire. It was crazy. Had he actually said it? She swallowed the aching dryness in her throat and tried to think. It had to be stress. He was so tired he was hallucinating. The more she stared, the more serious his face grew.

"I must not have heard you right," she finally said.

"Yes, you did."

The sudden urge to lash out at him surprised her. "You want me to believe that your father was what? Dracula?" She met his level gaze and waited for the punch line. "For chrissake! And that makes you son of Dracula?" she asked in a sarcastic tone.

Andrew said slowly, "It makes me a vampire."

"Stop it!" Monica shouted, getting to her feet only to realize her legs wouldn't support her. Taking hold of the desk she tried to reason with him. "You're obviously overwrought and you need rest." Stress had driven her husband to the edge, or so she told herself. "I don't want to hear anymore of this, Drew. This is the secret you've been keeping?" she asked, her voice rising with hysteria.

He went to her, pulled her to him. The urge to take the alarm from her eyes, to give her the time she deserved to absorb the unbelievable. "You need to know," he whispered, tucking her head under his chin. "It's true, like it or not, I'm a vampire. Thomas will tell you. It is true."

"You've gotten him wrapped up in your delirium too?" Monica exclaimed, fear had overtaken her and she tried to push him away.

"It's not delirium, Love," Andrew took hold of her arms, steadied her, and continued, "My father attacked me and when he fed on me, I became a vampire."

"No!" she shoved him away and started for the door.

Andrew stepped in her path. "Listen to me, Monica! You don't want to believe it, and I can't blame you. But time doesn't allow for denial and won't make it any less true." He waited for her to look at him, willed her frightened eyes to his, and reached for her hand. "Think about it. I don't go outside during the day and

I can't be exposed to sunlight."

"Let me go!" She was yelling now and at the top of her lungs. "You need help!"

"You're right!" he exclaimed, loosening his grip when she relented. "I do need help because I cannot go to prison." His voice was thick with emotion when he saw it. Something he prayed he'd never see in Monica's eyes. Fear. She was afraid of him and tears filled his eyes. "You never have to be afraid of me, Monica. I love you!" He was pleading with her even while she was backing away to the door.

"I can't take this," she muttered, shaking her head. "Why are you telling me this now?" She was crying now and could hardly see him through her blurred vision.

"Please sit down, I can explain." Andrew was crying now too. Her pain was his and it was excruciating. He would have given anything to erase the misery he'd put in her eyes. She was in agony. "I have more to tell you," he whispered.

"What more could you say?"

"I had to tell you, Monica. I had no other choice. I'm running out of time, I couldn't afford to wait any longer," he said as she staggered back and collapsed in the chair by the door.

"Why?" she demanded, clinging to the anger because without it, the pain threatened to swallow her whole. "Out of time? You're not making any sense."

"The charges against me are true," he shouted and saw her flinch as if he struck her. He clamped his eyes shut and forced himself to continue. "I attacked those people in California," he confessed quietly. Seeing the dread fill her eyes felt like a blow to his chest.

"You killed those people." Her voice was little more than a whisper. She pulled her knees to her chest and prayed this was a nightmare.

He shoved a shaky hand through his hair and dropped his hands to his sides, defeated. "Yes." There could be nothing gained by telling her about the other attacks as well but he owed her all of it. "I'm responsible for the killings here and a man's death in the Virgin Islands as well."

Monica stared at him, tears filling her eyes. "You're telling me the entire time I've known you, the entire time we've been married, years, you've been running around killing people for what? Their blood?"

"No!" he protested. "It wasn't anything like that; I never intended to hurt anyone. I couldn't control it!"

A powerful pain brought her to her feet. "I must be loosing my mind." She crossed to look him. "So I guess that means you can't stand fire, crosses or garlic?"

Andrew nervously ran his fingers through his hair. "Don't be silly, I rather like crosses, and a well contained fire can be quite nice," he said reaching out for her.

Monica got to her feet—needing distance and not wanting him to touch her, she stared at him for a long time. "If you're a vampire then prove it to me." It was a demand, a last ditch attempt, they both knew, to cling to a life gone like a puff of smoke.

Andrew looked at her seriously. "Prove it to you? Are you serious?" he asked. He hated where she was going with this but he had to let her pursue it. Surely, she didn't really want him to prove it? She thought she was calling his bluff and hoped to catch him in a lie. "You can't really want that! It...it would turn your stomach."

She lifted her chin and took several steps towards him. They were close enough now that she could feel his breath on her face. "That's exactly what I want. How else do you expect me to believe what you're saying?"

Frustrated and feeling cornered, he pushed past her and strode to the window. "You don't know what you're asking, love. Do you really want me to mutilate myself in front of you?" he asked with his back to her.

"Just do it!" she screamed. It took all the strength she had to keep from going over to him and smacking the troubled expression off his face. He turned to look at her. In a voice so soft he could barely hear it, she said, "I have to know...I have to see the truth."

"Fine," he said, his voice rising with irritation. He rolled the cuff of his sleeve up past his elbow and placed his hand on the blind that covered the window. "Haven't you ever wondered about my so called allergy to sunlight? Just remember you asked for it."

Monica watched in silence when he slid his arm behind the blind. After a moment, she could see the beads of sweat appear on his forehead and his jaw tighten. "What's wrong with you?" she asked, suddenly aware of the smell of burning flesh.

Andrew said nothing. He just stood there as the sunlight seared into his skin like a hot knife through butter. The smell and pain was enough to make him drop to his knees. Still, he let his torture continue, his skin being burned from his arm.

The awful smell drove Monica to put her hand over her nose and mouth. The unmistakable smell of burning flesh sickened her. This wasn't a trick or a fantasy he was living, it was reality. "Stop it!" she cried, hurrying to him and yanking on his arm and pulling him away from the window.

Andrew moaned and collapsed from his knees to sprawl on the floor. The pain was unbearable and the smell was worse. He lay on the thick carpeting near delirium when Monica dropped down beside him and brought his head and shoulders into her lap. Instinct was taking over now and her anger was gone. "I...I told you...it wasn't...a pr...pretty sight," he said through clamped teeth.

Tears filled her eyes—what had she asked him to do to himself? The damage to his arm was gruesome. But how could this be real? He didn't look like a monster, but if everything he claimed to have done was true, then that is exactly what he was—a monster. "Lay still, Drew. I'll get Thomas." She yanked at the phone cord until she pulled the phone down to the floor.

*

Thomas couldn't decide which one of them he was more upset with—Monica for making such an outlandish request, or Andrew for giving into it. "Really, Master Andrew, how could you be so foolish?" He scolded, as he examined the severe burn. "Look what you've done to yourself."

Andrew flinched as Thomas began to clean the burn. "She insisted on seeing for herself, Thomas. Believe me, I wasn't any happier about it than you," he defended.

"There were less dramatic ways to validate your story. Such as having her ask me, for instance. I don't suppose that ever occurred to you now did it?"

"I tried that but she wouldn't take your word for it either. At this point she either thinks I'm a raving lunatic or that she is," he hissed as cold salve covered his wound. "I don't think she's made up her mind yet."

Monica was sitting across the room in silence. It seemed from outside herself she sat listening to them talking. Unable to believe what she was hearing, she could only watch in gaped amazement. Maybe they were all crazy, she pondered. Yet Thomas appeared totally at ease with the situation. He wasn't startled in the least. Acting as if her husband's cooked flesh was the most normal thing in the world. "Why tell me this now, Drew?" she asked quietly in a voice devoid of emotion. "Why not just keep it to yourself like you have since we met?"

He looked around Thomas and still saw the shell-shocked glaze in her eyes, but at least her color had returned. "I would have preferred to never tell you but with circumstances being what there are now, I had no choice."

"You've made that choice for years, Drew. Everything, all this is about choices. All the times I asked you what was bothering you, you chose to betray me. You deceived me," she said simply. "Over and over again."

"I wanted to protect you, Monica. I deceived you yes, but you have to understand why." He closed his eyes when her expression turned cold. "Can you honestly tell me that if I told you from the beginning you wouldn't have run screaming from this house? Because that's what I was guarding against."

"And this is so much better!"

"Oh, bloody hell!" he said in frustration.

"That's not an answer."

"What's the bloody question?"

Thomas had become invisible while he was finishing the first aid on Andrew's arm. He was wrapping a bandage around it while the argument ensued. It was obvious they had forgotten he was even in the room.

"Damnit Andrew! You said you kept this from me because you wanted to guard against my leaving you. The question is, do you think the odds of my staying are better now as opposed to then?" she asked sharply.

Andrew threw his hands up. "The decision is entirely up to you! What answer are you looking for, Monica. Do you want me to say that I was hoping with the passage of time you would come to love me so much that you couldn't leave me!" he shouted, pushing Thomas out of the way and getting to his feet he continued, "There, I've said it! I'm a bloody sonofabitch!"

Thomas had heard enough. "All right, that is quite enough! Not another word from either of you!" They were both shocked by his outburst. They were looking at him with wide eyes, so he continued, "Before either of you say something you can't take back, shut up!"

"Easy Thomas, don't get yourself so upset," Monica said calmly.

"Master Andrew and I will leave you alone now. I'm sure you have a lot to think about. Andrew, let's go," Thomas said pulling him across the room by the arm. "If you need anything just let me know, Madam Monica," he said, pushing Andrew through the door. The door closed and they were gone.

*

Andrew walked into the living room and went straight to the bar. He was so angry his hands wouldn't stop shaking. He poured himself a glass of wine. Confusion over who he was most angry with, Monica or himself, nagged at him. He filled his mouth full of the strong liquid and let it roll around on his tongue. He wasn't sure if he should swallow it or not. It quieted his churning stomach and soothed his throat.

He dropped himself on the sofa and closed his eyes. The day had been endless and painful but he did expect it. And crushing his wife's trust in him wasn't supposed to be enjoyable. She just suffered a rude brush with reality. Thinking she had the perfect husband and learning he was anything but, shook her faith in her judgment. Her husband was a freak of nature. As naive as it might have been he had hoped she would take the truth better.

But Monica was lost to him. She was gone, the moment he said the words, the woman he knew, disappeared. A wall went up—she was still there in body but she was closed off, removed. The love he always saw in her was replaced with cold distance. There was no understanding. The only emotion available from her now was anger. All the anger she could carry within her body and soul.

Thomas came in and sat down next to Andrew on the sofa. He set the tray he'd brought with him on the coffee table. "It's tea time," he said, filling a cup. "Put that glass down and drink this. It will settle your stomach and if you're lucky, your nerves."

"I do not want any tea, Thomas. I want to be left alone in my misery, can't you see that?" Andrew had decided to be difficult. The whiny shrill of his voice revealed that much.

"Why? So you can pity yourself?" Thomas said, refusing to indulge his mood. "Drink it, or I dump it down your throat for you."

*

Andrew was still sitting on the sofa when Thomas returned to the living room a half hour later. His master was content to suffer alone in his misery, but he would not allow it. Monica was angry and hurt and she was entitled. What was troubling though was that not a sound could be heard from the room where she had taken refuge. Their next move rested on what she would do with the secret she now knew. And so, they would wait, entirely in the dark, praying she made a decision they could all live with.

"So then, this is what you intend to do with the rest of the day?" Thomas asked, coming around from the back of the sofa to face him. He looked at the sullen figure in front of him and sighed. "You've got to pull yourself together. She could come out of that office and say she never wants to see you again, that's true. But she could also say she loves you and forgives you, and we can move on."

Andrew laughed and finished off the last of his drink. "I think we better go with the former on that, old man. Even if she were to forgive me, I then have to broach the subject we've all avoided until now. How understanding will she be then?" he asked in a slurred voice.

"Let's not borrow trouble, Master Andrew."

"Oh please, stop with the 'Master Andrew' business! I've been after you for years to stop being so formal. All the times in my life that you've saved my ass should afford you that right at least."

"Fine. I'm trying to keep you from going overboard with your thoughts, especially given your present state," Thomas said with a smile.

"Oh, there's no need to be so kind, I'm drunk and intend to get drunker still!" Andrew admitted freely and without a hint of shame.

"Indeed. As of this moment there will be no more drinking. I insist that you go upstairs, take a cold shower, and pull yourself together." Thomas was looking him directly in the eye when he spoke so Andrew knew he was serious.

"Why would I want to sober up? I've been devoted to becoming stinking drunk for the last hour, and now you want to ruin what I've worked so hard to accomplish," Andrew said in a wounded tone.

"Well, let's suppose Madam Monica comes in here and wants to talk with you, do you think she'll be pleased to see you swimming in scotch?"

The smile left Andrew's face and he grew somber. "I suppose not."

"I'm glad you still have some sense about you. Now go," Thomas advised sternly.

*

Monica had been sitting by the window for a long time lost in thoughts too absurd to connect to reality. The room was quiet—too quiet. And in the silence she felt the distance between her and Andrew that was too great to bridge. She wanted this time alone and both Andrew and Thomas had given it to her. She wondered if given enough time she could accept the truth about her husband. As to whether or not she could forgive him or love him the same way, that was something else altogether.

The life she made for herself had been perfect until now. If someone had asked her just yesterday, where she saw herself in ten years, she could have told them without doubt. Now everything had changed and she had no idea where to go or what to do. Monica couldn't imagine a life without Drew in it. But life with a man capable of such violence—the real Drew, a stranger to her—seemed impossible as well.

How could the life she loved so much be a lie? She knew she would have to face him sooner or later. And what would she say to him when she did? He admitted to her that he killed those poor people in California and here in the city. What was she to do with such an awful truth?

Restless tension caused her to rise from the widow seat and pace the room. She replayed what she said to Andrew when she learned of the deaths over and over. She told him that someone capable of killing so viciously had to be a monster. Could she change her opinion just because the monster turned out to be the man she married?

She wondered just how her life became so unrecognizable to her so quickly. To wake up only that morning with absolute faith in her husband's innocence, thinking she knew him as well anyone could, only to be proven so horribly wrong hours later. She had questioned Drew's sanity, and now she had to question her own.

All the while, an undercurrent of fear moved through her. Did she now fear the man who only an hour before she loved without doubt? She was afraid to look Drew in the eye, afraid of what she might feel or say in her anger. Even after all the lies, the thought of hurting him was abhorrent to her. There was more than enough pain to go around, his and hers, without adding to it.

*

Andrew stood in the bedroom with a towel around his waist. Unable to move, the floor beneath him soaked with the water running off his legs, he never felt more a stranger to himself before. This limbo he forced everyone into was anything but comfortable. The coldness he had seen in her eyes as he left the office sent a shiver right through him.

It was more than distance. It was as if he was a stranger to her. There was no intimacy when she looked at him. It was gone. As she seethed with anger after learning the truth, the room chilled just as her heart did.

The alcohol deadened the sting of her rejection but Andrew was sober now and the pain returned. His stomach churning and his head pounding, his thoughts were bouncing like a ping-pong ball in his mind. In the cold light of reality, he had to prepare himself for the possibility that he could lose his wife. It wasn't a pleasant thought but he had to face it.

And as Steve had predicted, NYPD's Lt. Pillar and a technician from CSI would arrive to collect blood and hair for analysis within the hour. He tried to forget the humiliation of having to submit to the court order. And he tried to accept what would happen when he was linked to the Central Park killings.

His eyes hurt and his hair was wet and hanging in his face. Drops of water dripped off his chin while his knitted brow illustrated how pensive he was feeling. He felt like shit. In addition, here he was in their bedroom while Monica was downstairs deciding their future—and he could do nothing. Nothing, that is, but wait and hope.

*

The disorderly atmosphere of the station left Casey out of breath and irritable, but it did little to slow him down on his paperwork. He sat behind the desk temporarily assigned to him, and polished his reports until they practically gleamed from the effort. He would be allowed to extradite Andrew Carter back to California first thing in the morning, and he'd be damned if he would let red tape foul up those plans. Carter would face an arraignment hearing upon arrival, and the judge would decide if there was enough evidence to support the charge of murder.

The evidence was overwhelming. Casey had no doubt, and when the DNA results came back tying Carter to the Central Park murders he was certain they'd nail him. But, why a billionaire businessman, well respected by just about everyone who knew him, would be so twisted as to viciously attack and kill total strangers remained a mystery. That Carter didn't come across as somebody insane was the scary thing.

Casey motioned to one of the uniforms, "I need to speak with the police chief. Is your Captain in his office?"

"Nope. He's having an early dinner with his wife. Want me to tell him you need to talk to him?"

"That'd be great, thanks."

"You really gonna take Mr. Carter back with you, huh? I mean, do ya really think he did it? Killed those people I mean?"

Casey shook his head. "Looks that way, yes."

"Look, my name's Parker and this may not count for too much, but I don't think there's a chance in hell Mr. Carter did these things."

"What makes you so sure, Officer Parker?" Casey asked with great interest.

"Nothing specific. I've met and talked with Andrew Carter quite a few times, and his personality just doesn't mesh with this kinda crime. You know how much money he contributes to this city every year? It's an awesome amount," Parker said confidently.

"You two buddies?"

"Nah, not really. Point is, my gut says he loves this city and the people in it. It would take a totally different kind of man to do the things he's accused of doing."

Casey put his feet up on the desk and studied Officer Parker carefully. "You seem pretty sure about Mr. Carter."

"He helped me out awhile back when my house burned down. I was, for the most part, an absolute stranger to him. He overheard me speaking to my wife at the annual police ball, and he stepped right in to offer help. I turned him down flat. Three weeks later, I get this call from the bank telling me we could rebuild. Because of an individual who wished to remain nameless. It was Andrew Carter. I went to see him that very same day and he greeted me like an old friend. Somehow he knew my wife was due to have our first baby. He said I shouldn't have to worry about whether or not my baby had someplace to sleep. He's a good man, Captain Casey. You should know that."

"I have my doubts about whether or not Mr. Carter is a good man, I've seen his good deeds first hand, but even a saint can be a sinner given the right circumstances."

*

Monica looked at her watch and closed her eyes. She shoved her hair away from her face in a gesture that meant she was still trying to work out a problem. She'd been alone in the office for over two hours, and though she'd looked at the upheaval from every possible angle, she still didn't know what to do. But she had to face Drew sooner or later so there was no point putting it off any longer.

She had to look him in the eye and see if any part of the man she loved so much remained. With a deep breath of determination, Monica opened the door, stepped into the hallway to find the house quiet, and went in search of the man she wondered if she ever really knew.

*

Andrew dressed slowly, and he now sat on the edge of the bed trying to gather the courage it would take to face Monica again. He should have been stronger so he berated himself for no other reason than it occupied his mind and honed his thoughts. If he possessed enough strength in the first place, this madness would not exist. Then there would have been no need to tell her the truth, or at least he could tell her in a better way, at a better time. Then the world he built so carefully would be solid instead of shifting beneath his feet—but 'if onlys' would not change anything. He had to know what she was going to do—so they would have to talk, and soon. Time was running out, whatever she decided, his destiny had already been determined.

Thomas had gone off to take care of business. So it was just Monica and him together in the house. He looked around the bedroom and nearly winced from the ache. From floor to ceiling, every inch of the room made him feel safe, as did her presence. It was hard to accept that no matter what happened, he would never again feel as safe as he did the years he had lived here, both before Monica and after.

Andrew knew that somewhere downstairs Monica was angry, hurt, and unaware of just how much was riding on the decision that she would make. She could change their lives forever. So he walked out of the bedroom and down the hall wanting his wife and wanting it over. When he reached the stairs, he saw her standing at the bottom looking up at him.

*

Their eyes locked as he started slowly down the stairs towards her. Not a word was said between them because neither knew what to say. Andrew stopped on the last step from the bottom and opened his mouth to speak, only to have Monica put her finger to his lips and silence him. The hurt in her eyes remained but the fear was gone. This woman he so loved didn't cower from him because she was not afraid. She stood close enough for him to smell her perfume.

He wanted to touch her but she pulled away before he could. So, he stepped around her and walked into the living room. He could hear Monica behind him and was sure she made her decision.

"I have a lot to say to you, Drew," Monica said when he turned to face her. "I wonder if you're ready to hear it."

Andrew watched her walk to the sofa and sit down. "I'm as ready as I will ever be." He ambled to the bar. "Want a drink?"

"No thanks, I'd like to get this over with."

That settled it, he thought. 'Over with' didn't leave him much hope. "Absolutely. I'm quite sure I already know what you're going to say, but, by all means go ahead."

Monica snickered. "You know me so well. I wish I could say the same about you. What am I going to say to you?" she asked curiously.

"You're going to leave me, aren't you?" he asked, as he poured some wine and fought to keep his hands from shaking.

"You think I would have stayed locked up in my office so long if it's that simple?"

He sipped his wine and shrugged. "I've lied to you and hurt you. And I've hurt other people. It is that simple."

"It should be," she said.

"Do you still love me, Monica?"

The question threw her off balance. "I love the man I thought you were, yes."

"Can you forgive me?"

Monica was quiet for a long time and he watched her searching for an answer—and God help him, she humbled him. "I don't know. I know I can't imagine living without you. But knowing what you are…what you've done and what you are capable of…," she trailed off, sighed. "I don't know where to go from here."

"I don't have much time left, Monica. God forgive me, I don't wish to pressure you, but I have to know if you still want to be with me."

His eyes or the plea in his voice alerted her. "You're not talking about going to prison are you?"

"I cannot go to prison," he spoke adamantly. "I can't survive in that environment, Monica."

She lifted a brow and stood. "You have no intention of even standing trial do you?" Monica asked, coming to his side. She turned him around to face her. "What're you planning?"

Andrew didn't answer. He took a drink from his wineglass. He felt her breath on his neck and looked into her eyes, knowing he couldn't live without her. The softness crept into her slowly, and with it, he prayed there was hope.

She touched his arm. "You didn't answer me."

Andrew gulped the last of his wine, and shook his head. "I can't say anymore until I know where we stand. I love you Monica, I always have. That's not ever going to change. But telling you more will put you in danger, and I won't allow that," he said, touching her cheek.

"And I love you," she admitted. "So you owe me the truth."

Chapter 30

Monica and Andrew were alone in the living room for over an hour. Evening set in and the day had been a difficult one for them both. She said the words he longed to hear. She still loved him. And she was right, he owed her the truth. From that moment on, he began telling her. It would cost him everything he held dear, everything but her. But, as long as he knew she would stand by him, he could handle anything.

"It's crazy. I hope there aren't any more surprises in store," Monica said. "I'm not sure I could handle it." She was rubbing the chain around her neck as she looked off into space.

"I have something more to tell you. I want to get it out in the open so we can deal with it and move on," Andrew said, with caution. He watched as the expression on her face changed. "Shall I continue?"

Monica couldn't imagine hearing anything more startling then what she'd already been told so she took a deep breath and said, "Out with it."

"I've not told you how my father died and I think you should know exactly what happened." He walked over and sat down next to her on the sofa.

"Okay," Monica said. She fixed her eyes on him steadily and took another deep breath.

"Reginald was alive and well up until recently. Actually, he even dropped by here once or twice. Of course, I threw him out on his ass but that did precious little to keep him out of my life. He was a miserable bastard, and I loathed the very ground he walked on. He became insistent on meeting you, and he was angry when I refused his request. I didn't want you anywhere near him." Andrew was speaking softly, trying to distance himself from the memories while he recalled them for Monica.

Monica sat silently, watching Andrew's expressions change with the tone of his voice. More pain lay in him than she would have thought possible. He was quiet now, pausing to regroup, and though she wanted to reassure him, she waited for him to finish. Reaching over and touching his bandaged hand, she prompted him to continue.

"He continued to push his way into my life and when I still refused to let him see you, he tried to blackmail me. He threatened to hurt you and I couldn't allow that. He made it quite clear he would take special delight in telling you what I am. I couldn't allow you to hear it from him, of all people. And with his constant badgering, he left me no choice. He had to be dealt with. To be silenced, once and for all."

"What did you do?" Monica asked in a whisper. She watched him struggle with his words. "Just tell me, Drew, it can't possibly be any worse than what you've already told me."

Andrew leaned up to the edge of the sofa. He wondered if he should just blurt it out. "I hadn't seen or spoken to Reginald in twelve years when I met you, and that was exactly how I wanted it. Then here he was, back in my life, and I hated him for it. He loved to try enticing me into a frenzy, driving me over the edge. To make me return to the lifestyle I'd worked so hard to put behind me. I'd taken all I could from him, so I sent Thomas for him to bring him back here to me."

"And I don't suppose he went with Thomas willingly?"

"Thomas had to strike him over the head and when he awoke the plane was already in the air, well on its way here. When they arrived, needless to say, Reginald was less than pleased," Andrew said flatly.

"And where was I when all this was going on?" Monica asked.

"You were away on an assignment. And even if you had been here, you'd never have seen him, I took him down to one of the underground tunnels and held him there."

"There are underground tunnels?" she asked, registering all this in her mind." She pinched the bridge of her nose and decided to dissect the finer details later. "Okay," she managed. "So then what happened?"

"I locked him in a cell and we had a row," he confessed, and risked a look at her. "I smacked him around a bit," he said, sparing her the brutality of the truth.

"Charming," Monica said. "I don't think I want to hear the horrid details. Can we get to the point?"

"First though, I think you might want to hear the truth behind why I left Cambridge. Why I came here and why, except for my mother's death, I haven't returned." He met her eyes and saw the dread clearly. "Her name was Elizabeth. We began dating after my freshman year of college. I fell for her in the most affecting way, she was beautiful, and she was funny. And she had the ability to make me forget who, and what, my father was. Mother adored her as much as I did. I would have married her if...we'd been together for five years when my father opened the door of immortality and shoved me through," he sighed. This confession would be harder than he thought.

"Elizabeth noticed the change in me straight away—but I pacified her, put her off, reassured her. I was fine, I told her," he continued. "I tried to cover, to ignore the turmoil and the hunger," his voice choked with emotion. "But it came to be impossible."

Monica recognized the love mixed with pain, she heard it in his voice, saw it on his face for this woman. A woman she never knew existed. Yet, it wasn't jealousy warring inside her but love and understanding. She knew that kind of love. It was the same kind of love that she felt for him. "You must have loved her a great deal," she whispered.

"Yes, more than I can say. So much so, I never thought I could love that way again," he paused, smiled. "Then you came into my life." Andrew reached out and touched her face. "My secret was safe from her for an entire year. Many times, I came dangerously close to taking her blood but my will won out. I thought I could handle the urge forever. I was wrong. One evening we were out walking together by the moors and decided to sit along the bank and talk in the moonlight," he said, glancing at Monica, wondering what was going through her mind. "We talked for a long time, the way lovers do, the way we do. Then we kissed." As he laughed, his eyes began to fill. "And before long we were making love in the moonlight. I thought I had it under control...," Andrew wiped his eyes to dry them.

Her anger drained away as Monica moved closer to him and squeezed his leg. "It's okay, go on," she whispered as she pressed her mouth to his ear. "Go on."

Andrew closed his eyes tight. The memory of that night still tormented him. After so many years, it still felt as if it were yesterday. "And before I could stop myself I fed off her. She cried out in pain but I was lost to reason, filling myself with her blood. Elizabeth was my first. Up to then I'd been steering my hunger towards animals. But I couldn't stop myself. The need was unlike anything I ever experienced before and my vampire instincts took over before I could stop them. She was dead before I knew it. I watched her die right in front of me. The last word she said to me was to ask why." He looked up from the floor and saw tears on Monica's face.

Monica swallowed hard. "God. That's why you left England?" She stammered. "To avoid prosecution?"

"Yes," he said, "but there was more to it than just leaving. Elizabeth was the daughter of the head police inspector. When her body was found and they questioned me, in my grief, I snapped and confessed. Then, all hell broke loose. There had been rumors about my father, about his being possessed by some sort of evil for some time. God knows, he made no secret of his activities. So when I confessed, there was a public outcry for my immediate hanging. I was so consumed by grief, I agreed with them. I was more than ready to face my punishment but Reginald felt differently."

"Why? Your father had no use for you anyway, so why did your father care?"

"It wouldn't have been that simple. In England, there were whispers, legends of vampires. But no one had ever seen one. With me there would have been undeniable proof. Exposure would have wreaked havoc—they would've hanged me first, then severed my head and my limbs from my body."

"And your father thought he'd be next and couldn't allow that?" Monica asked.

"He went to Elizabeth's father and made a deal with him," Andrew replied.

"What kind of deal?"

"The kind that costs a tremendous amount of money."

"He bought him off?" Monica asked, amazed.

Andrew stood up and walked to the fireplace. "Yes. It cost my father and mother five million dollars to save their son. My mother would have given anything to keep me safe, but Reginald's only motive was to save his ass. He was angry I couldn't keep my mouth shut. He'd had it all worked out. He was going to dump the body in the woods and when she was found, everyone would just assume a wild animal killed her. It probably would have worked too, if my conscience had allowed it."

"This man took money for his daughter's death instead of justice?" Monica asked, angrily.

Andrew looked away from her. "It was more than money, I had to leave the country and never return. The public demanded it. If I had stayed, they would have hunted me like a dog. So, after I was gone Reginald let word get out that the plane carrying me crashed. He did this only to ease my mother's anxiety, not for me. Not because he cared one way or the other about what happened to me."

"You had a horrible life," she said.

"It could have been worse."

"I can't see how, Drew," she said. "There's something I don't understand, if I have my lore and legend correct, vampires lead a fragile existence. How are you so different? Vampires don't live like human beings but you managed, how?"

"It wasn't easy, I'll tell you that," he said. "Thomas came with me and it took him years to rehabilitate me. He started to feed me food slowly, a little each day. For weeks, I vomited endlessly. It was a nightmare. It took years, but I was finally able to tolerate food of all kinds. There was still the problem of blood, however. I needed it to survive. My special wine. It's as strong now as it was in the beginning, but over the years since I left England, Thomas has changed the ingredients drastically. They've changed from human blood to rodent plasma and chicken blood with just a small amount of human blood added. Up until the last couple of years it worked like a charm," Andrew explained. His face was hard and expressionless. He looked at Monica, surprised she was still there. After telling her about his wine, he was sure she'd be disgusted.

"What changed?"

"I fell in love." He shrugged. "Reawakened passion can trigger passions that are even darker."

"I...I caused this?"

He went to her and cupped her face in his hands, met her eyes. "Absolutely not—I don't blame you, and I'll not have you blaming yourself."

"And your father, where is he now?" she asked.

"I killed him." It came out quickly—too quickly, he realized when he watched Monica pale. "A silver bullet, blessed by a priest, straight through the heart."

"I feel like I'm in the middle of a bad movie."

"I had no choice in dealing with Reginald. It was either him or me, or worse yet, you. Believe me, if the shoe had been on the other foot he would have wasted no time in killing me."

"And the body?" Monica asked, as she watched Andrew pace across the room.

"I buried it in one of the tunnels below the mansion," he said. "It took some doing but Thomas and I pulled it off. First he was placed in a concrete casing and then he was covered with soil."

"Your father's body is underneath us right now?"

"Yes," Andrew said simply, and he took another sip of wine.

Monica looked at him in amazement. "And it doesn't bother you to have his body right under your nose?" she asked.

"Not in the least. And besides, it's safer that way." Andrew knew how odd this must sound to her but it made perfect sense at the time. After all, the rule is to keep your friends close and your enemies closer. Dead or alive, Andrew would always consider his father a constant danger to himself and anyone else he loved.

Andrew took her hand tightly in his and felt the tension between them as they sat beside each other on the sofa. She loved him, he knew that. But he wasn't sure things could ever be the same between them. It would take a long time to get back to where they were in their relationship before she knew the truth about him.

He felt her squeeze his hand, and looked at her and smiled. He could still see the confusion and shock in her eyes but it was fading. When she smiled at him and touched his face with her fingertips, Andrew could feel her struggling to come to grips with everything she learned about him in the last several hours. In time, maybe they would be all right.

"Are you ready to face tomorrow?" She asked, pulling her eyes away from him and looking away. "It could get very difficult, are you sure you can handle it? I'll be here for you if you need me. It's the least I can do, considering."

"Tomorrow's coming whether I'm ready for it or not. Those cops don't understand what their doing or what chain of events this could set off in the future." Andrew felt the awesome weight of what was about to take place sinking into his shoulders, and he was beginning to feel the pressure. "Knowing you'll be behind me will make it tolerable, I suppose," he continued in a voice more cheery than before.

"I do love you, Drew. And I'll help you deal with this the best way I can but beyond that, I just don't know where we stand. I'm going to need time to sort through all of this, I can't make you any promises," she said with pain refreshed in her eyes.

Andrew cleared his throat. "God forgive me for placing you in this position. With all these doubts you have about us, you still want to be a part of this? Our lives…your life will never be the same again. So much is about to change. Are you sure this is what you want to do?" he whispered the words that were full of emotion. "I love you too much to cause you any more pain. And I owe you the chance to start a new life without me."

Monica pulled her hand away and stood up. Looking out the window at the night sky, she said, "And so—what—you're giving me the chance to just walk away? My life will be better being the ex-wife of a serial killer?" Lifting a brow, she met his gaze squarely. "You're putting me in an impossible position. If I stay, it doesn't mean I've forgiven you. But I'll go along with this plan. Not because I think its right but because no matter what, I can't watch you suffer, however much you might deserve to. I've made my up my mind." She walked away without looking back, out of the living room, without another word.

Andrew sat listening to the sound of her high heels on the wooden floor in the hallway fading away. He was exhausted physically and emotionally, and he wanted to weep for the light he'd dashed in her eyes. His stomach pains returned, leaving him grappling with the sharp, knife-like twinges he now found so familiar. Thomas had to know about them, so they could be dealt with right away. The last thing they needed to worry about was another relapse.

*

Thomas locked himself in the library, and looking at the clock on the corner wall, he realized just how long he had been there. He needed a break but there were still details he needed to be sure were taken care of first. He was sitting in the leather chair his master had brought with him from England. England, where this nightmare truly began—where a sweet young man became a monster he couldn't control.

On the small table in front of him, lay two stacks of files. A red file contained the entire recorded estate inventory, and a black one contained all the new additions to the inventory that had yet to be recorded or appraised. Thomas went through each of them slowly reading. He had to be certain of which items would be missed and which ones would not. Even the smallest mistake could cost them everything.

Thomas spent the last several days making sure everything was ready, because there was no room for mistakes now. The covert visit to the medical building in the dead of night wasn't exactly the easiest matter to deal with, but somehow he had managed it. But the trip and the creature were the most important step of the plan and all was finally secure. He had to shower the grime and the stink off that he brought back from that vile alley in the most disgusting part of town. While there, he acquired one of the most revolting creatures God had ever seen fit to put on this earth. And it was now scratching around in its shoe box on the edge of the table.

An hour passed and Thomas was finally satisfied that he memorized everything in the black file. He closed the flap and pinched the bridge of his nose. He was too old for this type of nonsense anymore. He got up from the chair and stretched. His muscles and bones ached from stiffness as if to remind him he should be off playing golf instead of plotting and planning and bending the law to his purposes.

He walked to the door, opened it, and found the hall quiet and the mansion grown dark with the lateness of the hour. It was almost nine p.m. It took a minute for his eyes to adjust to the darkness, he'd spent too much time under a bright reading lamp. Of course that was the reason. He refused to consider it confirmation of his old age.

When he turned the corner, Thomas noticed the only light was coming from the living room. So, he walked down the hallway and went inside. He was not surprised to find his master standing next to the fireplace, deep in thought. As Thomas approached the fireplace, his master looked right at him. Andrew's resignation meeting Thomas' preparedness was the calm meeting the storm.

Though Andrew was troubled, he smiled at the old man. "You certainly give a man a start! How long have you been here?" he asked, turning his attention back to the spot on the wall he'd been staring at so intensely.

"I've only just arrived. Can I get you anything?"

"No, thank you, Thomas." He wasn't in the mood to talk. "Is there something you wanted? I really need to be by myself for awhile."

"I was concerned about how you're feeling since I gave you the injection," Thomas said, with a worried look.

"The pain's not as bad now. But I'll probably need another before going off to bed."

"All right, I'll prepare one for you then. You need your rest, there are many changes coming. Did Madam already go up to bed?"

"I don't know. I haven't seen her for hours." Frustrated, he backed away from the mantle and rolled his shoulders, trying to release mounting tension. "Make sure one of the guest rooms is prepared," Andrew said quietly.

After all she learned about her husband today, this reaction was to be expected. "I'll see to it. Has she decided what she intends to do?" he asked.

Andrew closed his eyes and said, "She has decided to stand by me."

Thomas raised an eyebrow. "And she knows the risks?" he asked, grateful but cautious. It would make all the difference to have her with them.

"Yes."

"She can accept them?"

Andrew thinned his lips into a hard line while he considered the same question, "So she says."

*

The hamburger and fries he ordered were served to him cold. Casey might have raised hell if he hadn't been so damn hungry. He worked right through lunch and dinner, and now his head felt like a punching bag. He reluctantly pushed aside the last of his paperwork and walked across the street to where he was now sitting. In a cheap hole in the wall, New York City diner eating food he knew wouldn't agree with him.

The food, though it was cold, satisfied his hunger and relieved the pounding of his head. Maybe now he could finish his work and get to sleep early. He had a big day ahead of him tomorrow. He and Andrew Carter were going to take a plane ride back to California. And his high powered attorney wouldn't be able to wave a magic wand and make it go away. The best part was the man was clueless it was even coming.

He arranged it so Carter's attorney wouldn't see the extradition paperwork until it was too late to do anything about it. He was throwing his ass in coach and flying back to California. It was a prick thing to do, but then, he was feeling a little prick-like at the moment. He wanted to put this case behind him. And, he wanted justice served.

He shoved the last piece of hamburger into his mouth and slurped down the last of his double thick milkshake. Looking at the bill he threw a ten in the middle of the table on a nine dollar and fifty-two cents bill, and got up to leave. He almost made it to the door when he heard his waitress yell at him.

"You call this a tip!" She looked pissed off when he turned and saw her expression.

"No, here's your tip, sweetheart—next time bring the food while it's still hot," he replied, a real smartass tone in his voice, and disappeared out the door.

*

Andrew went up to bed sometime after ten when he finished playing a game of pool with Thomas. He was willing to do whatever he could to keep from having to go upstairs and face the chill of his bedroom. He thought a game of pool might relax him but he was wrong. He was still on edge, and knowing his wife was three doors down the hall from him instead of lying next to him, would do little to improve his disposition. Thomas had prepared the guest room as he asked and that was where Monica lay with walls and his lies between them. He had no one to blame but himself. She hadn't even come down to say goodnight, which was something she'd always done.

So there he was. At the bottom of the bed in the master bedroom, feeling low and wanting nothing more than to kiss Monica goodnight. He ran his fingers through his hair and taking a deep breath, collapsed back onto the bed. He was so tired but knew he wouldn't sleep with his wife in another bed. Not with so many changes waiting for him when he awakened.

The injection Thomas gave him only moments before was taking effect and filling him with the warmth only feeding could supply. He allowed his heavy eyes to close. His breathing became deep and full. Just before sleep took him over, he felt something he rarely felt...the memory of his beating heart.

*

Thomas looked into the shoe box and took hold of it by the tail, holding it up for closer inspection. It was squirming around helplessly. He dropped it back in the box just as it was ready to take a large chunk out of his finger. This rat was hungry. He would do the job nicely.

*

Captain Casey's face tensed as he sat on the side of his hotel bed and listened to the incessant barking of the police commissioner through the receiver that was jammed to his ear. "Yes Commissioner, we'll be leaving on the ten o'clock plane. I can assure you, nothing will go wrong. Just keep the press away. The last thing we need is Andrew Carter being tried by the press and giving his attorney grounds for any legal miracles like a mistrial. I'll see you when we get there. Goodnight sir." With that he slammed down the phone, and cursed.

He walked across the room, letting his robe drop to the floor. He went into the bathroom naked and turned on the shower. The only hope he had of getting any sleep was to relax, but he was too anxious about tomorrow for that. A nice hot shower might work wonders. The weather was turning again and he couldn't wait to get back to California where the only season was summer and this damp weather eating away at his bones would be only a memory.

The water felt good on his back as he climbed in the shower. Grinning, he let the water soak his hair while his thoughts shifted to a guilty verdict. Andrew Carter might be sleeping like a baby now, but after tomorrow, he would never sleep so soundly again.

*

Andrew was startled when he woke to find Thomas standing over him. "It's time, Andrew," he whispered.

Andrew was frightened suddenly, "Oh God."

*

At three o'clock in the morning the streets of the city were quiet and there was calmness in the air. The roar of the explosion ripped through the mansion with a vengeance, sending pieces of shattering glass into the street and onto the sidewalk. Across the street the unmarked police car was engulfed in the intense heat as the two men inside were thrown back in their seats.

They shielded their eyes from the brightness of the fire that consumed the entire structure Andrew Carter called his home and his business. From inside the police issued sedan they immediately called for help. The sky was alight with fire—the city was no longer asleep.

*

The ringing of the phone woke up Casey. He was not at all pleased at being disturbed, he looked at the clock on the bedside table and groaned. He grabbed the phone and put it to his ear. "What is it?" he shouted, turning on the bedside lamp with his free hand. Suddenly, he darted up in bed. "What!"

"I said, Andrew Carter and his wife just got blown to hell and back! Whole building just went up in a damn fireball. It's bad Captain Casey, there's no way anyone's coming outta there alive. Man, ain't no way!"

"Are you sure!" Casey demanded, pulling his pants on. "Are you absolutely sure about this?"

"Captain, sir, hell yes I'm sure! Tibbs and me, we were sitting right across the street and the damn explosion almost blew us out of the car! You better get down here."

"I'm on my way!" Casey slammed down the receiver and pulled on a T-shirt, grabbed his key and gun and bolted out the door.

*

By the time he arrived the street was a sea of red and blue flashing lights and nosey onlookers. When Casey jammed his car into park at the end of the street, he was already muttering under his breath. It was no wonder he couldn't get any closer in the car. There were enough fire engines on the street to start a parade. He got out of his car and looked down the street at the mayhem. He'd seen the tell-tale amber glow in the sky when he jumped into his car at the hotel. The radio reported the fire from the explosion could be seen all the way in New Jersey.

He took off at a jog down the sidewalk, zigzagging his way through firefighters, EMT's, and newspaper reporters. He had to flash his badge to get past the blocked off area. The heat from the flames was so hot, in no time at all his face was slicked with sweat. It looked as if they would be fighting the fire until well past dawn. He looked on in shock. "Oh Jesus!" he said.

"Hey, Captain, some kind of mess, huh? And if you can believe it, it's worse then it looks," a short, light haired, uniformed officer said as he came to Casey's side.

"How much worse could it be? What's your name, son?" Casey asked, without taking his eyes from the blaze across the street. "Did I assign you to this detail?"

"Yep, name's Smith. You assigned Tibbs and me to stake out Carter's place. We sure never expected this kinda action though. Captain of the 55th fire department said it's gonna take eight maybe ten hours before the fire's completely under control."

"You're sure they were in there?"

"No doubt about it, Captain, they were all snug as bugs in rugs. Sound asleep, probably never knew what hit them," Smith said, shaking his head in disbelief. "What a way to go."

Casey jammed a cigarette between his lips and flicked the lighter he pulled from his jacket pocket. He inhaled deeply, and after a second exhaled the smoke and the aggravation. The top brass would be pleased they wouldn't have to waste the time trying Andrew Carter in a court of law. They would hold a press conference saying they felt just horrible about the loss of life.

Every man was innocent until proven guilty. But, secretly, behind closed doors, they would be thinking Andrew Carter got what he deserved. And if other lives were lost in the process that was just a mere misfortune, at least in the end some form of justice was served. The very thought made Casey want to puke, and he was the one who would have to deliver the news.

"You, Captain Casey?" a sweaty man in a fireman's jacket asked, approaching him.

Casey watched as the man wiped his soaked forehead and stopped in front of him, "That's me."

"Just thought you'd want to know the score here," he answered, half coughing, half gasping for breath.

"The score? Is this a basketball game?" Casey asked, only half joking.

"I meant the body count."

"Let's have it."

"Well, looks like three in the residence and two in the offices. It'll be awhile before we can get to the bodies though, or at least what's left of them."

"Two in the business offices?" Casey asked, confused.

"Yeah, two security guards on the night shift. This whole thing's a damn shame, really."

"Any idea what caused the explosion?"

"Won't know for certain until the fire marshal gets inside to take a look around, but there's a whiff of natural gas in the air. That'd be my bet. But by the looks of things, it could be awhile before he'll get in to sniff around."

Casey threw the butt of his cigarette on the ground and crushed it out. Exhaling the last of the smoke he said, "Great."

*

The sun came up with the fire finally under control and a large blanket of black smoke covering the city. If Casey inhaled deep enough he could smell death in the air. A grisly thought, he knew, but apt given the charred remains they were sure to find when it was safe to sift through the rubble. He was sitting across the street on the sidewalk, chain smoking, and trying to figure a way this could be a blessing in disguise.

He hadn't moved for hours. He just watched as the home and business of Andrew Carter burned. He tried not to think about his wife or the old man who tended to his every need. The EMT's brought him coffee, and passing firefighters kept him posted on the progress. The last report he had been given was one hour ago. And it would be after lunch before the fire marshal could get inside to start his report. The hot spots had to be dealt with first.

He had to call the commissioner before he heard about the explosion on CNN. Casey decided to go down to the police station and call in from there. He fully intended to accompany the fire marshal inside the remains of the building. He had to see for himself what happened. When he walked into the station, the whole place was buzzing with conversation about the explosion. Casey rubbed his neck, walked straight into the Captain's office, and closed the door behind him.

Casey stared at the phone on the corner of the desk. The commissioner was the absolute last person he wanted to talk too but he was left with no other choice so he picked up the phone. He listened as the long distance line connected and he heard the first ring.

The ringing of the phone and the barking from the dog at the end of the bed awakened them both from their sound sleep. The old man was less than thrilled to be awakened from his dreams of

335

fly-fishing and boating. The phone was ringing off the hook and his wife's dog was yapping at the bottom of the bed.

He turned on the light and muttered some four-letter words under his breath. He yanked the receiver off the hook and jammed it to his ear. "Hello!" he growled into the mouthpiece.

"Commissioner? It's Captain Casey, I'm..."

"Captain Casey, do you have any idea what time it is?" he demanded, as his wife tried to quiet the dog's barking.

"Yes, sir..."

"Well let me just tell you. It's three o'clock in the blessed morning, that's what time it is! I ought to have your ass busted back to traffic cop! You better have a damn good reason for waking me up at this hour!" he yelled.

Casey bit his lip and stopped himself from saying anything he might later regret, "I do. Andrew Carter's dead."

The commissioner was struck silent. "What?"

"Andrew Carter is dead. He died in an explosion earlier this morning. His wife, butler, and two security guards went up too. I thought you'd want to know right away."

"Yes, of course." He sat up and leaned against the headboard of the bed. "Explosion? Any leads?"

"There's nothing to go on yet, we won't know for sure what caused it until the fire marshal gets a chance to examine whatever's left standing. There's no way anybody could survive this kind of explosion. And even if by some miracle someone did survive, they burned to death within minutes," Casey said, as he flipped through a magazine that was lying on the desk.

The commissioner cleared his throat and kicked the dog off the bed. He gave his wife a dirty look and said, "Let me know when you learn anything."

"Sure thing, Sir. Sorry to wake you," he lied. He was anything but sorry. The old fart deserved to see how the other half lived, the kind of cops that bust their asses out on the street everyday. That was the kind of cop the commissioner used to be before he was promoted right into a cushy desk job. All he had to do was bark orders all day long.

Casey wasn't sure he was glad about not having to drag Andrew Carter back to California. No matter how you looked at it, it was one hell of a nasty way to die. What if by some miracle, he survived the explosion only to burn to death instead? What kinds of terrible thoughts went through his mind before he slipped away to death?

Maybe he was remorseful about what he'd done to those poor people in California with those last few breaths, and maybe he wasn't thinking about those people at all. Perhaps he was thinking about the people that meant the most to him. His wife, there was no doubt that he loved her very much and that she loved him. No matter what he'd done, it was an awful way to die. But in such horror, there was at least some form of justice.

*

The last flame was snuffed out at eleven thirty that morning and the dozens of firemen at the scene breathed a sigh of relief. They were dirty, tired, and hungry and their lungs burned from all the smoke they'd been forced to inhale through the wee morning hours. Still, their job was not over yet. Thousands of gallons of water needed to be sprayed on the remains of the structure to insure the fire would not kick back up on them.

And they had done their job with an audience—and the public spectacle the media turned every tragedy into—since the whole thing started. The street was full of spectators and gossips and the police had to call in reinforcements to send them on their way. People from all walks of life watching in stupefaction as their self-proclaimed hero and his castle vanished right before their eyes. They were firefighters and this call had to be like any other. It wasn't supposed to matter that the man who once lived—and now died—there had done so much for their departments over the years with his many donations and pledge drives. But it did.

*

Bill Moyer was the current fire marshal for the district in which Andrew Carter lived. And when he got the call, he wanted to turn the assignment down. He'd seen many explosions over the years but none as massive as this one, and the thought of having to navigate the never-before-traveled ground of being sought by reporters and city bigwigs didn't thrill him. However, he relented and now watched from the sidelines as the last of the water sprayed on the hollowed shell of the remains.

The force of the initial explosion had obliterated most of the structure. Even now, eight hours after the explosion, remnants of the building were still falling from the sky. So, he stood with the seriousness of the situation settling on his shoulders. Though he didn't mind the responsibility, Bill was certain this was the worse call he had ever seen. It was up to him to find out what caused such devastation.

Across the street, behind dozens of people, were large chunks of brick and huge slivers of glass and wood. This would not be an easy job. He hadn't seen anything come close except the bombing of the medical building in California.

What made this even more difficult to deal with was Andrew Carter had been a good friend for more than five years. They loved Monica and had dinner together with them in this very building. They had laughed and shared good scotch together and now his friends were gone. Bill was shocked when he first got the call and his wife was beside herself with grief. He didn't want to believe it but the proof was right in front of him.

Andrew Carter was a damn fine man as far as he and his wife were concerned. He didn't give a shit what the papers and the television news had to say. Monica was so talented, and a lovelier person than he could ever hope to meet. He hadn't known Thomas very well but he was always good to Andrew and that made him pretty special in Bill's book. Now they were all gone.

"When can I get inside?" Bill asked a passing firefighter.

"A couple of hours at least, Bill. Go get some lunch while you wait, it looks like you could use it. I know you were close with the family. I'm sorry."

"Thanks. They were good people. No matter what anyone says, Andrew Carter wasn't a monster. I'll miss him, he was a good friend. Beep me when you're ready for me," Bill said, tucking his clipboard under his arm and walking away.

*

Captain Casey was sitting behind the Captain's desk when he walked into his office. He glared at him and said, "Make yourself at home, Captain Casey." He slammed the door and tossed the files he was holding on the desk. "I guess I don't need to ask how things are going, it's a damn shame what happened to Carter and his family but when your times up, it's up," he said, taking a drink from the paper cup in his left hand. "If you don't mind I'd like to sit in my chair."

"I'm waiting on dental records now," Casey said, getting up from behind the desk. "There won't be much else to identify the bodies with by the looks of it."

"The whole city's a mess over this. To you he might have been a murder suspect but to this city, he was a Good Samaritan and a damn fine citizen. We'll be in mourning for awhile, Captain Casey, so just be careful what you say out loud. Most people might not care to hear it."

Casey smiled and shook his head. "I'll keep that in mind."

"Good."

It was becoming clear why he wasn't exactly popular in this city. New York loved Andrew Carter. It didn't matter that he was just doing his job. He was the bad guy here, not Andrew Carter. He couldn't wait to get back home and return to his normal life. The people of California would want some kind of justice but they wouldn't find it here in New York.

*

The mood at WNYC news was one of despair. Mr. Philips decided to call a staff meeting at noon to try to help his people deal with this tragedy. Respect and affection ran deep for Monica Banebridge-Carter at the station and throughout the news community. Her absence would be felt for a long time to come.

He found it hard to believe she was gone. He would miss her drive, her need to succeed, her appetite for besting the best of her competition. Her talent impressed him from the start, and executives at the network loved her wit, on camera charm, and off camera, no nonsense professionalism. Replacing her on air would be nearly impossible. The public loved her. They would resist accepting someone else in her anchor chair.

The halls were silent and the expressions on the faces of her colleagues were solemn. Monica had been more than a fellow news anchor. She had been a friend to everyone. The people of WNYC were family. This tragedy was a blow and the grief would be deep.

But Philips was a pragmatic man even in his grief. Sending out a news team to the scene wasn't easy, but he did it. This story was too close to home. The pain was too deep right now. No one spoke to anyone about anything. The quiet was so complete you could hear a pin drop.

Mr. Philips stayed in his office with his door closed for a long time. Not wanting to be bothered, he needed some time to pull himself together before he faced everyone at the meeting. What could he say to them? They would look to him for support and he didn't think he could handle the responsibility.

The president of the network called to express his sympathies. And it was obvious that he too was feeling the loss. He wanted to air a five-minute tribute to Monica at the end of the three editions of the news to air that day. Mr. Philips agreed it was a good idea and sent one of the editors off to find the best material he could and pull it together for airing.

The flowers started arriving after seven that morning and the green room was already full of arrangements from various other news media. Including magazines and television news programs like, Meet the Press and 60 minutes. Florists were delivering by the dozens. Soon the entire studio was wall to wall with roses, lilies, and carnations. At the end of the day, Mr. Philips planned on donating most of them to the hospitals around the city.

*

Bill Moyer's beeper went off while he was at home with his wife for lunch. She was dealing with the news better than she had been when he left her but still he hated leaving her alone. She insisted he go and do what he had to. So, he drove across town slowly, in no hurry, to walk into the rubble that was once such a beautiful home.

The street was quieter now and most of the emergency vehicles were gone. A few people were still hanging around across the street and it would be much easier to do his job without prying eyes and whispers. Bill pulled his car into a parking space on the same side of the street as the building's remains. The four feet of sidewalk in front of the building—now rubble, with large pieces of concrete blown away—forced him to improvise. He stepped onto the street and closed the car door. Putting his hardhat on, he headed into the reeking, charred hovel.

He had almost reached the building when a man came running up to him from across the street. "Name's Casey," he said, shoving his hand into Moyer's and bringing them both to a halt. "You must be Bill Moyer."

Bill shook the man's hand. "That's right. What can I do for you?" he asked.

"Well, I'm a Captain with the LAPD and I was wondering if I could get a look around in there with you?" he said, showing his badge.

"I'll file my report when I'm through," Bill said, looking seriously at Captain Casey. "I don't need or want you shadowing me, Captain."

The hard tone in Moyer's voice told Casey he was another card carrying member of the Andrew Carter fan club. "I'm just trying to tie up loose ends."

Bill took a deep breath and pulled his clipboard from under his arm preparing to get to work. "Suit yourself, but you stay out of my way or I'll throw you out on your ass, got it?" he warned.

Casey agreed with a friendly smile, "Got it."

*

Getting inside proved to be trickier than Bill anticipated and his guest trailing so close behind him didn't make it any easier. What remained of the entrance hall was barely recognizable and to the left what used to be the living room was now nothing but a charred windowless black hole. The smell was unmistakable. Beams and glass blocked the entrance into the kitchen and it took some careful footwork by both Moyer and Casey to make their way inside.

Bill let his eyes sweep around the room. The entire back wall was missing and he was looking right into the dining room. "Smell's unmistakable," Bill said, crossing the room. "Natural gas, I'll have to check behind the stove."

Casey nodded to the middle of the floor. "The stove's over here," he said.

Bill glanced over his shoulder. "Yeah, but it was hooked up over here," he said, jabbing a thumb at a piece of rubber hosing sticking out from the wall. "See, the line for the gas was right here."

Casey came up behind him and looked over his shoulder. "Is that where the leak was coming from?" he asked, watching Moyer finger the hosing carefully.

Taking off a flashlight from his work belt and turning it on, Bill stooped for a better look. "Probably a safe bet," he said, aiming the beam close to the hosing and studying it carefully. "There's some fraying here, cracks of some kind or another which allowed for a steady leak."

Casey was confused. "So someone would have smelled the gas?"

341

"Not necessarily. It most likely was a very slow leak to begin with and the leak in the line let loose sometime through the night."

"So the smell would eventually be noticed and someone got up to check it out, and without thinking flipped a light switch and blew the whole place off the map?"

Bill shook his head. "It only takes a spark," he said, sadly.

"Damn," Casey said in awe. "So it was an accident with no foul play involved?" he continued in a serious tone.

"That'd be the likely scenario."

"All right then," Casey said, and turned and stumbled through the doorway into the hall. "I had to be sure. I'm going to see if the coroner's got anything on the bodies."

*

Bill walked outside and went around to the side of the grounds and found Casey and the county coroner talking. "You retrieve all the bodies?" he asked.

The coroner looked at him and his face grew serious. "All but two. We figure it's the security guards that are unaccounted for as of now."

"What makes you think that?" Bill asked purposely looking away from the three body bags, at his feet.

"Because of where we found these bodies in relationship to the house and what little clothing was left on the bodies," the coroner explained.

"How long for positive ID's?" Casey asked, joining in.

The coroner thought for a minute and said, "Dental records are being messengered over to me," he considered, "maybe as soon as this evening."

"Good, let me know when you're sure," Casey said.

"It's really just a formality, Captain. You're looking at the bodies of Andrew Carter, his wife, and his butler."

Chapter 31

Casey was sitting behind a desk in the station when his phone rang. He was reading over some files that Bill Moyer had sent over the hour before and he really did not want to be bothered. He left word he wasn't to be disturbed unless it was an emergency, but on the third ring he knew whoever it was, they were not going away. "What is it?" he barked, sounding more than just a little annoyed with the interruption.

"Weren't you ever going to call me back with an update?" the Commissioner's voice came over loud and clear on the line.

Casey dropped the file he'd been reading and rolled his eyes. "I was planning to call you as soon as there was something new to report, sir. I didn't see any reason to run up my expenses by making too many phone calls. I know how you hate that," he said, drumming his fingers on the desk.

"Very cute. Now where are we on this explosion? Do you know what caused it? Have the bodies been positively identified yet?"

"Yes and no. The explosion was caused by a gas leak, well actually to be more precise, it was a spark from a light switch combined with the gas leak that sent them sky high. And, to answer your last question, I'm still waiting on confirmation about the bodies. But it's really no mystery. It's Carter and family, there's really no question. The dental exam is just a formality," Casey said confidently.

"And the gas leak?"

"No foul play involved according to the fire marshal. Look, I thought about foul play myself, but I was in what was left of that building earlier this afternoon. I saw the source of the leak with my own eyes. It was just a freak stroke of bad luck and bad timing."

The commissioner seemed satisfied. "Let me know the minute you have confirmation from the coroner's office," he said.

"No problem, sir, I will." Casey hated having the commissioner on his back all the time. He couldn't wait for his vacation next month. He needed it badly and would no longer push it off until a better time.

*

It was late, and a blanket of smoke covered the side of the city that held Andrew Carter in the highest regard and called him their favorite neighbor. The street was quiet again and the crowds had been gone for hours. All of them deciding it was time to return to their homes, their families, and their lives. Every one of them would look at their simple lives with a new respect and admiration. The void would be felt for a long time to come. The city was in shock.

In two days the city authorities would demolish what remained of the Carter mansion. Not only was the structure a reminder, to the city and its people, of the friend they lost, but it was also a safety risk. It would be done first thing in the morning to allow the crews the entire day to clear away the wreckage. For the moment, though, the ravaged ground in front of the building was covered with flowers, cards, condolences of every kind.

*

This time when his phone rang, Casey grabbed it on the first ring, "Casey."

"Captain, I've just finished my examinations of the bodies. I've matched the records with each of the bodies, I can say with certainty that these bodies are that of Andrew Carter, his wife Monica Banebridge-Carter, and his butler, Thomas Frampton Leavy," the coroner said.

"Okay. Thanks for the rush job, Doc," Casey said and hung up the phone. The positive ID didn't surprise him, he'd expected as much. Having confirmation closed the books on his case, which was just fine with him. He could return to California now and escape the glowering looks from the citizens of this fair city and stop being the bad guy in a story he'd wanted no part of from the beginning. To get on with his life as captain of the LAPD was all he wanted. Well, that and an ice-cold beer at thirty thousand feet. It, of course, was all good news to him. So why then did he feel he wasn't quite ready to leave?

He hadn't known Andrew Carter the man, just the suspect in a case that had fallen into his lap. They were anything but friends, yet he couldn't shake the sympathy that encased this city because of his unexpected death. He had spent his time in Carter's life trying to build a solid case against him for murder. So, his spontaneous decision to stay in New York for the funerals caught him by surprise. After all, the man had no family to attend the service and mourn him and maybe, just maybe, Casey thought, he would get a bead on the man who was a saint and sinner combined.

In the evening paper, he read an article on Andrew Carter and his obituary. His parents had died many years ago in a plane crash and he was an only child. It was probably a very lonely life for him until he met his wife. So at least the last year of his life had been warm and happy. Until something snapped, something broke inside and his kindness turned to killing. Yes, Casey would attend the funeral out of respect for the Andrew Carter he had been before, what he stood for and accomplished before his downfall.

This city would never believe in Andrew Carter's guilt. A few might gossip about it but the majority would hold true to their hero. And without a trial, Andrew Carter would remain innocent in their eyes. But the DNA would prove him guilty. Prove that he had been with, and most likely attacked the victims in the park. Though it would be weeks, maybe even months, before the results were in, and with his death the D.A. just might drop the testing all together.

In his heart, Casey knew that Andrew Carter was guilty of murder. But there was little satisfaction in that knowledge for him—Carter had just died a horrible death himself. An eye for an eye; justice had been served. So, Casey was going back to his hotel room and going to bed.

*

The sun seemed to come up earlier this morning as Casey rolled out of bed and groaned. The commissioner kept him on the phone for a half an hour when he called him to tell him about the positive ID on Carter, his wife, and his butler. The commissioner wasn't too happy about Casey's decision to attend the funeral of a suspected murderer but he gave in once Casey promised to get the first flight out of New York when the funeral was over.

The funeral was to begin at noon. The bodies were released to Steven Hardy, Carter's attorney and friend. Casey might have found that an odd choice if there had been any family of Carter's to take care of the arrangements. The remains were cremated, but there would be visitation at ten a.m. And Casey planned on attending the visitation hour, although he wasn't exactly sure why. His flight back to California wasn't until six thirty five p.m., so he had nothing but empty time on his hands.

He phoned room service and ordered eggs and bacon with coffee, and was eating by eight fifteen. Bed tempted him, but he turned on the shower and stepped inside to ward off the lingering affects of too little sleep and too much caffeine.

*

Steven Hardy walked into the Bentley Funeral Home at exactly nine o'clock. He was preoccupied with his thoughts and dreaded what was about to take place. The owner, J. Michael Bentley, greeted him warmly. They shook hands and exchanged a few words about nothing in particular.

"Is everything ready, Mr. Bentley?" Steve asked as he straightened his tie.

"Yes. They are side by side at rest in the lavender room. Would you like to go in and see them now?" Mr. Bentley asked in a soft voice.

Steve took a deep breath. "Yes, please," he said, and let Mr. Bentley lead the way.

*

The lavender room was large with plush chairs lined around the walls of the room. Steve was hearing music playing softly in the background as he focused in on the framed pictures atop the caskets. He looked down at his well-shined shoes and prayed he could get through the day. When he looked across the vast room, he allowed his eyes fall to each coffin in turn. Each of them had large arrangements of flowers resting at the heads of them on the floor, just as he had requested.

He could hear Mr. Bentley right behind him and wanted to be alone with his frazzled thoughts and sadness. When he drew to a stop in front of Andrew's mahogany casket, he released a breath he hadn't realized he was holding. He smoothed his hand over the glossy surface and cleared his throat. Most would be expecting Andrew, Monica, and Thomas to be laid to rest in the most extravagant style money could buy. But he was following Andrew's last request to the letter.

"I'll give you some time alone, Mr. Hardy," Mr. Bentley said, and then turned and walked out of the room.

Steve heard him leave but kept his attention on the caskets in front of him. He couldn't wait for this afternoon to be over. It would not be easy, but he made a promise to Andrew and he intended to keep it. His comfort with this situation was not important. Therefore, he would stand here and shake hands with everyone who would soon arrive to pay their last respects to

Andrew and Monica Carter and to their good friend and servant, Thomas Frampton Leavy.

*

Casey chewed the last piece of bacon while he tied his tie that was dangerously close to being dragged through the yolk of his fried egg. He drank the last swallow of coffee and decided to get moving. It was twenty minutes till ten and it would be crowded. If he wanted to get in and out quickly he couldn't be among the last to arrive.

*

The visiting line formed early and Steve began shaking the hands of all who had come to bid farewell to Andrew Carter and his family. He accepted hugs from the women at Carter Industries and from Sarah, who all but dissolved into tears when he embraced her. She'd come to care for Andrew over the years and loosing him was like loosing a family member. He felt awful for her but there was nothing he could say to ease her pain.

Some from the office stopped in front of his picture and touched it fondly. This made Steve uncomfortable, looking into their pain-filled eyes was too hard right now. He did his best to ignore it. He counted off the minutes until the service would start and they could all say good-bye.

Casey arrived and was now in the middle of the line. He was struck at how affected everyone seemed to be by their grief. It made him feel self-conscience by the open displays of respect and love in front of him. Nervousness overtook him and he started fidgeting with his tie. People were looking at him with cool, unwelcome eyes. Someone probably recognized him from his many pictures in the New York Times. It didn't take a genius to figure out that in this crowd he was definitely outnumbered.

When he came face to face with Steve Hardy, he wasn't sure what he should say to him. The last time they were face to face was to discuss his client's case. "I'm sorry we have to meet again under these circumstances, Mr. Hardy," he said after a quiet moment between them.

"As am I, Captain Casey. I must say, I'm surprised to see you're still in town."

"I wanted to pay my respects. I'm leaving this evening. I'm sorry this had to happen. Regardless of what he did, no one deserves to die like that. I wish it all ended differently."

Steve smirked. "*Allegedly did,* Captain. Careful or these people might erupt into an angry mob and lynch you," he warned.

"Listen, take care and no hard feelings, I hope," Casey answered with a smile.

"Have a safe flight home," Steve said, and watched as the Captain made his way through the crowd. At least he would be out of town by tonight he thought, as he took another hand in his own.

When Mr. Philips and his staff from the station arrived, the crowd had lessened quite a bit. Steve recognized them immediately and went to Mr. Philips, who had stopped in front of Monica's casket to put her station picture next to the more candid picture from the year before.

"Mr. Philips, I'm Steven Hardy. I was Andrew's attorney and friend and I just adored Monica. I know this must be a difficult time for you and your station. She was a special person and Andrew loved her more than life itself," he said with affection, placing his hand on the man's shoulder.

"Thanks for the kind words, we'll all miss her. I guess we should be thankful it was quick and painless,." Philips said through red-rimmed eyes. "I'd hate to think of her suffering. Is there any word from Monica's mother yet?"

"Nothing, I'm afraid. I've tried to reach her, but she's out of the country and can't be reached."

"This is awful. They hadn't seen much of each other since the wedding. She was planning to be here with them for Christmas this year, and now this had to happen."

"It's going to be hard for everyone to get past this. It's just going to take some time. I feel like I lost a brother, we were that close, Andrew and I," Steve said, emotionally.

Mr. Philips wiped his eye. "We would've come to the cemetery but I understand why you've decided to keep it private. With all the press it would be a nightmare."

"I'm glad you understand. I want to do this quickly and quietly, Mr. Philips. The last thing Andrew would want is for his burial to turn into a three-ring circus."

"Which cemetery?" Mr. Philips asked as he took the hand of a fellow staff member and tried to comfort her. "I'd like to visit the graves when everything quiets down."

"Our Lady of Mercy. I'm sure you'll be able to visit the graves tomorrow—it'll be more private that way. Now, please excuse me,

I need to see about transport to the cemetery. If there is anything at all I can do for you, Mr. Philips, please let me know," Steve said warmly, as he shook Mr. Philips hand. Then he left the room to find Mr. Bentley.

*

A cemetery had never been one of Steven Hardy's favorite places, so as a rule he avoided them at all costs. So when the limo he was riding in drove through the gates of Our Lady of Mercy Cemetery, he had to force the air out of his lungs. Driving through the cemetery's many hills took longer than Steve would have liked, so he spent the time studying the backs of both hands. When, after a few minutes, the limo stopped, he forced himself back to reality to look outside.

He stepped out of the car watching the caskets being carried to the open plots. They were side by side, which was just the way Andrew said he always wanted it. Crossing the plush green lawn, he felt the sorrow sink in. He was in mourning, like it or not. He stood tall and straightened his jacket on his way.

He saw Father Patrick standing to the side of the plots with a bible in his hands, his eyes closed, and praying. He waited out of respect and fondness, though he only had the way the man had treated Andrew for his basis on the last. When he saw the priest raise his head, open his eyes, and smile at him, he went over and they shook hands. "I'm glad you could make it, Father. Though Andrew hadn't known you long, he was quite fond of you."

"It's my honor to be asked. Is there anything you'd like to say before they lower the caskets, my son? I realize you want to be quick with the press climbing all around." Father Patrick spoke in his crisp Irish accent.

"I've already said my good-bye's, Father." He lowered his head and closed his eyes. "Go ahead," Steve said in a whisper.

Father Patrick said a prayer and the caskets were lowered into the ground. Steve stayed until each plot was covered and then got into the limo and headed back to town. This day had been anything but easy and his heart was heavy. He lowered his tired body further down into the leather seats and closed his eyes. He was hoping tomorrow would be easier.

*

Casey walked through the plane to find his seat and dropped into it with a sigh of relief. He had done what he'd set out to do before he left New York. He paid his last respects to Andrew Carter. And he even understood Steven Hardy's decision to keep the burial private and closed to the public. After all, with as many people that were mourning that place would have turned into a zoo. He was just thankful that his job here in New York was finished and he could go home.

The very first thing he planned to do was go to the YMCA and swim a couple dozen laps to try and work off some steam. Next, he was going to inform the commissioner that he was taking a few personal days to get his head on straight. He wouldn't like it, but Casey didn't care.

He needed some time to himself. As the plane taxied down the runway and lifted into the air, Casey smiled. He was leaving the ghost of Andrew Carter—and anything else connected with New York City—behind him on the ground.

*

Standing on the balcony of the estate he purchased in Australia, his mind drifted across the Outback to a different place and time. His jet-black hair had now given way to longer blond hair. He was also in the process of growing a beard to complete his transformation. But his mind was troubled and his thoughts were consumed with all he lost in just seven days. She was still with him but the relationship between them was strained and he doubted if there would be enough time on earth for them to find their way back to each other. It was after all, what he deserved.

The coolness of the night and the brightness of the moon comforted him as he worried about the future. Andrew Carter was dead and gone but in his place a new man had been born, Darius Kesslemen. It would take a great deal of time to grow used to the name but it was his now and he had to make it his own. Monica too was dead to be replaced with Nancy Kesslemen. She was less than thrilled with her new life but this was the choice she made and she was determined to make the best of it. Thomas was dead but Robert Stoffle was picking up the responsibilities and tending to his master's every need. He, by far, was dealing with it better then either of the two of them.

All the precision used to give them this second chance. Thomas breaking into the medical offices and destroying their records, creating new dental records, and taking the records of the bodies thought to be theirs back in New York, as their own. The bodies, or whatever was left of them, would have been so badly burned in the explosion, that's all the coroner would have to go on for identification. It all worked like magic, but Darius couldn't apply that same magic to his broken marriage.

"Darius," Robert said, coming out onto the balcony. There was no response. "Andrew," he said, sharply.

"What do you want, Thomas?" he asked without turning around.

"First of all, I want you to start responding to your new name and calling me by mine."

Darius turned and faced him. "I'm sorry…Robert," he said, biting back on the hostility. "What is it?"

"Your wife would like to see you in her bedroom."

"Would she?" he muttered. "Well I don't feel like going another ten rounds tonight."

"At least she's speaking to you, Darius. It could be much worse, Robert said, sternly.

"I truly can't imagine that." He shook his head and blew out a breath. Tension, so thick it was present in every room in the house, was a weight on his chest, making it hard to breathe. "She can't stand to be in the same room with me. The bloody arguments started the second we left New York and she realized what she'd given up to be with me. It was the dead of night, mind you, but she still had the presence of mind to throw my dishonesty—towards her and our marriage—in my face. I thought she understood. She did choose to come with me," Darius snapped, frustrated with the whole situation. "I didn't force her."

"She's going to need some time, that's all. You told her everything, and then just hours later you ask her to make a difficult, life-altering choice. She didn't have time to be angry with you, Darius."

"I hate that name."

"You'd prefer a prison cell instead? It's yours now so get used to it. Go and talk to your wife while she's still willing to talk to you," Robert demanded. He took Darius by the arm and pushed him into the house. "Go."

"I'm not in the mood to argue again. I can't get those men out of my mind. Two more innocent people are dead because of me."

"You're referring to the security guards killed in the explosion?"

"Who else?"

"It was unfortunate, but necessary. Now go to your wife."

*

Darius knocked lightly and slowly opened the door. They stood looking at each other for a moment and he remained frozen in the hallway. "You can come in," Nancy said softly, folding her arms across her chest and turning away.

"Thomas...excuse me...Robert said you wanted to talk to me."

"Yes," she said uncomfortably. "I know you're unhappy I moved into my own bedroom, but how could you expect me to do anything different? I need some time," she said, sitting down on the window ledge and trying to see her husband as more than a stranger.

"It's not that we're in different beds, Monica. Do you think I'm so bloody shallow all I care about is that we're not having sex?"

"My name's Nancy, remember?"

"Yes, damnit—I remember! How can I forget with Robert reminding me every five minutes I'm Darius Kesslemen, not Andrew Carter, that you're Nancy not Monica," he shouted.

"Don't yell at me!" she shouted back, and turning, looked out the window, blinking away tears.

He hadn't meant to yell at her. "I'm sorry," he managed, raking his hand through his hair, miserably. "We're so far apart from each other. I'm not used to this distance between us. You must sense it as I do. Can't we reach some common ground and start from there."

"You ask for so much in such a short amount of time. I'm not a business deal you can manipulate, she countered, icily. "Do you think just because I have to call you by another name that everything bad between us, the lies, the dishonesty, can be forgotten like Andrew Carter?"

"No, damnit, you're not hearing me. You made the decision to come here. Don't you see how I could presume you are willing to meet me half-way? This silence, this distance will only make it harder to find our way back to each other. We have to talk it out." Darius stared at her with cold eyes. "Or maybe you find it easier to punish me?"

Hurt by his words, she crossed the room and slapped him hard across the face. "How dare you try and turn this around on me! I'm here aren't I? Didn't I just throw my entire life away to be with you?" Anger throbbed, but it was hurt that propelled her, drove her across the room to put distance between them.

"Punish you?" she spat heatedly. "I could've walked away, kept my own life but I threw it away to be with you," she cried out in anger. She couldn't stop the tears now. "I'll never see my mother again. She thinks I'm dead, and I have to let her. *I* gave up everything, and I'm not trying hard enough for *you*? Go to hell!" she shouted.

"Well, at least you care enough that my words can still hurt," Darius muttered, rubbing his cheek. "Goodnight, Nancy," he said, and walked out of the room, closing the door behind him.

*

Epilogue

Ten Months Later

Darius Kessleman rushed home from his office building after a long, difficult meeting. He couldn't wait to get home to Nancy and the special dinner she was planning for them that night. Things were looking up for them. In Australia for only ten months and already it was starting to feel like home. Every day spent rebuilding the marriage that was very near death when they arrived was well worth it. They worked at it and slowly they found their way back to each other. Things weren't perfect but at least they were close again. And although they still occupied different bedrooms, Nancy had been spending many nights with Darius in his room. They were slowly finding their way back to one another.

Robert pulled into the long driveway and up to the covered overhang to shield Darius from the hot sun. Darius threw open the door and was inside the house before Robert could even close his door. It was no small miracle that his two favorite people in the world were growing closer every day. His master was stronger than he had been in years and it was due in no small part to his freedom from his secrets. Most of the credit however was due to the new series of treatments Robert had created and had been using for the last two months. Already he noticed a drastic improvement.

*

Darius found Nancy in the game room. She was relaxing in one of the large overstuffed chairs she had picked out herself when they moved in. "Hello, Love!" He went to her and kissed her cheek. "How're things with the book?"

She rolled her eyes. "If I thought deciding to write this book was tough, imagine my surprise at the difficulty I'm having actually writing it." She smiled. "How'd your meeting go?"

"Surprisingly well—I never thought I'd take to the world of fashion, but I'm getting the hang of it. Our first show will be in May," Darius said, excitedly.

"You'll do great, don't worry," Nancy said, and reaching for him, pulled him down on the floor and started rubbing his neck. "You need to relax. You've got softballs in here."

"What's for dinner?" he asked with a yawn.

"It's a surprise."

"I think we're going to be all right," he said softly, losing his battle with sleep.

"So do I," Nancy whispered. She kissed him as his head slumped back against her. She smiled again. For the first time in so long she was happy again. She accepted Darius for what he was now. And most important of all, she could live with it. "So do I."

finis